FROM A DISTANCE

Books by
Tamera Alexander

Praise and honors for Tamera's first series,
FOUNTAIN CREEK CHRONICLES

"Tamera Alexander's characters are real, fallible, and a marvelous reflection of God's truth and grace. Her stories unfold layer-by-layer, drawing you in deeper with every page."

Armchair Interviews

"[A] tenderhearted story of redemption.... Rarely does a debut novel combine such a masterful blend of captivating story and technical excellence. Alexander has introduced a delightful cast of winsome characters, and there's a promise of more stories yet to be told."

Aspiring Retail

"This second book in the FOUNTAIN CREEK CHRONICLES reveals the power of love and forgiveness. All of the characters in the story are interesting and complex, even if they play minor roles. A warm-hearted inspirational story."

Historical Novels Review

"Alexander again delivers a most amazing story. The characters are more than words on a page; they become real people."

Romantic Times

"This follow-up to *Rekindled* and *Revealed* is a rich historical romance by possibly the best new writer in this sub-genre."

Library Journal (Starred Review)

Rekindled was named to *Library Journal*'s Best Books of 2006 list,
was a nominee for *Romantic Times*'s
Best Inspirational Novel of 2006,
and was a finalist for the 2007 RITA Awards for
Best First Book and
Best Inspirational Romance.

Revealed won the 2007 Romance Writer's of America RITA Award
for Best Inspirational Romance.

TAMERA ALEXANDER

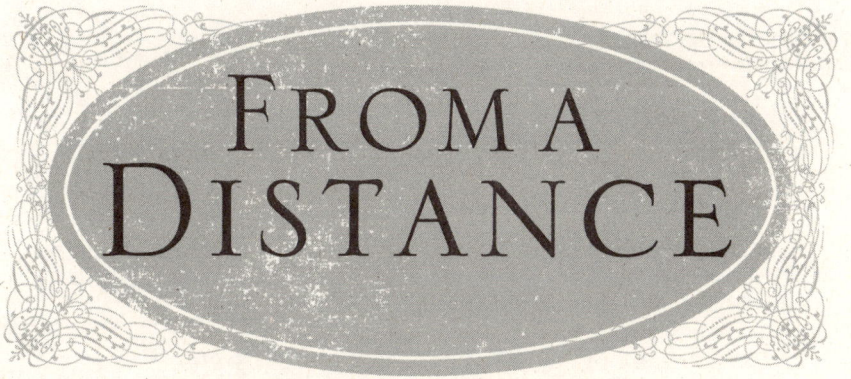

FROM A DISTANCE

TIMBER RIDGE REFLECTIONS

BETHANY HOUSE PUBLISHERS
Minneapolis, Minnesota

From a Distance
Copyright © 2008
Tamera Alexander

Cover design by Studio Gearbox
Cover photograph by Steve Gardner, PixelWorks Studios, Inc.

Scripture quotations identified KJV are from the King James Version of the Bible.

Scripture quotations identified NIV are from the HOLY BIBLE, NEW INTERNA-TIONAL VERSION.® Copyright © 1973, 1978, 1984 by International Bible Society. Used by permission of Zondervan Publishing House. All rights reserved.

Published by Bethany House Publishers
11400 Hampshire Avenue South
Bloomington, Minnesota 55438

Bethany House Publishers is a division of
Baker Publishing Group, Grand Rapids, Michigan.

Printed in the United States of America

Library of Congress Cataloging-in-Publication Data

Alexander, Tamera.
   From a distance / Tamera Alexander.
      p.   cm. — (Timber Ridge reflections.)
   ISBN 978-0-7642-0389-3 (pbk.)
   1. Women photographers—Fiction. 2. Colorado—Fiction. I. Title.

PS3601.L3563F76   2008
813'.6—dc22

                                                     2008002405

To Kelsey,
I'm so thankful God gave you to us.
But even more, that you
gave yourself to Him.

"All these people were still living by faith when they died.
They did not receive the things promised;
they only saw them and welcomed them from a distance."

HEBREWS 11:13A NIV

1

Elizabeth Garrett Westbrook stepped closer to the cliff's edge, not the least intimidated by the chasm's vast plunge. Every moment of her life had been preparing her for this. That knowledge was as certain within her as the thrumming inside her chest. At thirty-two, she still wasn't the woman she wanted to be, which was partially why she'd traveled nineteen hundred miles west to Timber Ridge, Colorado Territory. To leave behind a life she'd settled for, in exchange for the pursuit of a dream, for however long she had left.

A chill fingered its way past her woolen coat, into her shirtwaist, and through the cotton chemise that lay beneath. She pulled the coat closer about her chest and viewed the seamless river and valley carved far below, the mountains heaved up and ragged, draped in brilliant dawn to the limits of sight. She peered down to where the earth ended abruptly at the tips of her boots and the canyon plunged to breathtaking depths.

The *Chronicle* offices in Washington, D.C., were housed in a four-story building, and she estimated that at least ten of those buildings could be stacked one atop the other and still not reach the height of the cliff where she stood. She'd never before experienced such a sense of possibility. Standing here, she felt so small in comparison to all of this, yet in awe that the same Creator who had orchestrated such grandeur was also orchestrating the dissonant fragments of her life.

The competition had been rigorous, but she'd made it—one of three final candidates being considered for the position of staff photographer and journalist at the *Washington Daily Chronicle*. The other two candidates were men—men she'd met, liked and respected, and who knew how to frame the world through a lens as well as they did with words—which meant she would have to work extra hard to prove herself.

A breeze stirred, and she brushed back a curl. She inhaled the crisp, cold air, held it captive in her lungs, and then gave it gradual release, as the doctors had instructed. Hailed for its purity and ability to heal, the mountain air was even thinner than she had expected, and more invigorating.

Refocusing on her task, she strapped on her shoulder pack and checked the knotted rope encircling her waist for a second time, then untied her boots and placed one stockinged foot onto the felled tree.

She tested her weight on the natural bridge and judged it would more than hold her. Even though the tree looked solid, she'd learned the hard way that things were not always as they appeared. She trailed her gaze along the length of the gnarled trunk to where it met with the opposite ledge some twenty feet away. Heights had never bothered her, but once she started across, she purposed to never look down. Better to keep your focus on the goal rather than on the obstacles.

She adjusted the weight of her pack, concentrating, focusing, and took that crucial first step.

"Don't you go fallin' there, Miz Westbrook!"

Startled by the interruption, Elizabeth stepped back to safety and turned to look behind her. Josiah stood on the winding mountain trail, gripping the other end of the rope that was secured to a tree behind him.

Uncertainty layered his mahogany features. "I's just offerin' one last warnin', ma'am. 'Fore you set out."

Heart in her throat, she tried to sound kind. "I assure you, I'm fine, Josiah. I've done this countless times." Though, granted, never over so great a height. But be it eight feet or eight hundred, the ability to traverse a chasm successfully lay in focus and balance. At least that's what she kept telling herself. "But it *would* help me if you would stop your screaming."

His soft laughter was as deep as the canyon and gentle as the breeze. "I ain't screamin', ma'am. Womenfolk, now, they scream. Us men, we yells."

She threw him a reproving look. "Then, please . . . stop your *man-like* yelling."

He tugged at the rim of his worn slouch hat. "I won't be havin' to yell if you'd start actin' like a normal-headed woman. Instead of some . . . hoople-head traipsin' herself across a log for some picture of a bird's nest."

The felled tree was large, nearly fifty inches in circumference, hardly the *log* Josiah referred to, and crossing it to the opposite ledge would provide a better vantage point of the eagle's nest. The aerie was built on a precipice jutting from the side of the mountain, slightly below the level of the cliff and some thirty feet beyond. The photograph of the nest with the chasm below and the mountains in the backdrop would be breathtaking—if she didn't fall and break her neck first.

She'd crossed wider drop-offs on much narrower tree bridges than this. Doing such things always made her feel a little like a girl again, and took her back to a time when she hadn't yet been told that certain things were impossible.

"May I remind you that I'm paying you, very well"—she raised a brow, appreciating the ease of banter they'd shared since the outset of their association—"to carry my equipment and assist me in my work, not to offer opinions on my decisions."

"Ain't no extra charge for them, ma'am. They's free."

She shook her head at his broad smile. For the past week Josiah Birch had followed her instructions to the letter, as well he should. When properly motivated, the *Washington Daily Chronicle* had deep pockets.

Two other men had applied for the job as her assistant. They'd both seemed capable, but there was something about Josiah Birch that she innately trusted. He wasn't an educated man, but he knew how to read and write, and he'd learned to handle and mix the chemical solutions for her trade as fast as she had. And that he weighed twice what she did and held the excess in lean hard muscle and in an honest, open gaze had only bolstered his nonexistent résumé.

Focusing again, Elizabeth placed her right foot on the tree. Arms outstretched like a tightrope walker's, she compensated for the heavier-than-usual shoulder pack and took a carefully plotted first step.

Then a second step. And a third . . .

Approximately twelve feet below, a rock ledge protruded from the mountainside. It would break her fall should the rope fail for any reason, but the ledge only extended out halfway beneath the natural bridge. From there, it was a sheer drop down to the canyon floor. Not easily intimidated by heights, she kept her focus on her footing and occasionally glanced to the other side.

Inch by inch, the ledge disappeared from view. She resisted the temptation to look down at the river winding like a snake in the valley below. A gust of wind came from behind and pitched her forward. Loose curls blew into her eyes. She flailed for footing . . .

and found it. But the rope around her waist suddenly went taut and pulled her back.

"No, Josiah!"

Every muscle in her body tensed. Her back spasmed. She struggled to stay upright. The weight strapped to her shoulders tempted her to lean forward, but leaning too far could prove disastrous. Then she did what she knew not to do—

The snaking river below blurred in her sight.

She quickly pulled her gaze back to the ledge and, as taught from the age of six, imagined a ramrod extending from heaven's gate straight down through her spine and into the tree trunk beneath her. Slowly she felt her chin lift. As did her shoulders. Her legs trembled, but she regained her equilibrium and continued on across, one foot in front of the other.

With a rush of exhilaration she stepped from the tree onto solid rock again. *Terra firma.* She brushed back her hair and, masking her relief, looked at Josiah standing on the opposite ridge. "There, you see? I told you not to worry."

His dark eyes were wide, his knuckles a noticeably lighter shade as he gripped the rope. "You done scared ten years off'a me, ma'am. And they's years I coulda used." As if an invisible weight had been removed, his broad shoulders lifted.

Elizabeth set down her pack and opened it, excitement still coursing through her. A bit more excitement than she'd bargained for, but having made it across only sweetened the success. "I'm sorry, Josiah. That wasn't my intent. But I've been doing this since I was a little girl. I used to outrun and outclimb every boy I knew." She eyed the eagle's nest a good twenty feet away. "I could outride them too."

"Bet them boys liked playin' with you, all right."

"Actually . . . no. They didn't like it because I never let them win. Not when I could help it anyway." She unpacked her equipment, mindful of the rope still tied about her waist, and a particular memory came to mind. A memory of an afternoon at the riding stables, years ago. She'd felt similar exhilaration then as she did now—until her father discovered what had transpired. A bully of a boy had challenged her to a horse race. And she'd beaten him squarely. At the time she hadn't known that he was the son of her father's superior officer, and had not considered the possibility that her father and his fellow officers would catch her riding straddle-legged and wearing breeches beneath her skirt.

She'd long ago given up trying to forget the embarrassment that had darkened his face. And little had she known then what a defining moment that would be in her life.

Made of sticks and larger twigs, the aerie appeared to be at least seven feet wide and nearly that deep, and was built onto a ledge in the side of the mountain. Masterful. Even at this distance, she could distinguish feathers and tufts of grayish white down protruding from the sides. The nest was empty, for now. If only its occupant were nearby so she could capture a photograph of it too. Not that an eagle would remain stationary long enough for her to take its picture. That's what made taking pictures of animals—and fidgety people—such a challenge. If the subject moved, even the slightest bit, the image appeared ghosted once she developed it.

Since seeing the photographs of a place called Yosemite two years earlier, she'd dreamed of coming to the western territories, of taking photographs of the frontier—a place so far removed from the nation's capital and Maryland, her birthplace.

While landscapes such as the one before her were breathtaking, pictures of wildlife were what Wendell Goldberg, her employer at the *Chronicle,* truly wanted. *Spectacular photographs of wildlife* he'd written in a telegram days earlier—as if she needed the reminder. Along with those photographs, he wanted real-life adventures from people who lived in the West. Stories that championed the human spirit and that would entice would-be travelers and game hunters to venture west to the Colorado Territory—patronizing a travel company that was conveniently owned by the *Chronicle*'s largest shareholder, Adam Chilton.

The travel company was only a small portion of Chilton Enterprises. The bulk of the company's fortune lay in hotel properties, specifically resort spas. Word had spread back east about the therapeutic hot springs in this region. Their curative powers were the topic of conversation at extravagant cotillions and women's teas, and their attributes were lauded in the plush leather surroundings of gentlemen's clubs and smoking rooms. Chilton Enterprises requested that she take photographs of property in the area that they were considering for their next endeavor. And in exchange, their company would advertise exclusively in the *Chronicle*.

Wendell Goldberg was forever capitalizing on business opportunities such as these, and she considered it an honor to be personally mentored by the man—even if she didn't always agree with his tactics or his opinions.

"You best back away a mite, Miz Westbrook." Josiah's voice held gentle entreat. "Gonna be hard to help you from all the way over here. You liable to go slammin' into the mountain 'fore I can get you up."

She took a small conciliatory step back from the edge. "Satisfied?"

His cheeks puffed. "Ain't 'bout me bein' satisfied, ma'am. 'Bout you hirin' me to see you safe up these mountains and on back down again. I ain't been knowin' you but for a week, but you hangin' off the side of some mountain . . ." He scoffed. "I don't mean no disrespect, but that don't bode well for your soundness of mind."

Elizabeth laughed. "I appreciate your concern, but I assure you, my state of mind is quite sound. From now on, understanding that we'll be traveling together"—she attempted a somber tone—"I'd prefer it if you wouldn't sugarcoat your opinions, Mr. Birch. Speak your mind plainly, if you would. Without fear of offending me."

He mumbled something she couldn't make out, but could well imagine, and then took a cross-armed stance that reminded her of a famous Negro orator she'd once heard. "I just tryin' to do my job, ma'am. Like you hired me to do. That and keep the truth as plain-spoken as I can."

Plain-spoken truth . . . How refreshing that was. And she preferred that too, however abrasive or uncompromising, to the sting of having one thing spoken to her face and another behind her back—an occurrence she hoped she'd left behind her back east. "I think you and I will make a good pair, Josiah." However an unlikely one.

"I'm inclined to think that way too, Miz Westbrook. Long as you don't go do somethin' foolish and end up at the bottom of some mountain."

Choosing to ignore that last comment, she lifted the nine-pound camera from the bottom of the burlap bag and situated it as close to the edge as she dared so that it encompassed both the view of the eagle's nest and that of the valley below with the mountain range in the distance. She looked around for small rocks and placed them beneath the camera to balance it on the uneven ground.

Since she couldn't carry over all of her supplies, she had prepared the camera's wet glass plate beforehand and already had it inserted into its light-protective holder. Which meant only a short time remained for her to take the photograph, return to the other side, and develop the glass plate before the light-sensitive chemicals dried on the surface. It was a tedious process when she was in a darkroom, but was even more so in the field. If the glass plate dried out, or got the slightest crack, it became useless.

She lay flat on the cliff, arranging her skirt over her legs, and worked to get the image focused in the glass viewer.

When Josiah had met her with the horses outside the boarding-house this morning, darkness had ruled the predawn skies. They'd tethered the mounts at the base of the mountain an hour ago, and with the aid of lanterns, they'd started their trek. Then the eastern horizon had begun to stir, showing its intent, until finally dawn rose to reveal the before-hidden crevices and canyons, and the mountain peaks rising so high they disappeared into the pinkish-purple clouds.

"I'm bettin' you done real good in your schoolin', ma'am."

She smiled at his phrasing. "I did well enough, I guess." She lined up the viewer, making sure the North Maroon Bell showed clearly off to the right. The varying distances of objects would give the frame its needed depth. *Splendid.* "But one of my teachers, a Mr. Ainsworth . . . he shared the same opinion as the boys I was telling you about. He didn't encourage my athletic prowess."

"I take that to mean he didn't like your ridin' and climbin'?"

She chuckled. "No, he didn't like it one bit. He said I was . . . boyish and that my assertiveness was unsuitable and unattractive. Not qualities becoming of a young lady." Funny how she remembered Ainsworth's exact wording and could still hear his irritating nasally tone. The audacity of that pompous, overconfident—

"Don't sound like somethin' wise for a teacher to be sayin' to a young girl. 'Specially to one who prob'ly coulda whupped his hide." Josiah gave a high-pitched hoot, and his laughter echoed against the canyon walls.

Laughing with him, Elizabeth slid the protective holder into the camera slot and removed the exposure panel. She then uncapped the brass cover from the lens and let science work its wonder.

Her stockinged foot kept rhythm on the cliff as she silently recited the oft-remembered words from a speech given at an event her father had insisted she attend years prior. "*Four score and seven years ago our fathers brought forth upon this continent a new nation, conceived in liberty and dedicated to the proposition that . . .*"

It was a speech considered a disappointment by most in attendance that day, but not by her. Twenty years old at the time, standing hushed beside Tillie, her Negro nanny—whose full name of Aunt Matilda had been cast aside somewhere during childhood—she remembered every detail of that solemn gathering on the battlefield at Gettysburg, and would as long as she lived.

"The world will little note nor long remember what we say here, but it can never forget what they did here . . ."

The wind caught the feathers in the nest, and she wished she could capture this moment in a truer sense of time, so people would actually see those feathers moving and could hear the wind as it whistled low over the mountain and dove deep into the canyon below. An idea came for an article to accompany this photograph when she mailed it to Wendell Goldberg at the end of the week, and she tucked the thought away, hoping to remember.

When enough time had lapsed, she carefully replaced the lens cap and hurriedly repacked her camera. Now to get the exposed plate into the dark tent Josiah had set up across the ridge. She arranged the pack on her shoulders, checked the rope again, and shot him a quick glance before taking the first step.

The deep furrows lining his forehead stayed foremost in her mind as she made her way back across. The stocking on her right foot caught on a piece of bark, but a quick backward tug freed it. She stepped onto the opposite ridge and felt another sense of triumph. So much for Mr. Ainsworth and his assessment of her *boyish* skills!

She worked quickly in the tent—her makeshift darkroom— pouring a developing solution of iron sulfate and acetic acid over the photographic plate. The procedure turned the light-sensitive grains into a metallic silver that glistened in the half glow of the stubby, wax-skirted candle.

Witnessing this part of the process never lost its allure, and the image was stunning. She gave the glass plate a final water rinsing, which rendered it safe to the light again, and she reemerged from the tent.

As Josiah set to packing the equipment and loading it on the mule, she pulled out her notebook and recorded the date, hour, minute, location, and lighting of the picture she'd taken, along with a description. Keeping this information aided her understanding of how the various conditions influenced the success of her photographs.

She put her notebook away and bent to help Josiah pack, when her breath caught in her throat. Not much of a catch—just enough to gain her attention. She straightened and slowly inhaled, testing her lungs.

The doctors had made no claim there was a cure for her ailment, but they had encouraged that this territory's dry climate and mountain air should lessen the stress to her lungs. Their foremost recommendation—soaking in the region's hot springs—was a practice she looked forward to experiencing. In the past, she'd sought deliverance through physician-prescribed arsenic and chloroform remedies, and pungent mustard poultices. All hideous regimens that had brought no healing. On the contrary, they only seemed to have weakened her constitution and worsened her condition.

She breathed in and out again, beginning to think she'd overreacted. How she hated this weakness. Her health was excellent but for her lung ailment. She wanted to push on but didn't want that desire to blind her to her body's limits. Perhaps she should try and take the photographs she needed from the current vantage point.

"Are you certain, Josiah, that the view ahead holds more promise than this?"

He tied the last bundle onto the mule and pulled the strap taut. "This here's pretty, ma'am, but it ain't nothing compared to what's up ahead."

She nodded and, when he resumed the climb, fell in step behind him, trusting her own body's stubborn resolve as well as Josiah's judgment. So far he'd been right about everything—not that she would remind him of that.

Navigating the steep ribbon of switchback trail, she was grateful he'd insisted they travel this portion of the journey afoot. Shale dotted the path and made the ascent more difficult.

The weighted pack on her back grew more pronounced, and she paused for a few seconds to stretch and readjust the load.

"No need for you to tote that, ma'am. I can strap it on Moonshine, or I can tote it for you myself, if'n you let me. Like I said before, I be gentle with it."

She waved him on ahead. "It's not a bother, really. I just need to pace myself."

"Pace yourself . . . ? Sounds like you back there pacin' yourself right straight to death."

She laughed, despite the truth in his statement. "You haven't told me . . . why did you name that stubborn animal Moonshine?"

Josiah rubbed the bridge of his mule's nose. "I named him after somethin' my mama used to tell us kids when we was young. She used to say to us . . . that if ever we was to get parted from the other, we was to look up at the moon come night, and that no matter where she was, or where any of us was, we'd be together. Cuz we be lookin' at the same moon God hung in His heavens."

Elizabeth envied him that memory. What stories might her own mother have shared if she'd lived long enough to have the chance?

Josiah continued the uphill hike, and it took her three generous steps to equal his every two, her heeled boots and long skirt hindering her efforts. Her split skirt was in a trunk of clothing that still hadn't arrived from Washington, but she looked forward to the freedom and practicality it would allow.

Walking behind Josiah, she again noted the broadness of his shoulders, and the raised welts on the back of his neck. Once deep wounds, now long healed by the looks of them, the scars extended above his coat collar and blended into his hairline, giving insight into his past. Josiah Birch's physical strength was impressive, and he was proving himself an able assistant on these mountain treks. And quite entertaining.

But no matter how capable an assistant he might be, she always shouldered her own pack. Especially when it contained something so valuable. She'd saved for months to buy her camera, and it held the key to her achieving her dreams.

"Townsfolk don't much use this path." His deep voice carried to her over the plod of the mule's progress. "Too narrow and steep for 'em. Mostly the Ute who pass this way."

"The Ute . . . I'd like to meet—" Cold air prickled her windpipe as it fed down and filtered into her lungs. The higher they climbed, the thinner the air became and the more difficult to breathe. Studying the effects of higher altitude back east and now actually experiencing them were turning out to be two very different things. "I'd like to meet some of the Ute. If"—a painful stitch in her left side staccatoed her breath—"you could . . . arrange that."

"Only one man I know has any contact with the Ute, Miz Westbrook, and he ain't easy to find. I ain't seen him in a while, and he only makes hisself known when he has cause to. Which don't happen too frequent."

Massaging a pain in her side, Elizabeth skirted a larger rock in the path, aware of the loose shale close to the edge and of how unaffected Josiah seemed by the altitude. "This man . . . he sounds peculiar. Like . . . some sort of hermit."

"No, ma'am, he ain't no hermit. Just keeps to hisself. Likes it best that way is how I figure it."

A spasm started in her upper chest, forcing Elizabeth to slow her pace. It was a small one this time, and she managed to coax some breaths past the tangle at the base of her throat. She fixed her gaze to the trail and continued to climb. "How do I . . . contact this gentleman?"

"You don't. More like he finds you, if he has a mind to. Which he most often won't."

"And . . ." She breathed slowly, in and out, as physicians had instructed since her youth—advice more easily followed when one wasn't hiking up a fourteen-thousand-foot mountain. "Why is that?"

When he failed to answer, she looked up to find him halted on the trail, his arm raised, his rifle drawn.

She went absolutely still, grateful for the chance to gain her breath but with senses at alert. Crackling noises sounded from deep within the wooded ridge. Then the breaking of twigs, the faint rustle of branches. Wind whistled through the low-bowered pines and stalwart spruce, masking sounds that might otherwise have been detected.

She slipped a hand into her pocket as she scanned the wooded rise to their left—unsure whether her shortness of breath stemmed from her ailment or from whatever was out there . . . or perhaps both. Gripping the curve-handled derringer, an indulgent purchase she'd made before departing New York City, a measure of courage rose within her. Its .41 caliber ball would hardly deter a large animal, but it was better than facing one completely defenseless.

Josiah cocked his head to one side as though listening for something.

The first time he'd done this on the trail three days ago, she'd questioned him. After spotting the mountain lion, she'd swiftly learned to keep her silence. He'd shot at the animal and missed—by a wide margin if the splintered bark held truth—but his actions had apparently convinced the lion that they were unworthy prey.

It was unrealistic, she knew, but one photograph of that sleek, muscular predator would have all but guaranteed her the much sought-after position at the *Chronicle*. But in the flick of a second hand, the cougar had disappeared, taking her opportunity with it. And they'd spotted no wildlife since, other than the occasional bird and furry marmot—hardly prey capable of enticing travelers and game hunters west.

Josiah gradually lowered his arm and murmured low, a sound she'd heard from him before. "Felt somethin' on the breeze." His focus remained on the shadows beyond the trees. "Don't no more."

Elizabeth tried to respond but couldn't. A familiar ache wedged itself inside her throat, lodging like a fist in her windpipe.

Josiah looked her direction. His eyes narrowed. "You all right, ma'am?"

Elizabeth shook her head and groped at the high collar of her shirtwaist. The first two buttons slid free, but the effort earned her no relief. Each attempt to breathe ended in a pathetic wheeze, and her world took on that strange spiraling sensation she knew only too well.

She clenched her eyes tight—as if surrendering the ability to see might persuade her lungs to function. *Stay calm . . . steady breaths . . .*

"It be happenin', miz?" The deep cauldron of a whisper sounded close beside her.

Frantic, she nodded, furious at her body's betrayal. She'd warned him about this, just in case it happened while they were together. She hated being seen as weak; people treated her differently. She'd pushed too hard this morning. She'd known better.

Strength left her legs. . . .

Josiah eased her to the ground and pulled the pack from her shoulders. "Tell me what to do, ma'am! You got that medicine? One you told me 'bout?"

She shook her head, unable to answer. It was back in her room, and only a little remained. She'd been rationing it, waiting for a new shipment. No matter how many times she'd experienced this, it still terrified her.

He eased her onto the ground, her throat closing by the second. She stared into the sky, trusting God could see. She didn't doubt that. She only wondered if He would intervene. He had every time before, but it didn't mean He always would. She'd learned that early in life—when her mother died.

Her throat felt the size of a rye grass straw, and what little air she could inhale and expel hung in anemic wisps in front of her face. Elizabeth squeezed Josiah's hand and felt his flesh give beneath her nails. Yet he never let go. The panic in his eyes mirrored hers, and her body jerked as she fought for breath.

2

A moment passed. Maybe less, maybe more. Elizabeth couldn't be sure. But it felt like an eternity. Then the thinnest, most precious ribbon of air slid through the knot in her throat, loosening its hold.

Second by second, the spasm lessened.

Gradually, her throat relaxed and the sweetest rush of cool air trickled down into her lungs. Like a field hand parched from thirst, she was tempted to gulp it in but knew better. She filled her lungs slowly, deliberately, still suspended in that dreamlike state somewhere between consciousness and having been pulled under.

Josiah gently patted her hand. "This one don't seem to have hung on like the others you told me 'bout."

She nodded, his voice sounding far away. She couldn't speak, but he was right. This episode had been bad, but not as severe as the ones she'd endured on the journey west, the travel exacerbated by soot and ashes from the train and swirling dust from the stagecoaches.

For several heartbeats, she simply delighted in her lungs' obedience. And, as always in these moments afterward, there lingered the uninvited question of whether she would suffer the same fate as her mother, and at nearly the same age. Pushing away the thought, she indicated she was ready to stand.

Josiah offered assistance and held her steady for a moment, then retrieved her canteen from the mule. "Didn't I say you looked a mite peaked this mornin', ma'am?"

She took a long draw of water, choosing to ignore him. The western territories were more uncivilized than she'd anticipated, but the water here . . . She'd never tasted anything so cold and clean. She smoothed her shirtwaist and took another drink, choosing to leave the top two buttons at her neckline unfastened.

She dabbed at the corners of her mouth. "How much farther before we reach the ridge?"

Josiah shook his head. "It be just round this bend, ma'am."

He bent to lift her pack, but she motioned for him to leave it.

"You's the stubbornest white woman I know, Miz Westbrook."

She laughed. "So I still have some competition in that area, is that what you're saying?"

He scoffed and turned, mule in tow. She retrieved her pack and followed him around the corner, and found her breath nearly stolen away again. But this time for an altogether different reason. He had been right. . . .

The Rocky Mountains' renowned twin sisters, the Maroon Bells, rose like ethereal monuments against the pale azure sky. Capped in snowy brilliance, the north and south peaks splintered the morning light into a thousand sparkling prisms. Standing there, taking it in, she wished she could thank Wendell Goldberg again for giving her this opportunity, and for letting her choose this destination instead of sending her to California or to the Wyoming Territory, where the other two candidates for the position had been sent.

A lake, clear and smooth, filled the valley's floor, acting as the mountains' footstool and perfectly mirroring their splendor. If only her camera lens could capture the riot of nature's colors instead of portraying them in dull shades of gray.

She busied herself with helping Josiah unload the equipment from the mule. Then heard something in the distance . . . a rushing noise. It rose above the wind and their shuffling as they unpacked. She searched, and spotted it across the canyon—a waterfall cascading over boulders, some the size of a small house, down into a pool at least five hundred feet below. Gorgeous . . .

Wendell Goldberg's hunches were right. Easterners would pay an exorbitant amount of money to vacation here—*if* they could be afforded the same luxuries they enjoyed at home. Which, right now, was certainly not the case. But it soon would be once Chilton Enterprises constructed their new hotel.

"Why didn't you tell me there was a waterfall near here, Josiah?"

He dropped the folded canvas tent on the ground and looked at her as though she were daft. "Cuz you didn't ask me."

She dismissed his response with a smile. She hadn't confided in him about her association with the *Chronicle* for the same reason she hadn't told anyone else in Timber Ridge. All he knew was that she wanted to take pictures of nature, and he'd already agreed to accompany her on her expedition south to the cliff dwellings.

"Well, from now on, if there's a waterfall or hot spring or . . . anything like that within view of where we're standing, would you please tell me about it?"

Again, that look. "Yes, ma'am. I can do that." He went back to work. " 'Course, I guess I'm wonderin' why you can't just see it for yourself with your own eyes. God gave you two good ones, and it makes sense to me that . . ."

Ignoring his muttering, Elizabeth knelt and untied the straps to her shoulder pack and withdrew her camera, followed by glass plates cocooned in fabric and an assortment of bottles, each wrapped separately to prevent breakage. A glance confirmed that Josiah would soon have her dark tent set up and her supplies arranged inside. As expected from his previous routine, he'd pitched the tent as far away from the edge of the mountainside as possible, and on the most level patch of ground.

She readied one of the camera plates for exposure, cleaning the glass with a mixture of pumice and alcohol. She poured collodion onto the readied surface, tilted the plate at various angles until the entire area was coated with the transparent solution, drained the excess back into the container, and reached for a cloth.

Collodion stuck to nearly everything. She doubted whether she possessed a skirt, shirtwaist, or outer coat that didn't bear stains from the various chemicals used in her trade—a fact that irritated her father something fierce, fastidious as he'd once been with his blue woolen uniform and still was with his jacket and trousers for Senate meetings.

"It's all ready for you, Miz Westbrook."

Josiah lifted the front flap of the tent, and she crawled through the opening, wet camera plate in hand. A candle flickered burnished yellow in the darkness.

On her knees in the familiar half glow, Elizabeth dipped the plate, now tacky to the touch, into a light-sensitizing bath Josiah had prepared as she'd taught him. Twelve parts water to one part silver nitrate. Minutes later, once the surface of the glass was uniform and creamy white in color, she removed it from the bath, wiped the back of it with a clean cloth, and slid it into a lightproof wooden holder.

She emerged from the dark tent with the prepared plate, careful not to trip on the bulk of her skirt and coat.

Josiah had mounted the camera on its mahogany tripod. She rested the plate holder on a cloth on the ground and bent at the waist to view the upside-down scene through the glass viewer. No matter how many times she'd done this, capturing a slice of time on a piece of glass so that people far away could appreciate beauty they'd never seen always gave her a thrill.

She straightened and gestured to the tripod. "You chose the placement well, Josiah. Your efficiency at learning the camera's angle is commendable." She leveled her gaze, careful to keep her smile in check. "Even if your social skills leave something to be desired."

He laughed softly, the sound of it pure enjoyment to listen to.

"I thank you, ma'am, for that kind word. And I be doin' my best to work on the other. No doubt, given time, you'll teach me right." He dipped his head, not meeting her eyes straight on.

In that split second, Elizabeth caught a fleeting glimpse of Josiah's former station in life, or what she imagined it might have been like from the little he'd shared with her. He was more astute than any assistant she'd worked with back in Washington, and he possessed a subtlety of humor she admired. In her line of work, she often rubbed shoulders with such jesting from male colleagues, and whether Josiah knew it or not, his quick wit was serving to sharpen her own.

She'd never had a brother, or a sister for that matter, but if she'd had siblings, she imagined her relationship with an older brother might have been somewhat like hers with Josiah Birch, even in the short time they'd known each other. She guessed him to be roughly ten years her senior, though it was hard to tell. Thick muscle, similar to that of a younger man, layered his body. But within his expression lay a depth of emotion that bespoke age and experience beyond his physical years. And if the weathered wrinkles and shadows were telling, she read that the whole of his life had not been kind.

She bent to study the camera's perspective one last time. This was one view that never lied. It always mirrored exactly what was seen, albeit in reverse. And the upside-downness seemed to bring more clarity to the view. The trees stood taller against the swathe of azure blue. The mountains vaulted from the earth's belly with more startling strength when seen in reverse of nature's gravity.

She snuck a quick glance at Josiah and discovered him surveying the mountainside as well. The color of his skin was not a hindrance to their friendship in her eyes, just as she knew hers was not to him. But that was easier said out here, away from the confines of proper society and judging eyes. She wasn't blind to the looks they drew in town. She simply chose not to let them bother her.

As she turned and retrieved the light-protected plate, she heard Josiah's soft gasp behind her.

Straightening, she followed his line of vision, and in that moment she knew that, no matter her love of photography, her affinity for the English language, or her devotion to her career, words would fail to capture the majesty before her.

A bull elk—fully mature, judging by his massive size—had emerged from a clustered stand of Douglas fir. He held his head erect and his nose twitched, reading the wind as easily as she would a book. No doubt he smelled them. No doubt he *saw* them. Scarcely twenty feet separated them, a perfect distance to capture his image.

His enormous antlers extended skyward, and as she watched him, Elizabeth felt an overriding sense of awe. Already she could picture him filling the frame of her lens, as well as a frame in one of Washington's prestigious art galleries. The bull elk moved with deliberate grace. His rack—measuring, conservatively, five feet in height, twice that in span—punctuated the blue horizon at his back. He exuded an innate authority to rule and seemed almost conscious of his beauty.

This was the photograph she'd been praying for. The kind that would make Wendell Goldberg sit up in that fine leather chair of his and realize she was worth every penny he'd invested, and that *she* was the candidate who deserved to be the *Chronicle*'s first female photographer and journalist.

The mule brayed, and the elk's hindquarters quivered. Elizabeth held her breath, praying he wouldn't leap back into the brush. But he scarcely moved. This was every bit *his* mountain, and all four of them knew it, the mule included. Now if she could only get the plate into the camera without frightening him away.

Slipping the protective holder into the wooden slot caused a scraping noise, followed by an overloud click. The familiar sounds seemed inordinately bold against the hushed backdrop of nature, but the animal seemed unaffected by it all.

Convinced that the Creator had handcrafted this opportunity, she removed the lens cap, exposed the prepared plate to the light, and began silently reciting the speech she knew by heart. Things were going to work out for her—she just had that feeling.

All her life it seemed as though she'd been fighting an uphill battle. First with her health, and then in being excluded from opportunities due to her gender. Not that she wanted to be treated like a man. Not in the least. She simply wanted the same opportunities, to be allowed the chance to make the same mistakes. . . .

The morning sun broke through the clouds, spilling translucent sheets of silver onto the valley floor far below and reflecting off the rippled surface of the river.

Careful not to bump the camera or the tripod, she returned the lens cap to its place and admired the bull elk, which stood tall and proud, head erect. If this photograph exposed as well as she thought, it would rival any wildlife or nature scene captured in the western territories that she could recall. Even her mentor, Mathew Brady, would be envious.

Josiah raised a hopeful brow as she removed the plate from the camera. She nodded once and enjoyed the responding twinkle in his eyes. Now to get the plate developed. She tossed him a smile and hurried toward the tent, letting herself imagine in even greater detail the look on Wendell Goldberg's face when he saw the photograph of this bull elk set against the panorama of—

An explosion fragmented the silence.

Elizabeth turned to see the bull elk buckled forward, blood flowing from a wound directly behind his shoulder. The animal attempted a valiant stride and faltered, and Elizabeth had to stop herself from rushing toward him. Such beauty, such strength . . .

He keened low, a primal sound, a cry she knew she'd never forget. Then he crumpled forward—just as the glass plate slipped from her hand.

3

Daniel Ranslett knelt on one knee, his right shoulder still absorbing the impact of the rifle's discharge, just as it had thousands of times before. His focus remained trained on his target. His bullet had found its mark. Through the rifle's sights, he watched the magnificent beast falter, then crumple at the knees. For two days and nights, he'd tracked the animal to line up a clean shot, one that would be swift and humane, worthy of such a kill.

Watching the scene through his scope, a memory rose from years past, from another lifetime, and a better one. It lashed at his concentration, but with practiced control, he kept it at bay.

A strange and unexpected kinship rose inside him for the animal across the ridge, and he experienced an odd twinge of jealousy. He felt the strong, solid beat of his own heart while knowing that a short distance away, the precious lifeblood of his prey lay spilling out.

How had he, an agent of death for so many, escaped death countless times when innocent others had not?

A soft whimper sounded beside him.

"Steady there, Beau," he whispered, giving the beagle's head a quick stroke. "Not yet. You're getting impatient with age, fella." A trait he understood only too well.

He lowered his rifle and hesitated, spotting movement on the ridge opposite him. Daniel rose and squinted against the sunlight piercing the evergreen branches overhead. A woman walked from behind a stand of pine. A Negro followed. The two were a ways from his kill but were walking straight for it.

He grabbed his hat and his pouch from the rock beside him. Looping the pouch over his head, his long strides swiftly became a run. He reached the obscured crossing down the path in minutes, and the opposite ridge in another two, Beauregard fast on his heels. His tethered horse whinnied as they passed. Even in the cool of dawn, sweat slicked his skin from the run, and his cotton shirt soaked up the moisture beneath the hand-sewn leather jacket.

Only when he reached the familiar bluff did he slow his pace. His breath came heavy, his body weak from exertion and little sleep in recent days. The woman and man stood over the bull elk now lying on its side, surrendered to fate. Trickles of blood pulsed from the fatal wound, lessening with each fading heartbeat.

Only seconds remained. . . .

"*You're* responsible for this?" The woman made straight for him, her stance full of fight.

But Daniel found little left in him. Not looking directly at her, he nodded, keeping his voice low. "Yes, ma'am, I am." He whistled, and Beau dropped down beside him in the dirt, doleful eyes watchful, waiting. Daniel laid aside his rifle and his hat, and gave in to the fatigue weakening his legs. He knelt and stroked the elk's neck.

"You owe me an explanation, sir, for what just hap—"

"Ma'am—" He looked up at her, working to bridle his frustration. It'd been four months since he'd spoken to another human being, even longer since he'd had a yearning to. He had regular conversations with Beau, but it wasn't the same. Beau was much more pleasant than this woman promised to be. "Ma'am, I'll answer your questions. I'll even listen to your tirade . . . *after* I'm done here."

Stillness descended over the cliff—as if an unseen guest had been ushered in. Even the subtle chatter of wildlife fell hushed. The woman must have sensed it too, because her flow of accusations ceased. She stared at him as if she wasn't quite sure what she was looking at, but it was clear she didn't like what she saw.

Thankful for the reprieve, however brief, Daniel focused his attention on the elk. He could feel the powerful cords of sinewy muscle succumbing to the diminishing flow of life. How insignificant and small he felt by comparison, and what he wouldn't have given for his customary solitude in that moment.

He moved closer to the animal's head, and the memory he'd warded off moments earlier returned with a fierceness that made him shudder. He swallowed against the tightening in his throat, remembering the day he'd passed this tradition on to his youngest brother, Benjamin, on his first kill. Daniel kept his voice hushed, hoping only the dying elk—and perhaps Benjamin—would hear. "For your strength and bravery"—his voice broke—"I honor you. And for your sacrifice . . . my gratitude."

He could still see Benjamin's frail hand resting against the doe's throat as he'd repeated those same words, and the young, hot tears burning his brother's dirt-stained cheeks. "I killed her, Danny," his brother had whispered, over and over, his voice a blend of exhilaration and regret.

"You have reason to be proud, Benjamin. You did well. Our family will eat for a month because of your bravery, and this animal's sacrifice." The smile on Benjamin's upturned face had stayed fixed for at least a month following, and Daniel still knew it by heart.

From the corner of his vision, he saw the woman move closer. The memory of his brother's expression faded.

"Do you have any idea what you've cost me?" Her voice had grown softer, yet more strident.

Daniel raised his head and slowly rose to his full height. Her chin lifted in tiny increments as he did, the challenge in her eyes mirroring his own. To his surprise, she didn't back down—nor did she look like the type of woman who would. He didn't mind strong-spirited women. Out here, females toughened up real quick-like or they didn't last long. His guess was that she possessed enough stubbornness to persevere. If whatever was causing the shadows beneath her eyes didn't win out first.

"No, ma'am, I reckon I don't know. But I have a feeling you aren't about to let me off without telling me." He shifted, feeling the weight of past days—of past years—pressing down hard. "So why don't we just stand right here and let you get it off your chest so we can move on."

Her arrogant little jaw slipped a notch.

Good thing. It'd give her time to gather her thoughts, if she had any worth gathering. She was a Yankee—that much became clear the second she'd opened her mouth. Daniel swung his gaze to the Negro beside her. The man made no move to speak, but neither did he look away, as Daniel had half expected him to.

His stare was steady, solid, yet lacked overt challenge.

Daniel didn't hold anything against his kind, not really, and hadn't for some time now. He'd be the first to admit he hadn't known a Negro man in any way but one, and that world was long passed. The war had seen to that. He found the man's open-faced gaze uncomfortable to hold overlong and stooped to get his hat. He knocked it against his thigh. "While you're figuring out that cost, ma'am, I've got work to do." He smoothed back his hair and resituated his hat on his head. "It'll take me the better part of the day to get this animal field-dressed and back to town. Hopefully I'll make it before sundown." He'd never seen a woman's face go crimson quite so fast.

"You have cost me an opportunity that I'll likely not have again. The animal, the setting, the light . . . *Everything* was perfect. Not to mention my time here is limited." Her hands sliced the air as she spoke and seemed to fuel the upset inside her. "And your only concern is getting this"—she briefly glanced down—"*animal* back down the mountain?"

The only nugget Daniel had gleaned from her tirade was that her time here had a limit to it. Another good thing. Studying the firm set of her jaw, he was reminded again of why he'd moved to this sparsely populated territory a decade ago, and why he'd chosen to live a far piece from Timber Ridge. It wasn't that he didn't like people. He did. He just liked most of them better from a distance.

People were bringing change to these mountains. Change he didn't welcome. First the miners came, gouging and blasting a path to riches, leaving an ugly and indelible mark. Now opportunists from the North arrived, daily it seemed, promising to leave a similar legacy. Only they cloaked their business endeavors in the guise of progress, same as they'd done after ransacking his plantation and devastating his family. After crushing the South.

The woman before him lacked the grace and charm of a Southern-bred lady, but she wasn't wholly lacking in attractive qualities, despite the fatigue she wore. The color of her hair was fetching enough. A reddish-gold that captured the light and returned it. But the way she had it fixed . . . The masses of curls pinned tightly to her head reminded him of corkscrews—some long, others short—and they bobbed about her temples when she spoke, as though possessing minds of their own. And ornery ones at that. Not unlike their owner, it would appear.

Unbidden, an image came to him of what she might look like with that pile of curls unpinned and loosened about her shoulders. That would surely be an improvement, but as tempting an image as that created, that mouth of hers and where she hailed from canceled out any interest he might've pursued in another time and place.

Still, a good mother's training tended to reach deep inside a boy, setting roots that held fast, even when that boy became a man.

He tipped his hat back an inch to make sure she could see his eyes and looked squarely into hers. "My apologies for any harm I've caused you, ma'am. It didn't come by intention, I give you my oath."

"How kind and considerate of you, sir." Arsenic laced her pretty smile and dimmed her former beauty. "But your oath isn't going to get me back my photograph."

Why, the feisty little— Daniel's thought stopped short. Surely he'd misunderstood her. "Your . . . photograph?"

"Yes, my . . . photograph." She repeated the word as though trying to mimic him, but he doubted his tone was that arrogant, nor his accent that foolish sounding. "I'd just captured an image of the elk when your rifle went off, causing me to drop the plate." She motioned behind her. "The picture plate is broken. Ruined!"

All this fuss over a picture? His estimation of the woman slipped several more notches.

He glanced past her and spotted the wooden box balanced on a tripod. He'd seen similar contraptions back during the war. Photographers would swarm onto a field after a battle, like vultures scavenging a next meal. And their pictures of the wounded, or those begging for death to come, would show up early the next morning in newspapers or be found hanging in store windows. As if being there and seeing your childhood friends cut down, one after the other, hadn't been painful enough. Some things weren't meant to be made so public, and he didn't understand others' insistence that they should be. A photograph to remember wasn't something he wanted—or needed.

"Ma'am, as I see it, there's nothing much I can do about what you lost. I'd make it up to you if I could, but I can't. You've made that more than clear."

A storm moved in behind her eyes, but it was one he had no intention of weathering. A snap of his fingers brought Beau to his side. Daniel turned to go, aware of the murmur of conversation behind him. Knowing it wasn't directed at him, he started down the path to his horse—and then heard the distinct clearing of a throat.

"Perhaps there *is* a way for you to make restitution after all . . . Mr. Ranslett."

Daniel stopped midstride, already dreading the look that would surely accompany the woman's uppity tone, and knowing full well whom to thank for her learning his name.

The Negro turned away, but Daniel would've sworn he'd caught the man smiling before he did. In the woman's eyes, the storm had passed, but the steeled determination now in its place promised to be of no less trouble to him.

4

Daniel Ranslett strode back toward her, his gait purposeful, his expression amusedly bothered, and Elizabeth readied herself for a spirited exchange. She enjoyed debating about as much as she enjoyed Tillie's buttermilk pie.

One thing quickly became certain—she wanted to photograph this man.

Watching him, the memory of a mythological figure rose in her mind, born from a collection of stories her father had read to her at bedtime as a child. She could still recall many of the characters, larger than life, all of them, but the man who bore the weight of the entire world upon his shoulders stood out above all the rest. Atlas's physical strength had been renowned, but what she remembered most from the story was imagining the *tired* written on his face, the sense of fatigue in his every movement as the author painted his plight, and how, even as a child, she'd felt sorry for him.

The man walking toward her now shared similar markings of strength—and weariness.

He was dressed in buckskin, and dark hair hung loose and thick at his shoulders. His jaw bearded and unkempt, he looked as though he'd been living in the wilds for weeks, if not months, and that alone earned him instant respect. After spending a day hiking and taking photographs in the Rockies, she couldn't wait to return to the comfort and warmth of her room at the boardinghouse.

She might've thought him part native if not for the water green of his eyes . . . and that drawl. As soon as he'd spoken, his Southern heritage had bled unstanched. To say he was a simple-spoken man was undeniable, yet something about his manner kept her from thinking him simpleminded.

He stood straddle-legged before her, staring down, and Elizabeth fought the inexplicable urge to salute him. Much to her father's chagrin, she'd mastered the finesse of a military salute long before she'd learned to curtsey, and something in Ranslett's unassuming swagger and the way he carried himself goaded her to follow through. But she doubted he was the kind of man who would take that gesture kindly coming from a woman.

Which, heaven help her, just tempted her all the more. But if this man was her key to photographing the Ute people, as Josiah had whispered moments ago, she would refrain.

"Beg your pardon, ma'am?" His sharp features held suspicion.

Her right hand still itched to be raised, but she kept it stayed. "I said, perhaps there *is* a way for you to make restitution for your actions."

He stared hard. "For *my* actions?"

When she nodded, his eyes narrowed in a way that might have intimidated her, had her father not tried the same tactic many a time. She'd mastered the return stare by the age of seven.

Ranslett did a funny sideways thing with his jaw, as though he were trying to size her up. "And just how might you propose I . . . make *restitution*?"

He said the word in such a way that she wondered if he knew what it meant. Yet she resisted the urge to explain. "Is it safe to assume, Mr. Ranslett, that there are *other* elk populating these mountains? Or have you slaughtered every living creature between here and Wyoming?"

The green of his eyes deepened, but not with humor. "I don't know what you're getting at, but I tracked that bull for two days in order to line up a clean shot. To make sure he'd suffer as little as possible."

Surprising sincerity accentuated his features and threatened to soften her ire, but thoughts of her lost photograph kept it fueled. "Most impressive, I'm certain, but I'm not talking about killing another animal, much to your likely dismay. I'm talking about a photograph, Mr. Ranslett. My camera lens can capture images from a great distance, so there's no need to get this close again, though that would be preferred if you could manage it. I would require an animal of similar size and grandeur, one that will impress."

He removed his hat. His glance drifted casually to her left hand, then back again. "And just who is it that you're trying so hard to impress, Miss . . . ?"

She narrowed her eyes this time, not caring for the tone he'd taken. To hear him speak with that deep voice and smooth languid drawl, like molasses slathered over bread hot from the oven, he sounded for all the world like a properly bred Southern gentleman.

But the *manner* in which he'd addressed her—that held no semblance whatsoever to the Southern charm witnessed from Georgian and Tennessean delegates she'd met at political gatherings. Perhaps her father's assessment was correct—Southern charm was little more than oiled politeness and surface at best, a poor attempt by the lesser countrymen to garner favor with their victorious Northern cousins.

Still, she found herself unprepared for Mr. Ranslett's presence close up. His eyes, observant and full, gave the appearance of kindness, despite their penetrating quality. And beneath the rough exterior, there was a sense of civility to the man, a tenderness in his manner. He carried himself with an assurance that resembled nothing of an attempt to impress. On the contrary, he gave the distinct impression that being in another's company—hers in particular—was among the least of his desires.

And she still couldn't decide which of the two smelled more like a wild animal—him or the bull elk.

"It's Miss *Westbrook,* sir, and I'm not trying to impress anyone. I'm simply trying to do my j—" She caught herself before completing the word. But not soon enough by the look on Ranslett's face.

A smirk tipped one side of his mouth. "And just what exactly is your . . . *job,* Miss Westbrook?" He said the word as though he found it amusing.

Elizabeth felt her backbone stiffen yet held her temper in check. People always acted differently once they learned she worked for a newspaper. They grew more guarded, or depending on the situation, they sometimes stopped speaking with her altogether. For someone who'd never made friends easily, that part of working for the *Chronicle* hadn't served her well.

But she hoped to change that in Timber Ridge—by giving towns-folk the opportunity to get to know her first. Wendell Goldberg had initially suggested the idea, stating that telling people she worked for the paper at the outset would only alienate them, hinder her assign-ment. Best to win them over first, let them think that photography was her hobby, and then tell them when she was ready. While it felt the tiniest bit deceitful, she saw the wisdom in his counsel and wanted to do whatever she could to better her chances of getting that position.

She raised her chin a degree, having learned a thing or two about negotiation from eavesdropping on political discussions outside her father's office door. "You said you'd be willing to make restitution if you could, sir. And if memory serves, I believe you gave your word. Is that offer still on the table?" She paused, unsure from the set of his jaw whether this redirection would work. "Or is your oath of questionable worth?"

His smirk disappeared. He fingered the rim of his hat. "I can't guarantee we'll come upon anything, ma'am, but I'll give you a day—

one day—to see if we can scout out another elk. No promises. No guarantees. After that, my obligation will be seen to."

She started to push for more, then decided his offer was enough. For now.

Feeling empowered, she held out her hand. It was a custom just beginning to take hold back east but was one she favored. Men shook hands with one another when agreeing to something, why not with women? "Shall we strike hands on the deal, Mr. Ranslett? Make it official?"

He stared at her, then at her hand, and took a half step back. "I don't strike hands with women, ma'am. But I'll honor my word— don't you doubt it."

Feeling slightly embarrassed, she attempted a good-natured huff. "Come now, Mr. Ranslett. I am a woman who—"

"You won't get any argument from me there, miss. That's something we can agree on, at least."

His tone bordered on playful and caught her off guard, as did the mischievous arch of his brow. Unwilling to be deterred by some Southern yokel—no matter how impressive looking—Elizabeth summoned her resolve, her hand still extended.

"Surely you're not shy of such a thing. A grown man such as yourself."

"There's not much I'm shy about anymore, ma'am. And I don't say that to my credit. But striking hands with a woman . . ." He slipped his hat on and took his time in answering. "That's one thing I'll never do."

Feeling the fool, Elizabeth slowly drew back her hand. "Very well. I suppose I've credited the South with more progress than it's due." She meant for the comment to sting, as he'd stung her pride, and saw from his darkened expression that apparently it had.

"If that's your idea of progress, ma'am, then we define that word a mite different."

"There's probably a whole passel of things we'd define a mite different, if we studied it far enough." She did a fair job of mimicking his twang, her years of working alongside men having sharpened her ability to respond in situations like this.

Ranslett studied her for a moment, then tipped his hat in gentlemanly fashion and turned. His parting expression, a mingling of reproof and regret, stole whatever triumph she might have felt and left her wishing she'd used better judgment.

She stared after him as he and his dog rounded the corner and disappeared from view. Her gaze moved back to the elk that up until moments ago had ruled this mountain, and that now lay crumpled and defeated.

She'd seen Ranslett run his hand along the animal's magnificent rack and knew buyers back east would pay handsomely for it. He probably had a purchaser waiting in the wings. The thought sat ill within her, and it didn't take her long to figure out why. One of the main reasons for her coming to this territory was to encourage tourists to travel west. To stay in a luxury hotel complete with hot springs and a waterfall and . . . to game hunt, if they desired.

"You sure this is still a good idea, Miz Westbrook?"

She glanced over her shoulder at Josiah. "You're the one who told me his name a moment ago."

"I knows it. I know I did." He wagged his head from side to side. "I'm just thinkin' back on it now, is all." His brow furrowed in a comical yet serious way. "You happen to take notice of the way he looked at you, ma'am? And how he gave me the eye?"

Elizabeth studied her new friend more closely. "You're not . . . afraid of him, are you? Of how he might . . . mistreat you?"

Josiah's expression sobered. His gaze went distant, and she sensed the pages of his life turning back inside him.

"No, ma'am, I ain't afraid. Not of that. Not no more." His jaw went rigid. "Worst thing a man could do to me . . ." His voice dropped to a whisper. He bowed his head. "That already been done."

Elizabeth started to pose the obvious question, but better sense kept her from it. Her father had warned her about such times, when her natural curiosity was not a virtue but rather a fault, an intrusion. And hadn't personal experience confirmed that lesson as well . . . ?

"I just knows when a man is set on helpin' a person. And I don't get the feelin' that helpin' you is what Mr. Ranslett is set on."

Elizabeth tucked a wayward curl back into place. "I don't really care what Mr. Ranslett is set on as long as he leads me to another bull elk. And will somehow refrain from shooting it until *after* I've developed the image."

She had just prepared another wet plate when Mr. Ranslett reappeared over the rise leading his horse, his aging beagle in tow. The scowl on the man's face had deepened, which improved her mood considerably. Served him right, after what he'd done.

He wasted no time in situating the bull elk onto its back, not an easy task to manage alone. When he pulled his knife from his belt, she turned away. Some things she didn't need to see.

"You be needin' some help with that?"

At Josiah's question, she turned to answer him, only to realize he wasn't addressing her.

"No . . . thank you." Ranslett didn't bother looking up. "I don't."

Josiah hesitated, then moved away, his expression masking any affront he might have felt. Another lesson he'd learned from his former station in life, perhaps?

An hour and a half later, with her shoulders cramping and an ache spanning her forehead, Elizabeth slipped a total of four dried glass plates, developed and swathed for travel, into a pack that Josiah loaded on the mule. She massaged her temples, wondering at the frequent headaches she'd had in recent days.

Despite the earlier incident with the bull elk, she had to admit that the day had been a success after all. The panoramas should please Goldberg, along with Chilton Enterprises, while communicating to him her seriousness about this opportunity. She would also let him know she'd begun organizing a travel party for her excursion to the recently discovered cliff dwellings south of Timber Ridge. She planned to leave within the month, if not sooner. The photographs at Mesa Verde were at the top of Goldberg's list, and therefore hers too.

She stole a glance across the cliff. And now she had found someone familiar enough with the mountain passes—and the Ute Indians—to guide her there.

Ranslett hadn't said another word to either of them. Hunched over his task, he didn't look up when she approached. One glimpse at the bull elk reminded her to entertain her gaze elsewhere . . . and removed an appetite for meat anytime soon.

"We're going to head down now." When he didn't respond, she added, "Josiah and I," and then immediately wished she hadn't. It made her appear cajoling.

Ranslett stood and wiped his hands on the front of his untucked shirt, having shed his outer buckskin coat a while back. Watching the uncouth display, she got the feeling he meant for it to irritate her. Unwilling to take the bait, she looked down, feigning nonchalance, and it was then that she noticed his shoes. Made of soft leather and looped together on the top with strips of rawhide, they resembled what she'd seen natives wearing in photographs. What a strange combination of traits this man held.

The dog ventured closer, and she held out her hand to pet him. But a quick command from his master sent him scurrying back to enemy territory.

Her patience waned. "Mr. Ranslett, how may I get in touch with you? Once we're back to town."

He reached for his canteen and took a long draw. Water dribbled down his dark-stubbled chin before he wiped it away with his sleeve. "You won't, ma'am."

She waited, half expecting him to belch, but he spared her that indelicacy. "Then . . . how will we meet to—"

"Don't worry." Holding her gaze, he stuffed the cork into the canteen's spout with his fist. "Finding you won't be hard . . . *ma'am*."

Certain he was poking fun at her, she managed a single nod, authoritatively, as she'd seen her father do. "Very well. Then I'll expect to see you again . . . *soon.*" She arched a brow to make her point, but he'd already turned away. Feeling dismissed—and not liking it—she joined Josiah.

Before they rounded the bend on their downhill trek, something prompted her to look back. She discovered Ranslett watching her. He didn't bother to look away, and a slow smile tipped his mouth. Without returning it, she quickly faced forward and sauntered down the hill, wanting to be the first to silently dismiss the other this time.

The man might not know it yet, but she was confident she'd just found the guide who would lead her to the Ute people. And—if she played her cards right—who would lead her expedition south to the cliff dwellings.

5

A knock on her door the next morning roused Elizabeth from a restless night of little sleep.

"Good morning, Miss Westbrook. I'm leaving your tea service outside the room, dear."

Elizabeth rose on one elbow and rubbed her eyes, her world still blurry. She'd awakened often due to dreams during the night, yet she couldn't remember a single one. "My thanks, Miss Ruby."

The soft padding of boots on the planked wooden floor in the hallway faded, and Elizabeth pushed back the covers and shuffled from bed. A tremor tingled her right hand, and she clenched and unclenched her fingers in an effort to get it to stop. The same thing had happened last night as she retired, but she'd attributed it to writing the article for the *Chronicle*. She always wrote a first draft, made revisions to that copy, and then wrote a second. Tedious, but she prided herself on turning in a clean copy. Something Goldberg highly regarded.

A familiar scent slowly distinguished itself from the muskiness of the room, and a quick glance out the window confirmed her suspicion—it had rained sometime during the night. Which didn't bode well for her. Humidity always worsened her lung ailment.

She reached for the bottle on the bedside table and tilted it at an angle so the light spilling through the window shone through the amber-colored glass. She'd been rationing it in recent days, but only a couple of teaspoons remained. Not even a full dose.

She opened the door, carried the tea service into her room, and set it on the desk. Though it was far less formal than the coin-silver set back home, she suspected it was Miss Ruby's finest, which made her appreciate it all the more. Miss Ruby, the proprietress of the boardinghouse, already had the tea steeping in the pot for her, as she did each morning. It was a special herbal blend the doctors in Washington recommended for her ailment. Elizabeth poured a cup and stirred in the remains of Mrs. Winslow's Soothing Syrup and drank it as a precautionary measure.

The syrup was also something a physician had prescribed, and she'd quickly discovered that it had a soothing effect on frayed nerves, which might prove helpful after such a fitful night. Its bitter aftertaste had lessened over time, but it still burned a path down her throat. She'd recently started taking a dash of the syrup with her tea before retiring too, to help her sleep, but with the bottle being near empty she had foregone the ritual the evening prior.

She slipped down to the communal washroom and raced through her morning routine, eager to get dressed and to the store so she could mail the photographs she'd developed after dinner last night. With any luck her package would arrive at Wendell Goldberg's office before the other candidates' first submissions did and would be a silent indicator of her determination.

Pausing for a second, she stared in the mirror at the flurry of curls springing from her head. She tried to pull her fingers through but knew it was useless. The only time she could get a brush or comb through the mess was when it was wet, and she hadn't the time for that this morning. Oh, for hair black as a raven's wing, straight and silky like the woman she'd seen earlier in the week at Mullins General Store, instead of the wiry mass of corkscrew curls God had seen fit to give her. Any effort to groom it now would only tease it into a rat's nest, as Tillie had said all too often.

Tillie was about the *only* one who could say that to her, given that her own hair was also averse to the brush. She sighed and pinned the curls up as best she could.

If there was a way of contacting Mr. Ranslett, she could get an idea of when he'd be available to take her hunting. But she'd have to rely on him to get in touch with her. And if Ranslett failed to keep his word . . .

As soon as the thought came, it quickly left, finding no foothold. "*I'll honor my word.*" She thought about what he'd said to her yesterday and somehow knew he would do just that—keep his word—regardless of the obvious fact that he didn't care to.

Not until she'd climbed into her chilled bed last night had the idea come to her. Even as she'd tried to dismiss it, she'd found herself weighing its merit. She could have taken another photograph of that bull elk . . . afterward, with Daniel Ranslett standing beside it. Though the idea still made her shudder, she knew Goldberg would have wanted her to do it. A photograph like that wouldn't have made the front page, for obvious reasons, but could have been used to advertise to game hunters.

Still, taking a picture of something dead didn't sit well within her, even if it would win her Goldberg's favor.

She repacked her toiletries and headed back to her room. She fit the key into the lock, but . . . it didn't turn. She tried to force it, sighing in frustration. Miss Ruby had warned her it might stick on occasion. But of all the times . . . As it was she would have to rush to make the stage that carried mail to Denver every weekday morning, and she didn't want to wait until Monday to mail her photographs.

She shook the knob, then gave it a brute twist. That did the trick, and she rushed inside.

She dressed quickly, lacing her corset snug and pulling on her stockings. Hers was the only room located on the third floor of the boardinghouse and was more spacious than the rooms on the lower levels. It had plenty of space to store her equipment, but Miss Ruby had made it plain that she wasn't enamored with her bringing the various chemicals for her photography into the room. Yet she had nowhere else to put them. And she needed them close in order to develop pictures during the evening hours. Not the ideal arrangement, but she'd make it work. No doubt hauling the heavy equipment up and down the flights of stairs was growing tiresome for Josiah, yet he never complained about it.

In fact, she couldn't remember Josiah complaining about anything she asked him to do. He might sass her occasionally, but that was different and all in fun. And she enjoyed it. Their banter was reminiscent of her relationship with Tillie. Oh, how she missed that woman.

Elizabeth buttoned her dress and fitted the coordinating black cummerbund around her waist, then secured the fasteners and stepped back to eye the ensemble in the full-length mirror. The dress was by far her favorite. She'd spotted it on a trip to New York City with her father and had slipped into the clothier to buy it, only to discover the price. Exorbitant! So she'd sketched the gown and shown it to a dressmaker in Washington, and the woman had captured the lines perfectly. Wearing it made her feel more feminine, yet it had a businesslike quality about it too. Not too frilly. Not too plain.

The bustle in the back was a work of art and flattered her waistline. Which, her being thirty-two, had far more generous curves than a decade previous. But that was the beauty of a corset—it lessened the contribution of passing years. And its curse? Not being able to take a deep, satisfying breath. There were days she weighed the cost.

Checking the clock one last time and knowing it would be close, she grabbed the envelope of photographs addressed to Wendell Goldberg. Already the hot tea was taking effect. A calmness flowed through her even as she hurried out the door.

6

There's a lot of meat here, son. You sure you want all of it going to them this time?"

"That's what I said—all of it." Standing in the doorway of the butchery, Daniel turned to see Lolly sink his meat cleaver into the milky pink shank of the elk. Beau yipped at the sound, his tail wagging, but a well-aimed look from Daniel kept him stayed and gnawing on the bone Lolly had tossed him.

"All I'm suggesting is that you think on your decision again. I could put some of this aside, get a good price for it. The rack, especially." Lolly wielded the butcher's axe as if it were an outgrowth of his thick, beefy arm. A lifetime of butchering accounted for that. "Then you'd be set once winter comes again. Wouldn't have to worry none."

"I appreciate your concern, friend, but I'm already set for next winter. I typically don't worry about much. And the rack's already spoken for." Anticipating Lolly's scowl made it even more enjoyable when it came.

"Then tell me this, Ranslett . . . What price are you gettin' for this bull's rack? A goodly sum, I hope."

Daniel turned his attention to the boardwalk outside so Lolly couldn't see his smile.

"You didn't just give it away, did you?" Lolly ceased his chopping. "Please tell me you asked *something* for it."

The heat of Lolly's stare prickled the back of Daniel's neck, but he ignored it and knelt to give Beau's head a good rubbing. The dog rolled onto his side, tongue lolling from his mouth.

Lolly swore softly beneath his breath and resumed chopping.

Daniel helped himself to a piece of jerky from a jar and regretted—for the hundredth time—his agreeing to take Miss Westbrook hunting. Her request had been nothing short of foolhardy, but he'd felt partially responsible for what had happened on the ridge yesterday—at the time anyway. Granted, that sense of responsibility had lessened each time she'd opened her tart little mouth.

What she was doing so far west, traveling the Colorado mountains unescorted—or at least not properly so—wasn't clear. She and that Negro journeying together wasn't proper. Even being from the North, she should know better. He'd wager his rifle that she'd come west for something more than just a hobby of picture taking. She was hiding something. He felt it.

And the way she'd wanted to strike hands with him . . . He tore off another piece of jerky and tossed some to Beau. He did like her spunk, though, and she had plenty of it. Might be fun to take her out and see how she could handle a rifle, see how that spunk held up under pressure. Spending time with her might prove more entertaining than he'd originally thought.

"It's a wonder you got a spare penny to your name, Ranslett." Lolly humphed. "All my life I've waited for a kill like this, and you just pull up at my door, sled loaded with the biggest bull elk I've ever seen, acting like it's nothing. You and I need to discuss right priorities, son."

Daniel laughed to himself, appreciating the false censure in Lolly's tone, and that the man referred to him as *son.* Leaning against the doorpost, he watched the town of Timber Ridge slowly awaken. The

Maroon Bells stood sentinel over the town while rocky troughs and peaks rose and swooned around them in stony admiration.

Sometimes he felt almost one with this place, as though he belonged here, instead of like the misplaced son he knew he was. How could he have lived in these mountains so long when his heart, his thoughts, the root of who he was, lay buried on a battlefield back in Tennessee?

Then again, perhaps therein rested his answer.

He stretched his shoulders, tired and stiff from days of hunting. By the time he'd gotten down the mountain, it had been dark and he'd been bushed, so he'd bunked with Lolly last night, on a cot in back.

Directly across the street, the door to the boardinghouse opened and Daniel took a hasty step backward, hoping she hadn't seen him. With that riot of copper curls caught up and a package of some sort tucked beneath her arm, she set out at a swift pace, looking like a woman being chased by a fire.

People on the boardwalk turned and stared in her wake, yet she seemed unaware of the attention. Most folks waited until after she'd passed before leaning close to whisper to one another, probably thinking they were being mannerly. But in his estimation, anything you wouldn't do or say to a person's face shouldn't rightly be done or said behind their back.

Miss Westbrook took the corner at breakneck speed. Presented with her shapely backside, Daniel found double enjoyment—first, in watching the tempting sway of those hips as she moved. And second, in simply watching her go, knowing she wasn't his concern. Hard to say which gave him the greater pleasure.

"You sure don't seem to hang on to much for long, Ranslett. Except for that rifle there. Don't think I've ever seen you carry another one. Which strikes me as odd, if you're askin', you bein' a man who makes guns for a living. Which you didn't ask me, I know. But if you ever did"—the chop of the cleaver accentuated his point—"that's how I'd give answer."

Not one to require an abundance of company, Daniel did enjoy an occasional visit with Lolly. The man could carry a conversation all by himself, which suited Daniel just fine, and the gem of wisdom or insight that often fell from the man's lips kept him returning too. That and Grady Lolliford's unfailing honesty.

"Speaking of not askin' me . . ." Lolly blew out a breath. "You haven't asked whether I've gotten any orders for you lately."

"Guess I figured you would've said something if you had."

"Well, consider it said. An order came in this week."

Daniel looked back to find Lolly watching him, and he knew why. "Who's it from?"

"Fella new to town. Said he'd just left Mullins's store and didn't find the gun he was looking for. He's huntin' elk and bear, looking for a guide too. I told him about you, that you made the best guns I've ever shot with. Told him I wasn't sure when I'd see you next, but that I'd ask you when I did. So . . . you got any rifles ready?"

"I do. Two of them. I'll bring them in tomorrow and leave them with you."

Lolly laid his axe aside. "Glad to hear it." He wiped his hands on his apron. "Sounds like you're doing better . . . since the last time we talked."

Daniel approached the cutting table and fingered the rough edge of the wooden counter. "I am. It's just taken some time."

"Like I told you before, it wasn't your fault, son . . . what happened last fall."

Daniel nodded, having told himself that over and over.

"Thomas Boyd was a good man. He just wasn't a very good hunter. And that's no fault to you. You were teachin' him, but he wasn't ready to go out on his own. That's all there was to it."

Daniel stared outside. "Some people still think it was my fault— I can see it in their eyes."

Lolly moved from behind the counter, wiping his hands on his apron front. "They'll come around, given time." He sighed. "Something like this happens, 'specially to a good family like the Boyds, and folks look for a person to blame. Guess it helps them cope with the loss. Makes them feel like they're more in control, maybe. Less at the mercy of some fickle-handed fate. And you bein' so private a man . . . well, that doesn't help."

The blame Daniel had seen in Rachel Boyd's eyes at the funeral last fall had worn a guilty rut in his conscience. He wondered how she was faring, and her two boys, though he was none too eager to see her again. Nor she him, he felt certain. Which seemed odd after having grown up together. She'd tried to blame her husband's death on the gun Thomas had been carrying that day—one Daniel had custom made for him—but the rifle had been examined and had fired repeatedly without fail.

Lolly gestured to Daniel's rifle. "You ever want to sell that beauty, just say the word. Those Whitworths are rare. I know plenty of men around here who've admired it, and they'd pay you a sinful price for it too. I think they figure it'd be like owning a piece of history. Albeit from the losin' side of the war."

Stung by that last comment, Daniel knew the man meant no harm. He ran a finger down the overlong barrel. Lolly knew the gun's history, and his, yet had never judged him over it. "Much obliged, friend, but I think I'll keep her."

Lolly opened his mouth, then closed it and motioned behind him. "Help me with something out back?"

A whispered "Stay" kept Beau by the door, and Daniel followed Lolly to the icehouse. Though the man stood a few inches shorter in stature, his forearms were the size of Daniel's thighs. Whatever needed carrying, Lolly could've managed it himself. But Daniel appreciated being asked, while also suspecting an ulterior motive.

Lolly pointed to the other half of the elk hanging upside down from the rafters. "I told you he was a big one."

Daniel exhaled, his breath clouding the frigid air. "How did I ever get this thing back to town?"

"You didn't. That fine mare of yours did." He retrieved a saw hanging on the far wall. "Don't seem fair to me"—his gruff voice took on a shine—"you owning both her and that rifle."

"Tell you what . . ." Daniel gripped the lower portion of the carcass and secured it as Lolly started the cut. "You can have both of them . . . once I'm dead."

"That's a dangerous thing to say to a man who has a saw in his hands, boy." Lolly grinned as he sliced through meat and bone.

Knowing where this meat was going gave Daniel a sense of satisfaction. It always did. It took every ounce of strength to manage the elk quarter alone, but he wasn't about to ask for help. Lolly would never let him live it down. The man's kidding could be merciless.

Back in the shop, together they heaved the carcass atop the cutting block.

"Little out of breath there?" Lolly laughed and wriggled his bushy brows.

Daniel kept his grin from showing. "Maybe when I'm old like you, I'll be able to lift more."

Lolly popped him a good one in the arm. "Listen . . . ah . . ." He shrugged. "Why don't you take the meat on out to the Tuckers' yourself this time? It'd mean a lot to Mathias and Oleta to see you again. And the kids would like to see you too."

So that is it. Daniel had sensed something was coming. "I think it'd be best to have it sent over, like we've done the last couple of times. I'm not sure my going out there would be a good thing right now."

"Whose good are we talking about? Theirs? Or *yours*?"

Daniel crossed the room to retrieve his rifle. "There're times, Lolly, when your honesty oversteps its welcome."

"Surely you don't think the Tuckers will treat you any different than before. If you think they will, then you're not giving them enough credit."

Daniel picked up his rifle and got his hat from the rack. He knocked the hat against his thigh, and dust plumed. Truth was, part of him wanted to go back out to Mathias and Oleta Tucker's home, to see them and their children. He'd been thinking about it for some time now. None of the boys or girls were natural-born to the couple, but they loved and cared for them as if they were. But the kids had known Thomas Boyd, and they played with the Boyds' boys.

In the space of a breath, a memory sunk deep inside him worked itself loose and rose to the surface.

It was a fleeting glimpse, only a second or two captured in his mind's eye, filed away somewhere deep inside him all these years. Of his pushing Benjamin on a swing beneath a two-hundred-year-old oak behind their home. He was twelve or thirteen at the time, and Benjamin was just a little thing, tow-haired and smiling, not even walking yet. He'd built the swing as a Christmas present and remembered tying knot after knot after knot in that looped rope to make sure it held good and tight.

Little good did all his protection do in the end. . . .

A snap of Daniel's fingers brought Beau to his side. The dog had the elk bone wedged between his teeth. "I appreciate your work on the elk, Lolly. Be sure and keep a portion of the meat for your trouble." He paused in the doorway, hearing the resigned sigh behind him. He adjusted his hat, reconsidering, his eyes misting as he looked anywhere but back at Lolly. "Have the meat ready come morning. I'll pick it up on my way out to the Tuckers'."

He left the shop before Lolly could respond, and before he could change his mind. He headed down the street. Since last fall, he'd all but stopped coming to town, and when he did, he made extra sure he didn't go anywhere near the sheriff's office. With that in mind, he took the long way around town on his way to the general store.

7

When Elizabeth rounded the corner to the general store to post her package, she was greeted by the sight of the stagecoach driving off in the opposite direction. She stopped midstride on the boardwalk and let out a frustrated sigh—then bit back a much harsher response when someone plowed into her from behind.

She turned and glared at the man, and heard every word—including the not-so-watered-down expletives—he spat at her through his tobacco-spittled beard.

She stared at him. "Perhaps you shouldn't follow so closely next time. And give thought to a bath . . . that would prove useful." Seemed the farther west she traveled, the fewer people practiced good hygiene.

A vulgar gesture accompanied his sneer—a gesture she'd unfortunately seen used by soldiers and officers. Though she'd known many soldiers of upstanding character, the military seemed to also attract the worst of men. She chose not to respond and turned away.

So much for being the first to get her photographs to Goldberg. With heavy steps, she covered the remaining distance to the telegraph office. She'd have to settle for wiring Goldberg to notify him that she would mail the package on Monday, along with the next installment in E.G. Brenton's column.

Dreading having to cross the messy thoroughfare, she carefully negotiated the mud-caked steps leading from the boardwalk down to the street. She gathered her skirt at the sides, grimacing at the thick layer of sludge and muck left from last night's rain. And her with her favorite dress on. Not a good decision on her part.

Her second miscalculation of the day.

Whenever Washington received rainfall, the air was thick and muggy, pressing over the city like a wet woolen blanket. Why the forefathers of this country had chosen to build the nation's capital on a swamp, she'd never understand. Yet that wasn't the case in these mountains. Yesterday's dirt might've been churned to mud, but the air still felt dry and light. Pungent evergreen scented the chill along with a sweetness she would've sworn was honeysuckle, but neither scent improved her attitude.

She climbed the stairs to the boardwalk and arrived at the telegraph office, only to be stopped cold by a sign posted on the door. Her last strand of patience evaporated. She strode inside. "How long will the telegraph be down?"

The man behind the counter quickly rose from his stool, his once-white apron smeared with ink and dingy with stains. At least he wasn't the young boy who had assisted her earlier that week. It had taken that inexperienced youth three tries to relay the telegram to the next station. And even then, she'd wondered if Goldberg would ever receive it and if it would still resemble her original message in any form.

"Good day, ma'am." The man gave a conciliatory nod, his expression showing regret. "I wish I could say, but I'm not sure. They think it's a problem down in the canyon. I heard something about the rains causing a slide during the night."

"A slide?" She briefly glanced outside. "That much rain fell?"

"Doesn't take much here, ma'am—especially this time of the year. Not with the snows thawing and beginning to melt. If you want to leave your message with me, I'll send it as soon as they have the lines repaired. That way you won't have to come back in."

She reached for a slip of paper, aggravated at the situation but also with herself. "Yes, thank you. I'd appreciate that." It was her own fault she'd missed getting that package on the stage. Still, Timber Ridge was primitive compared to Washington—rain taking out the lines. She thought she'd factored in the remoteness and what effect it would have on her situation, but she hadn't.

She penned the brief message in her head first, and removed unnecessary words as she set it in ink, factoring each cent. As well as factoring the confidentiality of the man sending it. "Am I assured, sir . . . that the messages I send through your company are kept confidential within your office here in Timber Ridge?"

"Yes, ma'am." His expression and manner reflected integrity. "Only me and whoever's listening to the clicks on down the line will know what you sent. Unless you're telling someone how you're about to rob the bank." Humor crept into his features. "Then I might have to get the sheriff involved."

She liked this man. "Agreed. Please send word to me at the boardinghouse once you receive confirmation of receipt." She laid her coins on the counter.

He read what she'd written and nodded. "Will do, Miss Westbrook."

Only a few steps down the boardwalk, she passed a darkened office window. It was part of the same building that housed the telegraph office, but it occupied a larger portion, and she'd already been there once. Sketched in large white letters on the front glass window were the words *Timber Ridge Reporter*.

As was her habit when she traveled, she'd stopped by her first day in town to pick up a copy of the newspaper. A person could learn a lot about a town from its newspaper, and by meeting its editor. But Drayton Turner, the *Reporter*'s editor, had been out. "On *special* assignment" according to the young woman behind the front desk, as if Elizabeth should've been impressed by such a statement. The *Timber Ridge Reporter* was a leaflet compared to the *Washington Daily Chronicle*.

Her gaze fell to a placard in the window she hadn't noticed before. On it was listed the hours of business. She read it and smiled. *Closed on Fridays?* How could a newspaper office be closed on Fridays? No matter the day, the *Chronicle's* multi-office, four-story building was always abuzz. Even on Sundays—though she normally didn't adhere to working that day, unless she was far behind.

Taken by the quaintness of this little town, she continued on to the general store and was almost to the back counter when she would have sworn she was staring at an apparition.

Standing there transfixed in the middle of the aisle, draped from head to toe in black, the woman resembled a portrait of a Southern belle Elizabeth remembered seeing hung in Mathew Brady's art gallery. An invisible hedge encircled the dark-haired woman, and people in the store went out of their way not to brush the ebony lace of her full-tiered skirt or interrupt in any way the air that seemed to lay in quiet folds about her.

Elizabeth attempted to do the same. But when she glanced at the woman's face, she found herself unable to look away.

The woman was stunning, but it wasn't her beauty that so commanded Elizabeth's attention. It was the grief veiling her features that Elizabeth found so hard to turn away from.

Until the woman met her stare.

Elizabeth forced her gaze elsewhere, embarrassed at having intruded upon something that felt so intimate, while not understanding what it was she'd intruded upon. "I'm here to see if my medicine has been delivered." She heard the explanation coming from her mouth but didn't remember granting the words permission. "It should have been here days ago." What was this overwhelming need to explain herself to this lady? She looked back.

The woman's eyes were wide set and watchful, and Elizabeth

found herself imagining them as they'd surely once been—a luminous sparkling blue, instead of dull and near gray.

"We have a doctor newly arrived to Timber Ridge." The woman's voice came out soft, like a petal opened prematurely before the final frost. Yet Elizabeth understood every word. "He hails from New York, I'm told."

Elizabeth found herself nodding. "I didn't know that. I'm . . . new to town."

"I know." Something surfaced in the woman's expression and removed a layer of grief, if only for an instant. "I've heard about you."

Elizabeth didn't have a response for that.

The woman's arms rested gracefully at her sides, skimming the delicate fabric of her skirt while leaving no impression on the folds. Were Southern women taken aside at a young age, to a hidden parlor, perhaps, and taught how to stand with such a regal air that it appeared as though they were not so much supporting their own weight as they were being held aloft by invisible strings? Everything about this woman was graceful, yet she exuded a tension that was nearly palpable.

Perhaps the other patrons in the store felt it as unmistakably as Elizabeth did and that was why they kept their distance. Perhaps Elizabeth should've done the same. She was searching for something else to say when she heard the woman take in a sharp breath.

"Forgive my boldness, but . . . would you agree to come to my home and photograph my sons?"

It took a moment for the unexpected request to register, and for its subtle desperation to sink in.

Elizabeth had photographed only one child before, and that endeavor had not ended with success. The child wouldn't cooperate, refused to remain still. Other photographers were able to talk to children in singsong voices or cajole them with entertaining noises that bewitched them as the seconds passed, so the glass plate could be fully exposed. But not her.

It was absurd, really, but she wasn't at all at ease in the company of children. They made her nervous. She never knew what to say to them or what to do. And when they smiled she couldn't help but think it was at her expense. Her reaction was a throwback to less-than-fond memories of childhood but was real nevertheless.

The woman's black-gloved hands knotted at her waist. "I would be willing to compensate you, of course."

Elizabeth rushed to correct the misunderstanding. "No compensation is necessary, ma'am. I'd be happy to do it." She gave a soft laugh. "But I feel compelled to tell you that I'm not gifted in relating to children, so the end result may not turn out as you desire." Her mind skipped ahead to obvious questions—had this woman lost a child and therefore wanted images of her remaining children? Or was it her husband she mourned?

"Mrs. Boyd?"

They both turned at the man's voice. Ben Mullins, the proprietor, had moved from behind the counter and was holding out a bag. "Here it is, Mrs. Boyd." Mullins smiled at her. "It's not much, but I can order more—you just say the word."

Mrs. Boyd took the bag and drew herself up, squaring her shoulders as though she were about to enter battle. From the gauntness around her eyes and the pallor of her skin, it looked as if she'd already endured one.

"My thanks, Mr. Mullins." She swayed for a second, as though the task of remaining upright was demanding her last ounce of strength. "I'm sure this will be fine."

Mr. Mullins's expression held compassion. "It's good to see you again, ma'am. Tell your boys hello for me. I stuck a few gumdrops in there for them. Hope you don't mind. Lyda insisted on it. She's always been partial to your sons, as you know. Just like I have." His voice fell away. "They remind us so much of our own children."

One side of Mrs. Boyd's mouth trembled as though she were trying to form a smile but had forgotten how. She bowed her head, and Mr. Mullins shifted his attention.

"And about your order, Miss Westbrook . . ."

Elizabeth blinked at the sound of her name.

"Your shipment finally arrived, ma'am. I'll get it from the back." The blue-and-yellow gingham curtain guarding the doorway leading to the storeroom wafted at his passing.

"Seems you won't be needing our new doctor after all."

Elizabeth smiled at the faint whisper beside her. "No, it doesn't seem so." Not yet, anyway.

The woman's task seemed complete, yet she didn't turn to go. The thought was absurd, but Elizabeth briefly wondered whether the woman's boots were nailed to the floor, she was so still and unmoving, like a child who'd been told to stay put and wait to be gathered.

A man walked into the store, drawing Elizabeth's attention, and everyone else's, it seemed. His hat nearly brushed the top of the doorframe as he passed beneath it, and he paused just inside as though searching for someone.

When his gaze settled on Mrs. Boyd, Elizabeth noted a subtle change in him.

He walked in their direction, speaking to everyone he passed without exception, addressing each man, woman, and child by name. If first impressions counted for anything, Elizabeth guessed him to be an official of Timber Ridge. Perhaps the magistrate or mayor, though she'd never seen a mayor so well loved as this man apparently was, so she decided on the former. Protectors of justice inspired adoration like few others.

"Rachel . . ." He touched Mrs. Boyd's arm, and the imagined nails in the woman's boots loosened.

She leaned into him. "Thank you for coming back for me."

He kissed the top of her head and cradled it as he might have a child's. "The boys are in the wagon. We'll head home now." He tipped his Stetson in Elizabeth's direction. "Miss Westbrook, we haven't had the pleasure of meeting yet. It's nice to finally make your acquaintance, ma'am. I'm James McPherson, sheriff here in Timber Ridge."

Silently congratulating herself at having guessed correctly, Elizabeth peered up at him. More than just a hint of the South lingered in his voice, like another man she'd met recently. "The pleasure's mine, Sheriff. And should I be impressed or frightened that you already know my name?"

"Neither, ma'am." His soft laugh was convincing. "I just consider it part of my job to know who's coming and going through town." He considered her as he slipped an arm around Rachel Boyd's shoulders. "You're from our nation's capital, and from what I've observed, you have a particular interest in photographing our mountains. An uncommon pursuit for a woman."

"Very good, Sheriff. And yes, I do nurture a love for photography. It's a hobby I've studied for several years."

"James . . ." Rachel looked between them. "Miss Westbrook has agreed to come to the house and photograph Mitchell and Kurt."

Brief surprise lit his face. "Well, that's a fine idea. My nephews are good-looking boys, Miss Westbrook. I think your camera will take to their likenesses real quick, if they'll sit still long enough for you to catch them."

"I'm sure I'll find some way to persuade them." Although Elizabeth had no idea how. She'd agreed to the request only for Rachel Boyd's sake. Being in the company of someone grieving made people promise things they might not otherwise, in hopes of easing their pain.

Rachel reached out and grasped her hand.

Taken aback, Elizabeth stole a look at the sheriff, who seemed as surprised as she was.

Rachel's grip—not really a handshake, more like a clasping—was gentle and womanly, so different from what Elizabeth had worked to develop with her male peers. "I admire you, Miss Westbrook. It takes courage to leave your home and come to a place like this. And then to offer to share your gift with us . . . expecting nothing in return."

The tears in Rachel's eyes prompted a weight to settle in Elizabeth's chest. She silently accepted the praise while knowing herself unworthy of it. She'd hardly come to Timber Ridge expecting nothing in return.

Rachel was delicate in every way that Elizabeth was not. Her flawless ivory complexion, the way she moved—even her features seemed to have been crafted by a smaller, more skillful hand. And not a corkscrew curl on the woman's head. Elizabeth had always felt ill at ease around such women. Until now.

Rachel squeezed her hand one last time before letting go, and seemed to come closer to remembering how to smile before once again abandoning the effort.

Sheriff McPherson gently held Rachel's arm. "At your convenience, Miss Westbrook, please stop by the sheriff's office. It's just two streets over, on the right, and we'll arrange a day for me to escort you out to the house."

"I'll do that, Sheriff. Thank you."

Elizabeth followed their progress out the door and then walked to the front window and watched Sheriff McPherson assist Mrs. Boyd into the wagon. As they drove away, she spotted two redheads over the wall of the wagon bed but couldn't see the boys' faces. The wagon rounded the corner at the far end of the street.

The kindness in James McPherson's face coupled with the strength of his stature made for an odd, but powerful, combination. Especially for a lawman in such an untamed territory. If she'd been the melting type, she might have considered it a few minutes ago, but she had yet to meet a man who even came close to sweeping her away. Her career had become her companion and was filling that place inside her, satisfyingly so.

Tillie's oft-repeated mantra about the wisdom of remaining single came to mind. *"It takes an awfully good man . . . to beat no man at all.*" Elizabeth had been well into womanhood before comprehending the meaning of the saying, but life's experiences had proven the counsel trustworthy.

It didn't erase the loneliness she still sometimes felt, especially late at night, but it made it more bearable when she imagined being wife to one of the many ambitious soldiers who had vied for her affections, at least on the surface. In reality, most had been vying for a higher rank through an alliance with her father. A painful truth, but one that she'd accepted, and learned from.

She studied the faces of Timber Ridge residents as they passed by on the other side of the window. Some she recognized, though she had yet to make their acquaintances.

"Yes, ma'am, I'm just checking to see if those sights your husband ordered for me came in yet."

She recognized the voice instantly—just one aisle away—and peered over the shelf.

"And if you have some gumballs, would you add those to my order too? A box of them, please, ma'am."

Elizabeth waited until Lyda Mullins left to fill the order before she quietly sidled up to the counter, knowing her presence would be about as welcome to this man as an invitation to attend one of her suffrage rallies.

8

Gumballs, Mr. Ranslett? Somehow I didn't peg you as a man with a sweet tooth."

A faint grimace crossed his face when he saw her, but that was all the reaction she earned. "Miss Westbrook . . . I didn't see you when I came in just now."

Elizabeth laughed. "Well, if that's not the most honest response I've gotten in a while, I don't know what is. But that's all right, Mr. Ranslett. I'll take honesty over pretense any day. Blunt is so much better. Saves everyone time."

He stared at her for a beat. "At least that's something we see eye to eye on, ma'am."

He'd apparently bathed, because the wild smell from yesterday was gone, replaced by something still earthy but very pleasant. Either that or it had been the elk all along.

Ben Mullins returned. "Miss Westbrook, I've got a question for you." He gestured for her to follow him off to the side, then leaned closer. "I'm not sure that company sent the right thing. They sent bottles of syrup, like you said, but"—his voice lowered as he held out the bottle—"they're labeled for children, ma'am." His brows rose. "With teething problems?"

Elizabeth shot a look at Ranslett to see if he was listening, but he didn't seem to be paying her any mind. She couldn't explain why, but she did not want to be seen as physically weak in front of him and therefore didn't want him knowing that she took medicine. Everything about the man screamed strength and control, and she wanted to give the same impression.

His gaze settled on something in the corner behind her. Curious, Elizabeth turned, and quickly ascertained the object of his stare. Angled against the wall was a mirror, and from her vantage point she could see his image from the chest down. Just as she reasoned he could see hers—from behind.

As a test, she reached behind and smoothed a hand over her bustle. He quickly glanced away. She turned back, hiding her smile, and kept her voice soft. "They shipped the right medication, Mr. Mullins." Seeing as the proprietor would be receiving future orders, she decided it best to tell him. "My physician in Washington prescribes this particular syrup for my lung ailment. I've taken it for several months now, and it's actually working quite well. Even if I'm not the manufacturer's intended consumer."

"Well, whattaya know . . ." He adjusted his glasses and read the label to himself, his lips moving silently. He nodded, and continued in their conspiratorial tones. "Lots of folks with breathing problems end up out here. Colorado's air is good for the lungs, ma'am, has healing properties. So do our hot springs, they say. There's a spring not far from the boardinghouse where you're staying. You should try it out sometime."

"That's what I've heard, and I fully intend to do just that."

"You've got three big crates in the back too. Came fragile packed. Must be the glass plates and chemicals you told me about."

It tickled her the way he was still whispering. "I'll ask Josiah to pick them up this afternoon, Mr. Mullins."

"No rush—whenever is fine. If I see him first, I'll let him know they're here." He held up the bottle. "I'll go get the rest of these for you."

Mullins retreated, and Elizabeth stole a furtive glance beside her. Ranslett was watching her directly now, innocent looking as could be. Debating for only a split second, she stooped low enough to peer back at him in the mirror. "See anything interesting a moment ago?"

Expecting a sheepish look, she didn't get it.

A rogue's smile tipped his mouth. "When a woman wears a bow the size of Texas on her backside, she ought not be surprised if it draws a stare or two. You said we were supposed to be blunt. Right, ma'am?"

Elizabeth clenched her teeth to keep from laughing, but she couldn't prevent a smile. "Most certainly. That's exactly what I said."

His gaze swept her dress. "Just don't wear that thing when we go hunting. Bright colors don't blend in, and they tend to scare off the prey."

So he *did* intend to keep his promise about taking her hunting. That was good news. "And I suppose not shaving for days on end and wearing buckskin like a native attracts them?"

A dimple appeared in his stubbled right cheek. "I don't know that I'd recommend that for you, but it seems to work for me fine enough."

It sure did, but she wasn't about to agree. "Exactly when are you planning to take me on this hunting trip, Ranslett?"

His brows shot up. "First time I've had a woman call me by my surname. Is that part of this . . . *progress* you were telling me about yesterday?"

"Are you evading my question?"

"No, ma'am. How about tomorrow?"

She sobered, excited at the prospect. "You're serious?"

His smile deepened. "I am. I've got somewhere to go first thing in the morning, but I can take you up to—"

"Our agreement was to a full *day* of hunting, Mr. Ranslett. Not an afternoon." She already planned on using the trip as the basis for a column, recounting the experience for the *Chronicle* readers, spicing it up some if she needed to so that it would appeal to game hunters.

He did that sideways thing with his mouth again. "Are you always this demanding, Miss Westbrook?"

"Yes, I am."

He exhaled. "Best to know at the outset, I guess."

She ignored the gleam in his eyes. "What time do we leave?"

"How about I meet you at the butcher's shop at nine? It's right across from your boardinghouse."

"And just how did you know where I am staying?"

"I told you I wouldn't have any problem finding you." With a nod, he indicated her dress. "You don't exactly mix in with the rest of the folks around here."

Mrs. Mullins laid his bill on the counter. He read it, put down his money, then hefted the box of sundry items, a box of gumballs balanced on top. "Thank you kindly, ma'am."

"And here are your items, Miss Westbrook." Ben Mullins made the necessary change from the bills she handed him. "Sure is an interesting thing you do, ma'am."

"Thank you, I find it intriguing. It's a hobby I've studied for several years."

"Lyda and I would like to have you over for dinner this Sunday, if you're available, to hear more about it, and to get to know you better. You might consider setting your camera up some Saturday in the store here too. I know people in town would pay to have their pictures taken, if that wouldn't be something you're opposed to."

She was taken aback by his kindness and interested in his offer. "I'd appreciate both of those opportunities, Mr. Mullins. Thank you very much. Until Sunday, then . . ." She moved to lift her box, but Ranslett beat her to it. She caught up with him halfway down the aisle. "I'm quite capable of carrying that myself, you know."

He stopped and turned. "Did you hear me say you weren't?"

So soft was his voice, so neutral his expression, she knew he'd meant nothing by the gesture. He was just being mannerly. She felt awkward in the moment and somehow put in her place by his kindness. Her defenses rose accordingly. "I just want to be clear that I don't expect you to do those kinds of things for me." She glanced at the box. "I'm perfectly capable of managing on my own."

He stared, his expression inscrutable. Then he adjusted the crates in his arms. "Thanks for making that so clear for me." Without a word, he deposited her box in her arms and walked out the door.

She'd underestimated the weight and dropped her envelope of photographs in order to balance the load in her arms. She stared at Ranslett's back, half amused, but mostly annoyed that he would just dump the box in her arms and leave. She quickly glanced around to see if anyone had overheard their exchange.

Two women nearby moved away, while a man standing down the aisle a ways made straight toward her. He was rough looking and lacking refinement, the sort she'd seen when passing by the gaming hall in town. She couldn't believe he was coming to help her.

She glanced down at the envelope. "Thank you, sir. I appreciate your assistance."

But he didn't move. And from the thick bulge in his cheek, he was enjoying a distasteful pastime. "Out here, ma'am, we appreciate a woman who knows her place, and who remembers what that means. And who don't go traipsin' round town flauntin' some nigger on her arm."

Elizabeth's body flushed. She worked to keep her voice calm. "I know very well who I am and what my place is . . . *sir*, as I can clearly ascertain what sort of man you are."

His actions portended what was coming. The dark spittle landed squarely on the envelope. And with a parting glare, he turned and strode from the store.

Elizabeth saw Lyda Mullins approaching. Flustered, embarrassed, she glanced down at the man's parting gesture. "I'm sorry about what just happened, Mrs. Mullins."

Lyda patted her arm. "Don't you worry about it at all, and it's not you who needs to be apologizing." She retrieved the envelope and wiped it with a towel. "I appreciate what you're doing here in Timber Ridge, Miss Westbrook. I think it's mighty brave." Her smile was short-lived but genuine. She tucked the photographs inside the box. "Here's a letter that came for you this morning too." She slipped it in as well. "You take care now, and Ben and I are looking forward to Sunday lunch. Come about noon, if you want. Or earlier and go to church with us."

Elizabeth nodded. "Thank you," she whispered. "I'd like that."

She secured her grip on the box and continued down the aisle, peering to the side so as not to trip over anything and draw further attention to herself. She expected to find Ranslett waiting outside on the boardwalk and searched for him first in one direction, then the other. But he was gone.

———

Daniel awakened in a cold sweat, his flesh crawling. He bolted upright in his bed, blinking in the darkness, not sure where he was for a moment, only that the wraiths that haunted his sleep were pressing especially close tonight.

Beau whined and nudged closer, and Daniel ran a hand along the dog's back, gaining a measure of calm from the softness of his fur. He took in a lungful of air. Then another. This had been a bad one. Despite the many battles he'd lived through, two in particular reigned over his dreams—the night Benjamin had followed him . . . and the battle at Chickamauga he'd just dreamed about.

Passing years hadn't dulled the images. Lowering his face into his hands, he remembered everything—the smell of smoke from the Federals' campfires a mile away, and the pangs of hunger gnawing a hole in his belly.

The misty haze of a Georgia dawn had lain lightly on the north-west mountains, and trees stood stark and naked in the gray light, stripped by an early frost. His right cheek flush against the barrel of his newly requisitioned Whitworth, Daniel searched for his target in a sea of Federal blue. He'd practiced with the firearm but hadn't used it in combat yet—if these assignments they gave him could rightly be termed "combat." They were certainly part of the war and always ended in a death. Always. So he guessed they qualified just fine.

His superior told him that this gun, with its special sights, could accurately shoot a target up to a mile away. Even farther if you were really good, which he was.

The leafless branch at his back acted as both support and reminder of his lofty perch, and he blew into his hands, trying to warm them, loosening up the tendons. Temperatures had dipped low during the night as he'd dozed below with his regiment, slipping from wakefulness to sleep and back again. But long before dawn the cold had finally dispelled any hope of rest, and he'd risen to climb to his perch.

His stomach growled and he tried to ignore the pangs. His rations were gone. They'd stripped the bark from trees and had used water from the creek to make a bitter drink. It had done little to satisfy his belly and had only invited the chill deeper inside him.

No fires allowed—Major's orders—which made smelling the smoke from the Federals' camp that much harder. He had no socks, and the leather soles of his boots had worn through in spots, but at least he had boots. Most of the men in his unit didn't.

The cold steel of the Whitworth felt like a branding iron against his cheek, and he took a breath, held it, then exhaled, feather-closing his left eye in order to sharpen his focus. He secured his target, over a mile away, and watched the man through the crosshairs.

The colonel sat astride a bay mount, double rows of polished brass buttons lining his decorated uniform and glinting in the pale morning sun, easily distinguishing him from the lesser-ranking officers and soldiers standing nearby. Down to the last man, each Federal soldier gathered round their commander looked warm and well fed, and he couldn't help but envy them for that. But he didn't envy what awaited them on this side of the ridge—the Tennessee Army, crouched and ready to strike.

He snugged the trigger with his index finger, patient for the right angle. He'd only get one chance. Minutes passed, and he could feel the eagerness of his regiment awaiting his lead. *Relax, steady breaths.* He whispered a prayer, and fired.

In an instant, the world changed.

Stricken, the Federal colonel clutched at the hole in his chest even before the blood soaked his uniform. Through his sights, Daniel watched the commander fall headlong from his horse, a split second before the report of the rifle reached the Federal camp, though Daniel doubted the man heard.

But the colonel's men did, and they acted quickly. Confusion engulfed their camp, according to plan.

His assignment complete, Daniel sheathed the Whitworth and began his downward climb just as an eerie screech rose from the densely wooded hillside beneath him. One voice lifted at first, followed by another and another, until the unearthly, primal chorus flooded the forest floor and rose in a fearsome swell over the pike. His spine tingled with the chill of it, familiar though it was, and he wondered how any enemy could hear the rebel yell and not shudder.

Below him, his regiment pushed through thick stands of pine and prickly bramble until they crested the ridge. Eager to join them, Daniel had started to climb down when he heard a faint high-pitched whistle. It cut through the cacophony. He sensed it more than heard it and might not have done that much had he not had such experience with it on the opposite end. He placed the sound an instant before the bullet slammed into his back.

The force knocked him belly first over a limb, and he dangled there, suspended, momentarily blinded by the fire scorching his back and right shoulder. Distant gunfire registered and impulses collided inside him.

Strangely weightless, he hung there, able to make out the faint outline of someone climbing up to him. He heard his name being yelled.

Another distant whistle, similar to the first, and Daniel pictured his mother's face, regretting that he hadn't gotten back home in the past two years. The bullet hit somewhere to his right. The branch on which he hung cracked and gave way. He lunged at lower limbs in hopes of slowing his descent but couldn't get a hold. The bark stripped the flesh from his palms, and somewhere on the way down, he had blacked out.

Pushing the memory from his mind, Daniel climbed from bed and strode to the cabin door. He stepped outside into the crisp, cloudless April night and took a lungful. The moon cast a pewter spell over the mountains, and the chill felt good against his bare chest.

He breathed deep, trying to cleanse himself of the nightmare. Judging from the moon's position, it was somewhere between two and three o'clock. Ice crystals blanketed the blue spruce and lodge pole pines, and in the distance the low roar of the waterfall girded the night's busy silence.

His face was cold, and reaching up, he realized his cheeks were wet. He wiped them and stepped farther out into the small clearing. A trillion stars blinked down at him, and he couldn't help but wonder if they were portals to heaven, as his mother had told him when he was a boy. And if Benjamin was watching.

On nights like this it gave him comfort to think his youngest brother and his mother were together. That comfort swiftly fled when he considered that *all* of his family was now there, together, and he'd been left on this earth alone. For what reason? To what purpose? None that he could figure. God had simply forgotten to take the last Ranslett, and Daniel sorely wished He hadn't.

In that moment, he would have given all he owned to have been back in Franklin, walking the familiar hills of home, of his childhood, before the war had pillaged the land and taken his family.

Beau's whining from the doorway encouraged him back inside. Daniel shut the door and knelt down. He scruffed Beau behind the ears, grateful for the desire to please his master that shone in the dog's big brown eyes. Odd, but Daniel found himself a bit envious of Beau. For so long he and *his* Master had been at odds with each other, something that hadn't been true earlier in his life. He didn't know about God's feelings on the subject, but he was growing weary of the feud. Part of him wanted to try and mend things, but how could he when the only One who could have intervened that night, who could have saved Benjamin . . . hadn't?

He crossed the room and stoked the fire. Sparks flew up the rock chimney he'd laid by hand. Pencil-drawn pictures hung above the mantel took him back to better days. Mitchell Boyd had drawn the first—a picture of Daniel hunting. Daniel's body was as big as the mountain and his rifle just as tall, and on his face was a wide grin. Daniel found Kurt's picture more sobering. Again, it showed a child's rendering of him, but this time he stood over a bear sprawled flat on the ground. The bear wore a sad countenance. Which Kurt had explained, "That's because he's dead. You just killed him because you're the best hunter in the territory."

He remembered the night the boys had given him the pictures, two weeks before their father, Thomas, was killed. He hadn't seen them or their mother since then—except from afar, at the funeral—and he hadn't seen their uncle in a while either.

Thinking of home and family, he was reminded of the debt he still owed James McPherson. Though things between him and McPherson had become strained and they hadn't spoken in months, he stood by, ready to repay that debt whenever McPherson called it in. The man had saved his life, in so many ways.

He lay down on the bed again and pulled the blanket up over his chest. Beau hopped up beside him and snuggled close, contributing his warmth.

Nights like this made Daniel wish he could ask McPherson how he'd managed to start living again. How he'd gotten to the place where he didn't wake every morning having relived a battle like Chickamauga, where Daniel had been wounded. Or the terror on the battlefield that night in Franklin, within miles of his childhood home. Daniel closed his eyes and could still see row after row, layer after layer, of mutilated bodies—nine thousand of them, piled on top of each other so that the dead were left standing with no room to fall. The earth drank in their blood until its thirst was slaked and it could hold no more, so the ground pooled the precious sacrifice in hastily dug holes the soldiers had clawed out, seeking refuge and finding none.

Realizing sleep was futile, he threw off the covers. He filled the coffeepot with water and hung it on the hook in the fireplace, then lit the oil lamp on his desk and set out his quill and paper. Congress had yet to respond to any of his letters, but they couldn't ignore his requests forever. Surely he'd gain someone's attention if he kept writing. Sometimes he felt like the lone voice in a wilderness, but someone needed to stand up for this land and for the Utes' sacred cliff dwellings. Otherwise the heart of the Colorado Territory would be pillaged and lost forever, just as his beloved South had been.

To make matters worse, he couldn't seem to convince land developers that he didn't want to sell his land—any of it—to *any* company. Frankly, he didn't much care how his decision would affect the "expanding economy" of Timber Ridge, as Zachary at the title office tried to persuade him. In his experience, most folks tended to think they needed a lot more to get by on than what it actually took.

He poured a cup of coffee and settled at his desk. Only a couple of hours remained before he needed to head back down the mountain. He was actually looking forward to visiting Mathias and Oleta Tucker and their family. And spending time in Elizabeth Westbrook's company was higher on his list than he'd thought it'd be.

The woman was obstinate, opinionated, and he doubted whether the word *satisfied* was even in her vocabulary. But she would be a welcome distraction after the night he had just endured and would provide a nice buffer in case things at the Tuckers' were strained. But the best thing—Elizabeth Westbrook didn't have the slightest connection to him or his past in any way, which was what he needed. Someone who wouldn't remind him of what he'd done during the war, of what he'd once been.

He picked up the quill, dipped it, and began to write.

9

This 'bout it, Miz Westbrook." Josiah retrieved the last satchel of supplies from the corner, sweat glistening on his brow. "We ready to go soon as Mr. Ranslett shows."

"Very good. Thank you, Josiah. I'll be right down."

The satchel Josiah carried wasn't overly heavy, but he had already made five or six trips up and down the two flights of stairs. She really needed to find another place to stay. Either that or find a safe location where she could store her equipment and develop her photographs. Her room was coming to smell of chemicals, and Miss Ruby had kindly commented about that fact again this morning when delivering her tea.

Elizabeth took care in wrapping the camera lens in a soft cotton cloth before slipping it inside her pack. It was the single most expensive piece of equipment she owned and she hadn't the means to buy another. She could replace about everything else, but if this lens were to break, her dreams of winning the job would be broken too.

"What you doin' with all these books, ma'am?"

Josiah held up a McGuffey Reader, and she cringed, having intended to reseal that crate.

He'd carried three crates up to her room for her last evening, and at the time she'd been under the impression they'd all come from the same company and contained glass camera plates, chemicals, and other supplies she'd shipped from Washington. But as she opened them alone later, she realized her father had seen fit to send her a crate of supplies as a "welcome gift" of sorts.

Telling Josiah the truth about the books meant risking his being disappointed in her. And though it might have sounded silly to some, she didn't want him thinking less of her. She waved off his question. "Those were shipped to me in error." Which was partially true. What was also true was that she was responsible for that error.

"Want me to tote 'em on back to the store for you?"

"No, no, that's not necessary. We can take care of them later."

"Suit yourself, ma'am. Too bad we don't got us a schoolhouse here in town."

Josiah's steps retreated down the hallway and Elizabeth let out a sigh. Well, that answered one of her questions. She'd hoped the town had a school. It would've made her father's request a little easier to fulfill.

She reached for the letter and ran a hand over the broken seal on the back of the envelope. Her father was such a stickler for the details. This particular seal bore the imprint of the United States Congress and gave insight as to his frame of mind when he'd penned the missive.

She skimmed the page, taking comfort in the familiar slant and formality of his handwriting. She noted the date of the letter's author-ing—three weeks ago. Hardly a week after she'd departed Washington. Sooner than she would have guessed he would write.

My Dearest Elizabeth,

First and foremost, I pray this letter finds you, and then I pray that it finds you well. I have had occasion to ponder the map on my office wall and cannot quite fathom the miles that separate us. I pray you are finding the rest you need and that the air in those Rocky Mountains is as medicinal as our physician said it would be.

While my desires voiced to you the night before your departure remain unchanged—I would have you happy and fulfilled, preferably here in Washington—I understand this desire within you to stretch your horizons, as you so stated, and to discover what difference you might make in the world. It is not unlike what has long driven my own pursuits.

To that end, I am having a crate of slates and readers sent to your attention. All newest editions, of course. Additional teaching supplies will arrive at a later date, as I can arrange for them. Senator Wilkes, Director of Education, is indebted to me, and I will lean upon his good favor for your benefit. If Timber Ridge, Colorado Territory, is to have its first teacher, then they will have one supplied with the finest curriculum available. Which will no doubt be of higher quality than such a wilderness has ever beheld.

I look forward to receiving a photograph of you with your pupils, as I have no doubt you are still making time for the hobby you have so long esteemed.

Your father, both near and far,
Colonel Garrett Eisenhower Westbrook

She ran a finger over the dried ink on the elegant stationery, lingering over her father's signature, and closed her eyes. Guilt over her swiftly told falsehood retraced the miles she'd worked so hard to put between her and that particular evening.

She loved and respected her father and had fully intended to tell him the truth. She had entered his study the night before her departure, resolute to share everything—and had done just the opposite. She'd known in that moment what it must have been like for the hundreds of men who had once served beneath her father's command. The pressure to please him was overwhelming, and that he inspired that desire not from fear of him or his disapproval but from simply wanting to reach the aspirations he held for you . . . Well, that made her want to succeed in her endeavor here even more.

She read a particular line for a second time.

If Timber Ridge, Colorado Territory, is to have its first teacher, then they will have one supplied with the finest curriculum available.

A teacher.

That's what she'd told him she was coming out here to be. He'd questioned it only briefly, having already seen the advertisements in the *Chronicle* for teachers needed out west. She'd wanted to confess her true reason for heading west, but he'd never been supportive of her working at the *Chronicle,* much less her striving to be a photographer and journalist. Those were men's jobs and therefore unsuitable. It wasn't that he thought her incapable of doing them. That wasn't the issue. There were simply roles for men and roles for women, and those lines were not to be blurred.

She'd known he wouldn't approve of her *teaching* career, but he would object far less to that noble profession than he would the truth.

She slipped the letter back into the envelope, then into the desk drawer, and drank the last of her tea. At thirty-two years old, one would think she would've outgrown the need for her father's approval. Was she not capable of deciding her own future? Of course she was. So why did part of her still feel like that little girl with mud-splattered curls standing outside the horse stables, cringing beneath his stern frown while longing for his affirmation?

She checked her pack to make certain she'd included a full bottle of medicine and locked the door behind her.

Thinking of the crate of books up in her room, she was able to see a glint of humor in it all. A shipment of teaching supplies was on its way from Washington to Timber Ridge, and the town didn't even have a school.

She reached the boardwalk and spotted Josiah waiting across the street at the butcher's shop per their discussion, but she saw no sign of Ranslett. She checked her pocket watch—thirty-five past eight.

She was early—a by-product of being raised with a military father. He was a stickler for punctuality.

She thought again of how Ranslett had left her standing in the store. He wasn't late . . . yet . . . but in the event he'd changed his mind about taking her today, she and Josiah would make the short trek back to Maroon Lake, where they'd been yesterday afternoon, and she would finish taking photographs there. So their preparation this morning wouldn't be in vain.

She stood there for a moment, debating a quick errand, and then decided to chance it. She told Josiah where she was going, then cut a path down the street. To her delight, the office was lighted inside and she saw a man in the back.

She opened the door, knocking as she did. "Hello?"

As he drew closer and she got a better look, she guessed him to be Drayton Turner, the editor of the *Timber Ridge Reporter*. Who else would be working when everyone else was not? And would be wearing such a scowl?

He met her at the front counter, hardly looking at her. "I'm sorry, ma'am, but we're not open for business until nine o'clock."

His brusque manner was familiar and sparked an unexpected urge within her to be back in the throes of the bustle of the *Chronicle* offices. And why should she expect a newspaper editor in the Colorado Territory to be any different from one in Washington? They were an odd breed, editors, but a breed she understood. "Yes, I realize that, sir, and I didn't mean to bother you. I was hoping to pick up the most recent edition of your newspaper."

Recognition flitted across his face. "You're the photographer. I've seen you around town." His scowl softened. "A photographer is a welcome addition to Timber Ridge."

She could well guess why he felt that way. She'd seen his publication. Not a photograph to be found. But that was no excuse for her to act pretentious. "Yes, I am. Photography is a hobby I've studied for several years. Couple that with a fascination with the Wild West"—she said it with enthusiasm and widened her eyes—"and here I am." Aware of him watching her, she waited to see if he would buy the "coming west for adventure" slant.

Slightly taller than she, he was balding on the crown of his head but boasted a healthy stand of black hair elsewhere. Rather than increasing his years, the look gave him a distinguished quality that he carried off well. Thankfully he wasn't one of those men who grew his hair longer on one side and swept it across to the other to compensate. One of the reporters at the *Chronicle* did that, even adding a little twist on the top, for whatever reason, and he was forever being ridiculed by his peers behind his back. Though the habit was amusing and only drew more attention to what he was trying to hide, Elizabeth had always found it uncomfortable when the jesting turned to him.

"I admire that kind of courage, ma'am. Especially when I find it in a woman. I'm Drayton Turner, editor of the town's newspaper, the *Timber Ridge Reporter*. I own this building and am working hard to get Timber Ridge up with the times. We have a telegraph office, if you haven't noticed." An elitist air slipped into his voice and told Elizabeth all she needed to know.

"Elizabeth Westbrook. It's a pleasure to meet you, sir. And yes, I was recently in the telegraph office." It was all she could do not to mention it wasn't working. No need in getting off on the wrong foot. She extended her hand.

He looked momentarily bemused by the gesture, then shook her hand. "And you as well . . . *Miss* Westbrook?"

She nodded, answering his none-too-subtle question.

He reached to a stack on a nearby table. "Here's a copy of our latest edition. We publish every Monday and Thursday morning. But with the town's growth, I've been considering going to a larger format. Either that or going to a more frequent publishing schedule."

If Goldberg had handed her something like this, he would have been offended had she not read it right away. So she skimmed the front of the single sheet publication in half a minute, then turned it over, nodding as she scanned the back. She'd always been a fast reader.

"So, what do you think of it, Miss Westbrook?"

His tone cradled the real question. He wasn't asking for her opinion as much as he was asking for her praise, and she couldn't fault him for it. It was a loathsome dependence she shared. Every other Monday when E.G. Brenton's article hit the stands, she couldn't wait to frequent the local restaurants and shops in hopes of overhearing comments. The more positive the better.

"Your publication is very . . . informative, Mr. Turner. And well laid out on the page. Do you do your printing on site?" She decided it best not to mention the four misspellings she'd found.

His laugh was indulgent and his expression patronizing. "If my guess is right, and I'm rarely wrong in this regard, my little newspaper is none too impressive to someone like you, Miss Westbrook. Let me see if I can guess correctly . . . New York City?"

Elizabeth shook her head, seeing more similarities between him and Goldberg by the minute. Both were intelligent, capable, self-assured men—who wore their egos on their sleeves. The last character trait wasn't an admirable one, but it certainly made reading the men easier. The only difference she could detect was that Turner was younger, and significantly more attractive.

He held up a hand. "Wait, don't tell me." He smirked more than smiled. "Washington?"

"Very good." Though not hard to decipher. "But I've spent quite a bit of time in New York, so you weren't too far off there either."

Feigned yearning thinly veiled his envy. "I'm impressed, Miss Westbrook. I've never been to New York City. Came close once, but then my—" The confidence behind his smirk faded. "Let's just say that my circumstances changed. I'll bet being out here seems a world away to you, barbarous in comparison to what you're accustomed to."

"No, not at all."

"You can be honest, ma'am. We'll consider this conversation . . . off the record."

The statement made her go tight-lipped. How many times had she used that same phrase only to quote the person verbatim the following morning under the guise of an "unnamed source"? Once Goldberg had inserted the person's real name, against her wishes but at the insistence it would have been wrong not to expose the source. She hadn't agreed, but since E.G. Brenton's name was on the article and not hers, she hadn't had to deal directly with the aftermath. But as E.G. Brenton's "assistant," she'd lost a trusted source.

She used care in phrasing a quote-worthy response while thinking up a reason to leave. "On the contrary, Mr. Turner, I've been impressed with the beauty of Timber Ridge and its surroundings. Already I can tell that good, decent people live here. New York City may be exciting in many ways, as is Washington with its political climate, but neither of those cities has anything like your Rocky Mountains."

He chuckled softly. "Well done, Miss Westbrook. A truthful answer that deftly skirted the heart of the question. With such skill you ought to run for town council. Or better yet, come work for me!"

She joined in his laughter, hoping hers sounded natural, and glanced at the clock on the wall. "I have another appointment this morning, but I thank you for the newspaper." She opened her reticule. "How much do I owe you?"

"No charge, ma'am. Just consider it a 'welcome to town' from the *Timber Ridge Reporter*. And . . ." His expression turned decidedly less businesslike. "Feel free to stop by anytime. Perhaps I might persuade you to take some photographs for the *Reporter*. I'll publish them and list your name right alongside. Imagine it . . ." He punctuated the air as he spoke. "Elizabeth Westbrook, Female Photographer!"

How like Wendell Goldberg this man was. Goldberg had a way of knowing what would motivate a person and never failed to use that to his advantage. He also never wanted to be bothered with something until that *something* held an advantage for him. Then he could change horses in the middle of a stream faster than imagined and with nary a splash. Just like this man.

"I doubt my photographs of landscapes and wildlife would be of interest to you, Mr. Turner. Or to anyone else who lives here. You see both all the time."

"And who's saying you can only take photographs of landscapes and wildlife, Miss Westbrook?"

Elizabeth guarded her reaction. "Well, no one, of course. That's simply been the bulk of my choices thus far."

His area of focus briefly drifted to encompass more than just her face. "One of the beauties about being out west is that convention isn't so . . . burdensome a cloak in these parts. You'll find that, out here, you can explore . . . other choices. And I'm hoping you'll make time to do just that." He tilted his head and looked at her in such a way that told her he meant for the gesture to come across as promising, perhaps even enticing.

But his effort fell far short on her.

With a hasty good-bye, she hurried to meet Ranslett, not daring to look back, but could feel Turner's eyes following her. The attraction wasn't there for her, yet a small part of her appreciated his attention. Hadn't encouraged it, but appreciated it.

For the first time in years, no one around her knew of her association with the *Washington Daily Chronicle*. No one knew she was the daughter of U.S. Senator Garrett Westbrook, decorated colonel in the Federal Army, and strategist behind some of the North's greatest battle victories in the war—both distinctions coming with their own stigmas and preconceptions.

Here, she was free of those past identities. No one saw her as the woman she'd once been. They saw her for who she was now, and the anonymity felt . . . wonderful.

For the first time in her life, she truly believed she had the chance to be whoever and whatever she wanted to be.

It was two minutes after nine, and Josiah confirmed that Ranslett hadn't shown yet. Winded from hurrying back, Elizabeth peeked inside the butcher's shop, wondering why he'd suggested they meet here. She got a whiff of what awaited past the entryway and decided against venturing farther in, until she spotted the man behind the counter. Then she changed her mind.

He stood hunched over a slab of meat and repeatedly brought down his cleaver with a force worthy of his build. His shoulders matched the width of the doorway behind him, and his forearms and hands were massive. She stepped inside.

The smell of raw meat and its vestiges hung heavy in the small building, and an oversized slate board propped by the door quietly announced what cuts of meat were available. She looked for an icebox but didn't see one. Their butcher back home had a pristine ice-lined glass case where he displayed fresh cuts of beef, pork, chicken, and fish.

The man behind the counter didn't look up, so she took the opportunity to watch him, already knowing he would make an excellent subject for a portrait. She laid aside her pack and surveyed the room. Morning sun slanting through the front window would provide ample light, and the surroundings were perfect. Rustic, unrefined. Without a word, this setting, this man, would capture a slice of what it was like to exist on this frontier. Perhaps far better than the pictures of landscapes she'd been taking.

She couldn't say whether Goldberg would be won over by the photograph or not, but her instincts told her it held possibilities. Even more so if the butcher had a story to go along with the life experiences etched in his face. And she bet he did.

The man briefly looked up, away, and then back again.

He stilled, his meat cleaver paused midair. His bushy eyebrows met to form a single line. "How do, ma'am. Somethin' I can help you with?" He sank the cleaver into the edge of the table and swatted at an unseen fly.

"Yes, sir. At least I hope there is."

He gave her a quick up and down, then eyed her more closely. "Meat's out back in the icehouse. Got what's listed on the board right there—plus some elk I can sell you. Fresh. Just butchered yesterday."

Jars of jerky sat atop a shelf above the counter. She'd never cared for its salty taste or tough texture. "I'll take four slices of jerky, please." Her chances were always better if she purchased something.

"Peppered or no?" He tore off a piece of butcher paper.

"Not peppered, thank you."

He formed a sleeve and slipped the jerky inside. "Ten cents."

Handing him the coin, Elizabeth noticed the swelling around his knuckles and the scars crisscrossing the tops of his arms and hands. Butchering was a costly occupation. Maybe he'd be willing to let her take a photograph of him closer up, after she got his image with the butcher block and cleaver. "Sir, I don't mean to be too forward, but I—"

"In my experience, ma'am, anytime a person starts out with 'I don't mean to be too forward . . .' it usually means they're aimin' to be just that. They're just hopin' the other person won't take offense." He handed her the jerky.

She laughed softly, not having expected him to be quite so insightful, or forward. "I admire your candor, sir, and will come straight to the point."

"That's usually best, miss." He kept a straight face, but she detected a smile edging his voice.

"I'm new to Timber Ridge and have come here to photograph your beautiful mountains. But . . ." She tried for a shy smile. "I'd very much appreciate the opportunity to take your personal photograph, sir. I have my equipment here, and—"

He shook his head. "No thank you, ma'am. Not interested."

"No fee is involved. It won't cost you a penny."

"Good day to you, ma'am." He walked back to his table.

Elizabeth moved down a few steps to keep in his line of vision. She'd heard of natives who didn't want their picture taken for fear the image would steal a piece of their soul and they would enter the next world unwhole, but she'd never encountered a white man who held that belief. "It won't take but just a few minutes, and it doesn't hurt a bit." She ended on an upbeat.

He picked up his meat cleaver. "My answer stands."

Elizabeth tightened her grip on the jerky, and the paper crinkled. "May I ask why you're so averse to my proposition?"

He grasped his cleaver, brought it down hard, twice, and laid aside the two cuts of meat. "Maybe 'no thank you' means somethin' different back east, ma'am." Another clean cut, but this time with the crunch of bone. "But out here when someone says it, it's considered rude to keep pushin'."

"I don't mean to push, I just—"

"Morning, Lolly. I just got the meat from the icehouse and left those two guns in the back."

Elizabeth startled at the voice behind her and turned, hearing the butcher's deep grunt in response.

Ranslett's tone was all friendliness and welcome, but disapproval shaded his expression. And she noticed something else. His beard was gone. His jaw was smooth and clean-shaven; his hair looked freshly washed. A still-damp hank of hair curled at his temple and he'd traded the worn buckskin for a well-fitted shirt, vest, and dungarees.

The change was astonishing, and the question was out of her mouth before she'd thought it through. "Going courting this morning, Ranslett?"

He smiled and rubbed his jaw, his dimples even more pronounced without the beard. "Not that I know of, Miss Westbrook. But the day's young yet." He winked. "How 'bout I get back with you on that?" He glanced over her shoulder toward the butcher, his demeanor sobering. "Is there a problem here?" he whispered.

"No. No problem. I was just asking Mr.—" What had Ranslett

called him? "Mr. Lolly a question." She shot a glance at the burly man, who seemed absorbed again in his work.

"And I believe Mr. *Lolliford*"—Ranslett gave the name added emphasis—"gave you his answer."

She hesitated, not caring for the tone of his correction. "So it would seem. By the way . . . you're late."

"My apologies." He dipped his head. "I had a letter to post for Monday's stage." He gestured toward the door. "Shall we?"

She grabbed her pack and preceded him outside. The tan mare he'd had with him in the mountains was now hitched to a loaded wagon, and his beagle sat perched on the wagon seat. Josiah stood in the street, clutching the mule's reins.

She stopped short on the boardwalk. "Are we taking a trip?" Though she couldn't see his face, she heard his chuckle.

"I need to deliver some meat to a family outside of town. It shouldn't take us long. Then we'll see if we can find something worthy of that camera of yours. Something that will . . . impress."

She ignored the teasing in his tone. "Josiah has my equipment packed on the mule. Can we tie on to your wagon?"

"Fine by me."

She noticed Josiah didn't move but watched Ranslett instead. Not until Ranslett gave a nod did Josiah do as she had suggested.

"Mind if I ride in the back there, Mr. Ranslett, sir?"

Saying nothing, Ranslett unpinned the back hinge, lowered the railing, and made room enough for a person to sit.

"Thank you, sir." Josiah climbed in and situated himself.

Ranslett started around to her side of the wagon, presumably to help her up, but Elizabeth placed her camera on the floor beneath the bench seat and climbed up on her own accord. He smiled up at her, offering her a curious look, and moved to check the harnesses.

The beagle snuggled up, and Elizabeth held her hand outstretched for him to sniff it. He licked it, and she rubbed him behind the ears.

"Remember, Ranslett, you promised me a day of hunting and I want the full experience. Exactly what you'd do during a normal day of scouting out an animal to cut down in the prime of its life." She waited for his reaction and could tell he had one but hid it, because he purposefully wouldn't look at her.

"It's called tracking, ma'am." He leaned down to peer beneath the wagon. "And I told you before, I'll do my best."

She pulled the pad and pencil from her pack and made note of his phrasing, then slipped it back inside again. She'd already noticed what was beneath a blanket in the back. "Is the rack spoken for?"

He put his foot on the wheel to climb up. "Beau, to the back!" The beagle vaulted over the seat and climbed to where Josiah was seated. The dog began licking Josiah, which didn't seem to bother Josiah at all.

Ranslett climbed up beside her and sat down. The bench seat shrank by two thirds. Holding her camera, Elizabeth tried to scoot over so that they weren't touching so much, but her right hip met with the edge of the box seat. It wasn't as if she were some prim young schoolgirl who had never rubbed thighs with a man when riding in a carriage, but this seemed different. This seemed so much . . . closer.

She looked at where their bodies met, then lifted her gaze to find him smiling.

"There a problem, ma'am?"

She lifted a shoulder as nonchalantly as possible. "No, everything is fine. And you?"

"I couldn't be better."

"I am, however, still awaiting an answer to my question. . . . Is the rack spoken for?"

"Yes, ma'am, it is." He gave the reins a snap and the mare responded.

She gripped the bench seat. She didn't know how she would manage to ship something like that back to Washington but knew it could be done. And she also knew Goldberg would prize the gift. He'd be the envy of the other board members, and her thoughtfulness wouldn't hurt her chances at the job either. "What if I were to say that I'd like to buy it from you?"

"Then I'd have to tell you that I'm sorry, that it's already spoken for, again."

She weighed his answer. Her funds were by no means unlimited but the accommodations and food here were far less expensive than what she'd budgeted for, so she had some leverage room. "What if I offered you more than your current buyer?"

"I'm pretty sure you can't match his offer, Miss Westbrook."

"Try me."

He maneuvered a path around a freight wagon whose owner was unloading supplies at Ben Mullins's store, then pulled back on the reins and waved another wagon through the intersection. "I appreciate your interest, but . . . no thank you."

Elizabeth realized then that he'd been behind her in the butchery for longer than she'd thought. She sighed and stared off to her right. He probably thought himself comical at repeating what Lolliford had said to her. He snapped the reins again, urging the mare forward, and they rode in silence.

They were nearly out of town when she heard her name being called. She turned on the seat. Ranslett must have heard it too because he slowed the wagon.

Sheriff McPherson waved to them from the boardwalk and held up a hand, indicating for them to wait. He shook the hand of the man he was speaking with, then strode toward them. "I'm glad I spotted you, Miss Westbrook. My sister reminded me this morning to set a time to bring you out to the homestead for that photograph. Once she gets something in her mind, it's hard to budge it."

Elizabeth smiled at him. "I'm much the same way, so I understand."

McPherson's focus drifted. "Ranslett . . ." He nodded once. "How've you been?"

Ranslett shifted on the narrow bench beside her. "Fine, Sheriff. Keeping busy."

Sheriff McPherson acted as if he might say something else, but he didn't. A moment passed.

Elizabeth would've had to have been completely unobservant to miss the tension traveling between the two men. And she was fairly certain Ranslett hadn't been gripping the reins so tightly a moment ago.

"Rachel's eager to learn more about what brought you out here, Miss Westbrook, and about Washington. She asked for you to bring whatever pictures you may have of back east."

"I'll happily do that. I only hope my stories won't disappoint her. Washington isn't as exciting as people often imagine."

"Don't forget where you are, ma'am. Timber Ridge is a beautiful place, but it hardly matches the happenings in a big city. Rachel always dreamed of visiting places like Washington when we were growing up."

"And where did you grow up?"

"Little town south of Nashville, ma'am, called Franklin." Sheriff McPherson shot Ranslett a quick look. "You've probably not heard of it . . ." A shadow crept over his face. "Unless you knew somebody who fought there in the war."

It took a moment for the name of the town to register. And when it did, Elizabeth swallowed. "Yes . . . I—" She took a quick breath, wondering if she sounded as breathless as she felt. "I remember . . . reading about that particular battle." And hearing numerous officers recount what a great victory it had been for the North, and for her father in particular. He had been scheduled to be on the battlefield that day but was called back to Washington. His longtime military friend and colleague, and her "Uncle" Henry, took his place. And before the battle had even begun, Colonel Henry Jackson had been killed by a sharpshooter. After telling her the news, her father had never spoken of it again, but she knew he carried the burden of that day inside him. Just as she did the guilty gratitude that he hadn't been there.

Mindful of the heritage of the two men present, she suddenly grew conscious of her own heritage and stance in the war. "Sheriff, please tell your sister"—she pushed away thoughts resurfacing about the war and the number of soldiers killed in that battle—"that I look forward to seeing her again. I'm free to come out late tomorrow afternoon if that's convenient for her."

"Actually, tomorrow might not be the best day. How about . . . next Saturday? A week from today?"

As they settled the details, Elizabeth stole a glance beside her. Ranslett hadn't even attempted to join the conversation.

"Ranslett, you're welcome to join us too." The sheriff was studying the ground, but his invitation seemed sincere. "Might be good for you and—"

"I can't. But thanks."

Elizabeth sensed McPherson wanting to press the issue, and waited for him to do so. But he didn't. He simply gave a slow nod, tipped his hat to her, and walked on. As Ranslett drove the wagon from town, she thought again of what Lolly had said to her about not pushing a person. Especially when they turned the corner and Ranslett stole a backward glance in the direction the sheriff had walked.

10

They'd traveled nearly a mile before Elizabeth dared test the silence. Josiah hummed a tune from the back, one she remembered hearing at a rally she'd attended where the speaker had been a former slave. Somehow Josiah managed to weave the melody into the slow plod of hooves and the squeak of wagon wheels.

She moved her head slowly to the left, a fraction at a time, as though she were watching the rise and fall of the passing mountain peaks instead of sneaking a look at Ranslett beside her.

He seemed lost in another world, one in which she was not a part. He was an impressive-looking man, in a rugged, unconventional way, and vastly different from the polished, well-bred Southern boys she'd known who had attended Georgetown University before the war. His jaw was more square than her memory had assigned and his hair thicker, with a curl to it. His eyes turned down at the corners, giving him an almost boyish appearance, and a melancholy one. But the boyish look ended abruptly at his muscular neck and shoulders—at that point, *powerful* was the overwhelming descriptor she would choose to assign him. He and Josiah were very similar in that regard.

"Beautiful country, isn't it?" He looked her way.

She quickly focused on the mountains beyond him. "Yes, it is."

"You've never been out west before." It wasn't a question.

"No, I haven't." She smiled. "Why, does it show?"

"Not to a blind man."

She held back a laugh, still a bit peeved at his earlier behavior. A cool breeze, not too chilling, rustled the sparse grasses growing between boulders strewn along the path.

"What brings you out here, ma'am?"

She felt Ranslett's attention but didn't look at him. "I've always loved photography, and when I read about the Colorado Territory, I decided I wanted to see it for myself." Which was wholly true—it just wasn't the whole truth.

"Where'd you read about it?"

"Books, newspapers."

He grunted softly.

"What does that mean?" She imitated his grunt.

"Just strikes me as odd . . . a woman like you just up and deciding to leave Washington and travel all the way out here—to take photographs."

"Firstly, I don't care for your phrasing of 'a woman like me,' and secondly, perhaps it does sound odd if you don't have a love for nature and an appreciation for wildlife." Granted, her love for both of those things had been recently acquired, but nevertheless it was true.

His amused expression said he wasn't the least bothered by her comments. Nor fully convinced.

He slowed the wagon and negotiated a tight turn onto a washboard road. It smoothed out after a hundred yards or so, but not before Elizabeth wondered if her teeth would ever stop rattling. She took a deep breath of cool air and felt a tingle in her lungs. Not one that frightened her this time.

"Tastes good, doesn't it?"

She knew what he meant. "Yes, it does. The air here is much fresher than what I'm accustomed to."

"I don't doubt it." He sat up straighter and stretched his back and shoulders, then rolled his head from side to side. "You ever been married?"

"I beg your pardon?" Elizabeth was certain she heard a soft chuckle behind her.

"Just asking a question, ma'am. Making it blunt, the way you like it. And saving us both some time."

His attempt to copy her accent failed miserably. "No, I've never been married. If I had I wouldn't go by *Miss* anymore, now, would I?"

He shrugged. "Can't always tell by that these days."

She debated whether to counter the question and decided to match his boldness. "What about you, Ranslett? Have you ever been married?"

He huffed. "No, ma'am."

"Such a reaction might lead me to think that you don't esteem the institution of marriage."

"Then you would've made a hasty judgment, Miss Westbrook, and would have arrived at the wrong conclusion."

She stared at him as they rounded the bend. A cabin came into view, a modest dwelling set in a cleft of the mountain and bordered by evergreens. To the left sat a barn sagging with neglect and the weight of time. An empty corral adjoined it, its fence in need of repair—but it didn't really matter since there were no livestock present. A leaning structure squatted nearby, between the barn and the cabin, and Elizabeth assumed it was an outhouse.

A curl of smoke rose from the cabin's chimney, making the scene idyllic, in a rustic sort of way. She could already see the caption— *Primitive Colorado Territory Homestead, photograph by Elizabeth Garrett Westbrook.*

Silently, she framed the scene through the eye of her camera lens. Ranslett was already delivering on his promise of finding something *impressive* for her camera lens, not that she was going to tell him. She still wanted another bull elk.

And she still needed to broach the subject of his escorting her to the cliff dwellings. She would know when the timing was right, and this morning wasn't it. But soon. It was mid-April, and she wanted to be on her way no later than the first of May. Goldberg had set September first as the date to have all the photographs and articles into his office, and then the board would review the three candidates' work and make their decision. Allowing a month each way for the journey—perhaps longer if the terrain was difficult or if weather didn't cooperate—then a good two weeks to photograph the dwellings and the Indians, and then time to develop the prints and ship everything back to Washington, she should be able to have her submissions in around mid-August, with time to spare. Everything was going according to plan.

The door to the cabin swung open before Ranslett brought the wagon to a halt. A woman stepped out onto the front porch, wiping her hands on her apron. Her hair looked entirely silver, but her movements belonged to those of a younger woman.

She squinted and tilted her head. "Daniel Ranslett, is that you?"

"Yes, ma'am, it's me." He set the brake and jumped down. "Hope you don't mind us just showing up like this."

"Well, I'm expecting President Grant any minute for tea, but you can stay until he arrives." The woman's seriousness dissolved into a smile.

Elizabeth liked the woman's humor and was mildly impressed that she knew who the current president was. Except for Rachel Boyd and Drayton Turner, she'd gotten the impression that people in Timber Ridge didn't care much about what was happening back in Washington. Or back east, in general.

A child scampered out the door of the cabin, a little girl judging from the ragged dress. She worked her way into the folds of the woman's skirt, sucking her thumb and peeking out every few seconds. Another girl followed, a little older if her height was any indication, and not so shy. She was lithe of build and had hair the color of honey that hung straight down her back. She stared open-faced and curious. Three boys appeared from around the side of the cabin, all barefoot and dark-haired. They looked to be near the same age—could've been six or seven years old, or maybe ten. Elizabeth wasn't good at judging such things.

She'd have thought the woman on the porch to be beyond the age of having children so young, but people out here didn't seem to operate by the same rules as society back east. And apparently neither did the birds and the bees.

"Hope you don't mind some meat, Mrs. Tucker." Ranslett shoved his hands into his pockets. "Lolly had some extra again and asked me to bring it on out. I think Mrs. Mullins might've sent some gumballs along too—for you and your husband to enjoy, of course."

Elizabeth's interest piqued at the gentle lie he'd told. So this was what he was doing with all that meat from the bull elk. He should have said as much.

The older girl clapped at the news, while the boys whispered to each other. Mrs. Tucker laid a gentle hand on the tiniest girl's shoulder. "If Mathias can still manage a gumball, then I'm sure the president's carriage will be arriving any minute." She laughed and nodded to Elizabeth, then peered beyond her to Josiah. "Let me tell Mathias you're here. Then I'll call the rest of the children to help unload."

The rest of the children? Elizabeth stared. How many more could there be?

"I've got something for Davy too." There was a subtle change in Ranslett's voice. "If he's well enough to come out. If not, I can bring it in."

Mrs. Tucker paused in the doorway. "If it's what I think it is, we'd better bring him out here." She smiled and shook her head and disappeared back inside.

All five children shadowed her like little ducklings. Which, when thinking of her father's letter, gave Elizabeth an idea . . .

Ranslett made his way around to her side of the wagon, and she quickly laid her pack on the floorboard and got a foothold on the rim of the wheel. Halfway down, she slipped. She caught herself and regained her footing, noticing how Ranslett didn't come to her aid. Once on the ground, she brushed the road dust from her skirt and finally braved a look.

Ranslett wasn't exactly smiling, but his expression said he was thinking about it. "You made such a point of getting up there all by yourself, ma'am. I just figured you wanted to show me how you could get back down too."

Doing her best to appear indifferent, she glanced at Josiah and was certain she'd caught him about to smile. He quickly turned to untether the mule.

She retrieved her camera from the seat. "I might as well make the most of the opportunity. . . . I'll set up over there and get an image or two of the house and the mountains while we're here."

"So you wants me to set it all up, Miz Westbrook?"

"Yes, please, Josiah." She looked back down the road they'd traveled. "Right about there." She pointed.

Josiah tugged the mule's reins, but the animal went lock-kneed, obviously making a stand. Josiah walked back to the animal and scratched the place between its ears and whispered in a low voice. Never once had Elizabeth seen him whip the mule or treat it in brutal fashion. The mule finally relented, and the beagle shadowed Josiah's steps.

"Miss Westbrook, about the Tuckers . . ." Ranslett removed the blanket covering the rack and wadded up the cloth. "I'd like to ask something of you, if you don't mind."

Seeing the rack up close gave her pause. She'd seen similar ones, of course, but smaller, hanging in statesmen's quarters back home. The set of antlers looked even bigger separated from the animal, but definitely less impressive, and Elizabeth chose to remember them as she'd seen them the very first time. How she wished she hadn't dropped that glass plate.

"You were saying?" She raised a brow to remind him.

He stuffed the blanket into a corner of the wagon bed. "The Tuckers and their children are fine people. You won't find any better." He glanced back at the house. "Mrs. Tucker sometimes asks me to stay and take a meal with them, and I feel the need to—"

War cries and high-pitched squeals cut off the conversation, and they both turned in the direction of the house. Children ran full out toward them—Elizabeth counted seven, eight . . . *ten* in all—followed by Mrs. Tucker and a man she assumed was the woman's husband. He carried another young boy in his arms. That made eleven children!

The children's squeals quieted when they reached the wagon. The girls stared wide-eyed at the antlers, while the boys reached out to touch the points. Elizabeth studied Ranslett, trying to make sense of what was happening. Surely this family wasn't the buyer he'd referred to earlier. Some of the boys weren't even wearing shoes.

Ranslett met the parents by the front of the wagon.

Mr. Tucker balanced the boy in his arms and stuck out a hand. "Daniel, it's good to see you again. It's been several months."

"Yes, sir, it has been. I don't get to town as much as I used to." It seemed like a long time before Ranslett spoke again. "Davy, how are you, buddy?"

The boy shifted in Tucker's arms. "I'm good, Mr. Daniel."

Elizabeth saw something pass between the older gentleman and Ranslett, a look calling the boy's response into question. She studied the child more closely yet didn't see any signs of illness. She noticed his hair was the same honey color as the older girl she'd first seen with Mrs. Tucker.

Davy strained to peer over Ranslett's shoulder. "Did you bring Beau with you again?"

"I sure did." Ranslett motioned back behind him to where Josiah was setting up the dark tent. He put his fingers to his mouth and gave a sharp whistle. The dog came running.

Mr. Tucker took care when kneeling down with Davy, but

Elizabeth caught sight of the wince on the boy's youthful face. Yet all evidence of pain vanished when Beau reached up and licked his tiny chin.

Davy giggled and the rest of the children gathered round him, doing the same. It was odd—from what she remembered about children she would've thought they might have crowded close and pushed and shoved to get a chance to touch Beau. But not these children. Each took their turn, and the older helped the younger ones who acted shy.

When the moment quieted, Daniel motioned toward her. "Mr. and Mrs. Tucker, I'd like to present Miss Elizabeth Westbrook of Washington, D.C. Miss Westbrook, my friends Mathias and Oleta Tucker, and their children."

"Welcome, Miss Westbrook." Mr. Tucker included his wife. "We're glad to make your acquaintance."

One of the dark-haired boys raised his hand as though in school, and spoke when Ranslett acknowledged him. "Do you still remember all our names, Mr. Daniel?"

"Well, let's see. I remember Abby and Libby—" He lightly touched the heads of the first two girls they'd seen on the porch. "Luke, Mason, and Nathaniel." He frowned as though having trouble recalling a name, then tousled the hair of the boy who had asked the question. "And Zachary!" He smiled and the boy giggled. "And Bradley, Caroline, Ansley, Marshall . . . and Davy!"

Everyone clapped, and Elizabeth couldn't help but stare. Josiah had led her to think this man was a hermit, and he seemed anything but. The same dark-haired boy who had asked Ranslett to name them caught her eye and smiled. Her chest constricted. What if he asked her to recite their names? She'd just heard them but would never be able to remember them all. Except for Davy and Libby, with the golden blond hair.

She took a step back and looked away.

"Davy, I've got something special for you." Ranslett motioned for

Mr. Tucker to follow him to the back of the wagon. "It's something you asked me about a while back. You didn't believe me when I told you how they felt."

The other children smiled and watched for Davy's reaction. Elizabeth moved to where she could see his face too, and found herself tearing up.

Davy's bottom lip quivered. "You did it. You got it for me."

Mr. Tucker leaned him closer so he could feel it. "It's soft! Just like you said. You're the best hunter in the whole wide world!"

A shadow accompanied Ranslett's smile. "That's hardly true, but I may be the most persistent."

Mr. Tucker instructed the children to follow Ranslett's orders about unloading the meat, and they all started in on the task. Elizabeth felt a touch on her arm.

Mrs. Tucker leaned close. "I hope you can stay for lunch. Daniel said it's fine with him, if you can spare the time. It's not often we get to visit with guests. Especially one from so far away." She nodded toward Josiah. "We'd be honored to have all three of you share our table."

"That's very kind of you, but I really need to—" She felt a tug on her skirt and looked down.

The girl she'd admired earlier, Libby, stared up. "I like your hair. It's pretty." Her diminutive mouth tipped in a smile.

Elizabeth reached up and touched a wayward curl at her neckline. She couldn't recall anyone having ever said that to her before. Women with her type of hair usually had it ironed straight, which was more the fashion. She hesitated, considering Mrs. Tucker's question and thinking of the hunting trip and all she'd hoped to accomplish today. Then she considered again how many children there were. Enough to start a school . . .

She turned to Mrs. Tucker. "We'd be honored to stay for lunch. Thank you."

11

As soon as Mathias said amen, the chatter of conversation filled the cramped kitchen. Daniel tried to catch Miss Westbrook's attention from the opposite end of the table, but she wouldn't look his way. As long as she didn't ask what the meat was, he thought they'd be okay.

While he'd unloaded and stored the elk meat earlier, she'd gotten a photograph of the homestead and the barn. And, oddly enough, one of Beau. He was amazed the dog had sat still long enough. Meanwhile, he'd helped Mathias and the boys store the meat frozen in Lolly's icehouse into a box snugged into a hole out back. They'd packed it with snow and ice. With temperatures as cool as they'd been, and the nights still hovering at freezing or dipping just below, the meat would last the family for weeks. Made him feel good to be able to help them out.

The meal Oleta and the girls had prepared was simple, as always. Boiled potatoes, bread that never seemed to have gotten the chance to fully rise—no surprise with this many kids—and squirrel. He'd grown up catching and killing the rodents and broiling them over an open flame. It was a sweet meat and plenty tender, but he doubted Elizabeth Westbrook from Washington, D.C., had ever been introduced to the Southern "delicacy."

He'd counted four squirrels for sixteen people. Oleta had div- vied them onto plates before everyone sat down, and she'd divided one squirrel among him and Elizabeth and Josiah alone. Daniel hadn't interacted much with the Negro but could read the man well enough to know he'd eat whatever was put before him and be gracious about it.

As Elizabeth eyed the meat on her plate, Daniel silently offered up another prayer. He didn't want her to do anything that would offend Mathias or Oleta. To say that the woman could be demanding was like saying that Colorado winters could get a mite chilly.

Mathias passed the bowl of boiled potatoes. "Miss Westbrook, did I hear you tell Oleta that you want to get a picture of the children?"

"Yes, sir. If you don't mind." Elizabeth picked up her fork and peered on either side of her plate, presumably looking for a napkin. Knowing she wouldn't find one, Daniel was glad when she finally gave up the search—then cringed when she picked at something on one of the tines.

"Don't mind one bit. They'll have fun with it, I'm sure. What caused you to set about learning such a thing?"

Elizabeth made a dismissive gesture. "I happened into it, you might say. It's a hobby I've studied for several years now."

"I'll admit, I've heard about cameras like yours before." Mathias mouthed something to Luke, who took a potato and passed them on. "But I never saw one before today."

"I'll be happy to explain how it works after lunch. And I'll make a copy of the photograph of the children once I get back to town and send it to you via the mail service next week."

The children giggled, and Elizabeth's blue eyes went round.

Oleta, who sat next to her, reached over and gave her arm a squeeze. "The mail wagon doesn't run out here, dear. But Mathias goes into town every few weeks for supplies, and the children always race over to the store to check. Whenever you get the image made, you can just leave it for us there. We'll be obliged to have it."

Little Libby, who had clamored to take a seat beside Elizabeth, leaned forward. "We run like Mama says, but nothin's ever waitin' for us." Her tiny lips pursed. Libby was small for five, like her older brother Davy, but she was sharp as a whip.

Smiling, Elizabeth nodded and lifted her glass as if to take a drink, then stopped and peered into it. She frowned.

Daniel watched from where he sat and willed her to look past whatever it was and just take a drink. A little dirt wouldn't hurt her. He doubted she noticed that she'd gotten the only real glass the Tuckers owned. He and Josiah were drinking their water from saucers, which was how he remembered his grandfather taking his coffee, and the children shared tin cups they passed back and forth among them. Mathias and Oleta provided refills from two pitchers on the table and took sips as the cups passed.

Elizabeth's frown deepened. As did Daniel's concern.

She glanced at Oleta, who thankfully wasn't looking at the moment, and set the glass down. Daniel pulled off a piece of meat with his teeth and chewed. How could the woman not feel the hole he was boring through her?

"Mr. Daniel?"

Daniel looked to his left, where Davy sat.

"Thank you for my present." The boy's eyes lit despite the shadowed half moons beneath them. "It's the best thing I ever got."

Daniel couldn't answer right off. He smiled. "You're welcome, Davy. I wish I could've brought him here to you, so you could have seen him close up. He jumped heights that would've taken you and me a ladder to climb up. He was so strong."

"Was he m—" Davy's lips formed a thin line. A frown eclipsed his tiny smile.

"Magnificent?" Daniel filled in, remembering their past conversations and how he'd described the animal to the boy. "Yes, he was. I followed him for a few days, watching him, waiting so I could—"

"Get a clean shot, because something like him don't deserve any less."

Daniel's chest tightened. "You don't forget a thing, do you?"

"No, sir. When I grow up, I want to hunt like you. See faraway places, live in the mountains with a dog, just like you do. So I best pay attention—that's what Pa says." Davy forked a bite of potato, and that's when Daniel noticed them. The bruises on his arms.

Mathias had told him earlier about the bluish marks that had started appearing, for no reason that they could identify. If Daniel didn't know Mathias and Oleta as well as he did, he might've suspected they'd been harsh with the boy, but he'd known the Tuckers for almost ten years. Mathias would give his own life before he laid a harsh hand to any of the children. He and Oleta dedicated every ounce of energy to these kids, all of whom had been abandoned in some way or another.

"Thank you for the elk, Daniel."

Mathias's voice drew Daniel's attention. The older man's gaze traveled briefly to Davy, then back again. His expression held answer to the one question Daniel hadn't had the courage to ask Mathias yet. Daniel stared at the boy, watching him eat, refusing to accept the truth.

"Davy, I—" Daniel cleared his throat. "I'll get you a picture of an elk like that one so you can see what he looks like. Up close." His focus skipped to Elizabeth, who still wasn't looking his way. "I promise I will."

Davy smiled and stuffed his mouth with bread. When no one was watching, Daniel snuck the remainder of his meat onto the boy's plate, winking at him as if it was their secret. Smiling, Davy glanced quickly from side to side, then shoved the morsel in his mouth.

Lively conversation from the opposite end of the table garnered attention, and to Daniel's surprise, Elizabeth wasn't contributing to it. She only smiled and nodded when the children asked her a question. Either that or shook her head. For being so quick and detailed in telling him what to do, she had seemed awfully guarded since arriving.

Oleta extended the bread plate to her, and she took a piece. "Behind our house there's a real pretty stream, Miss Westbrook. It's a ways up the mountain but not too far a climb. The children go there to hunt and to play on the rocks. It's right pretty and might work nice for your picture box."

"Thank you, ma'am. It sounds like the perfect setting." Elizabeth picked up the meat on her plate, again glanced at Oleta, who was distracted with helping Abby, then took a discreet sniff. She looked across the table at Josiah, whose plate was empty, squirrel bones picked clean, and took a cautious bite.

"Up the stream a ways is where we caught them squirrels." Pride puffed young Luke's voice, reminding Daniel of his own childhood and stirring memories of having taught Benjamin to hunt. "Me and Mason and Zachary got us some traps up there. We'll show you after lunch, ma'am, if you're wanting to see 'em."

Elizabeth chewed good and long before finally swallowing. "Thank you, I'd . . . like to see your squirrels." She took another bite, and conversation around the table paused.

"See 'em?" Mason's puzzled look gave way to a grin, as if Elizabeth had just told a joke. "Won't be no more seeing 'em, ma'am. We done ate 'em."

Elizabeth's jaw froze midchew.

Mathias and Oleta exchanged a look and Daniel felt a rush of heat. The children started giggling. He had to admit, Elizabeth's expression was priceless, but he couldn't share the humor. She looked at him—*finally*—as though asking if she'd heard correctly.

With as inconspicuous a nod as possible, he answered her question, and she put a hand to her mouth.

She looked from child to child, all of whom were now laughing. It looked as if she might have managed to swallow what was in her mouth, with effort. But judging from the pallor of her face, Daniel wasn't certain that had been the best choice.

She choked a cough and her eyes watered, whether from embarrassment or because she was going to be sick, he didn't know—maybe it was both. But he wished he could help her.

One of the boys chose that moment to let out a loud burp, which challenged the others to try and outdo him, which just encouraged more laughter.

Amidst the fun making, Elizabeth took a sharp breath and leaned forward in her chair. It looked as if she was having trouble breathing. Daniel rose. Oleta covered her hand, concern filling the woman's expression. But it was Josiah who reached her first.

12

Elizabeth coughed and struggled to get a breath, hearing the children laughing at her. She'd tried to swallow the meat, but it hadn't gone down, and still wouldn't. The realization of what she'd been eating had caught her off guard, then made her gag.

"It's all right, Miz Westbrook." Josiah knelt beside her and discreetly held out his hand.

She knew what he was asking her to do but was loath to obey. She leaned to the side and spit the meat into her own palm. "Outside—" Breathing was like trying to suck air through a cracked reed. "Please . . ."

Josiah led her to the front porch, supporting most of her weight. "You needs your medicine, ma'am?" he whispered.

She nodded and motioned to the wagon. He sat her down on the porch steps and ran. Elbows on her knees, head in her hands, she leaned forward, wheezing. This didn't feel like a normal episode, as the doctors referred to them, but her condition made even the simplest problems worse.

An arm came around her shoulders, and her embarrassment deepened.

"What can I do to help, Miss Westbrook?" Ranslett knelt beside her on the steps.

Elizabeth shook her head, unwilling to look at him.

He moved to sit beside her, and his hand moved in slow arching circles on her back, comforting and soothing in one way—while not, in another.

Her wheezing grew louder. She concentrated on breathing and gripped the stairs until she felt the soft wood give beneath her nails.

Josiah ran past them back into the house, and returned seconds later with her glass. She didn't inspect it this time but downed the entire contents as quickly as her body would allow. The medicine tasted bitter without the herbal tea to diffuse it, and she shuddered in response.

"Is she all right?" Strain tightened Mrs. Tucker's voice.

Josiah spoke first. "She be fine in just a minute, Missus Tucker. Miz Westbrook just got herself a little choked up, is all. Happens to me too, whenever I'm eatin' too fast or tryin' to talk too much."

Elizabeth caught his wink meant just for her and wondered if Mrs. Tucker would believe his fabrication.

"Oh . . . I'm so glad." If Mrs. Tucker didn't believe him, she didn't let on. "I'll go tell the children. They were worried. Especially Libby." She went back inside, leaving the door open behind her.

The warmth from Ranslett's hand on her back penetrated her shirtwaist. "Does this happen often, Miss Westbrook?"

Choosing to answer from the standpoint of choking on squirrel, she shook her head.

"I think she be fine in just a minute, sir. The fresh air be fixin' her right up." Josiah gestured toward the wagon, the bottle of medicine tucked discreetly in his grip. "I put this back in your pack, ma'am. Then I get everything ready so we can make that hike upstream."

Elizabeth trailed Josiah's path with her gaze. Anything not to have to face Ranslett.

As the muscles constricting her throat began to relax, so did she. A warm flush spread through her body and the wheezing gradually lessened. Tillie used to tell her she sounded like someone on their deathbed from pneumonia during her episodes. Such a comforting thought . . .

"I'm sorry, Miss Westbrook." Ranslett's voice came out soft. "I should have warned you . . . about the squirrel."

"Yes . . ." She cleared her throat, testing her voice. "You should have." So he knew the reason for her choking. Mrs. Tucker probably did as well but was too kind to admit it. Oh, she felt so foolish, and more than a little miffed at him. "I thought we had an agreement to be blunt with each other."

"I tried. I just couldn't get you to look at me."

"Ah . . ." She looked at him then. "So it's my fault?"

His smile would have charmed a tempest. "I didn't say that, but what else could I do?" His voice lowered, reminding her of the open door behind them. "Announce that you're about to eat a rodent?"

"Yes, that's exactly what I wish you'd done." But she didn't really mean it. "I'll do the same for you if the time ever comes. But I have a suspicion . . ." She glanced behind them to make sure no one was there. "That with your upbringing, your dining habits encompass a broader and far less cultured fare than my own."

"Well . . ." He let out a low whistle and slowly pulled his hand back. Beau perked his ears but didn't move from the bottom step. "That was a mite tacky, ma'am . . . even for you."

Elizabeth let her mouth fall open. "*Even for me?* What's that supposed to mean?"

"It just means that people with"—he stared pointedly—"your upbringing aren't usually the most polite folks around."

His tone was teasing, but there was a seriousness to it that hadn't been there a moment before. "Listen, Ranslett, if I've offended you, I certainly didn't mean t—"

"Sure you did. You just meant to do it in a way that wouldn't make yourself look bad." He turned to look at her more fully, and his eyes narrowed, though not in malice. "When you've got something to say that isn't kind, Miss Westbrook, there's no way to couch it so that it is. Or to hide from how it makes you look when you do. That's something us good ol' Southern boys learn real quick about women." His accent thickened, comically so. "Your gender may say things with a smile, all soft and gentle-like, but some of you—granted, not all—have a dagger hidden in your skirts. Us country boys may not be as quick as some, ma'am, but it don't take us too long to figure out who those women are." He winked at her. "We just check each other's backs for the bloodstains." He stood and reached behind him as though feeling for something. "Yep, feelin' a little sticky back there."

Elizabeth sat for a few seconds, somewhat stunned. Feeling thoroughly, though gently, rebuked. While also surprised at the depth of this man's insight. Not that it was earth shattering. She just hadn't expected such an observation from him. Nor the smooth delivery. To say that Daniel Ranslett knew who he was, was like saying that the sun knew a bit about shining. This man was more comfortable in his own skin than anyone she'd ever met, and she found that quality attractive. No, more than just attractive. She envied him for it.

She accepted his help in standing, the kindness in his smile making her more aware of the warmth of his hand.

Later, as she took two photographs of the children by the stream, she saw the afternoon, and their hunting trip, slipping away. But after the conversation they'd had and knowing what greater request she had yet to make of him, she decided to let it go for now. As she worked, she took the opportunity to watch him. Daniel Ranslett acted the same, regardless of who was watching or what anybody else thought. Whether he was with a child of five or an adult of fifty-five.

By the time they reached the outskirts of town later that afternoon, she had decided how to broach the topic of his leading her excursion to the cliff dwellings. Now to wait for the right opening. She wanted it to sound casual, natural. As if she could find someone else if she so desired.

He hadn't uttered a word since leaving the Tuckers'. He'd spoken with Mr. Tucker off to the side before they'd left, and when he'd climbed into the wagon, the burden etched in his features had been enough to keep her quiet. Even Josiah had stopped humming a mile or so back. She turned around to find Josiah asleep in the wagon, Beau curled up beside him.

She loved dogs, but her father had forbidden them from having one, saying her lung condition wouldn't tolerate it. But she'd never noticed any difficulty in breathing around animals.

"You didn't get your picture today, Miss Westbrook."

"Ah . . . the man speaks." She looked over at him. "You're a man of very few words this afternoon."

He shrugged. "Maybe I only know a few, and used them all up."

She laughed softly. "From the thoughts I've seen playing behind those eyes of yours, I daresay that's not true. And no, I didn't get my picture." At least not the one he was referring to.

He guided the wagon down the street. "I promised you a full day of hunting and you didn't get it. If you're free one day next week, we'll go again. But this time you need to meet me up in the mountains, not long after daybreak." He glanced at her clothing. "Dress warm and wear gloves. Gets colder up there. And leave those fancy boots behind. I'm hoping you have the right gear for this."

She couldn't believe he'd mentioned having the right gear. This was too easy. "Yes, actually I do. I've got all the latest equipment for hiking and mountain climbing. Which brings me to something I—"

He started laughing.

"What?"

He didn't answer.

"What's so funny?"

He snuck a quick look. "We won't be doing any mountain climbing, Miss Westbrook, so you can just leave your little ropes and pulleys at home." He faced the front, still grinning. "I can almost see you trying to do it, though. That'd be a picture for your camera, all right."

The way he said it made Elizabeth wish she had a cliff right there. She'd show him. She'd practiced with ropes and pulleys on a two-hundred-year-old oak in their backyard and was quite good at climbing, especially if she wore her split skirt. Which her father said was the silliest thing he'd ever seen on a woman. Somehow she knew Ranslett's opinion would be even more severe. But what did she care?

The boardinghouse lay ahead, and the casual opening she'd been waiting for in the conversation was quickly disappearing. "I've got a proposition that I think will be a wonderful opportunity for both of us."

He peered over at her, his expression relaying doubt.

Not letting the rise of his brow throw her off, she kept on course. "I'm funding a private expedition to an area south of here, in the San Juans. Have you heard of them?"

He looked at her as though she was being obtuse. "I believe I have. Have you ever traveled those mountains?"

She scoffed. "You know I haven't."

He stared. "Go on . . ."

"Our purpose will be to make the trek to the dwellings that were recently discovered in some cliffs several hundred feet from the base of a canyon."

He brought the wagon to a stop in front of the butcher's shop.

"I've already calculated the time it will take." She wished she'd thought to bring her maps so she could show him the route she'd marked off. "If we leave the first of May and it takes us approximately a month to travel from here to there, then we should—"

"You can't leave the first of May."

She blinked, not appreciating the interruption. "And why not?"

"Too much snow." He set the brake and climbed down.

She glanced at the townspeople around them. Most were dressed in light jackets, some in shirt sleeves alone. "But the snow's already melting, and we've still got two more weeks."

"Sure, it's melting here, but not over the passes. You can't cross those for at least another month. Maybe two, if more snow falls between now and then."

Elizabeth glanced at Josiah, who was tethering the mule. Surely he heard every word, yet he acted as if they weren't even around.

Elizabeth climbed down and went to stand beside Ranslett as he unhitched the horse from the wagon. "I would like you to lead the expedition, Ranslett. I'll pay you, of course. But I would need to leave by the first of May."

He pulled a strap through the harness. "What are you taking these pictures for?"

The question was unexpected, but she had an answer. "I told you. I'm here to capture images of the landscape. Photography is a—"

"Hobby you've studied for several years. So I've heard you say . . . more than once."

She didn't like the way he was looking at her. As if he'd discovered something she didn't want him to know. It was impossible that he knew anything about the *Chronicle*. But even if he had discovered that she worked for the newspaper, or if anyone else found out, it wouldn't be the end of the world. She could still do her job, get the photographs she needed, the heartfelt stories she wanted—*if* people would still open up to her—and find out about the landowners for the hotel developers. Which reminded her, she had an appointment with the manager of the land and title office on Monday. She hoped Mr. Zachary would show up this time.

The conversation wasn't going as planned. Best to deal with Daniel Ranslett head-on. "I've asked you a question, Mr. Ranslett, and I'm still waiting for an answer."

He walked to where she stood. "My answer was no." Tugging on the leather strap, he took his time stepping back.

Elizabeth squinted. "Why are you saying no?"

"Because I'm refusing your proposal."

The vein in her forehead started to throb. It was a telling sign, and always had been. Her father still kidded her about it. Whenever she got angry a tiny vein, normally not noticeable, popped out. That it wasn't the most attractive thing didn't bother her; she had other shortcomings far worse. What she found so frustrating was that it so clearly announced her displeasure. People always knew when she was truly mad. Like now. And the look Ranslett was giving her wasn't helping.

His gaze slowly drifted upward.

She clenched her teeth, summoning patience. "I realize you're refusing. What I'm asking for is an explanation as to *why*."

"I believe you're a mite angry, ma'am."

Throb, throb, throb. "I'm a *mite* upset, yes. And I'd still like to know why you're refusing."

He shrugged. "Mainly . . . because I don't want to." He walked to the back of the wagon, leaving her staring after him.

13

Her vein was going to explode.

Right in the middle of the road in this tiny, one-horse, dot-on-the-map town out in the middle of nowhere Colorado Territory, where— Elizabeth stopped and took a deep breath, and remembered why she was here and what she stood to gain, and she slowly exhaled. Right in the middle of the Colorado Territory, where the breathtaking landscapes and gorgeous vistas were going to earn her the job she'd always dreamed of having. Of being a staff photographer and "recognized" journalist with the *Washington Daily Chronicle*.

A sudden calm flowed through her again.

Daniel Ranslett knew how to communicate; he'd already demonstrated that. He was just being difficult, and was enjoying every blasted minute of it.

"Fine." She walked to the wagon and retrieved her pack. "You don't want the job. I'll find someone else."

"Best of luck to you, ma'am." He tipped his hat in a kindly manner and whistled for Beau, who was sitting with Josiah on the boardwalk.

Infuriating, the way he acted like a Southern gentleman while basically telling her to take a hike. "You're right, you know." She waited for his head to come up. "What you said before . . . out at the

Tuckers'. But women aren't the only ones who have hidden daggers, Ranslett."

That seemed to bring him up short. He looked away for a second, then sighed. He came alongside her. "I'm sorry, Miss Westbrook. My mind's just occupied with other things right now. What I'm trying to say is that it's different out here. I've traveled these territories, and a person doesn't *tell* these mountains anything. Not when you're going to leave, not when you've got to get back. With all due respect . . ." He paused, and she sensed his genuine concern. "The mountains tell you. I've seen plenty of men try to dictate how it's going to be, and they paid for that mistake with their lives. And those of their families. So just be careful what you're aiming to do, and when." Taking the reins, he guided his horse free from the wagon and tethered it to the post.

Still too angry to be overly sentimental at what he'd said, she was practical enough to have heard him. "If something happened and it wasn't safe to travel, then I wouldn't go. I would wait, most certainly, and I would trust my guide's lead." Maybe that last bit would help persuade him, but his stance indicated that was doubtful. "From all accounts I've read, they say that traveling in the Rockies during the months of May through September are the most pleasant and beautiful." Memory had kicked in and she'd quoted that last line from an article she'd read. And it came out sounding rehearsed, even to her.

A smirk tipped his mouth. "And have *they*—whoever *they* are— traveled these mountains before?"

She could only remember bits and pieces from the account but was relatively certain it had been a verified source. "Of course they have."

A muscle flexed in his jaw. He stretched his shoulders and winced slightly. "I'm not going to argue with you, Miss Westbrook. And my answer stands." He turned to go, then stopped. "But I will disagree with them on the months. Those months are pretty, but the most beautiful time is the dead of winter, when the world turns white and everything goes frozen. The trees, the rocks, the river, the peaks, everything. Even your breath comes out white, and crystals form on your lips. The air is so cold you'd swear your lungs are on fire, and there's not a soul to be found for miles, just you . . . and the land . . . and the quiet."

His voice had gone hushed, making the mental picture he'd created within her even more powerful.

"I wish I were going to be here then, so I could see that."

He laughed softly. "So you could capture it with that camera of yours?"

She felt an affront. "So I could appreciate its beauty."

He nodded but didn't speak for a moment. "It changes you . . . once you've seen this land. Really seen it. You're different inside. I wish more people understood that—maybe then they'd be more careful with things." He stepped up onto the boardwalk.

She wanted to continue their conversation, but apparently he was through.

He stood inside the entry to the butcher's shop. "How about next Friday. For hunting?"

She didn't have to think long. "That will work nicely, thank you."

"I'll draw a map for you"—he indicated the boardinghouse with a nod—"and give it to Miss Ruby before I leave town."

"Leave?"

"I live a ways from here."

"Let me guess. In the mountains, all alone, by yourself. With your dog."

He smiled. "Yes, ma'am. Something like that. The best hunting I've found is on a ridge not far from my cabin. That'll be our best bet."

"If that's our best bet, why didn't you take me there to begin with?"

He glanced down the street, then slowly back. "To be honest, I wasn't properly motivated before now."

"And what was it that I said that changed your motivation?"

His smile faded. "Nothing you said, ma'am. Nothing from you at all, actually."

Again feeling gently put in her place, she stared. She knew deep down that no matter what else Daniel Ranslett might be—and certainly it couldn't all be good—he was an honest man at his core. "Well, whatever changed your mind, I'll look forward to seeing where you live."

He gave a short laugh. "Sorry again, ma'am, but you won't be seeing that."

"Don't tell me . . . you don't like people knowing where you live?"

"Don't take it personally. I just like my privacy."

"Some people might call that eccentric." She decided to have a little fun with him. "I'm sorry . . . do you know what that means?"

"Nope, but if you insist on telling me, the map I leave might have you ending up in Wyoming."

She laughed. "Then I'll try to refrain."

"You'll be bringing your man with you, right?"

Realizing who he was talking about, she glanced behind her at Josiah across the street. *"Your man."* She hadn't heard that phrase used in a while. And from Ranslett's expression, he was wishing he could take it back. Seeing that gave her another glimpse into who he was, or at least into who he'd once been. *"Josiah* will be accompanying me, yes. He's currently in my employ."

"Good. That'll work fine."

She peered at him. "Are you thinking I wouldn't be able to find my way without help?" She would never admit it to him, but a good sense of direction was something she'd never had. She could read a map well enough, but she wasn't one of those people who instinctively knew which way was north. Her father was. He'd once told her that even in the heat of battle, when the smoke was so thick he couldn't see but a few feet in front of him, he always knew his way. In a revealing moment in later years, moments that didn't happen often between them, he'd confessed that he thought God had given him that gift so that he could lead men into war. So that his men would be confident in following him.

Elizabeth hadn't said anything then, but she still doubted whether war was God's reason for giving her father that ability. Giving gifts so that men could better kill one another didn't line up with what she knew of the Almighty. Surely when God imparted those gifts, entrusting those small pieces of himself to people, He did it with greater expectation than that.

"You credit me with thinking too deeply, Miss Westbrook. My thought was that it would be good to have someone with you for safety's sake. These mountains can be harsh, and with very little warning. Good day, ma'am."

"Good day. And, Ranslett . . ."

He turned.

She gave a half nod, unable to resist. "In case Josiah and I happen by your cabin early on Friday morning, I take my coffee with milk, and no sugar." She smiled and turned on her heel.

———

She could tell by the look on Sheriff McPherson's face that he was surprised to see her. "Good morning, Sheriff. I hope I'm not bothering you. I know it's early for a Monday morning." She pushed the office door closed.

He rose from his desk, chewing and wiping his mouth. He swallowed. "Good morning, Miss Westbrook. And it's not too early at all." He rushed to her side of the desk and gathered a pile of papers and books from a chair. "Here, have a seat. Pardon the conditions—we don't get many women in through here. My sister's about the only woman who ever visits, or used to. She hasn't been in for a while." He stacked an empty tin with others on a table behind him and brushed what looked to be remnants of breakfast—or perhaps several meals—onto the floor.

"Thank you." She curbed a grin at his attempt at cleanliness, then glimpsed something smeared on the chair just before she sat down. She quickly caught herself and stood again.

Seeing it, he shook his head. "Why don't we go for a walk? That might be safer."

She let him lead the way. They turned right as they departed the office, then left at the next street.

"How are you adjusting to life in Timber Ridge, ma'am?"

"Quite well. I love your town and your people. Everyone here is so kind, and your mountains . . ." The Maroon Bells reigned above, etched steely and white against the brilliant blue. "My camera doesn't rightly capture their beauty."

"They are pretty, especially with the snow on them." They walked in silence for a few paces, and then he looked over at her. "But I'm thinking you didn't come to talk to me about the mountains." He smiled.

"You're right, I'm actually here seeking your advice on something. I'm planning an expedition to the cliff dwellings south of here that were recently discovered."

"For that hobby of yours?"

McPherson tipped his hat to a woman passing by. Elizabeth hoped the woman wasn't married—not with the look she'd just tossed in the sheriff's direction. Yet the man seemed totally unaware of it.

"Yes . . . for my hobby." Feeling a prick of guilt at the lie, she consoled herself with the fact that it *had* been a hobby for years. "And I'm in need of a guide for that journey."

"I've got just the man for you and you've already met him—Daniel Ranslett. Ranslett can track anything or anyone, even through water." His grin said he was kidding, but there was also a seriousness to it. "And he knows these mountains better than anyone else. I'd be willing to speak to him for you, if you'd like."

"Actually, I've already spoken to Mr. Ranslett about the opportunity, and he turned me down. Quite soundly, in fact."

McPherson laughed. "That sounds like Ranslett. He can be a hard sell at times."

"That's putting it mildly."

"But he's always honest. You never have to guess where he stands on something."

They took the path that circled Maroon Lake, where she and Josiah had taken photographs last week. The water was still frozen in patches and lapped at the mud bordering the banks.

"How did the two of you meet, ma'am? If you don't mind me asking."

"Not at all." She briefly told him of her and Ranslett's first encounter, and McPherson's laughter caused her to embellish a few of the details for humor's sake. "When I put to him that I wanted another day of hunting to replace the elk he cost me, I didn't really think he would agree, but he did."

"Consider yourself lucky, Miss Westbrook. Ranslett's not one to agree to such things. It's not that he's unsociable. He's just . . . taken to enjoying his privacy more in recent years."

"Am I right in guessing that you've known each other for a time, Sheriff?"

He didn't answer, and she wondered if she'd overstepped her bounds.

He finally nodded. "Ranslett and I go back a ways, yes, ma'am. He's a good man. And again, you won't find a better tracker or hunter in all the Rockies."

"That may be the case, but he's made it clear he has no interest in guiding me to the cliff dwellings. When I first arrived, I posted an advertisement at the general store and learned just this morning that one gentleman has responded—a Mr. Hawthorne. He left word that he's available to meet with me this afternoon. I was wondering if you would be willing to look at his letters of reference—or speak for his character, if you know him."

"Can't say that I do know him, but I'd be happy to look at his references for you. You want to be able to trust whomever you hire."

"Thank you. I appreciate that."

They rounded the lake and took the path leading back to town. "You know what's brought me west, Sheriff. But what about you? What drew you from your . . . obvious Southern roots?"

He smiled. "It was a lot of things, I guess. Mainly, though, life was different after the war. Houses were still standing, but homes were gone, families torn apart. And in a way it was too sad to stay there and face it every day. So I came west, not planning on staying here, mind you. Just wanted to see what everyone was talking about."

"And what took you from that to being sheriff of Timber Ridge? That's quite a leap."

"Something happened not long after I arrived here, Miss Westbrook. Something that . . . changed my view on life, you might say. I know this town may look rough to you, ma'am, having come from such a big city, but when I first got here there was no law at all. Not in a person or an office anyway. Every man just pretty much called things how he saw it. If there was a dispute, it was settled between the two having it. Sometimes more civilly than others." His eyes narrowed. "We had a killing . . . of a white man who was well liked in town. He'd been outspoken against the Negroes coming into Timber Ridge, about them taking up residence alongside the whites. You know what I'm talking about. . . . When his body was found outside of town, there was an uprising.

"White people demanded justice, and before anything could be settled, some of the men saw justice meted out—their own way. They accused a Negro man of the murder, and they hung him. . . ." A shadow encompassed his face. "Along with his wife and four children. I wasn't in town at the time, but I was told they hung the children first, starting with the youngest. Then his wife, and then him."

Elizabeth saw in the sheriff's face what could only be described as the rawest of pains. A question burned inside her, one she already knew the answer to. She swallowed to ensure she could speak. "The man was innocent . . . wasn't he?"

McPherson looked down for a moment, as though not wanting to answer. "He was. But things happened so fast, and those few who knew he didn't do it were too afraid to say anything. And even if he had done it . . . they killed his family!" He paused on the trail and nodded toward a stand of trees, just off the lake.

Elizabeth stilled beside him, not seeing anything at first, then . . . A sadness settled deep inside her. Crosses, six in all, arranged in a semicircle from largest to smallest, in a tiny cove of pine.

"Ben Mullins, who owns the general store, he and I buried them. Shortly after that I put my name forward for sheriff. And I've been here ever since."

She slowly exhaled, not having to wonder whether she would remember that story well enough to write it down later. She felt it burning in her down deep, and knew that E.G. Brenton's readers would too.

14

Later that afternoon Elizabeth took her place behind a line four patrons deep at the counter of the land and title office. She wondered if standing in line was necessary in order to speak with the manager, a Mr. Zachary, but with only the busy clerk behind the counter to ask, she chose to wait. Apparently everyone in town bought land on Monday.

She used the time to read the different advertisements on the bulletin board to her right, amused at the misspellings or poor wording on many of them. As Wendell Goldberg espoused daily without fail, *"No word should be uttered, much less written, without benefit of an editor."* No one would ever accuse the man of being humble.

She paid special notice to the posts advertising land for sale. The *Chronicle*'s investors had proposed specific requirements regarding the plots of land they wanted, and land suitable to construct a hotel with access to hot springs was primary. None of these notices described the various plots as having access to hot springs, but that didn't mean—

"May I be of assistance, ma'am?"

Elizabeth turned to meet a face she didn't recognize, but a swift inventory of his tailored suit and professional demeanor told her who he was. "Mr. Zachary, a pleasure to meet you, sir." The importance of knowing people's names was something her father had drilled into her at a young age. He still recalled the last name of every ranking officer who ever served beneath him, and many of the soldiers.

"Miss Westbrook, is it?"

She gave a half nod.

"My apologies for not keeping our appointment last week. I was called out of the office at the last minute." Mr. Zachary revealed a tendency to rock back and forth on the balls of his feet. "Don't tell me you've already fallen in love with our territory, ma'am, and are here to purchase one of our mountains."

Elizabeth's laughter came out higher pitched than she intended. The man was closer to the truth than he might guess. "Yes, sir, and I'll be paying in gold bullion to seal the deal. Do you find those terms agreeable?"

He had himself a good laugh, as did the other patrons in line who'd overheard.

"I *would* appreciate the opportunity to speak with you, Mr. Zachary, privately, if you have a free moment."

He motioned for her to follow.

This certainly wasn't the first time she'd played a role to gain information on behalf of the *Chronicle,* but this was the first time she'd ever felt a twinge of conscience while doing so. She entered his office and took the chair indicated by his gesture, then heard the door close behind her. In a big city like Washington, her chances of ever revisiting people she dealt with in this manner were slim. Especially after the *Chronicle* published the story being investigated.

But here in Timber Ridge it felt different somehow. More devious. Yet she had a job to do and a career to forge. . . .

"Would you care for something to drink, Miss Westbrook?"

No business owner in Washington had ever offered her refreshment. "No, thank you, sir, and I promise not to monopolize your afternoon."

His expression said he doubted that could be possible.

"Since arriving in your town, Mr. Zachary, I've heard people speak of the mineral pools in the area, and . . . I'm wondering if you have a plat that marks the locations of these springs."

He leaned forward on his desk, his pleasant gaze growing wide. "Oh, you're asking near the impossible, ma'am. There are so many locations scattered throughout the region, I'm afraid we don't have a map designating them all. But I can direct you to one just outside of town, if you're interested in *taking the waters,* as we like to say."

She gave a polite smile. "I should have been clearer in my request. I'm sorry. I'm only interested in looking at the . . . larger pools and springs."

Mr. Zachary steepled his fingers beneath his chin and gave a slow nod, a portion of his good faith noticeably waning. "May I inquire as to the nature of your interest in these springs, Miss Westbrook?"

"Most certainly." She and Goldberg had role-played this situation before she'd left Washington. "I'd like to photograph them during my stay here in Timber Ridge. And, from experience, the larger bodies of water are better suited for the camera's wide-angle lens." Which was true.

The lost measure of favor gradually returned to Zachary's countenance, and she remembered one of the last meetings she'd had with Goldberg before she left Washington. *"Managers of local title institutions control the reins on many levels, Miss Westbrook, and if they get wind of a large investor maneuvering to take controlling interest of their town's land, they might perceive it as a threat, which it isn't—it's growing their economy. Or they might reason it will go against the town's best interest, which it doesn't. And they could nix the deal before it even begins."*

So she decided to play the demure angle. . . .

Elizabeth scooted to the edge of her seat. "But if you think, sir, that taking photographs of your springs would be detrimental in any way, then I'll—"

"Not at all, Miss Westbrook. We'd be happy for you to take

photographs, but you need to be aware . . ." He rose from his chair. "The sections of land that have the larger springs are privately owned. You'll need to gain permission from the owners before taking photographs on their property. Most are fine with you being on the land, unless it's for hunting purposes. In that case, etiquette dictates that you gain their permission beforehand, for obvious reasons. Who wants to be shot at by accident?"

"Better by accident than on purpose!" She laughed along with him, rising from her chair. "I completely understand and will happily comply."

"Come with me, then, and I'll ask my assistant to pull those maps for you." Mr. Zachary approached a pretty brunette in the outer office. "Miss Carter, if you would pull the maps of these properties for Miss Westbrook." He scribbled on a pad of paper on the woman's desk. "And please answer any questions she may have."

"Miss Westbrook"—he tilted his head in acknowledgment—"the pleasure has been mine, and please don't hesitate to contact me should you require further assistance during your stay in Timber Ridge."

Elizabeth marveled at the ease of it all. Deeds were public record, but accessing similar documentation in Washington had never been so effortless. Without her identifying credentials from the *Chronicle,* she would never have gotten anywhere. "Thank you, Mr. Zachary, for your help."

"I'll get these maps for you, ma'am." The pretty brunette disappeared into a back room and returned minutes later. She unfurled large rolls of paper and secured their curling edges with polished rocks.

Elizabeth had studied maps of the area, so was fairly familiar with the land. Still, it took her a moment to gain her bearings on the exact locations of these plats.

"You'll see, Miss Westbrook, that the drawings list the name of the owner and date of purchase. Wherever there's an *X,* like right here"—Miss Carter tapped the paper—"that indicates the location of a hot spring on the property." She flipped to a map in the back. "And if you see this symbol here"—she pointed to a series of three short wavy lines—"that indicates a waterfall of some significance on the premises."

Even better . . . "Thank you, Miss Carter. This is quite helpful."

After several minutes, and with Miss Carter's assistance, Elizabeth isolated a map that contained what she thought would be the prime areas of interest to the *Chronicle*'s investor. "Here . . . this one." She smoothed a hand over the crinkled paper and pointed to a large area filled with straight horizontal lines. "What is this?"

"That indicates a substantial area of minor-surfaced terrain. Or in other words, it's flat."

Elizabeth nodded. Perfect place for a hotel. And hardly a stone's throw away were three large wavy lines and numerous *X*s. Unfortunately, the waterfall and hot springs fell on the opposite side of a dark property line. She pulled a pencil and paper from her reticule and jotted down the name of Travis Coulter, the man who owned the property suitable for a hotel. Then she slid her gaze across the bottom of the map to read the second name. Only to realize there was no need to write that one down.

The landholder was Daniel Ranslett.

15

Miss Carter tapped the collection of maps. "Someone else was in here looking at these recently. I remember now because of . . ." She glanced around, then leaned close. "The feud."

Elizabeth perked up. "The feud?"

"Well, it was more of a disagreement, really."

Elizabeth waited. That normally did the trick.

"The story goes"—Miss Carter's voice lowered—"that Mr. Coulter wanted to sell to a land developer from New York City. But the developer wasn't interested in his land without also acquiring"—she peered at the bottom of the page—"Mr. Ranslett's property. So the deal didn't go through. From what I heard coming from Mr. Zachary's office, Mr. Coulter wasn't pleased."

"Do you happen to recall the land developer? The name of the company?"

The woman shook her head. "I could ask Mr. Zachary, though. I'm sure he has record of it."

"Oh no, no, don't bother him. I was just curious." All she needed was to raise Zachary's suspicions again. Elizabeth wanted to ask if she could borrow the maps but knew that was out of the question. That would take Mr. Zachary's approval for certain. "I think I'll just study these for a minute, if you don't mind."

"Not at all. I'll check back with you."

Elizabeth pulled another piece of paper from her reticule and began sketching. She drew a crude map outlining how to get to the land, then went back and inserted the various relief markings along the way to help navigate and identify the path. The surveyor had been extremely thorough. A thought occurred, and she questioned Miss Carter when the woman returned. "Is the location of the owner's residence marked on the maps?"

Miss Carter looked more closely. "Sometimes they are, if the structure was in existence when the surveyor plotted the land, *and* if the surveyor remembered to mark it. Ah . . . you're in luck with this one." She pointed. "Mr. Coulter's dwelling is here. And let me check for Mr. Ranslett's. Mmmph . . ." She shook her head. "I don't see any . . . Wait! Yes, I do. Here it is. It's faded on the map, but you can see the outline of a square. That indicates a dwelling of some sort."

Elizabeth had a hard time containing her excitement. More than likely, Ranslett had tried to erase the marking at some point. As she hurried to her appointment with Mr. Hawthorne, Elizabeth had fun imagining Ranslett's expression if she were to show up on his doorstep, and knew she was drawing attention as she giggled her way down the boardwalk.

Elizabeth eyed the man across the table from her. He was not someone she would readily call a gentleman. In appearance, Mr. Hawthorne—the man who had answered the advertisement to lead her expedition—seemed a rough sort. A *backwoodsman* is what her father would have called him. Savvy about life in the wild but not about much else, she suspected. Perhaps time would tell . . . *if* she hired him to be her guide.

He leaned close over the map spread out between them on the table. "This is where you're wanting to go, ma'am?"

"Yes, Mr. Hawthorne. You've traveled the San Juans extensively —is that correct?"

"Yes, ma'am. I've been all over these mountains. Beautiful country. Peaceable enough with the natives these days too."

"Natives? Would that be the Ute?"

"Yes, ma'am. There's Ute. But I was speaking of the Cheyenne. They've been warrin' again recently."

He drained his fourth cup of coffee and, starting at the dot that marked Timber Ridge on the map, traced a path with his thick forefinger and trailed southwest to the location Elizabeth had marked at the bottom—the cliff dwellings discovered by William Jackson last fall.

"Just give me a minute here to work through the timeframe you gave me, coupled with where we'll be going. . . ."

As he considered the information, she ticked off items in her mind. She'd mailed an envelope of pictures to Goldberg that morning and had confirmed that her telegram from the previous week had finally been sent and acknowledged. In the envelope for Goldberg, she'd also included another article she'd written late last night following her Sunday meal with Ben and Lyda Mullins, a delightful couple. She'd been surprised to learn of the tragedy in their earlier lives, and hearing about it had only confirmed what Ranslett had said to her about these mountains. Not that she hadn't believed him, but hearing of the Mullins children—lost so young, and their parents' pain still raw after all these years—made it more real.

"What did you say you're paying me, ma'am?"

Elizabeth schooled her reaction to the premature question. "I haven't said yet, Mr. Hawthorne, because we haven't discussed terms of salary. In part, because I'm waiting for you to present your recommendations, as requested."

He leaned to one side in his chair, reached behind him, and pulled a wad of documents from his back pocket. He deposited them by her plate.

"There you go, Miss Westfork. I think they'll read to your satisfaction."

"It's West*brook,*" she gently reminded, for the second time. Noting the limpness of the papers and their discoloration, she lifted them by a corner.

"There's three in all, like you asked for. Two of the fellas live here in Timber Ridge. The other hails from Missouri, so you'll need to wire him if you want his second word."

"Thank you, Mr. Hawthorne. I'll do that." She unfolded Hawthorne's letters, trying not to imagine what had contributed to the dark stains lining their edges. She only hoped it was something as innocent as tobacco juice, as disgusting as that was.

She wished again that Daniel Ranslett hadn't been so set against the idea of guiding her trip. But he had been, and there was nothing she could do to change his mind. She reviewed Mr. Hawthorne's letters of recommendation. Definitely written in a different hand, each of them, she noted the qualities each letter listed—honest, reliable, hardworking, dependable. Had been guiding parties for a number of years. "Your letters seem to be in order."

"You feel free to check with any of those men. They'll stand behind what they wrote."

Hawthorne was able and willing. Add to that, the calendar pages were flipping by almost faster than she could count. Wendell Goldberg expected photographs of those cliff dwellings no later than the end of summer.

"So we have us a deal, ma'am?"

She'd known Hawthorne's type before and had managed fine. The key was to never let him forget who was boss. "Yes, Mr. Hawthorne. We *have us a deal*—pending the substantiation of your references. If they prove to your benefit, I'd like to leave no later than the first of May."

Stating it aloud made it seem more real, and imagining the adventures that lay ahead sent a buzz of excitement through her. Not to mention the affirmation from her colleagues that would accompany the special publication of her photographs in the *Chronicle,* perhaps followed by a showing to display her work, similar to an event she attended three months ago in New York to honor Mathew Brady.

As she walked back to the boardinghouse later that afternoon, she imagined her father attending such a gala event, with her as the honoree. And the image brought a smile, but only a fleeting one. Much remained to be conquered between this moment and that. Namely, making the journey to Mesa Verde.

She wanted to write about the adventures to be experienced in these western territories, certainly. But to do that well, she needed to live them. And she was ready!

———

"You still gots your mama with you, Miz Westbrook?"

"No, I don't. She died when I was five." Elizabeth stopped on the trail and checked her map again. She wished she'd taken more care to capture all the relief points as she'd copied the details to Travis Coulter's place from the surveyor's tedious rendering. "Do you think this is the right way?"

Josiah peered back at her. "I ain't the one that drew the map, ma'am. But I can read one, and this is the way your paper says. Look there . . ." He pointed upward to a snowcapped mountain peak. "That there's the South Maroon Bell. And this one here"— he pointed to the other white-crusted peak vaulting up by it—"it's the North. We done traveled them both in the past two weeks. You don't recall that?"

"Of course I recall it. I know the names of these mountains. I just don't know where I am right now."

He looked at her as if she'd grown a third eye. "The way you drawn it, which I's hopin' is right—" He gave a fatherly dip of his chin. "It says we been on this man's property for a while now. We should find his cabin over that ridge a ways. Why we up here anyway?"

"I . . . I want to take photographs of Mr. Coulter's land. I heard from someone in town that it's very pretty."

He blew into his hands, still holding Moonshine's reins. "Well, whatever we doin', we best hurry. Snow comin' in soon."

"But there aren't any clouds."

"I don't care. I just tellin' you that in my bones I feel snow comin'."

Elizabeth tugged her coat sleeves down as far as they would go. The temperature gauge outside the boardinghouse had read approximately forty-five degrees when they left. It didn't feel much colder than yesterday, but there was a moistness to the air today that chilled her from the inside out. At least she wasn't having any difficulty breathing. She had been drinking the herbal tea religiously and had taken to adding a dash of extra syrup to each cup. That along with this Colorado air seemed to be doing the trick.

They'd ridden a good hour and a half from town before coming to the cliff that marked the turnoff on the map. As customary, they'd left their horses at the bottom of the trail and had started on foot. She wriggled her numb toes in her boots.

"I mourn you losin' your mama so young, ma'am. It's a hard thing growin' up without knowin' your roots. And who it was you come from." His breath hung like a fog before disappearing. "Why you out here like this? Young woman like yourself, doin' what you's doin'? I bet your papa worries 'bout you. Your mama too." He glanced upward. "From her perch on high."

Elizabeth smiled at the personal nature of his question. "I used to study pictures of faraway places. I'd hear stories people told about their travels, what they'd seen and what they'd done, and I would wish I could have those same experiences. Then one day, I realized I didn't want to spend the rest of my life just hearing and never doing. Or living the life someone else had planned for me. I wanted something more."

"What you gonna do with all these pictures you're gettin'?"

Elizabeth watched her pointed boots appear and disappear beneath her skirt as she hiked beside him. "I'm going to take them back to Washington and show them to other people so that they'll know what this place is like." She felt him looking at her but didn't return his attention.

He made a sound like he'd just tasted something delicious. "Helpin' others find their way. This a good thing you're doin', ma'am. A good thing."

Culpability crept close in the lingering silence, and Elizabeth tried to think of something to say to fill the gap. The way he said it made her seem so noble, when she was anything but. Part of her wanted to tell him the truth about her coming here, but the greater part of her was afraid to for some reason.

"I'm guessin' you and me's more alike than we thought, Miz Westbrook."

That brought her attention back. "And how's that?"

"It was a paintin' I seen of a place out here that first set my sights west too."

"Really?" Relieved at the turn in conversation, her interest was also piqued. "What was the name of the painting?"

"Didn't have a name that I recall. I seen it in a store window, years back now. Came back there every day just to look at it. I'd stand and stare at them colors. Never in my days had I seen land bucklin' up so high in the sky. And the color of the water . . ." He let out a soft whoop. "They ain't got no water that color back in Georgia, to be sure."

"You're from Georgia, then?"

"Yes, ma'am. I's born in Atlanta, but I lived lots of places since those days. Before the war, I's in the Carolinas and Tennessee mostly. After that, I's all over. Wherever I wants to go, I go."

"Do you have any family out here?"

He looked skyward. "I reckon all my family's up there with your mama by now. Don't rightly know for sure, though. Weren't no records kept of where they sent us." His voice changed. It grew quieter, more flinty. "You just wake up one mornin' and they's loadin' you up. Then you's gone."

It took her a moment to realize what he was referring to, and the pain in his voice brought one to her chest. Something he'd said not long ago came to mind. About the worst thing in his life already having been done to him. "Josiah, you once said you'd already had the—"

He suddenly brought his arm out, impeding her progress. "What done happened here . . . ?"

She followed his line of vision to a point farther up the trail. To where a man lay motionless, his body half hidden in the brush.

16

"You stay here, ma'am, while I go check this out."

As Josiah approached the body, Elizabeth quietly followed behind, peering to one side so she could keep an eye on the man. He was clothed in dungarees, a wool shirt, and boots, pistol at his hip, and the upper half of his body lay sheltered beneath a low hedge of scrub brush. He didn't move as Josiah stood over him, nor as Josiah knelt and checked his wrist.

"Is he breathing?" she whispered.

Josiah spun, his eyes wide. "I done told you to wait over there. You ain't a listenin' woman for nothin'!"

Unable to argue with him, she stayed silent.

Frowning, Josiah licked his forefinger and held it beneath the man's nose. "No, ma'am, he ain't breathin' . . . cuz he's dead."

Elizabeth took a backward step. She'd seen dead bodies before but never one so . . . newly dead. New being measured not so much in time as in the lack of a coffin and a mortician's touch. She scanned their surroundings, wondering if they were truly as alone as it seemed. Thick brush and evergreens lined the trail on either side, and the path ahead curved up and around, making it impossible to see for any distance. The trail was dirt and rock, like every other trail they'd traveled so far. Nothing seemed out of the ordinary.

She laid her pack aside. There were no external wounds on the body that she could see, and his pistol was still fastened at his hip. "How do you think he died?"

"Do I looks like a doctor, ma'am?" Josiah rose, and his voice rose with him. "I ain't got no idea how this man passed. All I know is that he's gone!"

Elizabeth stared at him, unaccustomed to his speaking to her in such a manner. Then she looked from him to the man and back again. "Did you know him, Josiah? Was he a friend?"

His jaw muscles tightened. "I knowed him . . . in a way, but he weren't no friend."

"What was his name?"

"Don't know that neither."

"So in what way *did* you know this man?"

"I met up with him at the livery a while back, when I's workin' there. Month or so before you come to town." Josiah's features were tense. "He come in looking for Mr. Atwood—man who owns the livery. Man's wantin' to buy a horse. 'Mr. Atwood ain't in,' I says. 'You come back this noontime. Mr. Atwood be happy to deal with you then.' " Josiah shook his head. "But he already got his mind made up, and he been drinkin'. You could smell it on his breath. He had a meanness to him. You could tell it in the way he walked, the way he looked at you. He went on over to a stall, started messin' with one of Mr. Atwood's stallions. Rilin' him, yellin', gettin' all the animals worked up. Drawin' a crowd from outside. I asked him kindly to leave and come back later. But he wouldn't."

Elizabeth compared the dead man's build to that of Josiah's and found there was no comparison. The dead man was thick around his middle but was a good half foot shorter, and his arms and legs lacked muscle and were bony, like an old man's.

"He walked from the stall and picked up a hammer. He waved it at me. I says, 'I don't want no trouble with you, sir.' Then he looks down and sees he done stepped where an animal been. 'Pick it up,' he tells me, pointing to the pile. So I turn to get a shovel and he says, 'No, nigger, you pick it up with your hands.' "

Elizabeth burned inside as the scene unfolded in her mind.

"I go to get the shovel and somethin' hard hits me in the back of the head, knocks me down. I reach back and feel my own blood. He's still goin' on behind me, talkin' foolishness. I stand up and tell him we done fought a war over this and that I ain't fightin' it again with him. 'Mr. Lincoln signed something sayin' that,' I told him. But this man . . ." He scoffed, looking down at the dead man. "He says he don't give a—" Josiah closed his mouth. "His tongue had a foulness to it, ma'am. Showed what poison there was eatin' at him on the inside. He says he don't care 'bout Mr. Lincoln or the war, that a nigger will always be a nigger. And now look at him." He sighed. "Maybe not right away, but in the end . . . a man always gets back what he gives."

"Did he come to the livery again? Bother you in any way?"

"No, ma'am. But Mr. Atwood let me go after that, sayin' he don't want no more trouble at his place."

A bitter tang filled Elizabeth's mouth. "As if what happened was your fault."

"Don't always matter whose fault it is. Things is the way they is, and you just live each day with what comes."

She didn't know what to say. *I'm sorry* seemed empty and inappropriate. It was the dead man who should have offered apology. But if ever there had been a hope of his doing that, it had gone to the grave with him. Or soon would.

She reached out and touched Josiah's arm, giving it a gentle squeeze, then walked back to retrieve her camera pack where she'd left it. Josiah stood over the body, and she couldn't help but wonder what was going through his mind. Then something went through hers.

She looked at the dead man, then at the evergreens and the

Maroon Bells rising in the near distance. If she were to back up a ways . . .

No, she couldn't. It wasn't right. Even thinking about taking this photograph felt wrong.

She thought back to the day Ranslett had killed the bull elk, and of her regret afterward over not having captured the image for Wendell Goldberg. But this was a man, not an animal, however vile his behavior, or his heart, had been. Wondering what Goldberg would do, Elizabeth found she already knew. If he were here, Goldberg would have already had the tripod set up and the article half written.

She knelt and began unpacking her satchel. She heard the crunch of gravel.

"What you doin', Miz Westbrook?"

"I'm going to take a photograph."

"Of a dead man?"

Disbelief laced his tone, but it was all right. She couldn't believe she was doing it either. "Of life in the Rocky Mountains."

"Looks more like death in the Rocky Mountains to me."

She started cleaning a glass plate, wondering if she would have to set up the dark tent herself. She couldn't explain it, but this photograph felt outside the boundaries of Josiah's obligation to her, so she would set up the dark tent herself if she needed to. But she wouldn't ask him to do it.

"Why would a good Christian woman like you want a picture of a dead man?"

"It's not just a picture of a dead man." Elizabeth found herself moving faster than she normally did. Maybe it was guilt. Maybe it was nervousness over what—or who—had killed this man. But she wanted to get the picture taken and leave. "It's a lesson about reaping what you sow. Isn't that what you said a moment ago?"

She watched his worn boots in front of her and felt his stare, but she kept her head down. He shifted his weight. The leather on his right boot was worn clean through on one side. The other one would soon match it. How had she not noticed that before?

It seemed as if they stayed that way for a while, and she had the words on her tongue to excuse him from the task when he turned and strode back to Moonshine. Wordlessly they worked, Josiah setting up the tent and arranging her light-sensitive solutions. And she preparing the glass plate and adjusting the camera's placement and focus.

She ducked into the tent and finished preparing the glass plate by candlelight, then reemerged. She peered through the viewer of the camera one last time—checking the position, the view of the body—and adjusted the rear focus knobs to bring the man's image into clearer focus.

She fitted the light-protective holder into place within the camera, removed the slide and the lens cover, and started her silent recitation. The words to President Lincoln's address were especially meaningful in view of what Josiah had just shared. The sun slipped behind a bank of clouds that hadn't been there a short while ago, so she repeated the last half again to allow for a longer exposure time.

An hour later they had everything repacked on the mule and the glass plate was developed and dry, aided by a wind that had kicked up. Elizabeth swathed the plate in cloth and placed it in her pack.

Josiah started toward the body.

"What are you doing?"

He paused over the man. "I's gonna carry him back down the mountain to our horses. We got to take him into town and let the sheriff know."

"Yes, but . . ." Elizabeth glanced up the trail. "Can we not first go see if Mr. Coulter's home? You said yourself his cabin should be just over the ridge."

"You aim to leave this man out here all by his lonesome?"

"No, not for long. Just for a little while. Or you can stay here with him and Moonshine, and I'll go on by myself. It shouldn't take me long." She didn't like the second option and was relieved when his expression revealed the same.

Elizabeth pounded on the door to the cabin. "Mr. Coulter?" She walked to a window and tried to see inside, but dirt caking the panes prevented it. "Hello?"

"I don't think he be home, Miz Westbrook."

She rounded the cabin for a quick peek out back and stopped to stare. Through an opening in a stand of aspen trees, she saw a large meadow extending for at least a half mile before gently folding itself back into the foothills, ample space for a resort hotel with all the amenities. If she remembered the placement of this meadow on the surveyor's map correctly, then Daniel Ranslett's land began just over the next ridge.

A gust of cold wind sent her retreating behind the protection of the cabin, and she retraced her steps to the front. She knocked one last time and unlatched the door. Though Josiah said nothing, she felt his disapproval as she stepped inside.

If this was Mr. Coulter's main residence, he was certainly a frugal man. And not one prone to cleanliness. An assortment of smells greeted her, none of them pleasant. "You're right. No one's home." She stepped back outside and closed the door behind her, disappointed.

"Josiah . . ." She almost hated to say the words, feeling that she'd already pushed him. But Goldberg would want to show the view to the land developers. With a frown, Josiah started unpacking the equipment, not saying a word. She situated the camera far back enough to get the edge of the cabin in the picture for added depth.

An hour later, Josiah turned Moonshine around and they headed back down the mountain. Though neither of them said anything, Elizabeth was certain the same question plaguing her was also on Josiah's mind—was the dead man on the trail down below the same man they'd come looking for today?

Her mind sped ahead. If he *was* the same man, what did that mean in terms of acquiring this land for the developers? Would it be easier or harder for them to make the acquisition? And how would that play into her own situation if they weren't able to—

Hearing the vein of her thoughts, Elizabeth clenched her eyes, embarrassed. Down below a man lay dead on the trail, and all she was thinking about was how that development might affect her career. God was forgiving, but there were times she wished her thoughts could be hidden even from Him.

A light snow started falling and she grew cold. Her attention went to Josiah's boots. She'd worn thicker knit stockings in boots with no holes, so he had to be near freezing. Yet he said noth—

Josiah stopped the same time she did. They were to the spot where they'd discovered the man's body. Only . . .

The body was gone.

17

Night had fallen and the sheriff's office was dark when they finally returned to Timber Ridge. A blanket of snow covered the ground and Elizabeth's fingers were numb with cold. She blew into her cupped hands, vowing not to leave her gloves behind in her room again.

Josiah pounded on the door. "Sheriff McPherson, you in there, sir?" After several tries, he shook his head. "Best leave it 'til mornin', Miz Westbrook."

Elizabeth pressed close to the office window and peered inside. "Seems like someone should be here. Law enforcement should be available at all hours." She knocked on the pane, then tested the doorknob. It held fast.

"You ain't in that big, fancy city of yours no more, ma'am. You can't be expectin' the same here as you gots there."

"Do you know where the sheriff lives?"

"Yes, ma'am, I do. But it's a ways from town and it's freezin' cold. Besides, he got other duties when he gets home. To his widow sister and her younguns."

"What happened to her husband—do you know?"

"It ain't right to speak of the dead, ma'am. But since you're new to town . . . I only know what I heard—that Mr. Thomas Boyd was out huntin' and a bear got him. They says it was a sorry scene, what they come upon when they found him."

Elizabeth winced just thinking about it, then about Rachel and her two boys having to endure that loss. "So the sheriff lives with them now?"

"Yes, ma'am. Moved onto the ranch after it happened. Mr. Boyd, he left behind two good boys. One be eight and the other be six. I reckon they's growin' faster than Missus Boyd can keep up with. Mitchell, the older one, he got a likin' for huntin' like his papa did. And little Kurt, he aims to keep up with his big brother, no matter what." He shivered and rubbed his arms. "Listen, ma'am, I don't mean no disrespect, but that man out there, he was dead. What we gonna do? Travel all the way out to the sheriff's place just to tell him we found us a dead man and then done lost him?"

"It just seems like he should know about it."

"And he will, come mornin', ma'am. We tell him soon as he gets into town."

Snowflakes drifted down, and from the saloon two streets over, piano music traveled the chilled night air. She searched the board-walk in both directions. Deserted. "How does a corpse just up and disappear? Tell me that."

"It don't—leastwise not by hisself." Josiah turned and walked to where he'd tethered Moonshine.

Elizabeth didn't move. "And we're certain he was dead, right?"

Josiah gave her a look that said she'd asked a needless question. It was a look she was becoming accustomed to seeing from him. "Yes, ma'am, *we's* certain."

A thumbnail moon shone over the highest peaks, offering little in the way of illumination. Timber Ridge was advanced enough to have invested in coal-burning street lamps, but apparently not advanced enough to have round-the-clock law enforcement.

"Answer me this, ma'am. What you plannin' on sayin' to the sheriff when he asks you why we was up there to Mr. Coulter's place?"

"I'll tell him we were up there taking pictures."

"And what you got a picture of while you's up there, Miz Westbrook?"

Elizabeth smiled at his imitation of Sheriff McPherson, though she wasn't about to answer the question with the truth.

"A dead body, you say, ma'am. Well, now, ain't that interestin'. Why's a good woman like you takin' pictures of a dead man? And one you don't even know."

"All right, Josiah, your point is made. But I insist on telling the sheriff about what we found."

"I's all for that, ma'am. I just sayin' that we don't need to break our necks to tell him 'bout something that can wait 'til mornin'. More than likely, some animal got him, drug him off into the brush."

"I don't remember seeing any drag marks through the dirt." Not that she'd looked specifically. Some observant journalist she was turning out to be.

"We got bears that could pick a man clean up off the ground and carry him for miles. So that don't mean nothin'.'"

Shivering at the thought, she stepped down from the board-walk and walked beside him down the dimly lit street back to the boardinghouse.

Josiah made three trips up and down the stairs carrying her equipment back to her room, then said good night. Elizabeth closed the door and locked it tight, resisting the urge to crawl straight into bed. Instead, she spent the next half hour making a print from each of the two developed glass plates in her pack. Holding the photograph of the body brought the realness of it back again, and she imagined that same trail now, cloaked in the dark of night and covered in snow, erasing all traces of whatever had happened there. Not that they'd detected any.

Her thoughts drifted across Coulter's property line, to Daniel Ranslett's land. Or rightly, to Daniel Ranslett. She had a feeling that no matter what amount Chilton Enterprises offered him, he wouldn't sell his land.

She arched her shoulders and rubbed her lower back, rolling her neck from side to side. In the end, getting the landowner to sell wasn't her problem. She was just supposed to give Goldberg the names, which she would provide in a letter to him tonight.

Her gaze was drawn again to *the* photograph, and the confrontation Josiah had described played again in her mind. She sat down at the desk and pulled out a fresh sheet of paper and dipped her quill, then wrote the story as she remembered him telling it. She included a summary at the end about how a person reaped what they sowed and then finished with a mention of Josiah Birch, a man of courage and valor in the Colorado Rockies. Thinking that a good title, she added it at the top.

She scanned the four written pages. Not her best, but it was good. It would grab readers' attention too, especially the men, which is what Mr. Goldberg wanted. She signed her pen name at the bottom— E.G. Brenton—wishing she were signing her real name instead. In time . . .

After changing into her nightgown, she crawled into bed and blew out the chipped oil lamp on her nightstand. The sheets were cool against her bare legs and brought a chill. Shivering, she pulled down her gown from where it bunched around her hips, then reached for the blanket and tucked it snug beneath her chin.

It wasn't until minutes later, when she'd finally gotten warm, that she thought of Josiah. She rose on one elbow. Her gaze swung to the window. She'd never asked him where he lived or where he stayed at night. She pushed back the covers and padded across the bare floor to the window to see if it was still snowing. A deeper chill worked its way up her legs.

Hugging her midsection, she moved the curtain to one side and peered through a dirt-streaked pane. Pale moonlight mingled with the snow to outline the buildings and homes in burnished silver shadows. Her window overlooked the town, and the view was as she'd expected—desolate, ghostly white. Ranslett had described a similar scene so beautifully the other day, when everything was covered in frost and snow. Warmth from her breath fogged the glass pane, and her concern deepened as she imagined Josiah out there somewhere in the night.

She hoped he was someplace warm and dry. She'd paid him two weeks' salary in advance, so he wasn't without funds, which made her wonder again about his shoes.

Icy cold slipped through unseen cracks in the walls and floorboards, hastening her longing for her bed. As she turned to go she saw something move in the street down below. In the shadows.

She leaned close to the window, squinting. Waiting . . .

Perhaps she'd only imagin—

No, there it was again. Someone standing just inside the alleyway, on the opposite side of the street. Flakes of snow smudged the opposite side of the pane, and she tried to rub away the condensation with the ball of her fist.

Someone stepped from the shadows—a man, if the long duster and Stetson were any indication. He looked up one side of the street and down the other. Then just stood there.

She watched, curious. Why would someone be standing outside on a—

She pushed back from the window, heart in her throat. Whoever was down there had looked straight up at her window.

She consciously unclenched her jaw, waiting. The curtain swayed, betraying her presence, before falling back into place. There was no way he could see into a third-story room, but still she felt exposed.

She stared at the window, her mind racing. It was dark outside. The likelihood he'd seen her was slim. She could hardly see through the dirty panes herself. Still, she felt as though she'd been caught spying.

Seconds ticked past and she couldn't help herself. She moved closer again and leaned to one side. Careful not to disturb the draperies this time, she peered through a narrow slit in the fabric and watched the alleyway below, searching the shadows as best she could.

No one. Whoever had been there was gone.

Feeling suddenly brave in her sheltered tower, she nudged the curtain aside, and for the briefest second she expected to see the man standing below again, staring up at her like some seedy villain in a stagecoach novel. A shiver skittered up and down her arms, and she nearly laughed out loud at her own silliness.

She tried to see if she could make out the sheriff's office, but she couldn't. She could, however, see Mattie's Porch, the restaurant where she'd eaten yesterday—and that's when she spotted him again. Or she thought it was him.

A ways down the street, in a wagon, his shoulders hunched forward.

She pressed closer to the window. There was something in the wagon bed. A bundle of some sort . . . She couldn't make it out.

Her breath fogged the window again, and she impatiently swiped at the patch of moisture. She barely made out the outline of the wagon before the snow and the night swallowed it whole.

18

Morning couldn't come soon enough. Images of the stranger below Elizabeth's window last night kept blurring with those of the missing body and made for outlandish dreams, keeping sleep at a distance.

Eager to speak with Sheriff McPherson, she threw back the covers and shuffled from bed. Intermittent sips of tea sated her appetite as she hurried through her routine, and she was surprised when she went to pour another cup only to find the teapot bone dry. She must have been drinking more than she'd thought. No matter, she breathed in and out. Her lungs were clear and she felt surprisingly refreshed. If the sheriff wasn't an early riser, she was going to beat him to his office.

Some faithful soul had swept the boardwalks clear of last night's snow, but the frozen planks were still slick in spots. Her heeled boots didn't offer the best traction, so she stepped down to the street cautiously, gripping the railing, careful to hold on to the envelope she was mailing to Goldberg. Her breath shown in crisp puffs, and though the mud beneath her boots was frozen, she could well imagine what a horrendous mess it would be when the temperatures warmed.

The stage was pulling up in front of the store when she rounded the corner. Her timing could not have been better. She raced inside the store and paid the clerk at the mail counter, then handed the coachman her envelope. It felt good knowing that *the* photograph—as she'd come to think of it—along with the one of the meadow, and another article were out of her hands and on their way to Washington.

The townspeople of Timber Ridge were out early this morning. Especially the male population. At the far end of the street, a crowd of men gathered outside a building. Their murmured conversation drifted toward her, and several of them were shaking their heads. Her curiosity piqued, she decided to take that street to the sheriff's office in hopes of learning what the gathering was about.

She spotted Josiah standing on the outskirts. He saw her at the same time and met her halfway.

He looked tired, as though he hadn't slept well. "Mornin', Miz Westbrook. Word is, they come upon a body, ma'am. Only—" He glanced around, his deep voice anxious. "They come upon it somewhere here in town."

"Is it the same man?"

"I ain't seen him. Undertaker done had him inside when I got here."

"Have they given his name?"

"No, ma'am. But you and me got no idea what that man's name was anyhow."

She nodded, thinking. "Have you spoken to the sheriff yet?"

Josiah gave her a look. "Like I's just gonna walk right up to him and tell him I found me a dead white man?"

She took issue with his tone. "I was just asking if you had spoken with him yet, Josiah."

He gave a sharp sigh. "You a smart lady, ma'am, but you got a lot to learn 'bout how things work out here. Man like me don't bring up findin' no dead bodies to white men." He glanced around again and lowered his voice. " 'Specially when it's one of their own. I be findin' a noose round my neck real quick-like."

Her thoughts jumped to what McPherson had told her happened

in town years earlier, and it gave credence to Josiah's concern. "We found the body together. I'll speak on your behalf, if need be. I'll be your witness should any questions arise."

"I don't mean no disrespect, Miz Westbrook, but that gives me little means of comfort, ma'am. Not when you seen what I seen. I laid awake last night thinkin' on it. We got to tell him, I know that. It's the right thing to do, but it bein' the right thing don't mean I got to like doin' it."

She couldn't argue that point, and didn't try. He was right. Josiah had witnessed things, experienced things, that she'd only read about in her support of the abolitionist movement. As she'd been reading about it, he'd been living it.

"You're right, Josiah, of course. I'll tell him, and I'll be very careful in how I reveal the information to him."

Sheriff McPherson stepped from the building onto the boardwalk and the crowd's murmur fell away. She moved closer in order to hear. Josiah hung back a ways, then eventually followed. Behind the sheriff came another man, shorter and hunched. Whether by time or by nature wasn't certain, and he shuffled along more than walked.

McPherson stood at the edge of the boardwalk. "I appreciate your patience as we've begun investigating a discovery that was made early this morning."

The hunched man stepped forward and whispered something in the sheriff's ear.

McPherson nodded. "As most of you probably know by now, a body was found at daybreak this morning. It's that of Travis Coulter."

The reaction from the crowd was subdued. Elizabeth sensed Josiah's shudder beside her and felt one pass through her too. But just because it was the same man they'd gone to see yesterday didn't mean it was the same body, and it didn't implicate Josiah in any way.

But the coincidence *was* unnerving. . . .

"After Mr. Carnes's initial examination of the body"—Sheriff McPherson gestured to the hunched man beside him—"he's placing

Coulter's time of death within the last twenty-four hours. We've already sent a telegram to Denver asking for record of next of kin. If any of you know whether Coulter had any living relatives, I'd appreciate you getting with us on that." More questions were volleyed, and he raised his hands, waiting for silence. "Coulter's body was found behind the saloon."

A man close to Elizabeth laughed. "That ain't surprising, now, is it?"

"Mr. Carnes needs more time to examine the body before ruling on the cause of death, so we'll release that information when we have it. There'll be an investigation and I fully expect everyone in town to allow that investigation to be conducted without any outside interference. If anyone does choose to interfere—"

He scanned the faces as though trying to memorize them, and as Elizabeth watched him, the image of six crosses, arranged in a semicircle, from largest to smallest, rose in her mind. McPherson had to be thinking of that incident right now. How could he not? Surely others in this crowd had been in Timber Ridge long enough to recall it too.

"—then that person will be obstructing justice, and they'll be dealt with in the strictest sense of the law. If you know anything about what might have happened to Coulter, whether you think it's significant or not, I ask you to come and speak with me now. Thank you." He stepped from the boardwalk and was immediately engulfed by the crowd.

Elizabeth didn't say anything for a minute, aware of Josiah's reticence. "We have to find out if it's the same man."

"Yes, ma'am, we do."

"But we might as well wait here for a minute, until the sheriff is free."

Josiah nodded.

Her attention drifted, then eventually made its way back to McPherson. Just above him on the boardwalk, Mr. Carnes stood scanning the street as though searching for someone. The coroner stopped and scrunched his face, looking in the vicinity of where she and Josiah stood. Purpose flooded his expression.

Elizabeth glanced behind her to see what had drawn his attention, but no one was there. When she turned back, the man was on a path straight for her and Josiah, shuffling at a surprising speed.

She discreetly touched Josiah's arm, and it didn't take him long to follow her meaning.

"Oh . . . this ain't good, Miz Westbrook. This ain't good at all."

"Neither of us has done anything wrong, Josiah," she whispered, still watching Mr. Carnes. "Remember that."

"Miss Westbrook?" The coroner's voice sounded exactly as she would have expected—rusted, like an old hinge that needed a good oiling. Out of breath, he removed his hat and quickly glanced behind him in McPherson's direction. "You're the . . . woman photographer from . . . back east. Is that right?"

"Yes, Mr. Carnes, I am. How do you do?" She debated on whether or not to extend her hand in greeting, but then remembered McPherson's reference to the man examining the body and refrained. He had a peculiar smell about him. At first she thought it was a poor choice of cologne; on second whiff she cringed. It was formaldehyde.

Carnes smiled, and though it was a friendly gesture, it wasn't an altogether pleasant addition to his face. "I'm doing a whole lot better than the man back in my office—that's for sure. Listen, ma'am, I'm wondering if you could do the town of Timber Ridge a great service." His eyes were large and wide set, and one of them had a tendency to wander as he spoke. "Due to the circumstances of this case, I think it's imperative that a photograph be—"

"Carnes!" McPherson stared from across the street. He spoke briefly to the men encircling him, then started toward them.

"As I was saying, ma'am"—Mr. Carnes spoke in haste—"I think it's imperative that we have a photograph of the deceased for our case files. I wouldn't ordinarily ask this of you, dear lady, but the circumstances merit the request, and I—"

"Miss Westbrook, Mr. Birch, how are you this morning?"

Seeing McPherson's scowl, Elizabeth felt renewed respect for the authority he commanded both personally and as sheriff of this town. She also experienced a touch of apprehension for Mr. Carnes, and was glad she wasn't on the receiving end of the dark look.

Sensing the sheriff's greeting was more of a formality, she answered with a nod, and Josiah did likewise.

"Carnes, I advised you against doing this."

"But you did not forbid it, Sheriff. And I still hold that having a photograph of the deceased will prove beneficial in this case." He worried the frayed rim of his hat. "We've never had a photographer in Timber Ridge, and coroners back east routinely have their corpses—"

"This is not up for debate." McPherson turned to her. "My sincere apologies, Miss Westbrook. This isn't an appropriate conversation to be having in your presence, ma'am. And even less appropriate is what's being requested of you." His look silenced a fidgeting Mr. Carnes.

The coroner's mouth tightened into a thin line.

Josiah shifted his weight, and maybe it was her imagination, but Elizabeth felt his silent censure regarding the photograph she'd taken yesterday—as though she didn't already feel judged enough by McPherson's strong opinion on the subject. Thoughts ricocheted off one another. She needed to tell the sheriff about yesterday's discovery, but she wasn't about to have that conversation in front of Mr. Carnes.

She chose her words carefully. "I appreciate your concern, Sheriff. However, though capturing such photographs, as Mr. Carnes has suggested, doesn't fall within my usual practice"—from the corner of her eye she saw Josiah look at her, and her face heated—"I believe I could . . . tolerate doing this for you. For the overall good of the investigation." She purposefully did not look at Josiah. "But only with your permission, of course."

McPherson seemed to weigh her offer. He looked at Carnes, then at her. "May I speak with you privately, Miss Westbrook?"

She attempted to trace his footsteps in the snow but had to throw in an extra one every few steps. Grateful for the opportunity to finally speak with him in private, she hoped she hadn't overstepped her bounds in making the offer.

He led her to the end of the boardwalk and assisted her up the stairs. "I'm sorry you've been put in this situation, ma'am, and I appreciate what you're offering to do. But I fear that seeing this body will be upsetting to you. And I don't want to—"

"Sheriff, excuse me for interrupting, but . . . there's something you need to know. It may help in some regard."

He studied her for a moment, and she was struck by how gentle a man he seemed, and how handsome. Now, how to say what she needed to say to him with him staring at her in such a way. "Yesterday morning, we were near the Maroon Bells when—"

"We?"

"Yes, Josiah Birch was with me."

He briefly looked beyond her, then nodded.

"We were near the Maroon Bells when we found a man's body, on the trail."

McPherson showed no reaction whatsoever, which threw her, but only for a second. "Neither Josiah nor I knew his name or who he was. Josiah was going to carry him back to town, but when we came back a while later, the body was gone." Part of her last sentence replayed in her mind—*when we came back a while later.* That they'd left the body there sounded cold and without feeling, and she rushed to cover the awkwardness of it. "When we got back into town, we went straight to your office to notify you. But it was closed and no one was there. Since it was late and it was snowing . . . and quite honestly since the man *was* already dead, we decided to seek you out first thing this morning to tell you."

She could see him assimilating the information, piecing it together with whatever he'd learned that morning.

"So let me get this straight, Miss Westbrook. You found a dead man, and then you just left him there."

It wasn't an accusation *per se,* yet disbelief clipped his tone. "But we weren't gone for long. No more than an hour . . . or two, at the most."

"And where did you go?"

"On up the mountain."

His smile held understanding. "I'm trying to establish why you went on up the mountain."

Elizabeth sped her thoughts forward, feeling the sudden need to critique them as she went. "As it turns out, there's an odd coincidence linking our experience to what you found this morning. . . . I was on my way to see Travis Coulter in order to gain his permission to take photographs of his land." The statement was met with silence and the silence begged to be filled, despite something telling her not to. "If I know that a piece of land is privately owned, I always try and seek out the owner's approval before taking photographs." She offered a smile. "Consider it courtesy of the trade."

"That's very kind of you. And just how did you know that that land belonged to Coulter?"

She blinked. "I gained that information from a visit to the land and title office." She could just see Wendell Goldberg sitting back in his chair, shaking his head over how much she was divulging. "One of my first stops when I visit a town like Timber Ridge is to familiarize myself with the surroundings. And in your town's case, I wanted to see where the hot springs and the waterfalls were located. Those make gorgeous landscapes, as I'm sure you can imagine." In her mind, Goldberg's eyes lit with pride.

"I'm sure they do. I'd like to see some of your photographs sometime, Miss Westbrook, as would my sister. Remember, she's still planning on Saturday's visit."

"I haven't forgotten. I'm looking forward to it too."

"You seem to enjoy what you do, Miss Westbrook. I can see the excitement in your eyes when you talk about it." He briefly glanced past her. "Do you think you'd recognize the body you saw yesterday, if you were to see it again?"

"I'm certain I would."

He paused. "And do you think you could show me the exact location where you and Josiah found it?"

"Absolutely. We'd be happy to."

"Did anyone see you or Josiah, Miss Westbrook? Did you pass anyone on the way?"

"No, there was no one."

"You're certain?"

She nodded, then thought of something. "I did see someone from my window last night. He was standing in the alleyway below, opposite the boardinghouse."

His brow furrowed. "Did you recognize him?"

She shook her head, then described the sequence of events.

"And how do you think this relates to what we found this morning?"

"It probably doesn't. I just thought I should tell you in case it did."

Again that smile. Then he glanced in the direction of the coroner's office. "For now, the only thing that remains is for you and Josiah to view the body. I don't like putting you in this situation, but with what you've shared, I don't see any way around it. Then if you'd be so kind as to retrieve your equipment, we'll ask you to take a photograph for Mr. Carnes's files."

He gestured for her to precede him and they walked toward the coroner's office. Josiah and Mr. Carnes joined them on the way.

When they got to the door, Mr. Carnes went on inside but McPherson turned back. "Mr. Birch, would you wait out here for us? I'd like to speak to Miss Westbrook first. I'll return in a minute."

"I wait right here for you, Sheriff, sir."

Not wanting to, Elizabeth followed McPherson inside.

19

The past twenty-four hours had not been kind to Mr. Travis Coulter. But at least now Elizabeth knew why no one had been at home in the cabin. If she'd had a handkerchief with her, she would have covered her mouth and nose. The odors in the room could probably be attributed more to the routine duties performed in this office than the body, but she couldn't be sure.

An eerie sense of déjà vu crept into the room. She swallowed. "It's the same man."

"You're sure?"

She nodded.

She didn't know why, but she was more skittish viewing the body today than she had been yesterday. And it took her a moment to realize why. Yesterday the man had simply been dead. But today, he'd been murdered. Didn't the body being moved indicate that?

"Is there anything about him that looks different to you, Miss Westbrook? Any new marks on his body? On the clothing?"

The complexion was grayer than she remembered, which served as ample motivation for her to focus on other distinguishing factors. His boots looked the same, his pants, his shirt. The same girth around his middle . . . "I don't see any difference at all. I'm sorry."

McPherson gestured. "Did you happen to notice if Coulter was wearing a gun yesterday?" He slipped his own pistol from the holster on his hip. "Coulter carried a Remington single action revolver with a walnut grip. His had some fancy engraving along here"—he ran a finger along the barrel—"and on the chamber. It had pearl inlays on the sides of the grip too. He was real proud of it."

Carnes snorted. "He was a fool about that thing, is what he was. Showed it off every chance he got."

Elizabeth looked back at the empty holster on Coulter's body and tried to recall the picture she'd seen through the lens. Slowly, she nodded. "I do remember seeing a gun, though I couldn't tell you if it was as you described. Perhaps Josiah will remember more."

McPherson nodded. "That's real good, ma'am. It helps, thank you." He motioned to Carnes, who first draped a sheet over the body and then busied himself with mixing something in a bowl on a table in the corner.

McPherson gently took hold of her arm, much as he'd done with his sister in the store that day when she'd first seen them, and led her toward the door. Looking out the window, he exhaled—part sigh, part groan. Elizabeth followed his gaze and realized what—or rather, who—had inspired the reaction.

Coming up the street, like a man on a mission, was Drayton Turner. She hadn't thought about it before now, but she was surprised the editor of Timber Ridge's illustrious newspaper wasn't already on the scene, snooping for a story. Though she hardly knew him, she knew his type from years of experience, and could well guess what was in store for McPherson.

"He seems eager to speak with you, Sheriff."

McPherson gave a shake of his head. "You mean eager to speak with me *again*. He was already here first thing. Drayton Turner's an eager sort of fella. Typical newspaper man—always after a story. Whether one's there or not."

He wasn't looking at her, so Elizabeth didn't feel a need to guard her reaction. "That's a good thing, I'd think. For him to be ambitious in that way, since he's running a newspaper."

"Oh, I'm not faulting him for his ambition, ma'am. There's nothing wrong with that. Except when he goes for the trigger too soon and prints something that's not accurate. Which has been my unfortunate experience with those kinds of folk in the past."

"Those kinds of folk." Elizabeth couldn't help herself. "I would imagine it's hard to get all the facts straight all of the time. Surely Mr. Turner offers to retract any inaccuracies."

"He does. On the back page. A day later." He turned to her. "But the harm's already been done by then, now, hasn't it?"

She didn't answer.

"I'm of the opinion, Miss Westbrook, that it's best not to speculate when it comes to the truth. Best to wait until you've weighed all the facts; otherwise you can kick up a lot of dust for no reason." He shook his head. "But that doesn't serve a newspaper's deadlines. Or Turner's desire to sell more copies."

"But wouldn't you agree that sometimes it's difficult to know what the truth is? It may not always be what's staring you right in the face. Especially when there may be more than one version of it."

"Ah, but that's just it. There can't be different versions. Truth is constant. A person's perspective might be skewed, but that doesn't change what the truth is. All it means is that a particular person is . . . mistaken, for whatever reason."

She held his gaze, wondering how the conversation had turned so philosophical. "I couldn't agree more . . . for whatever reason." She smiled to lighten the moment.

The look McPherson gave her made her think of Daniel Ranslett, though she couldn't place why.

The door opened. "Sheriff, I'd hoped you'd still be here. I'm wondering if Carnes has confirmed how—" A smile accompanied Drayton Turner's surprise. "Miss Westbrook, how nice to see you again, ma'am."

She tilted her head in greeting, wondering at his hat. "And you, Mr. Turner."

"You're keeping that camera of yours busy, I hear."

She didn't know quite how to respond.

"Mullins tells me you'll be at his store this weekend, taking photographs."

"Oh . . . yes. He and his wife were kind enough to ask me, and I agreed. I just hope someone shows up, so they're not disappointed."

"Don't you worry about the people of Timber Ridge, Miss Westbrook." Turner glanced at papers lying beside him on a table, then turned his head slightly as though trying to read what was written. McPherson flipped the pages over. Turner's smile just deepened. "They'll be lined up in their Sunday best. Mullins already has signs posted in his front window."

She tried not to stare at Drayton Turner's hat—a feathered bowler that would have been considered the height of style back east. But in this rustic setting, it seemed out of place. Yet somehow it still suited his personality, and lack of discretion.

He fingered the hat's rim as though aware of her thoughts, then cast a glance at McPherson. Elizabeth could only interpret his look as puzzlement over why she was present.

"If you'll excuse me, gentlemen." She addressed McPherson, knowing she would also answer Turner's silent query. "If you're agreeable, I'll go get my equipment and be back shortly."

"I'll go with you," McPherson offered.

She shook her head, realizing that he would probably rather go with her than stay and answer Turner's questions. "Thank you, but Josiah will help me. *After* you meet with him, of course." She moved to the door, where Turner intercepted her.

"Miss Westbrook, if you're already taking a photograph of the body, might I impose upon you to make a copy of it for the *Reporter*?"

"I'll be happy to. If that's all right with the sheriff. . . ."

Looking none too pleased, McPherson nodded as he opened the door and motioned for Josiah to join him inside. "We won't be long, Miss Westbrook."

Apprehension showed in Josiah's features, and she willed him not to be nervous as she walked outside, aware of Turner following her. She took a few steps on the boardwalk and breathed in the fresh air. The temperature had climbed. "Tell me, Mr. Turner, does it always smell of fresh pine in this town?"

He sniffed. "I guess it does. You get used to it after a while."

"Mmmm . . . I don't think I would." Glancing his way, she decided to give him some of his own medicine. "What caused you to move out here, Mr. Turner? Why did the adventuresome editor choose the untamed west?"

"The truth?"

"Absolutely, and it'll be off the record." She winked.

"My wife decided she didn't want to be married to me anymore. The newspaper life wasn't for her. Or I wasn't. One of the two. Maybe both." He held her gaze. "How's that for truthfulness, Miss Westbrook. Whether on or off the record."

"I—" She searched for something to say. "I'm sorry. I didn't realize . . ."

His laughter broke the tension. "I'm only kidding, Miss Westbrook. You're far too gullible, but the trait becomes you."

Elizabeth smiled but didn't share his humor.

"I came out for the same reason everyone else did. To start fresh. To live in the Wild West before civilization catches up with it and tames it to boredom. Speaking of which . . . I'm still waiting for some of your photographs, ma'am. To publish in the *Reporter*."

She mentally flipped through the pictures she'd taken, realizing she'd been delinquent in cataloging them. "I did take one this week that you might be interested in. If you like children."

"I'm actually not too fond of them."

She stared, her brow raised. This man had to be Wendell Goldberg's twin separated at birth. "Well, then you probably won't be interested in this one."

"When I gave you counsel to branch out from your normal landscapes, I wasn't thinking of children but rather something with a little more risk, Miss Westbrook."

She thought of the photograph currently on its way to Goldberg. "I'll try and work harder on that in the future, Mr. Turner."

The door opened behind her, and she heard Josiah's voice before she saw him.

"You got any more questions, sir, you just let me know."

"I'll do that, and I appreciate your time, Josiah."

Josiah exited the building with McPherson, appearing decidedly more relaxed than before. Elizabeth gathered from his demeanor that the conversation with the sheriff had yielded no new information.

"Miz Westbrook, how 'bout I head on to the livery and pick up Moonshine. Meet you back over at the boardin' house?"

"Thank you, Josiah. I won't be long."

Josiah took the stairs from the boardwalk leading to the street at a quick jaunt.

Turner stepped forward. "You ready for me, Sheriff?"

"As I'll ever be, Turner." Playful sarcasm framed McPherson's response and drew a smirk from Turner.

"Our sheriff here doesn't hold my newspaper in very high regard, ma'am."

"That's not true and you know it." McPherson pushed the door open wider. "At times, I think I hold it in higher regard than you do."

Having no desire to get into the middle of their war of words, Elizabeth retreated a step. "If you'll excuse me, gentlemen, I'll be back shortly with my camera."

"One last thing, Miss Westbrook." Turner tucked his pencil in his pocket. "Would this afternoon be convenient for me to stop by and get the photograph from you? I'd like to use it in tomorrow's edition, if possible."

Knowing she would have wanted the same thing if she were in his position, she nodded. "Certainly. Give me until after dinner and then stop by. Will that work?"

"Like a charm, ma'am. Thank you." Turner walked on inside. From where she stood, she could hear him begin to pepper Mr. Carnes with questions.

She was almost to the stairs leading to the street when she felt a touch on her arm. She turned to find McPherson staring down, his expression inscrutable.

"There's something you need to be aware of, Miss Westbrook, and I didn't want to say anything in front of Turner, for obvious reasons." A woman and child walked by. He tipped his hat, sheriff's smile at the ready. "Mrs. Grady, little Caroline, how are you ladies today?" He waited for them to pass before continuing. "Josiah had a run-in with the deceased a while back at the livery."

"Yes, he's already told me all about it, Sheriff, when we found the man's body." Seeing the opportunity, she seized it. "Josiah is an honest man, Sheriff. Granted, I haven't known him long, but I believe him to be a man of outstanding integrity and character."

"And I'm not here to argue that. But I'm wondering . . . did Josiah tell you that Coulter threatened his life that day?"

Hesitant, she shook her head.

"Coulter promised to kill him. My deputy was outside the livery and saw and heard everything. Josiah controlled himself admirably, especially after Coulter came after him with that hammer. My deputy says Josiah fended him off, holding him by the throat at arm's length. Coulter struggled to get at him, mad as a hornet."

Elizabeth could picture it well and felt immense pride in Josiah's restraint.

"After Coulter left, my deputy made sure Josiah was all right. And he was. But he was angry too, and rightly so. It was what he said to my deputy that gives me pause today, ma'am . . . Josiah told him that he'd had a hard time not just snapping that little white man's neck clean in two."

The way the sheriff said it, Elizabeth could hear Josiah's voice.

"Problem is, a couple of other men in the livery heard Josiah say it too. I went and visited both of them right after, because I knew how they felt about Negroes. And I knew they'd side with Coulter if it ever came to something—no matter that they didn't like the man."

"But you can't fault Josiah for his reaction, understanding what had been done to him. Can you?"

"I don't fault him at all, ma'am. I'm sure I wouldn't have handled it nearly so well. I'm saying all this to make you aware of what happened, since Josiah's working for you. And to let you know that there are people in this town who know what Josiah said, and they don't hold kindly to Negroes. That's why I don't favor putting a picture of a dead body in the paper. I'm afraid it might stir things up that would be best left alone."

Elizabeth considered this, seeing both sides of this issue, as well as the overall issue in a broader scope. Maybe more clearly now than she ever had. "I understand what you're saying, but what am I supposed to do? Take the photograph, or not?"

"You take the photograph like you've agreed to do, and we'll see how things fall out. Pictures don't lie, Miss Westbrook, so I don't fear them." He rubbed the back of his neck. "Even though you're only here doing this as a hobby, what you've brought to Timber Ridge is the future. And it's coming, whether we want it to or not. What I fear isn't your lens, ma'am. It's what a handful of people will do when they see that picture without knowing the full story. And the conclusions they might jump to without taking the time to learn the whole truth."

His mention of truth burned inside her. She felt so . . . false, standing in front of him with his not knowing the full truth about her.

At the time she'd thought Wendell Goldberg's idea not to tell people about her true reason for being in Timber Ridge was wise counsel. And she guessed it still was, in a way. Because people were telling her things they wouldn't have otherwise. But every secret or personal thing they'd shared felt like a weight inside her now. The articles she'd written about them, and had yet to write . . . It felt as if she were handing out keys to houses that didn't belong to her.

"There's one more thing I need to tell you, ma'am. It came up as Carnes was examining the body this morning. But I asked him to hold off on saying anything publicly until he could do a more thorough examination, to make certain. I know how Coulter died." His intensity made her want to look away, but she couldn't. "And I won't be able to hold the information much longer."

She swallowed, praying she was wrong. "He died of a broken neck."

"Yes, ma'am. Snapped clean in two."

Later that afternoon, she waited in line at the telegraph office, carefully composing a message to Goldberg. He would salivate knowing this kind of story was forthcoming, and with photographs, no less, though her own reaction to it was far more guarded due to Josiah's connection with the victim.

She penned the message and handed it to the clerk, who, to his credit, didn't react in the slightest.

LOCAL RESIDENT MURDERED STOP ASSAILANT UNKNOWN STOP SCENE OF CRIME IN DISPUTE STOP PHOTO EVIDENCE AND DETAILS TO FOLLOW BY MAIL

20

Daniel made the outskirts of Timber Ridge by mid-Thursday morning. He reined in when he spotted a man working to free his wagon from a sludge hole. Temperatures had warmed enough yesterday afternoon for the snows to partially melt, and with this morning's sun blazing down, the rays were quickly making travel a muddy business.

Harnessed to the fellow's wagon was the finest pair of stallions Daniel had ever seen. They were huge, each at least sixteen hands, and black as night, every inch sinewy muscle and strength. Yet with the angle of the wagon and the weight of goods packed snug in the bed, the animals couldn't pull the freight wagon clear of the muck.

Daniel guided his mare closer. "Could you use a hand?"

Relief registered on the man's face. "I sure could." He rose from the bench seat, but Daniel gestured for him to stay put.

He walked to the back, rolling up his shirt sleeves. "You take the reins. I'll shoulder it from behind." He counted aloud to three, then put his full weight behind the stuck wheel as the man worked the team, calling the horses by name. Daniel slipped once in the sludge but regained his footing. The oversized freight wagon rocked, held fast, and then made a low sucking sound as the wheel finally began to budge from the hole onto drier ground.

It was slow work, and untidy. By the time they were done, Daniel's clothes were covered in mud.

The man set the brake and jumped down. He handed Daniel a rag. "Much obliged, friend. I was having a time of it there."

Daniel wiped his hands. "That's quite a pair of stallions you've got. Finest I've ever seen."

"Thank you. They're the finest team I've ever owned. Percherons, from France. Good temperament, hard workers too."

Daniel smiled. "Well, that explains it, then."

The stranger stared, obviously not following.

Daniel glanced back at the horses. "I thought maybe I hadn't heard you right—the names you called out a minute ago as you worked the wagon free. But I'm thinking now that I did."

The man gave a smile that could best be described as shy. He nodded. "Charlemagne and Napoleon. That was my wife's doing, I'm afraid. She insisted that animals from her native country ought to have French names." It was obvious from the spark that lit the man's eyes when he spoke of his wife that she was treasured. The freighter took the dirty rag from Daniel and tossed it in the back of the wagon. "I'm much obliged again for your help. If you ever need a load hauled in or out, I run freight to just about every town from here to Denver to Pike's Peak. I've got three other men working for me who run it farther south. I'll carry it for you at no charge. The name's Jack Brennan, and all you have to do is leave word with Ben Mullins at the store. He knows how to reach me."

Daniel gave his name but shook his head at the same time. "There's no call to offer that. All I did was shoulder your wagon out of some mud."

"My offer holds." Brennan grasped Daniel's shoulder as though they'd been friends for a long time and looked down at the mud caking Daniel's clothes and boots. "Anytime you need something hauled, Ranslett, you just let Mullins know when and where."

Daniel watched the freighter maneuver his team on down

the street, glad he'd decided to make the trip into town after all. He'd awakened early that morning thinking about Davy and the Tuckers . . . and peppermint. He was due to take Miss Westbrook hunting tomorrow, but if early morning skies held accurate prediction, snow was returning, despite the warmer temperatures.

Glad he'd brought an extra change of clothes along, he headed to a nearby creek that was fed by a hot spring. He stripped and rinsed his face, hands, and arms, then re-dressed and dropped his clothes off at a laundry in town. The Chinese woman behind the counter greeted him in an unfamiliar tongue, but somehow they communicated enough for him to know to pick up his clothes tomorrow.

His hankering for peppermint returned, the kind Mullins always kept in stock. But he didn't want some just for himself. And where he was headed today, he would need at least two full tins.

He hoped Miss Westbrook had a copy of that picture of the Tuckers' children too. If not, he planned on persuading her to make one right quick.

———

Close to noon, Elizabeth pushed back from the desk in her bedroom and yawned and stretched, ready for fresh air and exercise. The bright sunshine and warmer temperatures beckoned, and there was plenty of time before her appointment with Mr. Hawthorne.

She'd spent the morning cleaning and organizing her camera equipment and making certain she'd recorded the details for each photograph taken since her arrival at Timber Ridge. Her right hand ached from gripping the quill, and she wiggled her fingers to ease the tension. Feeling another headache coming on, she poured a cup of lukewarm tea and added an extra dash of Mrs. Winslow's Soothing Syrup. She ran a thumb along the edge of the nearly full journal.

The pages in this volume contained particulars for every photograph she'd ever taken, including those taken with Mathew Brady. Comparing the information always deepened her understanding of the use of light and shadow, and of the distance needed from an object in order to capture detail without sacrificing essence.

She looked forward to the hunting trip tomorrow with Daniel Ranslett. And since Saturday was slated to be spent visiting Rachel Boyd, and Sunday afternoon at the general store taking photographs of whoever showed, she'd spent the bulk of last evening cooped up in her room, making prints of developed plates, including the one Carnes stopped by to pick up. He was a peculiar little fellow with an odd way about him. It had taken her a moment to realize what he'd been doing, but he'd actually invited her out to dinner. Through a haze of formaldehyde, she had politely declined.

Not long after Carnes left, Drayton Turner had arrived. He'd been like a kid in a candy shop as he anticipated publishing the first edition of the *Reporter* to contain photographs. He'd already dropped by this morning to tell her he'd sold all his copies and was printing more. His highest distribution ever.

He'd been complimentary of the other photographs he'd seen in her collection, and she'd let him borrow two more for future publication in the newspaper. His praise was gratifying, and she had a feeling he didn't hand it out lightly.

She reached for her copy of the *Reporter* again and read her name beneath the photograph. Not *E.G. Brenton* but *Elizabeth Garrett Westbrook*. It felt good to see her name in the heavy-faced type. She'd been relieved to read that Turner had reported Coulter's cause of death as inconclusive. Not a single mention of Josiah either, thankfully.

She'd asked Josiah about his run-in with Coulter but hadn't said anything about Coulter dying from a broken neck. Josiah admitted the man had threatened him. "Stuff like that been said to me my whole life, Miz Westbrook. If I tucked tail and run every time a white man threaten me, I'da wore my legs off for sure by now." Seated on the boardwalk, he had leaned forward with his elbows on his knees, his hands clasped. "I gets up each day and I face what God gives me to handle, ma'am. Sometimes I fear it. Won't say that I don't. But knowin'

He's already sifted through it and that Jesus knows what's comin' before it gets to me . . . well, I reckon that ought to be enough."

Such wisdom and trust from a man who had been so misused in his life. How had Josiah developed such trust?

Elizabeth found herself wishing she had that kind of faith. It wasn't a prayer, really, more of a longing, but she felt it drift up and out of her, light and freeing, and she hoped God was listening. Then thinking of all that Josiah had endured in his life, she went still inside. Quickly, she tried to recall the thought, telling God it hadn't been a prayer. But somehow she knew it was already gone from her, and in His hands.

A knock on her door interrupted the moment, and she rose from her desk. If it was Drayton Turner again, she was going to send him a bill for taking up so much of her—

"Ranslett!" Seeing Daniel Ranslett standing there on her threshold pleased her more than she could have imagined. A thwacking on the wooden floor drew her focus downward. "And Beau too!" She reached down to pet him. "To what do I owe this honor, Ranslett?"

His smile was reminiscent of a schoolboy's. "We were passing by and thought we'd stop in and say hello."

Knowing that wasn't true, Elizabeth said the first thing that came to her mind. "Well, I'm very busy this morning, so you'll have to make it a quick visit."

"Okay. Well, good-bye, then." He walked down the hallway and only stopped when she started to laugh. He closed the distance between them again. "I'm actually here on a mission."

"I figured as much."

He held a frown for two seconds. "I'd like to have a copy of the photograph of the Tucker children you took the other day. And that one of Beau, if you have it."

She warmed, already guessing why he wanted them. "I've got the pictures for the Tuckers right here. I developed them last night. I was going to leave them at the mail counter at the store but haven't done it yet." She'd printed an extra copy of the children in order to satisfy her father's whim of seeing her "pupils." She would have to tell him the truth eventually, but that would be more easily done when she returned to Washington a success.

Ranslett pulled the photographs from the envelope. He looked at the picture of the children, then at the one of Beau, which had turned out especially nice. He didn't speak right off, but he smiled. "Well done, Miss Westbrook."

The sincerity in his voice was touching, and she guided him to the last one in the stack, anticipating his reaction.

He went still. "This is . . . How did you . . ." He traced a path over the picture, a smile slowly forming. "This is my favorite by far. Thank you."

His tender reaction brought about one in her.

"When did you take this?"

She swallowed to ease the tightening in her throat. "When you and Mr. Tucker and the rest of the boys were unloading the meat. All Davy wanted to do was to sit and stare at Beau. So it wasn't too hard to capture." Plus the fact that it seemed to hurt the boy to move, but she wasn't about to say that. Surely, Ranslett already knew. Two things had been obvious to her that afternoon at the Tuckers', and more so as the days had passed and she'd had time to consider it— Daniel cared deeply for the boy, and the boy was ill.

"You certainly have a gift, Miss Westbrook. It's just like looking at him."

She moved beside him to peer at the photograph. "Davy has a hard time holding a smile, and since I lack the ability to inspire one in my subjects, we decided to have him lying down just looking at Beau. And Beau looking at him."

"I can't believe Beau stayed still that long." He reached down and patted the dog's head. "Good boy . . ."

"Actually, he didn't. Or not all of him anyway. Notice his tail is ghosted. And so are his ears."

Ranslett softly laughed. "The picture is perfect, ma'am. Is there any way I could get a copy of the image for myself? I'll give these to the Tuckers."

So she'd guessed correctly. "Are you heading out there today?"

"Right after a trip to the store for some peppermints."

She half hoped he'd invite her along, even though she couldn't go. "I'll be happy to make you a print, Ranslett."

He eyed her. "What's it going to cost me?"

She pretended to think of something. "How about . . . a day of hunting."

He winced. "That's another thing I'm here to talk to you about. I know we set tomorrow to go but it looks like more snow's coming in. It'll be bitter cold, regardless. I think we ought to set it for another day next week."

She glanced to the window, then back at him, showing her suspicion.

"I know it's nice out right now, but trust me on this. The cold's coming."

"How do I know you're not just trying to get out of it?"

"Because if I'd wanted out of it, I wouldn't have come here to set another date."

She found his argument convincing enough. Though it was still hard to imagine more snow with such sunshine.

He held up the envelope. "The Tuckers will appreciate these. And I'll enjoy delivering them. Thank you, again."

"You're welcome, *again.* Oh . . ." She wondered whether to tell him her news, then figured he'd learn about it soon enough. "I found a guide to lead my expedition to the cliff dwellings." It was petty, she knew, but she rather enjoyed the surprise on his face. "I confirmed his credentials. He's reputable and experienced, and he's already working with Mr. Mullins to secure supplies. We leave one week from today."

He didn't respond.

"So if you happened to have changed your mind about my previous job offer . . ." She did a fair job of sounding serious, but her grin gave her away. "And you came here today with the intent of saying you're now interested"—she knew he wasn't—"then I'd have to tell you that I'm sorry, and that I've already hired someone else."

He bowed his head for a second before meeting her stare again. "Be careful, Miss Westbrook. What you're proposing to do is dangerous."

The change in his demeanor took her by surprise. "I was only kidding, Ranslett. Of course I understand the seriousness of what I'm—"

"You think you do, but with all respect . . . you don't. You've taken a few day trips in these mountains and now you think you're experienced. But you're not."

It wasn't easy, but she reined in the urge to argue with him. His caution, however well intended, picked at an old wound. If not for the tenderness in his delivery and having fought this battle so many times before, she would have retaliated. But nothing she could say would change Ranslett's mind. He was the type who had to see the outcome in order to be convinced. Just like her father.

And she planned on showing them both—along with everyone else—that she could do this. And do it well.

The planked walkway was unusually crowded for early afternoon, and after nearly colliding twice with two separate shoppers, Elizabeth opted for the street, watchful of the animal droppings littering the muddy path. Untidy streets was one unfortunate similarity Timber Ridge and Washington shared.

She met with Mr. Hawthorne at Mattie's Porch to go over the final details of their trip and to meet the other gentleman who would be joining them on the expedition. He seemed an upright man, younger than Hawthorne, accustomed to hard work, and experienced enough from the stories he told.

As they worked through each item on her list, Ranslett's cautions kept playing in the back of her mind. And repeatedly she put them aside.

Josiah joined them and they ordered a late lunch, though she didn't touch her food. She didn't have much appetite. Several women approached her table saying that they were bringing their entire families to the Mullinses' store for their first photograph sitting that Sunday. And when she stopped by the general store on the way home to thank Ben and Lyda Mullins for volunteering to host the sittings, she received several more comments from people who said the same.

By the time she returned to the boardinghouse, whatever trepidations she'd had about making the upcoming journey were a distant memory. She was actually making a difference in this town, in people's lives. She was leaving her mark. How she wished Tillie could see what her encouragement and challenge had accomplished.

Josiah was waiting on the boardwalk when she returned. Beside him were two large crates. "Clerk at the mail counter in the store left word that these come in on the stage for you. So's I hauled them over here for you, ma'am."

"Thank you, Josiah. What is it?"

"I ain't looked inside, Miz Westbrook. They got your name on 'em, ma'am, not mine."

She ran a hand over the top of one of the crates and read the originating address. Her father . . . An envelope was affixed to the side. She pulled it free and lifted the flap.

"You mind if I start takin' them on up, ma'am?"

"Not at all, Josiah. I'll be right there to open the door." She read the one-page missive.

Dear Elizabeth,

    Here are the supplies I referenced in my previous letter. As fate would have it, the morning after I sent the letter and books, I was in

committee with Senator Rochester, the current overseer of the Depart-
ment of Education. He recently acquired new furniture for the sixth
district, where his daughter instructs. You will remember her, his eldest
daughter who failed to find a suitor to her particular liking.

Elizabeth heard a slight *tone* in that last sentence. He'd often told
her she was too particular in her choice of men, and he'd given up
trying to pair her years ago, or to force the issue of marriage. She
was too much like him to ever be forced into a situation she didn't
desire, and he knew it.

Rochester was pleased when I told him your pupils in the
Colorado Territory could benefit from his generous donation of the
secondhand equipment.

Elizabeth shook her head, smiling. What else had her dear father
done . . . ?

To that end, these crates contain slates, chalk, maps, and a globe
(the old one from my office that you used to sit and study). Desks,
chairs, bookshelves, and other sundry items are shipping this week
by train and should soon arrive to your attention. I've instructed the
freighter to deliver the furniture to the schoolhouse in Timber Ridge,
so consider yourself forewarned, my dear.

I ponder the wisdom of writing these next words for fear they
will be misinterpreted on paper, but know that as I write them I am
feeling only the deepest love and appreciation for you.

Elizabeth felt an unease deep inside her.

When first you voiced your plans to move west, I thought them
foolhardy designs, dreams of a woman living too long in a make-
believe world. But your acceptance of this position—this grand
challenge—to be a teacher on the frontier has made me exceptionally
proud, Lizzie. Admittedly, through the years, your aspirations inspired
many sleepless nights for this father. Your sojourn at the newspaper

offered excitement, I'm sure, and I would have done my best to accept your decision should you have chosen an even more unconventional role for your life. But you have stayed the course, my daughter. You have listened to God's design and to His calling, and I could not be more proud to be your father.

    With eternal endearment,
    Colonel Garrett Eisenhower Westbrook

Her hands shook as a sick feeling curdled in the pit of her stomach. She closed her eyes and tears pushed out at the edges. Slipping the letter into her reticule, she took the stairs leading to her room at a fast pace, groping for her room key.

She dried her face as she went, determined not to let Josiah see her upset. Her father wouldn't approve of what she was doing now—that was no surprise. Tears threatened again. But to know, to *read* in his own handwriting, that he would have struggled to be proud of her if she'd chosen *an unconventional role* for her life. Which is exactly what she'd done. . . .

Josiah stood waiting at the third-floor landing. "I go get the other crate, ma'am."

Out of breath from the climb, she forced a smile. "Thank you . . ."

"And don't you go tryin' to lift this one yourself. It be too heavy for a woman. You'd tip right over, for sure. Even if you do have a mind to carry that big old camera of yours"—his voice grew fainter as he walked down the stairs—"strapped to your back, all by yourself, and with me standin' right there next to you, strong as a horse and doin' nothin' but watchin' you carry that for miles. . . ."

Normally his ramblings would have made her smile. She retrieved her key and tried to fit it into the lock, but her hands shook too badly. She paused, thankful she was alone, and took a calming breath.

This wasn't the end of the world. Despite their differences, she and her father had a loving relationship. He'd never pretended to understand her reluctance to marry at a young age, and had finally given up on trying to persuade her, as had everyone else. He'd abided her working at the *Chronicle,* but only because he knew, somewhere deep down, that he was partly responsible for her ambition. She sighed. She was her father's daughter. She saw the similarities between them—their independence and drive to achieve—and felt pride. He saw them and obviously felt regret. She tried the key again.

Why wouldn't the confounded thing fit! She smacked the door.

Finally, on the third try, the key slipped into the lock. She turned it. Or tried to. It stuck fast.

She leaned her forehead against the door, already hearing the heavy thud of Josiah's footsteps as he climbed back up the stairs. What was it she'd told herself just that afternoon? That she was making a difference in Timber Ridge. She was leaving her mark. She had friends in this town. People who liked her for who she was— a woman photographer. That had to count for something, even if not toward a father's pride.

She made another attempt with the key, this time holding it at an angle while also lifting up on the knob. The latch finally gave.

She pushed the door but met with resistance after a few inches.

Stopping short, she peered down at the rug on the opposite side to see if it had bunched up again. Or perhaps the housekeeper had left some cleaning supplies. Nothing. She gave the door a good hard shove, and that's when she saw—

Her stomach convulsed as if someone had delivered a blow to her midsection. Tears rose to her eyes. Bile rose in her throat.

"Oh, sweet Jesus . . ." Josiah's voice sounded from close behind. "What done happen in here?"

21

A pungent chemical smell hung heavy in the room, and Elizabeth could scarcely draw a breath. She grabbed hold of the bedpost for support, battling the familiar spasm at the base of her throat.

"You better sits down, ma'am. But not here, Miz Westbrook! Not here."

Elizabeth looked behind her on the bed and saw shards of glass. Glass on the bedcover, on the rugs. One of her dresses was balled up on the floor. She lifted the corner of it and crushed glass spilled out. They'd used the quilt on the bed, the rugs, her own clothes, to muffle the sound of the breakage, then had strewn the shards around the room. Her camera plates—all of them, from what she could tell—were destroyed. And whoever had done this hadn't just broken them but had done it methodically, with care, as though having taken pleasure in it.

Hearing the wheeze in her lungs, she allowed Josiah to lead her to a straight-back chair in the corner.

"Who would . . . do this? And why . . . ?" She couldn't help the high pitch to her voice.

"I ain't got no idea." He quickly searched the room. "But I gonna go get Miz Ruby from downstairs. She know what to do. You stay put right here, ma'am."

Elizabeth was grateful to Josiah for leaving the door open to the hallway. Strange, but whatever kinship she'd felt to this room before had been ripped from her, and she didn't want to be alone in these quarters. Not anymore.

She spotted something in the corner, and a soft cry threaded through her lips.

With effort, she stood and picked her way across the room, bits of glass crunching beneath her boots. She knew what she was looking at, yet at the same time wasn't fully able to grasp it. The well-oiled mahogany wood was familiar, but the box was smashed beyond recognition, the glass viewer crushed, the protective plate holders bent back, splintered, cast off to one side.

She knelt and gently fingered the pieces of wood. Dried silver residue from the collodion and other chemicals marked the larger pieces. Her hands trembled. Her gaze went to the nearest corner, where a piece of clothing—one of her shirtwaists—was stained dark brown. She carefully unfolded it and found jagged brown glass from her bottles of chemicals inside.

Never could she have imagined this happening, much less what it would have felt like. The sense of loss and violation. She put a hand to her mouth, thinking she might be sick. Then swallowed the bitter reaction and searched through the debris, looking for the camera lens, praying that perhaps it—

Inhaling sharply, she winced and turned over her hand—a fragment of glass was embedded in her right palm.

A bright trail of blood trickled down the pale underside of her wrist and beneath the hem of her sleeve.

"Oh, mercy, ma'am, you's bleedin'."

Josiah's hand came beneath her arm and Elizabeth heard a gasp behind her.

Miss Ruby stood frozen in the doorway, her expression mirroring the shock Elizabeth felt.

"What happened?" Miss Ruby's gaze swept the room. "Are you badly injured, Miss Westbrook?"

Elizabeth shook her head, unable to find her voice.

"We come back just now and found it this way, Miz Ruby. Some dark evil done worked its way in here." He took hold of Elizabeth's injured hand, but she instinctively jerked it away, fearing the pain. "I ain't gonna hurt you, ma'am." Josiah's voice was tender. "But I need to get that out of your hand. You just turn your head away for a second."

Elizabeth did as he said, her head spinning, her throat closing.

A sharp prick was followed by a warm gush. . . .

She felt pressure on her palm and turned back to see Josiah pressing his own shirt against the wound. Her body broke out in a cold sweat.

"You best see the doctor, miz. This gonna need stitches fo' sure." He turned to Miss Ruby, who stood in the crushed glass. "I get her on over there, and then I come back here and clean this up."

Elizabeth groped at her high-buttoned collar. "I can't . . . bre—"

"Where's your medicine, Miz Westbrook? Where'd you put it?" She tore at the buttons.

"It in your bag, ma'am? Where's your bag?"

She fought to pull air in only to have her body refuse the simple command. The more she tried to stay calm, the faster her pulse raced. And the narrower her throat seemed to constrict.

A portrait of her mother flashed in her mind. Mama at the same age as she was now, their features so strikingly similar. And painted only three months before Mama died.

Elizabeth's legs gave way. For a fleeting second, the image of her body lying sprawled amid the glass took perfect form. She felt herself being lifted.

A woman's voice floated somewhere above her, followed by a deep, low rumble against her left ear. Then she was running, only it wasn't her. The hard jostle of each step rattled her teeth. Strong arms crushed her close, almost to the point of hurting.

She was a lifeless rag doll with tufts of cotton for a throat.

A rush of cool air hit her in the face but stopped just inside her mouth. The pounding from the running matched the pounding in her temples, and a hole somewhere deep inside her opened up.

She teetered there on the edge, able to feel little else than a high-pitched hum coursing through her body and the crushing weight inside her chest. And that's when Elizabeth knew . . .

She was going to die, just like her mother.

22

Sucking on a peppermint stick, Daniel rode back into Timber Ridge. The look on Davy's face when he saw the picture of him and Beau had been nothing short of precious, as his mother might have said. And better than any picture of an elk he could have given him.

He'd stayed at the Tuckers' an hour longer than planned, just sitting with Davy, talking about hunting, and letting the boy hug and love on Beau. Mrs. Tucker had been real complimentary. "I promise you, Daniel, that dog of yours is better than any medicine any doctor ever made." It wasn't as if the Tuckers didn't have a dog. They had three. But none like Beau.

Daniel glanced down at the dog he'd raised from a pup. Beau looked up at him at the same time, trotting alongside the horse, tongue lolling as he panted. Knowing how much Davy loved the dog, and how much Beau loved the boy, it occurred to him that letting Beau stay with the Tuckers for a few days would be a kind thing to do.

And yet—he felt like a child admitting this, even to himself—he couldn't imagine not having Beau with him out at the cabin. After all, the dog had been his companion for fourteen years. Still . . . next time he was in town for an overnight stay, he pledged to run Beau out to the Tuckers' and let him stay the night with Davy.

He glanced up at the boardinghouse as he passed by, wondering if Miss Westbrook was in her room. He really should stop and apologize to her. It was the woman's own business if she went traipsing off on a journey like the one she had planned. He'd offered his opinion where none had been solicited, and he hated it when people did that with him. Yet from the way she'd closed the door in his face that morning—quietly but firmly—he doubted his face at her door was what she'd want to see right now.

He was to the end of the street when he heard his name being called. He turned to see Josiah running toward him, Miss Westbrook limp in his arms.

"Mr. Ranslett! Help me, sir!"

He jumped down and met Josiah as he climbed the stairs to the doctor's office. He opened the door and Josiah rushed inside. No sign of the doctor.

"Lay her here." Daniel pointed to the table. "What happened?"

As Josiah gave a quick account, Daniel checked her pulse and could barely feel one. Her lips were a light shade of blue.

"She gots a problem with her lungs, sir! She takes medicine, but I can't find it in that room!"

"Go find the doctor, Josiah. Now!"

The door slammed against the wall as he ran out, and nearly closed back again.

"Miss Westbrook!" Daniel slapped her cheeks.

She didn't respond.

He'd been around enough doctors and makeshift hospitals during the war to know something of what a doctor would do first. Try and get air in.

He took her face in his hands and pried her jaw open. He pressed his mouth to hers and blew air in. Her cheeks inflated. But he felt the pressure of his own breath returning to him. He tried again, watching her eyes, waiting for the rise and fall of her chest, for any sign that it was working.

Nothing.

He checked her pulse. And didn't feel anything. He looked around, not knowing what to do next.

"Is she wearing a corset?"

A man's voice came from outside. Daniel couldn't see him but had heard him clear enough. He ran his hands along Miss Westbrook's rib cage. "Yes! She is!"

"Take it off!" The man came running up the stairs and through the door, out of breath. "Cut it off if you have to."

Daniel yanked Elizabeth's shirtwaist free of her skirt. The corset was laced up tight. He pulled the knife from his belt and, slipping his left hand beneath the corset to shield her skin from the blade, started to cut.

The doctor came alongside him. He checked Elizabeth's pulse and pushed up her eyelids. Her eyes rolled back into her head. "Have you tried breathing for her?"

Daniel knew what he meant. "Yes. Nothing happened." Then he saw the blood. "Her hand!"

"I'll tend to that, you keep cutting."

As the doctor inspected the wound, Daniel made a clean slit up the length of the undergarment, unable to completely detach himself from what he was doing, and seeing. He cut part of her shirtwaist at the top but left the thin white chemise intact beneath. He'd apologize later.

Her chest rose slightly with the freedom, and a wheeze slipped past her parched lips.

"Roll up her sleeve." The doctor grabbed a bottle and syringe from a shelf.

Daniel did as asked, watching him prepare it. "What are you giving her?"

"Morphine." He slipped the syringe into her arm. "It'll relax the muscles around her bronchial tube." After a few seconds, the doctor withdrew the empty needle and put his ear next to her mouth.

"It's normally used as a painkiller, but patients with lung problems respond well to it." He checked her pulse again.

Daniel was certain her skin was paler and her lips a deeper shade of blue. "How long should it take to start working?"

"Not this long." The doctor grabbed a black bag and another bottle and syringe. "Can you carry her?"

Daniel gathered her in his arms and followed as the doctor ran down the boardwalk and across the street toward a wooded area. When they reached the opening in the stand of fir trees, he realized where they were taking her. And as he stepped inside, he heard Josiah and McPherson calling out behind him.

———

Elizabeth floated on a wave, away from the shrill hum that had all but quieted inside her now. She gave herself over to the tranquil dream, floating there—cocooned in darkness—not wishing to awaken. Because if she did, the pain would return.

Never had air felt so intense against her skin. Never so smooth and slick, so warm . . . *liquid*. It washed over her in waves.

Was this what it felt like to be dead? Like her mother . . .

Distant voices, indistinguishable, hovered closer. The high-pitched humming began again inside her—a slow, steady thrum.

She shook her head, not wanting to leave this place, wherever *this* was.

A sharp prick, like the tip of a saber, sent a tingling sensation shooting up her left arm. It sped through her torso to her other limbs and returned to explode in her chest.

Her lungs screamed. Frantic, she fought for air.

She arched her back until she was certain her spine would snap, and blinked to clear the fog before her eyes, but to no avail. Every sound echoed back tenfold. She had to get out of here. But where was *here*? And was it real, or her imagination?

Hands were on her body. Touching, restraining. *Those* were real.

She struggled to break free in the chest-deep water, and the stench of sulfur lay thick in the close space. It tasted bitter on her tongue. Through a heavy mist, she made out the blurred outline of a man moving toward her.

Pale light atop the warm water shone a path to the outside world and she lunged for it, nearly going under. She brushed the slick bottom of the cavern with her foot before strong arms penned her back from behind.

The outline of the man to her left loomed close. He took hold of her chin. She tried to scream but lacked the breath.

"I need to get her mouth open!" The unfamiliar voice ricocheted off the walls of the cave.

Elizabeth firmed her lips and turned away. But the arms encircling her from behind forbade her efforts and forced her head back. She clawed at the restraint, digging her nails deep into skin. Her jaw was forced open and in poured liquid fire.

Gagging, coughing, she choked on the liquid now scorching a path through her chest. She spit out the remains and, for a second time, went for the arms restraining her—

"Elizabeth!"

At hearing her name, she stilled—winded, wheezing, heart pounding in her ears.

"The doctor's trying to help you, and so am I." Arms held her immovable. "If you still have it in that stubborn mind of yours to go hunting, you'd better hold still and do what he says. You hear me?"

More obedient to the drawl in his voice than the gruffness of his command, she nodded—gasping, coughing—and pushed a mass of sopping curls from her face. Daniel Ranslett's grip loosened a fraction, and she felt the sharp rise and fall of his chest against her back, matching her own. It gave comfort.

The man in front of her, *the doctor* as Ranslett had referred to him, stepped closer again. "I realize this is easily counseled, miss"—his voice bounced off the cave walls—"and much harder done, but you must try and stay calm. I don't like being in here either. But please take some breaths, and let's see if your air passage is responding to the medicine."

She tried to swallow past the ache in her throat and told her lungs to fill. And to her surprise, they obeyed. A fraction. A whistling sound accompanied the effort, but at least she was breathing.

Seconds passed, and the pain moved further into the distance.

"Have you previously experienced this classification of seizure, Miss Westbrook?"

From what little she could see of the doctor in the dim light, his formal tone far outweighed the youthfulness in his voice—a requisite of his medical training, perhaps.

"No. Not this bad." She swallowed again and cleared her throat. It was so sore. "But I *have* had them before."

"You suffer from a lung affliction."

It wasn't a question. "Yes, sir. I do."

"May I?"

Through the fog, she saw the shadow of his hand before her face but wasn't entirely sure of his intentions. Yet understanding that he had most likely just saved her life, she nodded. "Certainly."

The doctor's hand disappeared beneath the surface of the water and came to rest over her heart. She didn't know this man but was familiar enough with examinations by physicians to recognize their routines. The slightest movement in the water sounded overloud in the narrow cavern. She had intended to visit the territory's hot springs, eventually, only under far different circumstances.

"How long have you suffered from this affliction?" The doctor moved his hand and gently pressed it against the underside of her throat.

She felt the faint throb of her pulse against his fingertips. "As far back as I can remember, but it wasn't until my seventh year—" she stopped for breath—"that I started having seizures. My physicians back east tell me that my lungs are being . . . compromised with each episode."

The arms around her waist loosened but didn't let go.

"Mm-hmm . . ." The doctor cupped her face and ran his fingers up and down the sides of her throat, then across the base of her neck.

But it wasn't the doctor's touch that captivated her attention.

Ranslett stood directly behind her, his hands on either side of her waist, his fingers spread over her abdomen. With curiosity, she followed their progress and with every labored breath, she became more aware of him.

The doctor paused and gave an abrupt laugh. "I'm Dr. Rand Brookston, by the way. We had no opportunity for introductions earlier, Miss Westbrook." He probed her throat again, but she knew his search would prove vain. He wouldn't find any lumps or swollen nodules.

He sighed. "No lumps or swollen nodules. . . . Have either of your parents suffered from this affliction?"

"Yes, sir." These were familiar questions. "My mother."

"And what is her current state of health?"

"She . . . died at the age of thirty-three."

Dr. Brookston's hands stilled. "My deepest apologies, Miss Westbrook. Was her passing . . . a result of the ailment?"

She nodded. "It was."

"And may I inquire . . . as to *your* age?"

Despite the intimate proximity she and Ranslett shared, Elizabeth didn't wish to answer the doctor's question in his company. She cleared her throat again. "I am . . . within two months of the age of my mother when she passed."

The hands about her waist tightened ever so slightly.

"I see." Dr. Brookston said nothing for a moment, then gave her shoulder a slight squeeze. "Then we will work together to make certain that a similar fate does not befall you."

Tears rose to her eyes at his words and as the realization of what had nearly happened to her became more real. She nodded, her voice fragile. "Thank you, Doctor."

Moments passed as he examined her, checking her pulse, listening to her breathe. Once Dr. Brookston declared her lungs cleared to his satisfaction, he led the way around the corner toward the cave's entrance.

Ranslett released her and she followed, trying to match the doctor's pace in the chest-deep water. Nearly losing her footing, she reached out to steady herself against the rock wall and winced at the ache in her right palm. Then she remembered . . . the gash from the broken glass. Deciding to use her other hand instead, she reached across toward the opposite wall. Almost there . . .

Her feet went out from under her. About to go under, she managed a quick breath—

Ranslett grabbed her from behind, so quickly he must have been anticipating it. She spit out the bitter water and tried to find her footing.

"Having some trouble there?" His deep whisper drew no echo. His hold on her remained steady.

"I seem to be. . . . Thank you for your assistance."

"Pleasure's all mine."

His grip around her rib cage made her breathing more pronounced, but something else felt different about it too. She laid a hand on her abdomen and suddenly realized what it was. Flabbergasted, she couldn't believe she hadn't noticed before. She was without her corset! Not the first time she'd lost a corset to one of these attacks, but this time . . .

She quickly felt for her shirtwaist and discovered it unbuttoned, but her chemise seemed intact. A possible scenario came to mind, and thinking of Ranslett, she hoped the removal of the undergarment had been the doctor's doing. Entertaining the other possibility sent her imagination reeling.

Chancing it, she turned. Daniel Ranslett stood close, *very* close. And when he smiled, she would've sworn the water jumped by ten degrees.

"You all right, ma'am?"

She blinked. "Yes, I'm fine." His hair was also wet. She must have given him a run for his money.

A moment passed.

"Would you, ahh"—he glanced past her—"like for me to take the lead?"

"I can't believe I'm saying this, but yes, I think that might be best. Thank you."

She waited for him to move, then felt something on her rib cage. What was he doing? A slow smile came. He was drumming his fingers? "Ranslett, I'm fine now. You can lead anytime you'd like."

"Well, that's awful generous of you, ma'am. And I'll do just that . . . as soon as you get off my toes."

"Oh! Sorry!" She stepped away and braced herself against the wall.

He held out his hand. "I promise not to dunk you . . . intentionally."

"I appreciate that." With a flourish, she swept back a mass of soaked curls. "I wouldn't want to get my hair wet."

His laughter echoed and she found herself staring up at him. The more she got to know this man, the more different he was from what she had first thought him to be.

He climbed out and reached back to assist her up the rocks. The weight of her sodden skirt made maneuvering more difficult, but she managed not to slip again.

Conversation floated toward them, and she gathered that a crowd was waiting beyond the stand of trees. Clear of the cave's warmth, the air took on a chill, and she peered down at her clothing, shivering. The wet shirtwaist hung open and the thin chemise clung to her curves.

Feeling Daniel's attention, she turned away and slipped the buttons through the holes, then crossed her arms over her chest for modesty's sake.

"Here . . ."

She looked over her shoulder to see him taking off his shirt. "It's wet, but it's thick. I've got a coat out there you can borrow, but . . . you probably need a little something more before we get to it."

She nodded, self-conscious, but only a little. He was acting as though the situation wasn't anything out of the ordinary, which made her feel more at ease. She slipped her arms into his shirt and pulled it together in the front. "Thank you, Ranslett."

He lifted a damp curl from her shoulder and rubbed it between his fingers. "You're welcome, Elizabeth."

It was the second time he'd used her Christian name, and she liked it. She also liked what he looked like without his shirt. But just as he hadn't stared at her—much—she forced her gaze upward and followed him beyond the shelter of the fir trees.

A fading April sun sat wedged between the Maroon Bells, their highest peaks towering over Timber Ridge. A chilling wind swept down from the north, quaking the newly budded aspen and reminding her of how quickly the weather could change in the mountains.

Several people stood waiting, among them a man Elizabeth assumed to be the doctor, since he was the only other person soaked to the bone. Dr. Brookston was indeed young looking, perhaps a few years her junior, and handsome, in a dashing sort of way.

Daniel's beagle ran to greet his master, and the first pair of eyes Elizabeth connected with were Josiah's.

With a broad smile, Josiah ducked his head as he approached. The front of his shirttail was stained with her blood. "You done gave us a scare, Miz Westbrook. You doin' all right now?"

She smiled up at him, her emotions raw when remembering what they'd discovered in her room at the boardinghouse. "I am. Thank you, Josiah, for all you did."

He waved away her thanks. "I jus' carried you to the doc's. It was him and Mr. Ranslett here"—something flickered in Josiah's eyes before he glanced down at Ranslett, who was slipping on his boots—"who knew what to do and gots you over here."

"Miss Westbrook . . ." Sheriff McPherson tipped his hat. "It's nice to see color in your complexion again, ma'am. I hear pale skin is all the rage back east, but the pallor of your face when Ranslett carried you in there . . ." He shook his head.

Ranslett stood and gave a casual nod, but she sensed something more intimate in his gaze. "That was a mite too high fashion for my taste too, ma'am. If you don't mind me saying."

"For mine too, I would imagine." Elizabeth felt a lick on her hand and reached down to rub Beau's head. "I'm most grateful to you, Dr. Brookston, for your quick action. And to you too, Mr. Ranslett, for your . . . thoughtful assistance."

Dr. Brookston gave a gentlemanly tip of his head, while Ranslett merely shrugged.

"It was nothing, ma'am." A wry smile tipped Ranslett's mouth. "Once the doc went inside, Sheriff and I just drew straws." A glint deepened his green eyes. "Mine came up short."

Everyone laughed. Everyone but Sheriff McPherson.

"Ranslett's being far too modest—while also seeking, I'm sure, to protect my . . . fragile reputation. You see, ma'am, I . . . ah . . ." McPherson toed the dirt with his boot. "I can't swim. Tried to learn when I was younger. My best friend growing up tried his best to teach me, but . . ." McPherson shook his head, glancing at Ranslett. "Water and me don't get along real well. Never have."

"Well, after all these years, that finally explains the smell around here," a man said from the back.

"Watch it there, Lewis." Sheriff McPherson's tone became worthy of his office. "I've got three empty cells around the corner. I might have to haul you in for disturbing the peace."

That drew more laughter, and slowly the crowd began to disperse.

But the comment from the gentleman made Elizabeth self-conscious about the smell on her clothes, and on her skin. The sulfur water had a distinct and . . . none too pleasant odor.

Black leather bag in hand, Dr. Brookston bowed slightly at the waist, his black hair plastered against his head. "I'll also take my leave, Miss Westbrook. But I'd like to examine you in my office . . . after you've changed into some dry clothes and had a chance to eat something." He gently took her hand and turned it over. The gash appeared puffy and red but thoroughly cleansed. And had stopped bleeding, for the time being. "We must have lost the bandage in the hot springs. This will need a few stitches, but we'll see to that when you come."

She rubbed her arms, grateful for Ranslett's shirt. "Thank you, Doctor. I'll be over shortly."

The setting sun illuminated a dark bank of grayish-purple clouds in the west. Perhaps Ranslett was right about the snow after all.

A coat came about her shoulders. Ranslett tucked it close beneath her chin. "I'll drop by tomorrow and pick it up."

Smiling her appreciation, she pulled the lapels closer and caught a whiff of seasoned leather and of something spicy, a decidedly male scent. Fresh scratches on his arms drew her attention, and stirred the vaguest recollection.

Sheriff McPherson followed her gaze to the marks. "Looks like Miss Westbrook put up a fair fight in there, Ranslett."

She winced. "Did *I* do that to you?"

"It's nothing that won't heal. I'm fine." He shot a weak grin at the sheriff. "She's stronger than she looks—that's for sure. And that's meant as a compliment, ma'am."

McPherson scoffed. "If that's your idea of a compliment, Ranslett, you need help in that area."

Listening to their banter, Elizabeth got the feeling she'd underestimated their connection. "My apologies, Ranslett. But when I can't breathe, I tend to get a little . . . worked up."

"If what happened back inside there was you being 'a little worked up,' then I'm not sure I want to be around when you're really riled."

She laughed, aware of how Ranslett's gaze swept her, from head to toe, in none-too-hasty a fashion, before settling again on her eyes. He had a way of smiling that made her wish she knew his thoughts, while also making her think she might blush blood red if she did. Something about the man fanned a flame inside her. How often had she prided herself on not being the swooning type? But apparently a tiny part of her still knew what it felt like to melt over a man. Thankfully, it wasn't a part that showed.

"Miss Westbrook . . ." The sheriff's tone had shed its humor. "I'd like to accompany you back to the boardinghouse to see your room. I sent word to Miss Ruby and asked her to leave things exactly as they were until I could take a look."

"Yes, Sheriff, of course. I'd appreciate your doing that."

"I think I'll take my leave, ma'am." Ranslett tipped his hat. "Dry clothes sound pretty good about now."

"Mr. Ranslett, sir." Josiah stepped up, having been unusually quiet. "I tied your horse up behind the doctor's for safekeepin'."

Ranslett eyed him. "I appreciate you thinking to do that. Thank you . . . Josiah."

Elizabeth looked between the two men, wondering if Josiah sensed what a step that was for Ranslett. Somehow she thought he did.

She and McPherson walked back to the boardinghouse, Josiah following them. As they rounded a corner, a chilling wind hit her full in the face and she shivered. Thoughts of what awaited at the boardinghouse brought a host of emotions to the forefront. Not the least of which were disappointment and anger. Who would have done this? And why?

"This may sound strange, ma'am, especially since you're newly arrived to Timber Ridge, but . . ." The sheriff assisted her up the stairs to the boardwalk. "Do you have any idea who might have wanted to do this to you? Or why?"

Her laugh was without humor. "That's just what I was wondering." Faces of people she'd met since coming to Timber Ridge flitted through her mind. And one by one she dismissed them all. If they were back in Washington, she could think of a couple of people who might feel strongly enough against her and her association with E.G. Brenton, but that was a world away. And even then, she was only Brenton's assistant in their eyes. "Everyone I've met here has been so kind and welcoming. I don't think I've been here long enough to make any enemies."

"Don't necessarily think of whoever did this as being an *enemy,* ma'am. Chances are pretty good you've met the person, that you've spoken with them in Mullins's store or here on the boardwalk. Think of it in terms of anyone who might have wanted something from you. Or who was looking for something. Did you notice anything personal missing when you first saw your room?"

She bit back an unexpected retort. Why was it people never understood how personal her equipment was to her? How much of *her* was wrapped up in it? Aware that McPherson had intended no offense, she let it pass.

"Everything was in chaos, Sheriff, as you'll soon see. I didn't have time to determine if anything was taken, but I'll look through the chifforobe to be sure. That's where I keep my money, my clothes, and what jewelry I have."

Reality quickly set in—regardless of the answers to the *who* and *why,* she had no equipment left. It would take a month or more for glass plates and chemicals to be ordered from back east and to arrive in Denver. A new camera would have to come from the American Optical Company in New York City and would be a special order. And very expensive. She had saved for months to pay for that camera.

Having one had been a prerequisite to her being considered for this new position at the *Chronicle*.

Considering her remaining funds, the likelihood of meeting her deadlines—much less pursuing her dreams—was quickly fading. She had a better chance of winning a footrace across the Rockies than being named the *Chronicle*'s next journalist photographer.

Hearing the thread of her own thoughts, Elizabeth suddenly felt selfish and petty. Here she was, alive and breathing, when by all accounts she shouldn't have been. She had much to be thankful for yet couldn't dismiss the underlying feeling of loss.

They arrived at the boardinghouse, and McPherson held open the door. "Mr. Birch, would you be so kind as to wait here? I'd like to speak with Miss Westbrook alone. But I'd appreciate speaking with you shortly as well."

"Yes, sir, Sheriff. I wait right here for you, sir."

Elizabeth and McPherson climbed the stairs to the third floor and the door to her room came into view. Foreboding moved through her, starting at the base of her spine and inching its way upward. She paused.

She'd promised to keep Wendell Goldberg abreast of her progress, but this wasn't something she could report to him. No, telling him this would be admitting defeat, and that was something she couldn't do. Not to him or her father. Not even to herself. Not yet. Not until she was aboard a train back to Washington, failed career and bruised pride in tow, would she relinquish hold of this dream.

God had put the seed of this ambition in her heart ages ago, and to return to Washington with anything less than that position as hers would feel as if she were giving up on herself, and Him.

23

Elizabeth stood still in the hallway, light-headed, staring at the door to her room, not wanting to go back inside.

"You okay, ma'am?" McPherson touched her arm.

"I think so." Her right hand ached and she cradled it with her left, noticing a tremble in both. The sheriff was with her. She had nothing to fear. "I'm just tired, and a little hungry."

"I promise I won't keep you long."

McPherson took the lead. He started to turn the latch, and paused. "Are these yours?" He indicated the crates Josiah had left in the hallway.

"Yes, they arrived earlier today. Josiah was bringing them up when we discovered what had happened inside."

Nodding, he opened the door and slowly pushed it back as if to get the full impact of the scene all at once.

The lamp on the bedside table cast an orange halo on thousands of tiny glass fragments littering the bed, the rugs, and the hardwood floor. A chemical odor lingered, but thanks to an open window, it wasn't nearly as strong as before.

"Was the lamp burning when you left, Miss Westbrook?"

"No. I assume Miss Ruby lit it, but I'm not sure."

His boots crunched on the shattered camera plates as he walked the length of the room and back. He sniffed. "Do you smell that? Something bitter."

She tried to detect the scent and couldn't. "All I smell are the chemicals. But I may just be accustomed to them."

His gaze traveled the room. "They sure tore up your equipment, but did it in a neat fashion, compared to how they could have done it—using the bedclothes and your dresses to cut down on the noise. . . . But it looks like that's all they did. I don't see any damage to the furniture, to the room. Just your camera and what went along with that. Tell me . . ." He didn't speak for a moment. "Yesterday you said that you believe Josiah to be a man of outstanding integrity and character. What do you actually know about Josiah Birch's background? Where he's been and what he's done?"

Elizabeth's heart did a painful flip. She swallowed, feeling a strong urge for a cup of tea. "I'm not sure what you're getting at, Sheriff."

"I'm just asking if you know what manner of man he is."

"Are *you* questioning what manner of man he is? Look at what he just did for me. He saved my life."

McPherson walked to where she stood, his expression open and sincere. "I'm just asking questions, Miss Westbrook. Trying to learn more about your situation so I can fit things together, try to help you. I'm not accusing anyone of anything." His brows slowly rose in question.

She firmed her lips together and nodded once. "I met Josiah when I first came to Timber Ridge, only three weeks ago. But I would vouch for his character as I would other men I've known the better part of my life."

He gave her an appraising look. "Once someone wins your confidence, Miss Westbrook, seems they've gained a strong ally."

"That may be true. But be assured, Sheriff . . . my confidence isn't something easily won. Be that to my credit, or otherwise."

That patient stare of his again. Not condemning, not pardoning. Just assessing. Finally, he blinked. "I'd say that's to your credit, ma'am." He bent and picked up a piece of splintered wood. "Is there anything left of your equipment that's salvageable?"

She removed Mr. Ranslett's coat and laid it aside but kept on his shirt. She was eager to change into dry clothes, but it was important she survey the damage, and being out of the wind, she wasn't nearly so cold now. She spotted a protective plate holder half hidden beneath the washstand and retrieved it. The slender wooden box was bent back, its hinge sprung, yet the wood hadn't splintered. "This can be mended." She handed it to him, and then her gaze fell to the edge of the bed.

She stooped and pulled out a box from the shipment Mullins had received late last week.

He knelt beside her. "What are those?"

She opened the box, mildly encouraged. "Fresh camera plates. At least they spared these."

"Fresh . . . What does that mean?"

"It means I haven't used them yet. They haven't been exposed or developed."

"So these don't have pictures on them yet?"

"That's right." She briefly explained the process to him. " . . . then once the plates are removed from the camera, they have an image burned into them through a chemical process that's light sensitive. They have to be developed quickly, before the plate dries, in a darkroom. Then I can make multiple prints from them later. Like the ones I made of Coulter's body for Mr. Carnes and Mr. Turner."

He nodded. "Interesting. And impressive, Miss Westbrook. I take it you have a fairly good knowledge of science, and chemicals in particular."

"More of chemicals than science. And only the ones I use regularly. I'm in no way a chemist, Sheriff. But I *am* highly respectful of the solutions I use. Some of them can be toxic if not handled correctly. But so can a lot of other common solutions we use every day."

"True . . ." He stood, sighing as he did. "You go ahead and check your personal items. I'll keep looking for something that might shed some light on this."

She turned to the task, ready to have it done. Atop the desk, papers and files she'd last referenced remained undisturbed. As did books on a table in the far corner of the room. She moved next to the chifforobe and pulled open the top drawer. She stilled, frowning.

Things weren't as she'd left them.

She skipped the other drawers and yanked open the door of the chifforobe where her dresses hung. The gowns had been shoved to one side and a green chiffon lace lay crumpled at the bottom of the closet.

She dropped to her knees and clawed through layers of lace and silk to get to the boxes stored at the bottom, vaguely aware of the sheriff kneeling beside her. The boxes were shuffled, some on their sides, but it was the burgundy leather cigar box, one of her father's castoffs, that was the object of her search.

Her fingers touched on something. She felt a measure of relief but held it at bay until she opened the lid. . . .

Empty.

She let the box drop and dug her hands into the still-damp curls at her temples. She squeezed tight. *Oh, God . . .*

"Your money?" McPherson whispered beside her.

She nodded.

"All of it?"

She nodded again, wishing she were alone so she could give in to the moan wrenching its way up her throat. Silent tears slid down her cheeks. "Except what little I have in my reticule."

All her life she'd wanted to do something special. Something that would make a lasting difference. That would set her apart in her father's eyes. And she'd been foolish enough to think that God had been preparing her for something like that. *But you were . . . weren't you?* Had she misread Him? Why would He place this love of words and images inside her if not to use it for His glory? As the *Chronicle*'s next journalist photographer she could have accomplished so much good. Could have helped open the door for other women to follow. . . .

She took a steadying breath. She was through in Timber Ridge, and for that matter—at the *Chronicle*. Her former position had been filled, and Goldberg had communicated that nothing was guaranteed for the two applicants who didn't win the position. She wiped her tears, knowing she would never see the cliff dwellings or see her pictures of them hung in any gallery.

Everything was over for her, even before it had begun.

24

Daniel left the general store and headed to the boardinghouse, Beau close on his heels. He didn't know if something special was happening in town, but the hotel was booked up and the board-walk was still lively with folks. Lolly could always be counted on to let him stay in the back room of the butcher shop. Daniel tugged at the collar of his new shirt, it being fresh from the shelf at Mullins's store. He'd stopped to buy a change of clothes, his other still being with the launderer here in town.

Night draped Timber Ridge in shades of pewter gray, and coal-burning streetlamps perched upon wooden poles above the board-walk encouraged evening walkers after sundown. He quickened his pace, mindful of the covered tin of food in his hand, and of Elizabeth Westbrook.

She had looked tired when he'd left her, understandably so.

He didn't hold photographers and their profession in high regard—or hadn't in the past—but what had happened to her was cruel. Part of him wished he could do something to help her, while the other part wondered if the destruction might not be God's way of preventing her from going on her ill-conceived expedition. Especially after what he'd overheard her say when she wasn't quite conscious back in the cave. Medicinal tonics made people run off at the mouth. He'd seen it plenty of times before.

Doc Brookston said you couldn't pay attention to what people said at times like that, but he disagreed. Seems people spoke exactly what was most important to them at times like that. Or at least what was weighing heaviest on their hearts.

Which made him wonder what was weighing on hers, and who—or what—Goldberg was.

In a flash, the image of her lying there on the table, his knife poised at the base of her corset, came back to him. Why women wore such contraptions was beyond him, particularly when the woman had no need of it. He'd followed the doctor's instructions as quickly as he'd been able. And though he'd tried hard not to, he'd seen more of Miss Westbrook than intended. He felt a fraction of guilt over it... yet couldn't help appreciating what he'd seen—she was a beautiful woman. His mouth went dry again remembering just how beautiful. So he tried not to think about it.

But that was one scene that would stay in his memory for a long time to come.

Beau ran on a few paces ahead of him, then stopped and glanced back, one of his front paws tucked beneath him as though he were pointing at something. Wild flowers usually grew alongside this stretch of road, but it was much too early for them. The snows had yet to finish their work.

Ever since Beau was a pup, he'd loved flowers. Loved smelling them, rolling in them, wreaking havoc with them. Even eating them sometimes. Daniel remembered discovering Beau in his mother's flower garden shortly after he'd gotten the dog. The shock on his mother's face was as clear to him now as if he were standing again in that moment. The memory drew forth both a warmth and an emptiness.

"Daniel Wayne Ranslett! How can something so small make such a mess? Just look at my flowers!"

"I'm sorry, Mama. I'll clean it up." Almost eighteen years old, he had gathered the broken stems and the chewed up white petals, vowing to plant new ones. Apparently, daisies were Beauregard's favorite. His mother had so few pleasures in life and the flower garden was her haven—the one place she could go where Nathaniel Thursmann, her second husband, didn't follow. "I'll replant everything for you, Mama. I'll even build a fence around it so Beau won't do it again."

When she didn't answer, he turned to find her kneeling on the cobblestone path, her head bowed.

Sick inside, he went to her. "Mama, I'm sorry. I give you my word I'll—"

His mother had scooped up Beau and was cradling the pup in her arms, cooing and kissing his little black nose. "He's precious, Daniel, even though he *is* in my bad graces at the moment." She gave the pup's tiny head a rub and laughed when he tried to lick her face. "You were right to choose him over the others. He may have been the scrawniest, but he's the sweetest. He'll grow into his ears soon enough, and just look at those eyes. He has it in him to obey—you can see it. He has that desire to please...."

Still cradling Beau in one arm, she held out a hand and Daniel helped her up. The sun shone on her blond hair, making it glimmer golden red in the light. With another kiss on the white tuft atop Beau's head, she transferred the puppy to Daniel's arms.

"And don't build a fence, Daniel. Teach him, instead. I may lose a daisy . . . or twenty"—she smiled—"but it'll be worth it in the long run." Her attention trailed to the main house a good distance from where they stood. "Fences can be prisons, in a way. They're necessary for those incapable of learning restraint, but they diminish life. If I had my way, I'd tear down every fence in Williamson County and across the state of Tennessee."

He knew she didn't mean it literally. At least he didn't think so. "But what if Beau gets into your flowers again? What if he tears up something else?"

She turned back, her eyes wistful. "Then you'll teach him again, until he's learned. Just as I've done with you boys. That's what God does with us, after all. Puts us out into the world where the only real boundary is that of His love. His love either compels us, or restrains us. There is nothing stronger, Danny."

She brushed her fingers through the hair at his forehead. "Looking at you is like looking at your father, God rest his soul. You have his strength and his humor, you know—more so than your brothers." Her voice went soft; the edges of her mouth trembled. "And his green eyes." She glanced away for a second, then scratched beneath the pup's chin. "I think you've found a good companion here, and a loyal one. Give him the care he deserves and the discipline he needs, and he'll give you more love than you'll know what to do with."

"Miss Charlotte! You best come quick, ma'am!"

They looked up to see Maida running full out, half dragging little Benjamin behind her. Daniel caught the sheen of fear in his youngest brother's eyes as his little legs pumped hard to keep up.

Maida's coffee-colored skin glistened in the sun as she shooed Benjamin toward them. "It's your husband, ma'am. Master Thurs—" She paused, her ample chest heaving, hands braced on her thighs. "Master Thursmann sho' done it this time! He sho' did. Hades itself is rainin' down, ma'am."

"Daniel, keep Benjamin here with you!" After giving Benjamin a hug, she set off for the house.

Daniel pulled his brother close and felt him trembling. "But what if—"

"No ifs," she called over her shoulder. "You keep your brother safe! Above all!"

As his mother and Maida ran for the house, he looked beyond them and saw a wagon full of slaves pulling up, and a line of slaves being formed down the drive. He recognized the wagon as belonging to Ralston Stattam, one of Nathaniel Thursmann's business partners, who had a plantation in Nashville. What had Thursmann gambled off this time? Or traded? Something of his mother's, no doubt. Of course, it all belonged to his mother at one time. Nathaniel Thursmann had always chosen whatever caused her the most pain.

Daniel felt a nudge against his leg and blinked. He looked down, half expecting to see six-year-old Benjamin there, clinging to him, his eyes wide and questioning. Instead, it was ol' Beau, panting, touches of gray around his muzzle, his tail thumping the dirt. But Daniel could still imagine his brother's face, as well as his mother's, and could smell the scent of her flower garden on the wind.

He took a deep breath and exhaled. The scent was gone. Just like his mother. And Benjamin . . .

Beau whined and took a step toward where the wild flowers would soon be growing.

Daniel patted his head. "It's too early, bud. There won't be any—" He couldn't believe his eyes. "Well, what do you know. . . ."

———

Elizabeth stood and wiped her tears. "I'm sorry, Sheriff. I don't normally do that in front of people."

"What, cry?"

The way he said it tempted her to laugh. "Yes, that."

"Nothing to be ashamed of, ma'am. You've been through a lot, and I'm not talking about just today. Takes courage to come out to a place like this, all by yourself, and to do what you're doing. You have a strength about you, ma'am. A strength that's admirable." He reached for his hat he'd hung on the bedpost. "I'm heading down to talk to Josiah—just to get to know him better," he added quickly. "We'll be at my office for a while, in case you need anything." He glanced around. "I'll see that this is cleaned up while you're at the doctor's this evening. Then you can come back and get some rest. It's been a long day."

"One of the longest I can remember." She looked down at the cut on her hand. And the day wasn't over yet. She doubted she'd be able to sleep in this room again, even after it was cleaned up. But after what the sheriff had just said, she couldn't bring herself to admit that.

The memory of Tillie's voice came back to her, as clear inside her head as if the woman were standing in the room. *"As long as you're still breathing, child, you still got choices."* Thinking of Tillie again made her tender inside. She wanted to trust Tillie's wisdom, but she saw no choices at the moment. None but to return to Washington. And that wasn't a choice she was willing to make, not as long as she had breath. Which might not be long in her case.

"Thank you, Sheriff, again, for your help."

A creak in the hallway drew their attention to the doorway. Her eyes went wide.

McPherson chuckled softly. "Looks like you've got yourself some company, ma'am."

There in the middle of the threshold sat Daniel Ranslett's beagle . . . with a bundle of yellow flowers dangling from his mouth. Beau stared at her, then tilted his head to one side, his ears flopping forward.

A soft whisper from around the corner brought the dog to his feet, and Beau wriggled with excitement. An eager bark cost him the flowers, but he managed to pick the bundle up in his mouth again after two tries. He glanced back into the hallway as though awaiting further instruction.

Elizabeth's reaction came out part laugh, part exhausted cry. *Adorable.* Both the dog *and* his master.

The sheriff walked to the door. "We'll talk tomorrow sometime, Miss Westbrook." He gave the beagle a pat as he left. "How you doin' there, Beau."

A murmured exchange in the hallway, followed by the snap of *someone's* fingers, and Beau came bounding toward her.

She readied herself in case he jumped, but he didn't. Accepting the flowers from between his teeth, she couldn't decide whether he really wanted to give them up or not. She bent to his level and kissed the soft white tuft of fur between his eyes. Once, twice. Which only encouraged his wriggling. She tipped her head back so he could lick her neck.

"If I'd known what reception a few wild flowers would get, I would've delivered them myself."

The slow, measured drawl of the deep voice encouraged her to smile, in the midst of the chaos surrounding her.

Ranslett leaned against the doorway, freshly dressed, one long leg crossed in front of the other, with a cloth-covered tin in his hand. Better that than between his teeth. . . .

He touched his coat on the desk chair as he passed. "Thanks for taking care of this for me."

"Thank you for lending it to me."

He came and knelt beside her, his close attention giving silent comment on her damp clothing. "As I recall, Doc gave you two orders earlier this evening, ma'am. I figured I could help with the warm meal"—a wickedly charming smile tipped his mouth—"but I can't do much about the other."

Elizabeth could only stare. How could he say something like that—with that scoundrel's grin—and still sound respectable? Her thoughts went to whatever was on that plate. It smelled *delicious*!

He rubbed the scruff of Beau's neck. "I'm sorry about all this mess, and about your money." He nodded toward the door. "McPherson told me. It's not right what happened in here."

His compassion evoked emotions best left untouched, and she forced them back down. "I appreciate that."

His eyes narrowed slightly. "I'll understand if you want to keep a formality between us . . . Elizabeth. But . . . in my mind, we kind of got a jump on things today, and I'm wondering if you might consid—"

"Are you going to hold that plate all night, Daniel?" Seeing the dimples in his stubbled cheeks, she knew she'd read him correctly. "Or will you allow me to eat sometime before sunup?"

He lifted the cloth to reveal a tin full of fried chicken and mashed potatoes, along with three biscuits, sliced and slathered in butter. Two cookies hugged the side of the metal plate. Oatmeal-raisin if her nose was correct. Her favorite. Her mouth watered. But how much did the man think she could eat?

He covered the plate again, rose and helped her to her feet. "Lest you think this is all for you"—he gave her a wink and walked to the door—"why don't you go ahead and get changed and come on downstairs. I'll find us a place to eat, then walk you to the doc's."

———

"You don't have to look if you don't want to."

Daniel smiled down at her. "It doesn't bother me to look." But from the pallor of Elizabeth's face, he guessed it *did* bother her. Good thing she was lying down atop the doctor's table. Bad thing was . . . the doc hadn't started stitching her yet.

"Would you like a shot of whiskey, Miss Westbrook?" Dr. Brookston held up an earthenware jug.

"I beg your pardon?"

The young doc grinned. "Part of working in such a remote area is making do with what we have on hand. Customarily, I'd administer a mild dose of ether to dull the pain as I suture, but my shipment hasn't come in yet. So . . ." He lifted the jug again. "I'm afraid this is the best I can do. It won't take much, ma'am. It's powerful stuff. Locally brewed from the mountain streams, they tell me."

She shook her head. "I do not partake in libations, Dr. Brookston. I'm sure I'll manage fine without it."

Daniel watched her as she watched the doc thread the needle, and he doubted whether *fine* would describe her state of mind once things got going in a minute. He was tempted to encourage her to have just a nip or two—the nerves in the palm could be awful sensitive—but he recognized the prideful little jut in that jaw of hers. She'd made her mind up, good and hard, and he'd be wasting his breath to try and convince her otherwise.

Unlike earlier, her breathing wasn't erratic. She might get close to swooning from the doctor's stitching, but he didn't think she'd pass out completely. Daniel didn't peg her as the swooning type.

Although . . .

He hid a rueful smile, remembering how she'd gotten all still and quiet when they were alone in the cave. He might like to test that swooning theory in other ways, given time, if that Yankee mouth of hers could ever be tamed, which was doubtful. But what an interesting challenge it would make.

He hadn't held a woman in years, and—God help him—even under the circumstances, he'd enjoyed being close to her. Of course, she hadn't been talking to him at the time, which might account most for the pleasure he'd gained from the experience.

He countered another smile and took the opportunity to look at her, focused as she was on the doctor's preparations.

There was nothing like the softness of a woman. The smell of her hair, the way she moved, the curves of her body that God had fashioned uniquely in the fairer sex. And Elizabeth's curves were *nicely* fashioned. She was an assertive sort and could be downright difficult when she put her mind to it, but she possessed a vulnerability that he found attractive. And that hair . . .

It spread full across the doc's table in a riot of reddish curls, some of them still damp, spilling over the side and brushing against Daniel's thigh. Seeing her lying there sent his thoughts over the edge and careening down a hill he hadn't traveled in a long time, one that left him short of breath and glad for the cool breeze issuing through the open window.

She had reawakened something inside him that made him remember what life had been like before the war. Before the loss. Before he'd learned how cruel life could be.

Fear sharpened her features. Her uninjured hand trembled as she fingered the tiny buttons on her shirtwaist. "I don't particularly care for needles, Dr. Brookston. Despite having much experience with them."

"Really? I'd hardly noticed." The doctor shot Daniel a discreet wink. "If it comforts you at all, ma'am, when someone else is doing the suturing, I don't particularly like them either." Dr. Brookston gently took her right hand and positioned it, palm up, by her side. "Now just lie still and I'll be done in no time. You'll be happy to know that, with the direction of the gash, there'll hardly be any scarring."

She exhaled through pursed lips. "A comfort indeed. Scarring is *just* what I've been lying here worrying about."

Her sarcasm earned a grin from Dr. Brookston and a quiet shake of Daniel's head. Even under duress the woman's mouth didn't let up. He thought of something else the doctor might want to sew up once he finished with her hand but kept the thought to himself.

He peered over her body to observe the doc's handiwork. He'd seen his fair share of suturing back in the war. Had even done some himself in emergencies, but he lacked the finesse of this young physician.

Sounds of the night and of a passing wagon drifted in through the window. The doc's office apparently served as his home, as Daniel saw a cot nearby, as well as trunks and boxes piled in a corner. From what he saw, the man hadn't been in town too long.

Softly humming a familiar tune, Dr. Brookston had completed his third suture when Elizabeth's eyes started to flutter and roll back in her head. Daniel took hold of her free hand and gently rubbed it between his own, anticipating the move might catch her off guard.

She snapped back, blinking, her cheeks flushing a healthy pink. He thought he heard the doctor chuckle but on closer look realized he was mistaken. The man was hunched over her hand, intent on his task, still humming away.

In a bolder move and wanting to see what she'd do, Daniel brought Elizabeth's hand to his lips and gently kissed her fingertips, tasting remnants of oatmeal cookie. With little effort, he took on a deeper accent from home. "It's all right, darlin'." He kept his voice hushed. "Just concentrate on something else. Whatever comes to your mind."

Her no-nonsense look communicated more than words could have, and he admired her ability to say so much without even opening her mouth.

"And just what is it . . . Daniel, that you think might come to my mind other than this needle of Dr. Brookston's"—she winced—"weaving its way in and out of my flesh?"

Her pasty expression lacked bravado, but her tone didn't. And she'd called him Daniel, on her own, with no prompting. That was something.

He laughed and was pleased when she did too, shaky though her laughter was. But he wasn't giving up. "Tell me what brings you out to this territory. A young woman . . ." He chose his next words intentionally. "Traveling on her own—independent, tenacious . . ."

"Tenacious?" A familiar edge lined her voice. "What makes you think I'm tenacious?"

She was too easily baited. "Would you prefer *persistent*?"

"I'd prefer to be off this table and"—she winced again—"on my way to Mesa Verde."

That reminded him of an apology he'd intended to issue. "About earlier today, when I warned you off your expedition . . . I'm sorry, Elizabeth. It's none of my business what you do. I know it doesn't help the situation, but my concern *was* genuine."

"Well . . . it's a moot point now anyway, isn't it?" Her voice went flat, all playfulness gone.

Daniel clenched his jaw. This wasn't the turn in conversation he'd anticipated.

"We're through, Miss Westbrook." Dr. Brookston slid back the stool he'd been perched on and rose. "I'll bandage this and send you home with instructions, which will include a good night's rest."

Doc Brookston wrote something on a slip of paper and handed

it to her. Daniel helped her sit up, watching for signs she might still be dizzy.

She read the paper. "There's no medication you want me to take? Seems doctors are always prescribing something."

"No, ma'am. Nothing besides this." He handed her a small container. "If you'll rub this salve on the cut, twice a day, morning and night, it will help with the healing and will minimize discomfort. I'm also prescribing rest, Miss Westbrook. Your lungs are clear, for now, and rest will aid in strengthening them." He paused, his brow knitting. "You've referred to this ailment from which you suffer as a lung condition, and I'm assuming that's what you've been told."

"Yes, all my life."

"I believe, as do a growing number of my colleagues back east, that, in cases such as yours, the problem may actually originate here." He touched her throat. "In the air passage, rather than in your lungs. However, over time the lungs will indeed be compromised due to the struggle for air, as your lungs clearly have been."

She nodded. "Is there anything I can do to avoid a recurrence of what happened today?"

"Unfortunately, we don't always know what triggers these attacks, and this one was especially severe." He seemed to be contemplating something. "You handle various chemicals in your avocation, do you not?"

She nodded again. "But I'm familiar with each of them, and I assure you, I take necessary precautions."

"For my benefit, ma'am, would you list the chemicals currently in your inventory?"

"You mean that *used* to be in my inventory." She sighed. "There's pyroxylin, ammonium iodide, and ammonium bromide." She glanced at him and he gestured for her to continue. "Iron sulphate, pyrogallic acid—"

"Which is classified as a mild poison." The doctor's tone adopted an instructional quality. "And can be absorbed through the lungs.

At which time difficulty in breathing will ensue. It causes extreme irritation to the respiratory tract, and if absorbed through the alimentary canal, it can—"

"Cause damage to the liver and kidneys. Yes, doctor, I'm fully aware. That's why I'm especially careful when handling that solution."

Elizabeth's tone was genteel. A bit *too* genteel, Daniel noted, for the glint in her eyes. However, Dr. Brookston's stare remained patient, unruffled—a clear sign for her to continue.

"There's also silver chloride, sodium hyposulphite, silver nitrate, and potassium cyanide."

The doctor's expression sharpened. "Before the seizure, Miss Westbrook, how long had it been since you'd eaten?"

"I wasn't hungry when I first awakened. I had a cup of tea for breakfast later in the morning, and then another cup around noon. I didn't eat any lunch. Why do you ask?"

"Because the reaction a person has to some of these chemicals can vary widely depending on two things. The strength of the body's immune system—we already know yours is weakened—and the amount of food present in one's stomach when they imbibe or inhale the substances. Potassium cyanide is worthy of extra caution, Miss Westbrook, especially in your instance. Even in small doses, it can be lethal, and can produce effects quite similar to the seizure you had today, and far worse."

Daniel observed a sobering in her, and was glad to see it.

"I understand what you're saying, Dr. Brookston, and promise to be more careful. Now, is there anything *else* I can do to keep this from happening again?"

"Many people opt for a more . . . sedate lifestyle." A shy smile crept over his face. "But I suspect you would hardly ascribe to that, ma'am. There *are* stronger medications available, such as opium and morphine, that have been used with limited success in cases such as yours, but . . ." He shook his head. "I'm cautious in prescribing those due to adverse secondary effects that accompany their prolonged use. A person can become dependent upon them, and there's reason to believe that when taken over time, they can actually exacerbate the problem."

Daniel was familiar with both of these drugs. Physicians on the battlefield had administered morphine liberally, much to a wounded soldier's appreciation. But the doc was right, overuse exacted a severe price. And the cost still haunted Daniel.

Dr. Brookston reached for a colorful metal tin on the cabinet shelf behind him. "In lieu of those drugs, Miss Westbrook, I'd recommend a tea that has been known to provide comfort in these cases."

"Thank you, Doctor. I'm already familiar with the teas and use them liberally." She reached for her reticule and withdrew some coins. She laid them on the table. "But I appreciate your recommendations, and your services."

"My pleasure, ma'am. And hopefully I won't see you again for a couple of weeks. Come back then, and I'll remove the sutures. One final thing before you go, and I realize I'm swimming against the current in making this petition, ma'am."

Sensing what was coming, Daniel gestured toward the door. "I'll wait outside." Coat in hand, he closed the door, but the open window prevented the privacy he halfheartedly sought to give. Beau hopped up from where he'd been lying and came to stand beside him.

"Even before I became a physician, I never ascribed to the use of restrictive feminine garments . . ." Daniel imagined the drop in Elizabeth's jaw. "And I would highly encourage you to consider eliminating that unnecessary garment from your daily assemblage."

Silence. Then a more muted exchange he couldn't make out.

Trying to muster as innocent an appearance as he could, Daniel met her at the door and assisted her down the front stairs.

She wouldn't look at him.

As he walked her to the boardinghouse, he thought twice about offering his arm. Not because he didn't want to, but because it had been so long since he'd attempted the gentlemanly gesture. But when he offered, she accepted and tucked her left hand into the crook of his arm, and the pull of time tugged hard, as did the remnant of his past life. A life of gentility and innocence he'd thought gone forever.

Their steps found a rhythm on the planked walkway. She was unusually quiet, which he attributed to fatigue.

McPherson had told him in the hallway outside her room that he was convinced whoever had broken into her room had a purpose other than just looking for money, and after witnessing the extent of the damage, Daniel agreed. Her camera hadn't been merely broken beyond use. It had been demolished past recognition.

His overriding concern was similar to one McPherson held— whoever did this had gained some kind of pleasure from the act. Either that or was sending Elizabeth Westbrook a strong message. Perhaps both.

Today was the most he and McPherson had spoken in months. Since last fall, when Thomas Boyd had died.

They got to the corner and Elizabeth paused, still not looking at him. "*You* cut off my corset?"

Unprepared for the question but not altogether surprised, Daniel waited until a man and woman had passed before answering. He'd heard embarrassment in her voice rather than anger. "Yes, ma'am, I did. You weren't breathing, and what I'd already tried . . . wasn't working. The doc—"

"What you'd already tried?"

He nodded and let his gaze slip to her mouth. Recognition slowly dawned in her expression. She touched her lips in a way he might have considered flirtatious had he not known her better. Yet the effect on him was the same.

"But that didn't work?"

"No, ma'am." Not in the way she meant. He smiled in hopes of easing her discomfort. "So the doc told me to cut off your corset, and I did."

In the glow of the coal-burning streetlamp, her struggle was evident, as was her fatigue. She pressed her lips together. "Was my . . . Did you . . ."

No matter that she couldn't get the words out, Daniel knew what she was asking. "It was just me and the doc, Elizabeth. Your modesty and decency weren't compromised in any way."

She smoothed a hand over the buttons of her coat. "So . . . you and I . . ." She gestured between them. "We're . . . all right, then."

He liked this side of her—very much—but was torn between not being completely honest and coming off as some mannerless rogue. He decided to try and split the difference. "You and I are just fine, Elizabeth."

She exhaled, obviously relieved.

"But may I say that you are one . . . beautiful . . . woman."

25

Daniel tried the doorknob, then held out his hand. "May I have your key?"

Wordless, Elizabeth retrieved it from her reticule and handed it to him, still thinking about what he'd said. *"You are one beautiful woman."* She knew she wasn't all that pretty, but she liked that he thought she was.

After two attempts, the latch clicked and Daniel pushed the door open. "Stay here." His soft command brooked no room for argument, not that she would have given any. She still wasn't eager to return and, though exhausted, didn't think she would sleep a wink.

She stood outside, Beau sitting beside her, while Daniel lit the lamp and checked the windows, then peered beneath the bed, and—from the telling creak—looked inside the chifforobe.

"Everything's in order. Or mostly so."

She stepped inside, surprised at the cleanliness of the room. But like a glass camera plate with an image developed into it, the image of what the room had looked like in its disheveled state was burned into her memory and made it difficult to see it any other way.

Beau sniffed at several places on the floorboards and sneezed.

A silver tea service adorned the desk and—*bless that Miss Ruby*—the pot was warm to the touch. Elizabeth poured herself a cup.

"If that's tea, you might consider foregoing it. You'll sleep better tonight."

Her back to him, Elizabeth opened the desk drawer, relieved to see the bottle of Mrs. Winslow's Soothing Syrup still there, and added a portion of its contents to the china cup. "On the contrary. This is an herbal tea my physician prescribed for my lungs and that you heard Dr. Brookston recommend this evening. Miss Ruby delivers a pot every morning and evening, per our arrangement." She stirred and sipped, closing her eyes as the warm liquid burned its way down. Its bitter taste was a deceitful precursor to a promised calm.

Daniel stared from across the room. "Are you having trouble breathing right now?"

She shook her head, finishing that cup and preparing a second. "And I'm determined not to. Would you like some? I can get another cup."

"No . . . thank you."

She looked around the room, trying to convince herself she could stay. And failing. "I can't be in this room, Daniel."

"We can leave for a while. Go for a walk and let it air out some more if—"

"No, I mean I can't stay here anymore."

He considered her from across the room. "All right, then, we'll find you another place to stay. Maybe Miss Ruby has another room. I'll go ask in a minute. I know the hotel's full, because I already checked there."

Elizabeth nodded and ran a hand over the books on the shelf, mentally counting the volumes as she went, in case any were missing. They were all there.

"Miss Westbrook?"

Turning, she saw who was peering through the partially open door and felt the tea churn in her stomach. What timing. "Mr. Turner . . ."

She acknowledged the illustrious *Timber Ridge Reporter*'s editor, then shot Daniel a glance. Daniel did a quick back step behind the chifforobe, his hand motions clearly communicating that he preferred to remain invisible. Considering the occupation of their visitor and his eagerness to uncover stories, she was inclined to agree. She didn't need Turner writing anything about her entertaining some late-night visitor. . . .

"Good evening, ma'am. I was hoping to find you in, though I'm sorry to be calling at so late an hour. I heard you've had a pretty hard day."

Elizabeth stepped closer to the door, aware of Beau's watchfulness and praying he wouldn't follow her. "It's had its challenges, and I'm glad it's almost over." She guessed why Turner had come to visit and hoped he would take her hint.

In her peripheral vision, she saw Daniel pressed back against the wall, his expression comical. He motioned for Beau to move closer to him, and the dog obeyed but with some hesitation.

Turner tipped his bowler—sporting a different feather in the rim, if her memory served. Quite the dashing reporter. "When I heard about what happened, I tried to get over sooner, but duties at the *Reporter* kept me confined overlong this evening." He gestured at her hand, frowning. "Were you in some sort of struggle? Was an assailant involved?"

She lifted her bandaged hand. "No, no, there was no struggle, and no assailant. I cut my hand on a piece of glass. It happened afterward. All very boring."

"Ahh . . ." He proceeded to pull out a pad and pencil from his coat pocket. "I'm sure you're still in shock, but I'd like to ask you some brief questions, if that'd be all right."

"Actually, I—"

"Do you have any idea who might have targeted you in this way, Miss Westbrook? Or why?" He waited, expression expectant, pencil poised.

Elizabeth studied him, and a single niggling thought begged

answer—was her own inquisitive nature ever perceived this way by people? She identified with his eagerness for a story, and shared it. But his abrasive manner . . .

"I'm more than open to speaking with you, Mr. Turner. But it's rather late, and as we've both said, I've had a very long day. I'm certain you'll under—"

"I know, and I apologize again for that, Miss Westbrook. But I'm publishing a special edition of the newspaper tomorrow and would like to get your version of what happened. I've already spoken with the deputy—the one who supervised the cleaning of your room. He gave me his side of things, but I'd appreciate the chance to get my facts straight before we go to press in the morning." He gave her a smile that said he knew he was being forward—just like Wendell Goldberg—and that he hoped she would be forgiving.

She didn't know which bothered her more—the fact that this . . . violation she'd endured would be splashed in black-and-white all over the *Reporter* for everyone in Timber Ridge to read over breakfast, or that she recognized Turner's pressure tactics as ones she had used herself on occasion.

"This won't take long, ma'am."

She acquiesced, familiar with that line too, and laid aside her teacup. She directed him to a bench in the hallway, glad Daniel was nearby and especially glad Turner didn't know it. "I'd feel more comfortable meeting out here, if you don't mind." She left the door ajar.

"Certainly, Miss Westbrook. It still smells a bit strong in there. The deputy told me it was the chemicals you use in your work."

"Yes, all of the bottles were broken."

As soon as she'd sat down, she heard a faint thumping coming from inside the room. When she realized what it was, she cleared her throat. Twice. The thumping stopped. Turner didn't seem to notice.

"If you don't mind, before we discuss the crime that took place here, I'd like to ask a few questions about this hobby of yours. Give readers a glimpse of the woman behind the camera."

Elizabeth smiled at the overly dramatic flair in his voice—a clear attempt to ingratiate himself with the interviewee. She'd done that too, and now cringed, remembering. "That will be fine."

"Oh, and before I forget—you don't happen to have a photograph of yourself taken alongside your camera, do you? That would be a wonderful accompaniment to go with the—"

"No, I'm sorry. I don't." She smiled to soften the interruption.

"Well, I guess any photograph of you would do, then. Whatever you'd like to give me."

"Again, Mr. Turner, I'm sorry. But I don't have any photographs of myself available."

"None?" He seemed surprised, then gave a small chuckle. "That's sort of like a cook who doesn't eat her own food, isn't it, Miss Westbrook?"

She didn't care for his tone, or this particular topic. "I'll be happy to answer a few questions, unless you'd rather—"

"Very well." He looked slightly disheartened. "Tell me, how did such a . . . *mature* woman like yourself take up the hobby of photography and decide to move out west?"

Mature woman? The phrase was jarring, like a note sung off-key in full voice. Her thoughts went to Daniel, sequestered in her room, listening to everything they said. No doubt he was enjoying this. It wasn't the first time she'd been described in that manner, and it certainly wouldn't be the last. In fact, she'd heard it stated in far less complimentary terms. She hadn't been much past the age of eighteen when it first began. For years she'd told herself it didn't bother her, and most days it truly didn't—not anymore.

She pasted on a smile, knowing how to guide an interview. She only hoped Turner would take notes on *that.*

"My love for photography, Mr. Turner, grew out of my love for science and nature. In the fall of 1861, in New York City, I met a

Mr. Mathew Brady when he was photographing the late President Lincoln. I had the good fortune of assisting him in that session, and that's when I realized that I had a strong affinity for . . ."

Over the next fifteen minutes, no matter what question Turner posed, she responded with information *she* chose to give. Finally, she rose, signaling the interview was concluded.

Turner followed her lead.

"I appreciate your time, Miss Westbrook, and your clever insights. You've been so open, and helpful. Nothing irritates me more than printing something that's not accurate." He retrieved his hat from the bench. "Just one last query and I'll be on my way. You know a man by the name of Josiah Birch, do you not?"

She sensed he was toying with her, and she didn't like it. "Yes, I do. You saw him this week, in fact, when we met at the coroner's. Mr. Birch is in my employ and is a fine, upstanding man."

"You know . . ." He tapped his pencil. "I wondered if that was him. Are you aware that this Negro—" He paused as though catching himself. "This fine, upstanding man," he added quickly. "The one in your current employ . . . is wanted for the murder of a white man in the state of Tennessee? Shot a defenseless man in the back. The poor fella never knew what killed him."

Like a pendulum suspended in midair, the moment hung. Fractured. Separate. The only sound Elizabeth could distinguish was the soft whoosh of wind outside the hallway window.

"I'm sorry if I've spoken out of turn, ma'am." Turner slid his pencil and paper into his pocket. "But I take it from your reaction that you weren't privy to this information before hiring him."

She tried to swallow, but the dryness in her mouth prevented it.

"It's none of my business, and you're free to tell me so, but . . . I'd advise you to be careful whom you associate with out here. People tend to judge a woman by the company she keeps, and things can get . . . complicated if she insists on keeping close company with a Negro. This isn't Washington, as I told you before, ma'am, and you'll quickly discover that folks in these parts don't appreciate being led on. They don't take kindly to pretense." His eyes were bereft of warmth. "And they won't care much that you're the daughter of a United States senator."

Elizabeth was too stunned to speak. A creaking noise sounded behind her and she turned to see her bedroom door move an inch. Then another. She prayed Daniel wouldn't show himself and that he hadn't heard what Turner had just said.

Then she saw it, a black button nose edging its way toward the threshold. She saw it clearly from her vantage point and wondered if Turner could. A soft shuffle and the nose disappeared.

For a second she thought Turner might go investigate.

His smile was presumptuous. "I didn't know you were entertaining company at this late hour, Miss Westbrook. I hope I didn't interrupt anything."

Her face heated. "It must be the wind, Mr. Turner. You know how drafty these clapboard buildings can be. Like you said, this isn't Washington."

He studied her for a moment, then walked toward the stairs. "You be sure and stop by the *Reporter* sometime tomorrow, Miss Westbrook. I'll have a special edition out." At the staircase he turned back. "And I always make sure our lead story gets a complimentary copy."

26

Standing in the hallway, Elizabeth could only stare at Drayton Turner as he disappeared down the stairwell. The word *under-estimated* rose in her mind. Yet part of her, a very small part, actually admired the tactics he'd used. His skill lay beyond what she'd credited him. His main reason in coming here tonight had been to spring the information about Josiah on her. His inquiries about photography had been a ruse, and she'd fallen for it, partially out of a desire to impress him with her experiences with Mathew Brady and President Lincoln. How foolish . . .

And Josiah, wanted for murder. Impossible. There had to be some mistake.

But what would happen to him when Turner printed the condemning assumption in the morning paper? And without question, Turner *would* print it. He would likely begin with something about her father being a U.S. senator, then add a line, maybe two, about her photography, then he would list the charge against Josiah. She knew that's what Turner would do because that's what Wendell Goldberg would've done, *and* what Goldberg would have instructed her to do.

She wanted the position at the *Chronicle* more than anything else. That's what she'd been working toward for the past ten years.

But there were times when she questioned whether she had what it took to do the job.

Turner might toss in the term *alleged,* which would matter little to the people of Timber Ridge. Once readers of the *Reporter* saw the word *murder* and they discovered, if they didn't know already, that Josiah was a Negro—which Turner would mention without fail— Josiah would be linked to the death of Travis Coulter, and his fate would be sealed.

She had to tell him. Get to Josiah and warn him. But she had no idea where he was.

Daniel . . .

She turned to find him standing in the doorway of her room. Discovery shaded his features, telling her he'd heard every word of her conversation with Turner. He slipped his hat on and whistled low for Beau. The dog appeared around the corner.

The sheriff had said Daniel could track anybody and anything, and that he knew these mountains. But she also knew how Daniel felt about Josiah, about his people in general. He didn't hate them as some did, but he clearly didn't see them as his equals. Following that thread of prejudice, she doubted whether he would be willing to help her.

"Do you have any idea where Birch is right now?" Daniel asked. "Where he stays?"

The concern in his voice surprised her. "When I asked him a few days ago, all he said was God had given him plenty of forest. And caves—he did mention caves. Does that tell you anything?"

"Yes, ma'am. . . . It tells me he could be anywhere within a five-hundred-mile radius of here." A smile tempered his sarcasm. "I'll find him. Hopefully before sunup."

As he passed her in the hallway, she stopped him. "Thank you, Daniel. And it won't take me but a moment to get ready."

He glanced down at her hand on his arm, then looked as if he might offer disagreement. "I'll get my horse from the livery and meet you outside."

"He didn't do it." Her voice came out more hushed than she'd wanted.

Daniel paused, then brushed back a curl from her face. "How can you be sure?"

"Because I know him. It may sound strange to you, I realize, but I know the heart that beats inside of that man. And he didn't do it."

He covered her hand. "A man can do a lot of things in his life, Elizabeth. Things so opposite each other that, over time, he can bear little resemblance to the person he once was."

"Josiah doesn't have it in him to kill a man. Not in that way."

Daniel's eyes narrowed and went dark and deep as seawater at midnight. "And just what way would that be?" A hardness had slipped into his voice.

"Josiah might kill to protect himself, but he would never kill a defenseless man, Daniel. That would be cowardly and cruel, and beneath a man of honor."

Daniel stepped back, looking as if she'd slapped him. "Beneath a man of honor?"

She wondered at the question in his tone. Perhaps she'd under-estimated his animosity toward Negroes after all.

"I'll meet you downstairs in a few minutes. And I'll do my best to find him."

———

Daniel assisted Elizabeth into the saddle, mindful of her bandaged hand, and then pulled himself up behind her. Her judgment from moments ago still burned inside him. *Beneath a man of honor.*

If she felt that way about Josiah being accused of a murder, how would she feel if she knew *he'd* killed countless *defenseless* men? He told himself it was different and wanted to believe she would see it that way too. It had been war, and though the men hadn't known they were about to die, they'd hardly been defenseless. They'd served as the masterminds of death for thousands from their pristine offices back in Washington or from their tents far removed from the heat of battle. Yet the faces of those very men, their sudden shock as they realized their fate and surrendered to it unwillingly, still haunted him. And would until the day he died.

He reached around Elizabeth for the reins. "You comfortable enough?"

"Yes, thank you." Her voice was soft, and she sat up straighter, putting some space between them.

He prodded the mare but kept her at a gentle pace. Beau jumped up from where he'd been lying and trotted behind. The town was quiet, and rightly so. It was late. Daniel hadn't checked the time but figured it had to be well past midnight.

With everything she'd been through today, she had no business going with him, but he knew she wouldn't have accepted his saying no. Not tonight. Not when he already knew she didn't want to stay by herself.

He'd dropped by the sheriff's office on his way back from the livery to see if McPherson was there. He wasn't. Daniel knew he'd want to know about Josiah Birch, so he figured they'd ride to the Boyd home. Then he and McPherson could head out to look for Josiah, and Elizabeth could stay the night in the cabin with Rachel and the boys. He didn't think Rachel would mind some female company, though she surely wouldn't be pleased at seeing him again.

Elizabeth turned to look back but stopped quickly and reached for the back of her head. "I think my hair's caught somehow."

He reined in, rose up in the stirrups, and she swept her curls over one shoulder. He eased back down behind her. "All set now?"

"I think so." She laughed softly. "But a cup of coffee would be nice if you could manage it."

He nudged the horse again. "I actually make a very good cup of coffee. But I don't happen to have any with me at present. How about

I bring some with us when we go hunting? I know you don't have your camera anymore, but I could show you some of the countryside, some real pretty spots you haven't seen before."

She looked back and her cheek came close to his. "That's very sweet of you. I'd like that very much."

Defeat softened her tone, and a rush of anger tore through him again at whoever had done this to her.

She faced forward. "Thank you for searching for Josiah."

"You're welcome." Her hair smelled faintly of sulfur, not the most pleasant scent in the world, but he was accustomed to it, having taken the waters in the area for years. He preferred the springs on his land. They didn't have near the smell of the ones in town and were considerably clearer.

He hadn't given her a choice on how to ride. He wasn't sure how skilled Elizabeth was on a horse and didn't want to take the chance of her slipping off the back and adding a broken arm to an already injured hand. McPherson and his sister didn't live more than fifteen minutes from town, but a part of the trail included a steep incline, then a narrow ridge overlooking Timber Ridge, with the remainder being winding mountain trail.

Daughter of a United States senator. Who would've thought . . .

The words played in his mind as they rode past the outskirts of town. He felt bad even thinking about this now, given the current circumstances, but when he'd heard Turner say that about her, his first thought went to whether she might be willing to help get his petitions before the members of Congress. If anyone should be able to bend the ear of a senator, it would be that man's daughter.

But what kind of man allowed his daughter to travel the western territories unescorted—or at least not properly so—taking photographs with a Negro man? Didn't make any sense. At any rate, now definitely wasn't the right time to bring up that subject. And that time might never come. Though he hoped it would.

There, he noticed it a second time—how she kept sitting up

straight, putting distance between them. He peered over her shoulder to see her holding on to the pommel. "You can relax. I won't let you fall off. Don't worry."

"Oh, I'm not worried." But neither did she let go.

He took the turnoff to the Boyd place, which started the steep incline. Elizabeth sat straight, gripping the pommel with her left hand, even leaning forward, until she apparently couldn't manage it anymore. She slid back into him, and Daniel was ready.

Holding the reins with one hand, he rested the other on his thigh, easily supporting her weight. She felt good against him. "There now, is that so bad?"

"It's not bad at all. I was just trying not to squish you."

He laughed. "*Squish* me?"

She giggled, and it was a nice sound. "It's sort of like being squashed, except I think it hurts more."

"Well, ma'am, if this is pain, then bring on the full load." That earned him a sharp nudge in the ribs. He smiled. "If there's one thing I don't think we have to worry about, it's you squishing me."

The land leveled out, and he noticed she didn't go ramrod straight again. He glimpsed the top of the Boyds' cabin through the trees but didn't see a curl of smoke coming from the chimney. He hadn't been here in months. But he remembered good times spent in the Boyd home, warm times with laughter shared over delicious meals, and the excitement when Thomas and Rachel's two boys were born.

"We're coming up on the sheriff's place. I figured we'd go ahead and stop by here first. He'll want to know about Birch and what's happening."

The mountain trail opened up into a cove where the cabin sat nestled in thick stands of aspen and spruce. It could have been a hollow in the Tennessee hills if not for the rugged mountains towering above the single-story roofline. He glanced toward the barn and, even in the dark, could picture Thomas Boyd standing there, with an arm outstretched in greeting.

He wondered if other men carried around the weight of regret that he did inside him. If he'd known beforehand how things were going to play out, he never would have encouraged Thomas and Rachel to move out here. Thinking of how Rachel would likely react to seeing him again, he decided he probably needed to provide Elizabeth some insight on the family's recent history.

"McPherson lives here with his sister and her two boys. Last fall, he moved out here to help after Rachel's—"

"Husband was killed." Elizabeth nodded. "I remember hearing about that."

Daniel guided the horse to the post in front of the cabin, wondering what else she'd heard about it. He dismounted and helped her down, then tethered the mare.

Lightly holding Elizabeth's arm, he climbed the stairs to the darkened porch. No light shone through the windows. He knocked, and it didn't take McPherson long to answer. He'd always been a light sleeper.

"Ranslett . . . Miss Westbrook . . ." An oil lamp in one hand, he rubbed his eyes with the other. "Come on in." He held the door open. "What's wrong?"

They stepped inside. Hoping they wouldn't wake Rachel, Daniel filled him in on what had happened. " . . . and Turner told Elizabeth that he was going to print the story in the morning, which gives us about six or eight hours, give or take, to find Birch."

"Sheriff, we're both assuming Turner *will* include that part about Josiah in his account." Elizabeth cradled her right hand close to her waist. "I fear what might happen if we don't find him first."

"You can count on Turner printing it, Miss Westbrook. And I fear the same." McPherson sighed. "Sometimes I wonder whether or not the good of having a town paper outweighs the bad."

Daniel waited, half expecting her to mention something about her father being a senator, since Turner was sure to print that too. But she didn't.

"I'll go change, Ranslett. Then we'll head out. Miss Westbrook, you can have my bed and get some rest."

She glanced from one to the other. "But I thought I might go along." She turned to Daniel. "To help you look."

Daniel gently squeezed her shoulder. "McPherson and I can move faster and cover more ground if you stay here. You've been through enough already today. And remember what Dr. Brookston—"

"James, who is it?" A light shone in the darkness behind McPherson, then the hushed patter of steps. "Is everything all right?"

Daniel resisted the urge to move into the shadows. This moment was inevitable, but it still felt too soon. Soft footfalls came closer, and McPherson threw him a look that said he understood but didn't know what to do.

"It's okay, sis."

"James, who's calling at this—" Rachel appeared beside her brother, a candle's glow illuminating her face.

Rachel had always been a beauty, even as a child, and the years had done nothing to alter that fact. Daniel remembered how he and McPherson had enjoyed intimidating every lovelorn boy in Williamson County who had set his cap for the hand of pretty Rachel McPherson. Daniel never had sisters of his own, so over time, Rachel had become like his. And for years, things had stayed that way between them—until last fall.

"Daniel . . ." His name left her like a pained sigh, and a frown eclipsed the question in her expression. Her face had thinned in recent months. The smile lines around her eyes and mouth seemed more pronounced.

Her gaze didn't stay locked on his for more than an instant before she looked away, and Daniel was grateful. Looking at her only reminded him that Thomas wasn't here anymore, and that she blamed him for that.

Daniel swallowed to remove the knot in his throat. "Rachel . . ." He caught himself before asking how she was. Any simpleton could see she still wore her grief. Even Beau seemed to sense the discomfort and remained quiet at his side.

Rachel's attention shifted to Elizabeth, and she laid a hand on her older brother's arm. Daniel knew what she was silently asking, and so did McPherson. Ever the Southern belle, Rachel was a stickler for doing things the proper way, and always had been, even if she was in her nightclothes.

McPherson nodded. "Rachel, I'd like to introduce Miss Elizabeth Westbrook from Washington, D.C. Miss Westbrook, may I present my sister, Mrs. Thomas Boyd of Timber Ridge, by way of Franklin, Tennessee."

Rachel offered a slight curtsey. "Pleasure to *formally* meet you, Miss Westbrook. And, please, call me Rachel."

"Pleasure to meet you as well." Elizabeth smoothed a hand over her skirt, and Daniel sensed self-consciousness in the act. "And I'd prefer Elizabeth, if . . . you don't mind."

Rachel smiled. "Elizabeth it is, then. I'm so sorry for all you've endured today. James told me what happened. You must be completely exhausted."

"I am rather tired. I think it's catching up with me." Elizabeth's gaze flitted to Rachel, then back to him, and confusion lined her expression.

"I'll fix you some warm milk and move my things to the boys' room. You can have my bed."

"Let her sleep in my bed, Rachel. I've got some business to tend to anyway. Daniel and I are about to head out."

A shadow darkened her face.

"Don't worry. . . ." He reached over and squeezed her hand. "It's not dangerous, but I may be gone for a while."

Daniel attempted to form a smile when Rachel looked at him. But before he could accomplish the feat, she turned away, twisting the invisible knife in his gut.

He gave Elizabeth a last look. "Get some rest, Elizabeth. I'll ride back with news as soon as we find him." He whistled for Beau to follow and walked to the barn to saddle McPherson's horse.

Fifteen minutes later, the plod of their mounts' hooves trumped the night's quiet.

"So when did we move to a first-name basis with Miss Westbrook?"

Daniel smiled at the question. "I think it was somewhere after I cut off her corset and before she nearly clawed me to death in the hot springs."

McPherson laughed. "She's a handful, that woman. And mighty pretty."

Daniel let the comment lie.

"Sometimes not saying anything speaks louder than if you did, Daniel."

"And sometimes, James . . ." He remembered a saying from their childhood. "It's best for a man to be thought a fool instead of opening his mouth and removing all doubt."

James laughed again, and they rode on for a few paces, side by side. Daniel had missed this friendship.

"Her father's a senator."

James whistled low. "She sure didn't advertise that fact, now, did she? She's hiding something else, you know."

"Mm-hmm, I do." Daniel wasn't surprised that James already suspected something. The man could wheedle secrets from a wishing well.

"I don't think it's anything bad, mind you. More like she's running from something. I think she'll tell us, given time."

"I'd normally say you're right. You can be persuasive, but she's about as obstinate a creature as I've ever met. I agree, though, there's something she's not being honest about. And she's not a very good liar, to her credit."

"Remind me again, where were you when Turner was in the

hallway asking her all those questions and telling her about Josiah Birch?"

Sensing James intended to poke fun at him, Daniel decided to beat him to it. "I already told you. I was with Beau, hiding behind her chifforobe."

They paused on the ridge overlooking town. In the daylight, every road leading to and from Timber Ridge could be seen from this vantage. Now, however, the town below lay blanketed in darkness, the only light an occasional flicker from the distant coal-burning lamps lining the main thoroughfares.

A wolf's howl rose in the darkness, lonely, haunting, reminiscent of another time. Hearing it, Daniel felt a peculiar corkscrew sensation working its way up his backbone. For reasons he couldn't explain, even if pressed, he kept his voice hushed. "Sometimes, late at night, when everything's still and you're almost asleep . . . do you still hear it?"

The breeze of a winter overstaying its welcome whistled down from the north, weaving an unseen path through tree limbs and into the opening of Daniel's jacket. He pulled it closed.

"No matter the number of my days on this earth, Danny . . . I'll never erase that sound from my memory. Never . . ."

Daniel let out his breath, comforted by the response and by James's use of his childhood name. For years, he'd wondered if he'd left behind his last shred of sanity on the battlefield that night in Franklin.

James's horse whinnied, and he reached down to stroke her neck. "Rachel still loves you, Danny. Just like she did when we were kids. Thomas was a farmer and a rancher and a good man. But he wasn't a hunter. He wasn't ready to go out alone like that yet. Deep down, Rachel knows it. She just misses him—that's all. Give her time."

Daniel fixed his gaze on some distant peak. "I miss him too. And Rachel and the boys . . ." Unable to deal with the tangle of emotions inside him, he intentionally turned his thoughts to Josiah Birch. "Where to now?"

"That depends . . ." James paused. "Give me your best guess as to where you think he might be."

Daniel weighed the possibilities. "Normally I'd say the shanties. But with Coulter showing up dead and knowing that Josiah had a run-in with the man not long ago, I don't think Birch would do as was his custom right now. I think he'd stay clear of town." He leaned forward in the saddle. "As I've headed back home around dusk recently, I've seen three fires burning. One's coming from south of town by Salter's Mines, another one's over by Crater Lake, and the third is by the springs near the Fraziers' place."

"I've watched him from my office window in town, coming and going. He never follows a pattern that I've noticed. Which doesn't make him guilty, just careful. And smart."

Daniel reached into his saddlebags for his gloves and tugged them on. The cold was moving in. "My best guess would be Fraziers'. Less populated, no main roads, and some deserted mining caves are nearby. They'd make good shelter. But Crater Lake is closer to town."

"Let's try Fraziers' first." James prodded his horse. They skirted Timber Ridge by way of a cliff and picked their way through the darkness, aided by a waning half moon.

A clearing loomed ahead. Arriving at the edge, they dismounted and tethered the horses. After searching the area, they found remnants of campfires and droppings from a horse or mule, but no Birch. They rode on down the ridge and across to Crater Lake. After combing the shores of the lake and the outlying areas with no success, they moved on to Salter's Mines. But found nothing.

The sun shone pink in the eastern horizon, but Daniel couldn't go back and tell Elizabeth they hadn't found him. So they pushed on, searching every nook and cranny they could find. When dawn lit the eastern horizon, they rode down the mountain and into town.

McPherson stopped by his office to see if anything had been reported to the deputy.

Weary from the saddle and the search, Daniel dismounted, eager to stretch his legs. He walked the brief distance around behind the building to the small stream, and kneeling down for a drink, he saw him. Naked and bleeding, on the opposite side of the streambed.

27

Tired of waiting, Elizabeth headed to the barn to saddle up Rachel's horse. Halfway there, she heard the frantic pounding of hooves coming up the path. Daniel rounded the corner on his mare, sending bits of gravel flying. He reined in sharply, and she ran to meet him.

Weariness weighed his features, but the urgency in his eyes gave her hope.

"You found him?"

He dismounted. "You need to get your things, Elizabeth. And come with me."

She looked past him. "But where's Josiah? Didn't you find him?"

A muscle flexed in his jaw. Something flashed in his eyes, and if she hadn't known better, she would have thought he was angry with her.

"We did find him, just a while ago, in town behind a building."

Instinct sent her back a step, and she pushed away the image forming in her mind. "Is he all right?"

"He's been beaten pretty bad." Daniel grimaced. "We took him to the doc's, and Brookston was working on him when I left. Said he needed to stitch him up."

She shuddered, remembering her own procedure. Tears rose to her eyes.

"Josiah's asking for you. And th—" His jaw went rigid. "There's something else." He pulled a piece of paper from inside his coat pocket and held it, tight. She recognized the typeface. The newspaper crinkled in his grip. "Turner's 'special edition' came out this morning."

Anger rose inside her, imagining what falsehood Turner might have written about Josiah, and what it had spawned. "They're lies, Daniel. All lies. Josiah couldn't have done what Turner said he did last night. Josiah's a good man. And good men don't—"

"Good men make mistakes, Elizabeth. They do things they regret." Daniel exhaled and looked away, shaking his head. When he looked back, his eyes were moist. "Whatever Josiah's done or hasn't done, don't add the weight of your disappointment to his burden. He's carrying enough on his own right now."

Her throat tightened as the impact of his words hit her square in the heart. She clenched her jaw, and a single tear slipped slowly down her cheek and into the corner of her mouth. The salt from it was bitter on her tongue, as was the reminder of her father's disappointment in her.

Daniel held out the newspaper. "You need to look at it."

Something inside told her she didn't want to. "I'll go get my things."

He took hold of her arm as she tried to pass. His grip was gentle but unrelenting. "Read it, Elizabeth."

Something in his voice made her lift her chin, and his pained expression made her wish she hadn't. She took the paper and opened to the front page. Reading the banner across the top, she sucked in a breath.

WASHINGTON CHRONICLE REPORTER
VISITS TIMBER RIDGE

Then just below that, in slightly smaller type—

MURDER SUSPECT SOUGHT IN SOUTHERN SLAYING

She reached out for something to hold on to, and Daniel was there. He held her steady, close beside her, yet felt so distant. Her hands shook as she struggled to focus on the page.

Elizabeth Westbrook . . . employee of the *Washington Daily Chronicle* and daughter of a United States senator . . . photographer for specious eastern publication comes west seeking adventure . . . armed with her camera and enough determination to conquer anything that stands in her path . . . working in conjunction with a land developer to . . .

She felt naked and exposed, and the more she read, the more vulnerable she became.

Plagued with lung disorder . . . benefited from the expertise of the town's new physician . . . ostensibly was acquainted with the late President Lincoln . . . her room was ransacked . . . expedition south to cliff dwellings could be in jeopardy . . .

Her conscience aching, she moved down the page, wishing she could throttle Drayton Turner.

Josiah Birch . . . former slave of the state of Tennessee and alleged suspect . . . accused in the murder of plantation owner . . . November 11, 1866. Body discovered . . . wooded area . . . cause of death, broken neck. Birch suspected of accessory . . . freed under suspicion due to lack of evidence. Sheriff seeks Birch for questioning in Coulter murder . . . Birch made recent threat on Coulter's life.

She'd eaten nothing since last evening, yet her stomach churned. Shame sluiced through her. She felt Daniel looking at her but couldn't bring herself to look at him.

"I can explain," she whispered.

He let go of her. "Not right now. We need to get back to town."

"What Turner has written isn't all true, Daniel. I can prove—"

"Just get your things, Elizabeth. Please . . ."

She hurried inside and told Rachel only that they'd found Josiah, then grabbed her coat and reticule and met Daniel out front. He was astride the mare and waiting by the bottom step. Holding her bandaged hand close to her chest to protect it, Elizabeth gripped his hand, slipped her left foot in the stirrup, and swung up behind him. All without looking at him.

He urged the mare down the path. She tried holding on to the cantle but there wasn't enough of the saddle's edge to grip without getting too close to Daniel. She nearly slipped off and quickly grabbed the back of his coat.

He reined in. "Put your arms around me."

She placed her hands on either side of his waist.

"Around me, Elizabeth."

When she didn't, he took hold of her left hand and drew it snugly around him. "Give me your other."

With care, she reached her bandaged hand around. He gently took hold and pulled her forward until her chest was flush against his back.

"Now hold on."

The horse's gait was smooth and fleet, and the mare seemed to anticipate the challenges of the mountain terrain as well as her master did. Elizabeth would never have attempted these trails at this speed with her horse, but not once did she feel endangered.

Evergreen boughs laced with ice glistened in the morning sun. Daniel's leather coat was soft against her cheek, and she relished his warmth as they rode. The snows hadn't come yet, but the biting cold promised they would.

She didn't know how Turner had discovered her affiliation with the *Chronicle,* but she was going to face him and demand that he correct the errors he'd printed. But as Sheriff McPherson said, the damage had already been done. She couldn't account for it, but the pain she'd experienced yesterday after finding her equipment destroyed and her money gone somehow hurt *less* than the sense of betrayal and deception—and disgrace—filling her now.

In the distance, a sharp wind cut over the top of the North Maroon Bell and sent a plume of ice and snow into the atmosphere. She watched it float and swirl, descending, drifting on a current, falling and falling, until it finally dissipated into nothing.

She tightened her grip around Daniel's waist.

———

Once down the mountain, Daniel skirted town by way of a trail that emptied out near Dr. Brookston's clinic. Beau was on the board-walk, right where he'd left him, lying at the deputy's feet. Daniel dismounted and helped Elizabeth down, noticing how winded she seemed, and remembering how tightly she'd held to him. She looked ashamed, and defeated, and angry—all at once.

He walked up the stairs, hearing her steps echoing his. "McPherson had some fires to tend to at his office. He asked me to bring you by after we're done here." He acknowledged the deputy, then paused before opening the door to Brookston's clinic, not knowing what they were walking into. "You ready?"

Her head came up. Her blue eyes wide, curls falling in disarray down her back, she opened her mouth to say something, then pressed her lips closed and nodded.

The doctor was pulling a sheet up over Josiah as they walked in, and Daniel stopped midstep, then relaxed when Dr. Brookston tucked it around Josiah's shoulders.

The doctor motioned them forward. "Come in, Miss Westbrook, Mr. Ranslett." He retrieved a jar from a shelf. "Mr. Birch was asking for you earlier, ma'am. He's heavily medicated at the moment"—he shot Daniel a look—"so he's slipping in and out."

Daniel saw the open bottle of "medication" on the shelf but he didn't think Elizabeth did.

She took hesitant steps forward and laid a trembling hand on Josiah's chest. Tears slid down her cheeks.

When he'd read the headline this morning and then learned she was in the area on behalf of land developers, that had surprised him. He'd suspected she'd been hiding something, but nothing like that. Developers coming in was a volatile issue, and Timber Ridge was divided over it. But at least he knew now why she'd singled him out—for his land.

Bandages covered the right side of Josiah's face, hiding a deep gash that had, thankfully, missed his eye. His left arm was swathed in gauze, then wrapped close to his body to be immobile, not surprising considering its odd angle when they'd found him. But at least the bone hadn't been broken. Eyes closed, his chest rose and fell in a strong, even rhythm, a good sign.

"Is he going to be all right?" Elizabeth whispered.

Dr. Brookston unscrewed the lid to the jar. "If determination counts for anything, then yes, I have every reason to believe he will be, given the opportunity to heal. I don't think I've met a man who possesses a stronger constitution." He gestured. "Speak to him, if you'd like. He might well respond to the sound of your voice."

She exchanged places with the doctor beside the table and leaned close. "Josiah?" When he didn't respond, she waited and tried again, louder the second time.

Josiah's eyes fluttered, then closed. "Miz Westbrook . . . that you, ma'am?"

She hiccupped a sob. "Yes, it's me." She lightly patted his arm. "I'm so sorry, Josiah."

With his good arm, Josiah reached over and stroked her hair. "Oh, ma'am, don't you be carryin' no burden for this. This ain't your fault."

"Y-yes, it is. What's in the paper this morning . . . I caused all this."

He took in a deep breath and slowly let it out. "That's not right thinkin', ma'am. I know it for sure . . . cuz I done laid by that stream most of the night."

Daniel saw Elizabeth bow her head, probably thinking what he was—that they had passed not far from that streambed shortly before midnight. It had gotten bitter cold, and Josiah had been stripped of his clothing.

Dr. Brookston dipped his fingers in a creamy salve and began applying it to the cuts on Josiah's arm. Elizabeth eased the jar from his hand and resumed where he'd left off.

Josiah blinked slowly and managed to open his eyes. "It's good to see your pretty face, Miz Westbrook."

She gave a sharp laugh. "Clearly the . . . *medication* Dr. Brookston is administering to you is affecting your eyesight."

Daniel smiled—so she *had* seen the bottle. Dr. Brookston's eyes widened as though he'd been caught red-handed.

Josiah tried to raise his head. "You okay, Miz Westbrook? Any harm come to you?"

"No, no harm."

"Then why you cryin' so? I's the one laid out on this table!"

His deep laughter filled the office and drew theirs out too. Elizabeth laid her pale hand on his dark forehead and Josiah sighed. "Your hand feels good, ma'am. It's cool, like you been dippin' it in a mountain stream."

As Daniel watched from a few feet away, he witnessed the friendship between them. In her tenderness and respect, in Josiah's laughter and protectiveness, and it was a friendship like he'd never seen before. Not with this particular type of pairing, anyway.

He moved to sit on a nearby stool and felt the pinewood floor give beneath his weight. He hoped Brookston was as handy with a hammer as he was with a needle. On the table next to him was the leather pouch he'd found not far from Josiah's body. He had briefly looked inside. It appeared to hold a collection of notes, like pages from a journal, most of them many years old by the looks of them.

Josiah winced, and Dr. Brookston poured more whiskey into a cup. Elizabeth intercepted it and supported Josiah's neck as he took sips. Once the cup was empty, she eased his head back onto the pillow.

"Minute ago, ma'am . . ." Josiah closed his eyes. "You say somethin' to me 'bout that newspaper. What's in there—" he took a breath— "that's got you thinkin' this was your fault?"

"Mr. Turner wrote articles about me, and about you. Some of what he said was not favorable, nor kind."

"What he's sayin' about you . . . Is it true?"

"Some of it is, and some of it isn't."

"Is it the truth got you upset, ma'am? Or the lies?"

She took a wet cloth from Dr. Brookston and smoothed it across Josiah's forehead. "A little of both, I guess."

"Way I see it, Miz Westbrook, if you mad 'bout him writin' the truth, you gotta ask yourself why. But if it's lies he's tellin', some folks'll believe 'em. Some won't. Best thing you can do is live a life that makes *him* the liar."

Daniel weighed the man's counsel and found it sound. Dr. Brookston sat hunched on a stool across the room, grinding something in his mortar and pestle, privy to every word. The tick of a mantel clock bracketed the silence.

Elizabeth leaned close. "Can you still hear me, Josiah?"

"Yes, ma'am, I hear you fine. My eyes is just tired."

She took hold of his hand. "I want you to listen to me, then. . . ."

To Daniel's surprise, she turned and looked at him. She held his stare, and he saw it cross her face—that instant where a person wonders whether they should tell the entire truth or not. When they weigh the choice and the risk of trusting someone, against the advantage of keeping their cards tucked close against their vest.

If he was reading her right—and countless hands of winning poker said his instincts were good—Elizabeth Westbrook was about to lay down and come clean.

28

I have lied to you . . . Josiah. Photography isn't just a hobby for me. I . . . I work for a newspaper back east . . . called the *Washington Daily Chronicle*."

Daniel could tell by the quick breaths she took that this was difficult for her. And yet she never broke his gaze. She had addressed Josiah, whose hand she still held and who lay on the table between them, but Daniel knew she was addressing him too, and he felt privileged to be the one she was looking at.

"I'm a secretary and the assistant to—" Her expression reflected distaste, and she started again. "I write articles for the newspaper, and I'm here on a . . . job interview, if you want to call it that. These photographs I've been taking"—her voice grew stronger—"and the ones I was going to take at the cliff dwellings, along with articles I've written, were going to be part of my portfolio that would be considered when they decide who the new staff photographer and journalist will be."

Daniel nodded once in silent acceptance of what she'd said, and wondered if Josiah had fallen asleep.

"You done speakin', ma'am?" His eyes still closed, Josiah's voice came out strong. "Ready for me to say my piece yet?"

"No," she said quietly. "But almost."

Daniel held her stare, not in the least tired of looking at this woman. Or of listening.

"I've also been here looking at land for a company that wants to build a hotel. That's why we went to Travis Coulter's that day, and why I was so insistent about going on to the cabin. I'm not associated with the company in any way other than taking photographs of land and finding out who the various landowners are. That's all." She struggled with emotion. "I never intended to hurt anybody or to use anyone like I have. And I regret any misunderstanding I've caused." Slowly, her shoulders relaxed. "All right, I'm done, Josiah. You can say your piece."

He laughed softly. "All I got to say is . . . I had a feelin' there was more to you, Miz Westbrook. I just didn't know what it was."

Daniel smiled. He liked this man more all the time.

"But somethin' else I wanna know, ma'am." Josiah lifted his head from the pillow. "Does your papa know what you doin' out here?"

Daniel waited, interested in this answer.

"No, he doesn't." She looked away. "He thinks I've come out here to be a teacher, to start a school. And in an effort to *help me*"—sarcasm laced the word—"he spoke with a colleague and arranged to send all those supplies—the books and slates you carried to my room. Any day now, a shipment of furniture is set to arrive as well."

"Your papa a teacher?"

The first hint of a smile appeared on her face. "No, my father's a senator in the United States Congress. That's part of the government in Washington."

Josiah let out a gentle whoop. "You's a real important woman, Miz Westbrook."

Her smile faded. "No." She shook her head. "I'm just the daughter of a real important man."

———

Daniel waited on the boardwalk outside the sheriff's office. He rubbed his face and sighed, tired from lack of sleep. Beau rested at his feet.

Over an hour had passed since he'd escorted Elizabeth inside to speak with James. She'd looked frightened. James was a man you wanted on your side at times like this, but he hadn't faulted her for being nervous. One thing you didn't want to do to James McPherson was lie.

The door to the sheriff's office opened and Beau jumped up.

James closed the door behind him, looking as tired as Daniel felt. "Willis is going to stay with her awhile, and Lyda Mullins is bringing her some lunch." He motioned. "Let's take a walk. I think better when I move."

Daniel fell into step beside him, and Beau followed without command. James set out on what used to be their customary route.

"I feel better keeping Miss Westbrook in my office than letting her walk around town right now."

Daniel slowed his steps. "Do you think she's in danger?"

"Not with us watching over her. But talking to her just now makes me think that whoever was in her room yesterday was looking for something. Oh, they took her money, all right, but I don't think that's what they went there for." James looked over at him. "Did you know she took another picture of Coulter's body?"

It took Daniel a second to track with him. "You mean besides the one Turner printed in the paper?"

James relayed what Elizabeth had told him, and as Daniel listened, it struck him that she really was a reporter, just like Turner. No, that wasn't fair. She was nothing like Drayton Turner. Elizabeth might share a similar curiosity, but he couldn't imagine her printing some of what Turner had published in his paper in recent months.

Beau ran on ahead and with a whistle, Daniel encouraged him back. "Can she get you that first photograph?"

James paused at the edge of Maroon Lake. "She's wiring her

employer at the *Chronicle* today to ask them to send it back. It might take two or three weeks, she said. But that's one picture I want to see. I talked to her about Josiah too. I've got a telegram on its way to a judge in Tennessee. If anything doesn't check out about Turner's story, we'll know it soon enough. Turner says that what he printed about Birch is true." He stooped to pick up a rock, then hauled back and threw it. It angled sideways over the water—one, two, three skips—before plopping full under the surface.

Well-chosen stone at the ready, Daniel followed suit. One, two . . . five, six. His stone skimmed farther across the lake, leaving barely any wake. He heard a snort of disgust beside him.

"How do you do that? You've always shot farther and thrown longer than anyone I know."

"I had to have something. You could outwrestle me and every other man in Tennessee."

For a moment, neither of them said anything, and Daniel's thoughts centered on Elizabeth and what she would do next. She obviously wouldn't be going on the expedition, which was a good thing in his mind. It was a dangerous undertaking. Not for the weak of heart—or lungs.

Standing there, a familiar sense of ease settled between him and James.

"It's good . . . to be doing this again." James gestured between them. "It's been too long." He stared out across the lake. "Which makes what I have to say all the more difficult."

Daniel attempted to read his expression, and couldn't.

"When I became sheriff, I took an oath to do everything in my power to keep the people of Timber Ridge safe. And it's not safe for Miss Westbrook or Josiah to be in this town right now."

"So send her to Denver for a while. Josiah too. Until things blow over." As soon as he'd said it, Daniel realized he hadn't suggested sending her back to Washington. And from the look James was giving him, so had he.

"I could do that. But I've spent quite a while talking with her just now, getting to know her better, weighing her options . . . and only one makes any real sense to me. And, for what it's worth, I talked with Josiah earlier, and he's in agreement."

The moment seemed to hang.

Realization crept over him and Daniel shook his head. "No . . . James. I won't do it. I've already told her I wouldn't take her, and I gave her my reasons."

"I'm not just thinking of her, I'm also thinking of you. Have you considered that her father's a U.S. senator? You've been writing those letters for how many years now? Three . . . four?"

"Seven. But I'm not going to use her just to get to her father." Though that thought *had* occurred to him.

James frowned. "I'm not suggesting that and you know it. I'm asking you to use this opportunity. Show her the territory. Let her know what you're trying to do. You've said yourself, countless times, 'If those people in Washington could only see this land, they'd do something to protect it.' Well, let them see it! She can do that for you. And she would, if you'd just ask her."

Daniel raked a hand through his hair. He couldn't believe they were having this discussion. "Even if she got there, she has no camera. There's no reason for her—"

"We've already worked that out. Timber Ridge has wanted a school for a while now, and it seems her father is sending everything but a teacher. He's already provided the books and slates, and Miss Westbrook tells me furniture is on its way. Seems only right that the town should buy her a camera and some equipment in exchange for all that. We'll order the camera and supplies from back east—then all we'll need is to find a way to ship it from New York to Mesa Verde."

The freighter he'd recently met came to mind, but Daniel wasn't about to mention him. "You saw her last night, James. She's not healthy enough to make the trip, and neither is Josiah."

"You may be right about Josiah. The doctor seems to think it's possible he could travel. He'll make the call when the time comes. But Elizabeth is determined to do this, and I think she can. What's more—" James laughed softly—"I want to help her do it."

"Then you take her!"

James shot him a look. "Brookston thinks her problem yesterday was the chemicals in the room. Keep her away from the concentrated fumes and that shouldn't happen again."

Though he was out in the open, Daniel felt as if walls were closing in on him. "It's too hard a trip. Too risky for someone like her." He scoffed. "I don't even know if she can ride!"

James turned to face him. "You know . . . you're not the same man you used to be. You used to claim you could hunt anything, climb anything, teach anybody to do the same—and it wasn't a lie. You could. But now—" Something akin to pity clouded his eyes. "Now you seem scared of stepping too far from your own shadow."

James always had a way of getting to the truth. It was infuriating at times, like now, and heat poured through Daniel as he recalled a childhood wish. To be able to knock James McPherson—just once—flat on his face.

"What are you afraid of, Daniel?" James asked the question as if he already knew the answer.

"I'm not afraid of anything." Daniel's throat tightened and he turned away.

"You know these mountains better than anybody. You've made the trip to Mesa Verde several times."

"By myself!" Too late, Daniel realized what his quick response had revealed.

The ripple of wind over water filled the empty space between them.

"So that's what this is about. Still . . . after all these years . . ."

Daniel looked anywhere but at James. "I won't be responsible for something bad happening to her, James. Josiah either."

"I could stand here and tell you that nothing bad's going to happen. That you'll all get there safe, but we both know that may not be the truth. But I do know this—if anything happens along the way, it won't be due to your negligence or lack of experience. Elizabeth and Josiah couldn't be in better hands. Why do you think I'm entrusting you with this?"

Daniel stared out over the partially frozen lake, glad he didn't have to respond.

"The war is over, Danny," James whispered. "You've got to find a way to move past what happened back there."

Daniel shook his head, hoping his voice would hold up. "You think I haven't tried?" He winced. "I still see Benjamin's face . . . *every day*. Him looking up at me for the last time. I carry that inside me, James. That and my mother telling me, over and over, not to let anything happen to him."

A frosty breeze carrying traces of pine caused Daniel to turn up the collar of his coat. He willed his friend beside him to hear the silent question he couldn't bring himself to ask.

James studied his boots for the longest time. "I wish I could tell you that I put all that behind me, Danny. But I still carry it with me too, every day. It just doesn't rule me anymore like it used to. At first, I cried so many tears I wondered if I was still a man. But it was either that or . . . stay there on that battlefield in my mind, lying among my fallen brothers. Except they only died once, Danny, with glory and honor. You've been dying every day since then, holding on to the past, to something you can't change. Let Benjamin's death mean something. Be the man he saw in you, the man who he loved." James's tone grew more resolute. "And about Miss Westbrook . . . I'm not asking for you to do this anymore. I'm relying on your honor."

Recalling the debt was like a knife in Daniel's gut. "You know that doesn't count for this. It can't."

James laughed softly. "You mean your honor has limits now?"

"You know exactly what I mean."

"Your pledge years ago was that if I ever needed anything, *anything*, you'd be there. And I need this. Because I can't afford to have something go wrong. Not like it did before in this town."

Daniel knew what he referred to. He could probably see the graves from where he stood if he turned, but he didn't.

"Rachel and the boys depend on me now. That's a burden I willingly took on. I love my sister, and I love those boys. But trying to enforce the law in a place like this while having the responsibility of a family . . ." Sincerity layered James's voice. He'd never been one for anything less. "That gives some people a target. I'm fine with them coming after me. I knew that risk when I took this job. But if my trying to protect someone else resulted in anything happening to one of them, I don't know what—"

"I'll do it," Daniel whispered, only too aware of the price Thomas and Rachel, and their sons, had already paid for their decision to move west, and at his encouragement, no less. "But if Elizabeth Westbrook shows the least sign of being unable to make this journey—same for Josiah—or if the passes are too risky, I'm turning back. I'll take them to Denver and get them situated there."

James held his stare. "Agreed."

As they walked back to James's office in silence, all that could go wrong on such a journey ran through Daniel's mind. He didn't know what he would do if something happened to her along the way. Elizabeth Westbrook already meant more to him than any woman ever had, and far more than he'd ever imagined she would.

29

She stared up at him with eyes the fragile blue of a robin's egg, frowning as if she thought she'd misunderstood him. "So . . . you're taking me?"

"I am." Daniel detected suspicion in the way she glanced at the door, then back at him. And it only fed his irritation.

"Is Sheriff McPherson forcing you to do this?"

"It's my choice, Elizabeth." He moved to James's desk.

"But you told me you wouldn't. Remember that day when you said leaving early was a bad idea. I—"

"The reasons I gave you before for not wanting to leave that early in the season are still valid. And leaving a week earlier is even worse. But circumstances have changed, so we'll adapt. Where are your supplies being stored?"

"In Ben Mullins's back room."

"I need a list of everything you've already purchased. Once we leave Timber Ridge, it'll be two weeks before we pass another settlement. And it's not really a town, more of a miners' camp, but they sometimes have supplies, depending on how long it's been since the freighter came through. Do you have gloves?"

She nodded.

He looked at the pair lying atop her reticule. "Other than those?"

She shook her head.

He picked up the quill and a piece of paper. "From there, it'll be another two weeks until we reach Mancos, which is near the cliff dwellings. So whatever we need, we take. Or we do without."

The delicate lines around her eyes and mouth framed her smile, and chipped away at his frustration. "I promise I'll follow your lead, Daniel, like I said I would. I won't be difficult and I won't complain."

He dipped the quill. "May I have that in writing, please?"

She slipped it from his hand. "The list of what Hawthorne purchased is in my room. Should I contact him about not—"

"I'll do that. If there's anything you can think of that you need, write it down. Starting with gloves. We'll go to the store first, then to your room at the boardinghouse, then to check on Josiah. We're staying with James and Rachel for the night, and we leave at daybreak. Do you know how to ride?"

"Yes."

"Do you know how to cook?"

She blinked. "Of course." She quickly bent over the paper. The scratch of the quill filled the silence. A stained indentation marked the inside of her third finger on her right hand, where the quill fit perfectly.

He hadn't known what to expect when he'd walked back in here to tell her the decision, but whatever he'd imagined, he hadn't been prepared for the submissiveness he was seeing now. Neither was he fool enough to think it would last.

At the moment, Elizabeth Westbrook was beaten and bruised, as surely as Josiah was down at the clinic. Only her bruises didn't show. But you could still see their effects, in the way her gaze wouldn't hold his overlong, in the quick way she agreed with everything he said, and in the lack of fire in her eyes.

She raised her head. "What about Josiah?"

He wondered when she would pick up on that. "He might not be well enough to travel. We'll make that decision tomorrow morning."

"But I can't—" She caught herself and gently closed her mouth.

Her restraint was admirable, and Daniel could see her filtering what she'd been about to say.

"Perhaps we could wait a few days until Josiah's well enough to join us?"

"I'd prefer to do that, but we don't have the time." He gestured to the window. Snow had started falling as he and James had walked back. "We either make it across the pass and out of here tomorrow, or we're stuck here for a while." He grabbed his coat, indicating for her to do the same. Beau jumped up from his spot by the coal-burning stove.

The temperature outside had dropped in the last hour, and the wind made it seem colder than the twenty-seven degrees registering on the gauge hanging outside Mullins's store. Daniel left Elizabeth at the counter with Lyda Mullins searching through a thick catalog for a camera, while he spoke with Ben about the supplies and freighter in the back room.

Mullins nodded. "Brennan told me whatever you wanted shipped within his territory was to be done at no charge. I'll see to it for you, Ranslett. You just tell me what and where."

"Thank you, sir. Miss Westbrook is making her selections right now. I'll be back in a couple of hours with a wagon to get these supplies."

After a stop by the telegraph office for her to wire Goldberg, they went to the boardinghouse and packed what she wanted to take with her. It took three tries, but they finally pared down the wants to the needs and fit them into one large duffle. He was encouraged when she tucked a journal entitled RECIPES inside. Years of bachelorhood had forced him to learn how to cook, but it would be good to share that responsibility. Especially since most everything else would be on his shoulders.

The snowfall was steady. Almost to the doctor's clinic, they heard the shouts before they rounded the corner. He spotted James on the boardwalk, his hand poised on the gun at his hip. A dozen or so men pushed their way up the stairs while James and two of his deputies barred their way.

Daniel took hold of Elizabeth's arm and pulled her back into an alley. "Change of plans."

She opened her mouth, then promptly closed it. If he'd known she could be this compliant, he might have been tempted to agree to the trip from the very beginning.

"You'll see Josiah, but not now." He led her through a series of back alleys to his horse behind the sheriff's office. Fifteen minutes later, they were atop the ridge overlooking the town on their way to Rachel's. He looked in the valley below to see if he could tell which building was the doctor's clinic and found it easy to distinguish. It was the one with the crowd gathered out front.

For the tenth time in half that many minutes, Elizabeth pushed the curtain aside and stared out the front window into the darkness. A slivered moon's pale light illuminated millions of feathery flakes as they drifted downward. Thankfully the wind had died some.

Rachel came alongside her. "James won't let anything happen to him. You can count on that."

Elizabeth wanted to be certain but couldn't. There had been so many men and only James and two deputies—and Daniel, who had gone back to town with the wagon to get their supplies. *Their supplies* . . . She couldn't believe they were leaving tomorrow. Daniel had seemed none too pleased when telling her his decision earlier that day, but—whatever caused him to change his mind—he had given her back her dream. And she was determined to do everything within her power to see it succeed. Now if she could only get word about Josiah.

Rachel's sons were seated at the kitchen table with their dinner. She assumed Mitchell's and Kurt's red hair reflected their father's coloring since Rachel's hair was dark brown. Although they did have their mother's eyes.

She'd shown Rachel the newspaper article earlier, wanting to be honest with her too. She'd hoped she and Rachel Boyd would be good friends. And still did. If Rachel's kind response to her confession had been any indication, that hope still held promise.

"Are you hungry yet, Elizabeth? The stew's ready."

"No thank you. Not quite yet." The silence lengthened. Elizabeth glanced up, then away again. "I-I'm sorry about the loss of your husband, Rachel."

A fleeting smile. "Thank you . . ." Her voice went hushed. "I miss him, very much."

"Have you ever thought about returning to Tennessee?" The question was out before Elizabeth had thought it through. She reached out. "I'm so sorry, I didn't mean to imply that your staying here was in any way—"

Rachel gently shushed her. "It's a perfectly normal question. I did think about it, at first, but . . . with both sets of our parents gone, and with James and Dan—" Her jaw went rigid. "I decided to stay here and give our sons the life Thomas wanted them to have. That we both wanted them to have."

A distant pounding brought them both to their feet.

Elizabeth raced to the door with Mitchell and Kurt on her heels, but Rachel put a hand against it before she could pull it open. Elizabeth turned, and her eyes went wide.

The graceful Southern belle cradled a rifle in her arms. "Just until we're sure who it is."

Elizabeth couldn't help but be impressed. So much for the little derringer in her pocket. "Is that something you learned out here?"

"No, I just grew up surrounded by boys." Rachel motioned for her sons to stand around the corner, then peered outside. They waited, and her face gradually brightened. "It's Uncle James." She threw open the door.

McPherson and one of his deputies reined in.

Elizabeth met them at the bottom of the stairs, careful of the ice and snow. "Where's Josiah?"

McPherson dismounted. "Daniel's got him. Dr. Brookston should be with them too."

"Should be?" Elizabeth looked between him and the deputy who'd stayed with her earlier. "So you saw them leave?"

"No, ma'am." Fatigue lined McPherson's features. "And hopefully nobody else did either." He motioned for them all to go inside.

They gathered around the fire. The sheriff and deputy wrapped their hands around cups of hot coffee and stood close to the hearth as Mitchell fed another log to the flames.

McPherson blew across the top of his mug before taking a sip. "Some of the men in town were upset this afternoon. They got the impression that Mr. Birch had done something he hadn't." His carefully chosen words were confusing at first, until Elizabeth saw Mitchell and Kurt sitting on the edge of their shared seat, in rapt attention. "So I talked with them and let them know that they were mistaken."

"Did they believe you, Uncle James?"

Kurt nodded at his older brother's question.

"Not at first. And they were mighty angry. But Willis here, along with Stanton, who's still in town, helped me to convince them otherwise."

"Did you have to shoot any of 'em?" Kurt's eyes went to the pistol at his uncle's hip.

Elizabeth could tell McPherson was tempted to smile.

"No. Thankfully, it didn't come to that." But the discreet glance McPherson sent his sister said it almost had.

A dull thud sounded on the front porch. McPherson left, then returned moments later. "Would you come with me please, Miss Westbrook?"

Elizabeth grabbed her coat.

He led her to the barn, where Dr. Brookston stood waiting in the shadows. "Did it work, Sheriff?"

"I think so. Nobody followed us. We doubled back twice to be sure. Stanton will keep watch in town through the night." McPherson peered into the darkness behind him. "How is he?"

"I don't think I've seen a tougher man. He fared the trip well enough, but it's cold. We need to get him inside."

Elizabeth followed them to a stall where Daniel was kneeling over Josiah, with Beau close beside them. Josiah looked surprisingly warm to her, wrapped in a fur of some sort with only his face showing. The men carried him into the house and situated him on blankets and cushions spread out before the fireplace. The boys were nowhere to be seen.

McPherson introduced Brookston and Rachel. Rachel greeted the doctor warmly but didn't so much as look at Daniel. Not even a cursory glance. Daniel's manner didn't reflect it, but Elizabeth sensed his unease.

Dr. Brookston opened his medical bag and peeled back the blanket of fur from Josiah's upper body. He pressed the stethoscope against Josiah's chest. "I administered a healthy dose of laudanum to Mr. Birch before we left, so he'll probably sleep for a while."

Elizabeth settled beside him on the floor. "How did you get out of town without being seen? Last I saw, a crowd was gathering out front of your clinic."

"Turns out the building my clinic occupies wasn't constructed with the finest workmanship." Dr. Brookston looked at Daniel. "Ranslett here noticed some loose floorboards when he was there earlier and made quick work of them tonight. He lowered Josiah through the floor while the sheriff and his deputies kept the crowd occupied out front. Of course, now I need a carpenter."

The men kidded Daniel about needing to fix what he'd broken. Daniel offered a timid smile but no further explanation. Watching him, Elizabeth felt an unexpected flush of pride.

"Mama, who is it?"

Mitchell and Kurt peered around the corner, and in unison, they yelled, running full out, "Uncle Daniel!"

Daniel dropped to one knee and grabbed them both in fierce hugs. The boys' momentum nearly sent him falling backward, but he managed to keep his balance.

"We haven't seen you in a long time!" "Do you still have your dog?" "Have you been huntin' again?" "Where's Beau?" "Did you bring us any claws this time?"

Daniel tousled a red mop of hair with each hand, smiling. The boys tried to duck and get away but weren't fast enough. Beau joined in the fray as Daniel caught Mitchell and flipped him up over his right shoulder, then grabbed Kurt and carried him around like a sack of potatoes. Laughter filled the room.

Elizabeth sat speechless at seeing this side of Daniel. Grinning, she looked at Rachel, expecting to see joy—but discovered tears instead. Rachel met her gaze, then quickly bowed her head and left the room. Daniel's own smile faded as he watched her go.

Elizabeth looked between the two of them, wondering at their history, and her first inclination was toward the romantic. Rachel Boyd was mesmerizing. What man wouldn't be attracted to her . . . And they *had* grown up together.

At James's insistence, Daniel took his bed, and Rachel insisted Elizabeth share with her. Josiah awoke briefly and ate some broth before slipping back into sleep, and the other men made pallets on the floor.

Elizabeth finished her tea in the kitchen and quietly crept into Rachel's room, uncertain whether Rachel was already asleep or not. As she pulled the covers up around her, Rachel stirred, and Elizabeth heard a muffled cry.

"Rachel," she whispered after a moment, staring into the darkness. "Are you all right?"

An unsteady breath. "No . . ."

Elizabeth tensed, not knowing what to do. She kept her voice hushed. "Do you want me to go get James?"

"No . . ." A hiccupped sob. "I want that man out of my house."

Josiah . . . She hadn't considered the fact that just because McPherson was accepting of Negroes, Rachel might not be. "I'm sorry, but he was injured and there was—"

"No, not Mr. Birch." She sniffed. "Daniel Ranslett."

Daniel? She thought of him lying in the bed just beyond the wall beside her. "I . . . I don't understand. Why is it not all right for him to be here?"

Darkness stretched the seconds taut, and Rachel exhaled a shaky breath. "Because he killed my husband."

30

Elizabeth awakened to hushed voices beyond the bedroom door. Yawning, she sat up, blinking, letting her eyes adjust to the darkness while she gained her bearings. Her bandaged hand was sore but not as much as yesterday, and a slight throb pulsed in her temples. The voices grew more distinct.

"You know what you did! We *both* know what you did!"

"Rachel, you have no right to speak to him that—"

"Thomas is *dead*, James!" A sob cut short. "And he's the reason for it!"

"Lower your voice. . . . The boys are going to hear you."

Recognizing McPherson's commanding tone, Elizabeth rose and padded to the closed door. The voices fell silent, but even with the door separating them, she felt the tension. The conversation wasn't hard to follow remembering the last thing Rachel had said to her last night. The floor's chill seeped through her socks, and Elizabeth glanced at the window. Still dark outside. Despite having had tea late last night, she craved another cup.

With painstaking care, she turned the knob and opened the door inch by inch, wincing in anticipation of a squeak.

"I'm sorry for what happened, Rachel. I know that doesn't change a thing, but if I could go back and have a second chance to—"

"My husband wanted his sons to be proud of him. That's all, Danny. Do you know that? That's why he went out there that day."

"Thomas asked me to take him bear hunting, Rachel. To show him what to do. So I did. I had no idea he would try and go out on his own like that. I told him I'd go with him, anytime. All he had to do was—"

Elizabeth heard a hard slap.

"How dare you make this out to be Thomas's fault! If you hadn't filled the boys' heads with tales of tracking and hunting, this wouldn't have—"

"Rachel!" McPherson's hushed tone was harsh. "You're out of line. You know better than anyone that when Thomas got it into his mind to do something, nothing could change it. You miss Thomas. . . ." His voice softened, and Elizabeth could imagine his expression doing the same. "We all do. But trying to blame this on Danny is wrong, and you know better. They need to get on the trail, so I want you to . . ."

Soft crying masked whatever else McPherson said, and Elizabeth closed the door, feeling guilty for having eavesdropped, while also grateful to finally know what had happened between Daniel and Rachel, painful as it was.

A knock sounded, and she opened the door again.

Daniel slowly raised his head. "Morning . . ."

"Morning, Daniel." She didn't ask how he was. The droop of his shoulders, and what she'd overheard, told her well enough.

"We leave in an hour, at sunup. Josiah insists he can travel, and Doc Brookston says he thinks he can make it, stubborn as he is." A smile colored his tone, though none touched his face.

"I'll be ready." She started to close the door but paused when he made no move to leave.

He sighed, and the words seemed to come hard for him. "Something else . . . before we set out. I want you to know that I'll do my best to get you to Mesa Verde . . . so you can meet this deadline of yours. But if either of you shows signs of not being able to make it, I'll turn back. Not out of spite and not because I disagreed at first with you making this trip, but because I won't risk anything happening to you—to either of you. Are we clear on that?"

She nodded once. "Perfectly."

"I'll go load up."

She penned a hurried letter to her father, telling him she was fine but preoccupied with settling in and with her "new job." And that she might be too busy to write for a while. James agreed to mail the letter for her. She would write her father again when they reached Mesa Verde, so he wouldn't worry over not hearing from her.

An hour later they were saddled and ready to embark. Dingy clouds filtered the pale sunlight, and a feathery, persistent snow drifted down, adding to the night's accumulation. Daniel gripped the reins of the two packhorses. She'd offered to lead one, but he had declined in a tone that left no room for negotiation. For now, at least.

She looked at Josiah beside her, concerned, despite Brookston's permission for him to travel. "You sure you're ready for this?"

"Sure I am, ma'am. Like I said at breakfast, I wouldn't be missin' this for the world, Miz Westbrook. And I do fine. Won't be no problem for Mr. Ranslett, or for you. I give you my word on that."

"If there's one thing you could never be, Josiah, it's a problem to me. Thank you . . . for doing this."

His smile stretched wide. He'd eaten a hearty breakfast, and Doc Brookston had assured her his injuries weren't life threatening. She'd overheard Brookston telling Daniel that stopping early for the first few days would be best, to ensure Josiah got enough rest.

McPherson fingered a strand of leather hanging from the bridle of Daniel's horse. "Send word when you get there. And along the way, if you can."

Daniel nodded. "We will."

"And remember what I said to you . . . earlier."

Daniel dodged his gaze. "I will." Then he glanced back at the house. "Tell the boys I'll bring them each a—" His eyes narrowed. "Just tell them I said to be good for their mother."

The cabin door opened, and as if on cue, the boys ran out, coats half buttoned, boot laces trailing. Rachel stood inside watching, arms clutched over her chest.

"Uncle Daniel!"

"You almost left without seein' us!"

Mitchell reached him first, but Kurt was fast on his heels. Daniel jumped down and caught them both in a fierce hug. He kissed their foreheads.

"Will you bring us back a bear claw?" Kurt's eyes went wide.

"Or maybe one from a mountain lion?" Mitchell's expression said he clearly thought his idea outweighed his younger brother's.

"I'll bring something back for both of you, but only if you promise to be good . . . and to help your mother."

"We will, Uncle Daniel."

"Uh-huh, we will."

Mitchell approached Josiah's horse. "Me and my brother, we'll take care of Moonshine for you, sir."

"Thank you kindly, Mr. Mitchell." Josiah touched the rim of his hat. "He too old to be goin' on a trip like this. He do better stayin' here with you."

Daniel tousled the boys' hair before climbing into the saddle again. Turning to McPherson, he whispered something low, then gave a sharp whistle that brought Beau running. Daniel glanced back and Elizabeth read his unspoken question. She nodded, sensing his apprehension and excitement, and sharing them both.

He formed the lead with the two packhorses, and she followed him with Josiah behind. At the end of the road, she turned back to see McPherson's hand raised in farewell, and Rachel's covering her heart.

The morning passed with little conversation other than Daniel's occasional warning of icy spots on the trail, which suited Elizabeth fine. She used the time to sort out the jumble of emotions inside her. Was she prepared for this? What would she do if her efforts for the position at the *Chronicle* weren't enough?

The morning breeze gave way to an afternoon wind that blew frigid against them the higher they rode. Beau's energetic romp finally slowed, and Daniel stopped, brushed him clean of snow, and put him in a pouch on the side of his saddle. It looked like it had been made especially for him. Beau poked his head out the top, contented as could be, and Elizabeth could tell they'd traveled this way before.

A tremor worked its way through her and she shuddered. Not traveling with camera equipment meant faster progress, both from the standpoint of ease in transporting the load and also from not stopping to capture images. But if she got to Mesa Verde and her new equipment wasn't waiting, the trip would have been made in vain. She simply had to trust that the freighter Daniel had hired would prove reliable.

A fork emerged in the trail and Daniel chose left. Every instinct within her told her the other way was correct.

She read the dingy sky, trying to decipher the sun's position. "Are you sure this is the way to the pass?"

The pace slowed. Daniel stopped and turned in the saddle. "Yes, ma'am, this is the way to the pass. Unless you carved out another one during the night." His manner not inviting a response, he faced forward and continued up the trail.

Elizabeth prodded her horse but glanced behind her at Josiah, expecting commiseration, but instead got a look that said, "That's what you get for asking."

The snow grew deeper the farther they climbed, until it finally reached the horses' knees. She hoped Daniel would stop soon for lunch and build a fire. Not only was she cold but she wanted a cup of tea. Her nerves were on edge and a cup would bring the calm she needed.

They continued on up the mountain, the swathe of white-billowed sky narrowing above them as sheer rock walls rose higher on either side. Daniel reined in. He studied the cliffs above, then dismounted and tied the packhorses to a branch.

"The pass is just ahead." Voice quiet, he eyed the highest point on the walls. "You both stay here. I'm going to ride ahead a short ways. Now would be a good time to eat lunch, if you're hungry. Be sure and drink your water, whether you're thirsty or not. Your body needs it for the altitude. No time for a fire. We need to get through the pass and get another four or five miles behind us before making camp for the night." He looked at her. "You warm enough?"

Frustrated about not being able to fix her tea, Elizabeth nodded, lying. She was frozen to the bone but wasn't about to complain. Not after she'd made such a point of telling him yesterday while at the general store that she had the latest in travel gear for her and Josiah—the warmest coats, boots, and wraps available. Apparently the New York manufacturer hadn't field-tested their apparel in the Rockies. Even with the gloves Daniel had recommended, her fingers ached with cold.

He looked back at Josiah. "You warm enough?"

"Yes, sir, this fur's right toasty, thank you." Daniel and Dr. Brookston had wrapped a bearskin around Josiah once he was saddled, tucking it around his legs for added protection from the wind and snow. Elizabeth was envious of his warmth.

Daniel rubbed Beau's neck before climbing into the saddle.

She flexed the fingers on her left hand for warmth, hardly able to feel them. It especially hurt to flex her right, with the bandage. "If you want, just call back to us if the pass is clear and we'll ride on through. No sense in you riding all the way back." Or in them sitting waiting and her freezing to death.

A gleam lit Daniel's green eyes as though she'd said something amusing. "I'd suggest you not call out anything while I go through there . . . unless you want to come back and dig me and Beau out midsummer." He winked at her. "And if you don't mind, get any sneezing done before I start through there too."

Feeling completely incompetent, and knowing she appeared that way, Elizabeth studied the layers of snow cascading over the peaks.

"Watch the wind patterns." Daniel's tone was attentive, but not in the least patronizing. "See how it swoops down over and through the pass. The wind lays the snow flake by flake on the edge of the mountain, creating a kind of shelf. Only there's nothing to support it from beneath. It's frozen during the winter so it doesn't carry the same danger then. But when warmer weather comes and the layers melt and refreeze, melt and refreeze, it weakens the—"

"Structure of the shelf. Yes, thank you, Daniel. I understand." Her tone came out more sweet sounding than she'd intended. She wasn't angry as much as she was embarrassed. She'd assumed those were rock ledges where the snow had settled but should have known better. "That was foolish of me. I'm sorry." The admittance didn't gall her as much as her lapse in memory did. She'd read about avalanches and had even seen pictures of the aftermath.

Daniel held her gaze for longer than necessary, and then his focus drifted upward to her forehead. "No need to get angry, Elizabeth. I just wanted to make sure you understood."

"I'm not angry, Daniel."

His expression said he begged to differ, and she gradually realized what he was looking at. The blasted vein on her forehead!

Tossing her a smile, he rode slowly down the path and disappeared around the bend.

"You sure you warm enough, Miz Westbrook?" Josiah whispered from behind her.

Elizabeth found herself not wanting to turn for fear her saddle would squeak and kill them all. "Yes, I'm fine."

"You needs to tell him if you's cold, ma'am." He kept his voice hushed. "He gots another one of them furs packed in the back. He get it out for you if you just ask him."

"I'll be fine once we're moving again. Don't worry about me." She was glad when he didn't say anything else. She reached behind her into her saddlebag and her hand brushed against the bottle of syrup. She withdrew it, then looked back at Josiah, who was eating a cold biscuit stuffed with sausage, compliments of Rachel, and studying the rock ledges overhead.

She untwisted the cap and took a quick drink, then another. The syrup burned a familiar path down her throat and, within minutes, something inside her responded. She felt herself begin to relax. She reached back for her own biscuit with sausage and ate a few bites, staring above, waiting, listening for the slightest crack or snap.

Relief flooded her when Daniel reappeared. Dressed in his customary buckskin and with his dark hair brushing his shoulders, he looked part renegade native, part wounded soldier returning from battle, and desire stirred inside her. Her mouth went dry at where her thoughts took her next. What would it be like to be close to him, to be held by him? To be loved by him? He'd told her she was one beautiful woman, and she wanted to believe that he found her attractive. But at times, she knew things she said didn't sit well with him. Yet she said them anyway. It was almost as if she couldn't *not* say them.

Dwelling on how different they were, the longing inside her ebbed. Their worlds held little in common, and regardless of his heritage, this was his home now. The mountains, the pristine wilderness. While hers waited a world apart back in the hustle and bustle of Washington.

The stern set of his mouth was telling. "Once we start through, we stay together. If I raise my arm, you stop. Keep a firm grip on your reins and follow my path. Don't wander to either side. The snow's masking a ditch on the right, and another one farther down a ways on the left. Any questions?"

Elizabeth couldn't have spit if her life depended on it. "How long will it take us to get through?"

"In summer, Beau and I fly through here in no more than three minutes flat. But today, we'll just take it slow and steady. If you need to talk, keep it to a whisper. You'll hear cracking as we're going through, but don't jump to conclusions. It's just the ice." He retrieved the packhorses.

Elizabeth shifted in her saddle, a dreadful headline forming in her mind. Something about a *mature* woman's newspaper career being cut short due to overzealousness. Pushing the thought away, she prodded her horse forward and followed Daniel.

Snow drifts threatened to reach chest high on the horses in places, but she kept the pace and path Daniel set, checking occasionally on Josiah behind her, who kept watch on the walls of snow above.

Daniel pointed high up to the right, and balanced on boulders nearly forty feet above were two bighorn sheep, just standing there, staring down. And her with no camera. Not that she could have stopped if she had it. The sheep leapt from rock to rock, with as little effort as children playing a game of hopscotch.

Treacherous and unforgiving, this land held beauty unimaginable to those who'd never experienced it. She could have lived her whole life and never seen such wonders, and would have been the lesser for it. Deprived in a way she never would have known. But God had known, and he'd led her here to experience it, to fulfill her dreams.

They cleared the pass and she half expected Daniel to stop and comment, or for them to take a moment to celebrate their accomplishment. But he kept riding, and at a quickened pace. The wind took on a grueling chill as they came up and over a ridge, and her entire body shook. She'd never wanted to be huddled close to a fire more in all her life. All the nights she'd thought her bed sheets had been cold . . . She hadn't known cold until this moment.

Two hours later, her pride frozen clean through, she opened her mouth to ask Daniel for the second fur when he reined in and dismounted. He withdrew his rifle from its sheath and turned a shoulder toward the wind.

"Wait here," he shouted, and disappeared between a cluster of ice-crusted aspen. He returned a moment later. "We'll camp here. In a cave beyond the trees. Big enough to shelter the horses."

He led the way, and Elizabeth was surprised at how large the opening to the cave was, and how dark. The walls narrowed the farther they went, but he was right, there was ample room for them and the horses inside. The cave had a musky scent but was not dank, as she'd expected it to be.

Darkness obscured the cave's depth, and as Daniel built a fire, she stared into the pitch black, wanting another dash of syrup from her pack and wondering if something was in the cave with them.

Daniel reached for more kindling and shook off the snow before feeding it to the fledgling flame. "Don't worry. Nothing else is back there. I'll show you, if you want, after I get the fire built."

Mimicking his actions, she knocked loose snow from the naked branches and handed them to him. She didn't like being so easily read. "I'm not scared, just curious."

"You picked us a good place to rest the night, Mr. Ranslett, sir." Josiah looked around, nodding. "Real good."

"Beau and I have camped in here before, a few times. Only once did a cougar show up during the night. He didn't bother us and we didn't bother him, so the three of us got along just fine."

Elizabeth studied him for a second; then he and Josiah started grinning. Masking her irritation, she smiled and threw what little kindling she had left in her hand at Daniel's head. He ducked and it missed him.

"He sure had you goin' there, Miz Westbrook." Josiah let out a soft chuckle.

"I didn't actually believe him." She held her hands out over the fire, relishing the warmth but not the unpleasant tingling in her fingertips. She didn't know if they would ever be warm again. Or stop trembling.

"I'll see to the horses while you and Josiah get dinner started. The food stores are—" He reached for her hands. "Are you okay?"

She pulled her hands back and shoved them into her pockets, feeling strangely on edge. "I'm fine. I'm just cold."

Josiah stepped forward. "I can help with the horses, sir. I'm able enough."

Daniel stared at her for a second longer. "I'd welcome the help, Josiah, but Doc told me this morning that you should take it easy for the first two or three days. Once we're past that and we know you're all right, I'll gladly share the chores with you."

"Least let me help by gettin' 'em brushed down. I can do that good enough one-handed, sir."

Daniel finally nodded, then focused on her again and motioned to a satchel by the fire. "Rachel packed fixings for corn bread. There're some beans you can warm up and some bacon to fry."

Elizabeth didn't move. She stared at the satchel, wishing she could volunteer to unpack the horses instead. When he had asked her if she knew how to cook, she'd answered from a desire to appease him. And impress him, perhaps. She knew how to make tea and could scramble an egg, most times without crisping it too badly. But the finer points of cooking had fallen through the cracks somewhere, aided by servants employed in her father's household.

"You did say you were handy with cooking. Right?"

Her temper flared. "Of course I know how to cook. I'm not a child!"

"I didn't say you were . . . Elizabeth." Daniel looked as though he might say something else, then apparently decided against it.

He and Josiah saw to the animals, and she rifled through the satchel, recognizing all the ingredients, just not knowing what order they went in or how to cook them. She poured the beans into a pot, covered it, and set it in the fire. Easy enough. She slid the iron skillet into the flame as well, then layered the bacon inside and covered it. By the time she got to assembling the ingredients for corn bread, she was feeling confident.

That's when she smelled something burning.

The pot of beans was smoking. She lifted the lid about the same time her brain fired off a warning not to. "Ahhh!" The lid was scalding. She dropped it into the fire and bit back an unaccustomed curse. The beans were burned. Using the hem of her skirt, she pulled the pot from the flames and dragged the iron skillet out too. The lid slid off and hot bacon grease popped and sizzled. Flames sprang up and she backed away, holding her hand.

Footsteps sounded behind her.

"Are you all right?" Still wearing his gloves, Daniel retrieved both the pot and the skillet, then fished the lids out with a stick. "What were you trying to do?"

His tone resembled one he might use with Mitchell or Kurt, and a rush of defensiveness rose inside her. "I was trying to make dinner—like you asked me to!" Her voice came out shrill and tense, and she hardly recognized it.

He stilled. Surprise cooled the concern in his expression. "I was just asking a question." His eyes narrowed. "Are you sure you're all right?"

"I'm fine!" She backed away, gripping her hand, tears threatening. "I just—" She looked around for her pack. "I need my pack. Where is my pack?"

Daniel came to her. "Give me your hand."

She shook her head. "I'm fine."

He gently but firmly took hold of her wrist and turned her hand over. A red mark throbbed where the lid had burned her. He left and returned with a packed ball of snow and a cloth. He wrapped the cloth around the snow. "Don't put the snow directly on the burn but hold this against it. It'll help the sting. When I finish with the animals, I'll fix dinner."

She wanted to protest but knew it would be useless. She would only make a further mess of things. As soon as he left, she found her pack and took a swig of the syrup. The bottle only held enough for one more day, but she had several more bottles in another bag. She knelt by the fire, feeding it kindling and watching the flames eat up the branches and twigs. By the time Daniel and Josiah returned, her mood had improved.

Daniel stoked the fire and repositioned the iron skillet between two rocks. Josiah hunkered down beside him with a fork and tended the bacon. Daniel added fresh snow to the sticky muck of beans and put them back over the flame, though Elizabeth doubted that would help the burned taste. Then he started mixing the corn bread.

She tried to catch his gaze and failed. "I'm sorry, Daniel. I should've told you I can't cook. I just didn't want anything to interfere with—"

"With my saying yes to taking you." He looked at her, and the disappointment in his gaze was numbing.

Nodding, she lowered her chin.

He whipped the batter. "I thought you were finally being truthful about everything. At least that's what you told me . . . told *us*," he added more softly. "Or was that a lie too?"

His reproach seared her conscience. Her eyes watered. "I'm sorry. It just seemed like such a small thing at the time." As soon as she said it, she wished she could take it back. It made it sound like small lies were all right. Which they weren't, but she'd treated them as if they were. A tiny lie here to smooth things over with someone. Or a half truth there in order for things to work out in a way that was best for everyone. She'd even done that in her writing, in her E.G. Brenton column. Tweaking facts to make them more interesting, to capture the attention of readers. Wendell Goldberg had taught her well.

The blade of truth sliced through her—so delicate, yet so painful—and she got a glimpse of what she must look like to the men on the other side of the fire. And she didn't like what she saw.

They ate dinner—scorched beans, crisply fried bacon, and golden baked corn bread so delicious it melted on her tongue. Yet it sat like ash in her stomach. Daniel and Josiah talked about the trip ahead and traded stories of nights they'd spent in caves. She listened but didn't have anything to contribute.

When it came time for bed, she looked around for a place to relieve herself, but privacy was almost nonexistent. When Daniel and Josiah went to check on the horses one last time, she braved the darkness of the cave and prayed the men wouldn't return too soon— and that nothing was waiting for her in the shadows.

Next, it came time to change clothes, and she realized it was useless. What was she going to change into? Her gown? She would freeze. She gathered her blankets from the pile to make a pallet next to the fire. Josiah did likewise. Then he took the medicine Dr. Brookston had prescribed and was asleep almost before she had her pallet arranged. He had his fur draped over him and she stared at the other one against the wall. Daniel would be using it, so she wasn't about to ask for it. That would mean admitting defeat yet again in that she hadn't packed correctly. Which she hadn't.

Beau found a spot on Josiah's fur blanket and nestled against him. Josiah didn't move.

She buttoned up her coat, put on her gloves and scarf, and lay down on her pallet, her back to the fire and to Daniel, who had returned from gathering more kindling outside. She cradled her head and stared into the darkness. Silent tears slid across the bridge of her nose, and the crackle of flames against wet wood echoed in the cave. It struck her as a singularly lonely sound, and she curled up tighter.

Daniel's movements quieted. She waited, figuring he was asleep.

Her back was somewhat warm, but her front side was frozen. She turned over and found him lying on his side, staring at her. She kept her eyes on the flames and curled up again, pulling her expensive but nearly worthless blankets up around her chin.

"The recipe book you have," he whispered. "What's in it?"

She watched a persistent flame eat its way through a frozen branch, lick by fiery lick. "Formulas for chemicals I use in developing photographs."

He laughed softly. "Makes more sense now."

She didn't share his humor. A question surfaced, and it was one she wanted answered. "Why did you agree to take me on this trip?"

He didn't blink. "Because I want you to see this land, this territory. I want you to feel it inside you, Elizabeth, so that it's not just something you take pictures of, but something you care about."

She stared at him for the longest time, disquieted by the unexpected response and yet understanding it. Already, she'd begun to feel what he was describing; she simply hadn't thought of a way to put it into words. Which didn't boost her confidence in herself as a journalist.

"Are you warm enough?"

Sick of deceit, no matter how thinly veiled, she refrained from nodding. "I'll be fine."

"Under normal circumstances, I wouldn't suggest this, but . . . would you like to share my bearskin? From the looks of things, I'm betting it's warmer than what you've got."

So cold, she considered it for a moment. He was fully clothed, as she was, but it still didn't seem right. She shook her head.

He rose and came to where she lay. "I'd give it to you, but then I'd freeze and who'd get you to Mesa Verde?"

Without asking, he lay down behind her and drew the fur over them both. Lying on her side, facing the fire, she didn't offer argument. And within moments, the warmth, both from the bearskin and from him, seeped through her clothes to her skin, and she shivered as it worked its way into her muscles and eased their trembling.

"Thank you," she whispered, still turned away from him, facing the fire. "Will you be warm enough back there?"

He didn't answer for a second. "I'm plenty warm—believe me."

He shifted behind her. "About dinner . . ." His voice was close. "I know how to cook, and so does Josiah, so it's not that huge of a bother."

"It is to me."

"I can tell, and I appreciate that." He touched her shoulder. "That's why I want you to know it'll be all right."

Tears swelled in her throat. "I can learn."

"I know you can. I plan on teaching you."

She laughed softly and turned over onto her back. He was on his side, looking at her, and the desire for him she'd felt earlier in the day returned. In the darkness and relative privacy, with Josiah asleep, images of what it would be like to be intimate with Daniel became even more vivid. She was no novice—she'd been kissed before. Twice, in fact. And by two different men. The second time, the shared embrace had been quite passionate and had lasted for at least ten seconds. Maybe longer. But she'd never wanted to be close to any man as she wanted to be close to Daniel Ranslett. The way he looked at her now made her more aware of being a woman. And made her grateful she was one.

He reached out and touched her cheek, and with gentleness that spoke deeper than words, he slowly traced the curve of her jaw. His focus went to her mouth and warmth spread through her.

Abruptly, he withdrew his hand and turned onto his back.

Wishing he hadn't moved away, she stared at his profile in the burnished glow of firelight. She didn't know when she'd first started to care so deeply for him, but she knew that at whatever that point had been, she was way past it now. When the time came for her to return to Washington, either with success or in failure, she had a feeling it would mean leaving behind someone she'd been waiting for all her life, and had begun to think might never come.

"We leave at sunup, Elizabeth." He didn't look at her. "We best get some sleep."

Facing him, she curled onto her side. "You'd have a better chance at sleep if you'd close your eyes."

"I'd have a better chance at sleep if you'd turn back the other way." The tiniest smile edged one corner of his mouth. "Please . . ."

Grinning, and taking her time, she did as he asked.

31

Daniel awakened during the night and checked the horses. The snow had stopped and the wind had died. Beau trailed his steps and only lay down again once Daniel added more wood to the fire. The dog knew the routine, and it didn't hurt Daniel's feelings that Beau sought Josiah's blanket again. Especially when he thought of what waited beneath his own.

He lay down beside Elizabeth and pulled the bearskin up, smiling to himself at the irony. He'd never known a woman, not in the biblical sense, and now here he was sharing a bed with one, except not really. It hadn't taken him as long as he'd thought to get to sleep. Not because he hadn't been tempted but because he was plain exhausted.

He closed his eyes, not daring to look at her beside him, or to dwell on those curls that glowed like copper in the firelight. Unbidden, the image of her without her corset appeared in his mind again, as it had last night as he'd touched her face, and he put an arm over his eyes in hopes of dispelling it. He finally turned to face away from her and attempted to redirect his thoughts. He started calculating how far they could travel each day if milder weather set in. He factored that in with when she needed to be back to Timber Ridge in order to mail her pictures of the cliff dwellings to Washington. It would mean a hastened trip, but they could do it.

The image of her still lingered.

So he started composing a letter in his mind; one he would send to Congress if she agreed to help him in his endeavor by supplying pictures of the territory. If Congress could only see this land, Mesa Verde in particular, they would understand and agree that it needed protection from individuals and companies who sought to exploit it. The possibility of success renewed his hope, and after penning the letter four times in his mind, sleep finally came.

He awakened again sometime later and rose on one elbow. Faint light from a gray dawn filtered in through the mouth of the cave. He needed to get up. He looked down at Elizabeth sleeping beside him and ached to touch her again, knowing he couldn't. She was so beauti—

"Mornin', Mr. Ranslett, sir."

Daniel's pulse shot up. Josiah was awake and staring straight at him. At them both.

Daniel easily read his thoughts and shook his head. "She got cold. I shared my bearskin with her . . . and that's all." How odd it felt to be explaining himself to a Negro, and yet he felt the need to.

Josiah didn't say anything for a minute, then finally nodded. But he didn't go back to sleep. And Daniel still felt his watchful eye when he returned from feeding and watering the horses a while later.

Elizabeth was awake and boiling water in a pot, apparently for her tea. She wore a scowl around her eyes.

Daniel squatted down beside her and added more wood to the fire. "Good morning."

"Morning, Daniel." Her smile resembled an afterthought, and she rubbed her temples.

"Did you sleep well?"

She glanced briefly at Josiah. "Yes, I did. Thank you."

"How're you feeling?"

She winced. "Well enough, except for this headache. The tea always helps."

He hadn't thought anything about her drinking the tea, at first. But as he'd been with her in recent days and saw her drinking it morning, noon, and night, he'd begun to wonder. It wasn't the tea that concerned him so much—his mother had adhered to herbal remedies—but rather what Elizabeth added to it that concerned him.

When she finished adding the syrup to her cup, he motioned to the bottle in her hand. "What's that you're putting in there?"

"Something my doctor recommended. It's for my lungs."

He nodded, not doubting that. He just wondered what was in it. "May I see it?"

Her brow creased. She handed it to him.

He turned the bottle over and read the brief description on the back, aware of Josiah watching them. The bottle was almost empty. He thought he remembered her opening this one at Rachel's house, just two days ago. "Mrs. Winslow's Soothing Syrup . . . for children?"

She took the bottle from him. "Like I said, it helps my breathing."

"I haven't noticed you having any problems breathing."

Her look was almost comical. She dangled the bottle in front of him. "And you wonder why?"

He stood, deciding to let it go. She was a grown woman and could make up her own mind. And would, regardless of what he said.

As they packed and loaded the horses, Josiah remained solemn, quiet, and watchful. Daniel felt like a cowed youth, as though Elizabeth's father were there, observing his every move.

Drifts on the trail were deep in places, but there was little wind and the snowfall had ceased. The mountains were shrouded in white, all glistening ice and sparkle. He occasionally glanced back at Elizabeth, knowing she wished for her camera. He wished she had it too so she could take some photographs for him.

They stopped midday for lunch and made a fire. They were making good time and the sun was out, warming the temperature. They had another pass to cross today, a shorter one, and then the next two or three days would be easier traveling. Josiah looked weary to the bone and only picked at the corn bread and bacon left from last night's dinner. Elizabeth, on the other hand, had talked most of the morning and was having her second cup of tea, emptying the last of the bottle's contents.

Daniel refilled Josiah's tin with coffee. "You feeling all right?"

Josiah took a breath in and let it out as he spoke. "Yes, sir. I doin' fine. Just a mite weary." He pulled the fur tighter around his chest and stood. "I need to excuse myself for a minute, but I can keep ridin'. Don't be thinkin' I can't." He walked behind a thick stand of evergreen.

With Elizabeth's help, Daniel doused the fire, cleaned the lunch dishes, and repacked the supplies. From a satchel strapped to one of the packhorses, he withdrew a tin of peppermint and offered her a stick. She accepted. He broke another in half and tossed it to Beau, who chomped it in two bites. He saved one stick out for Josiah, then put the tin away, and as he did, a note sticking out drew his attention.

Recognizing it, he handed it to her. "I meant to give this to you a couple of days ago. I stuck it in here and forgot about it."

She took the note from him, and as she read it, she smiled.

The Tucker children had given it to him the day he'd been at their house. It was a letter thanking Elizabeth for the photograph she'd taken of them. They'd each signed their names, which took up nearly half the page, and someone had drawn a little squirrel in the bottom corner.

She pointed to the squirrel. "Do you think he's laughing? Or just smiling?"

Daniel leaned closer to get a better look. "Actually . . . I think he's choking."

She giggled and tried to punch him in the arm, but he caught her hand—the one she'd burned last night—and held it. Then, on a whim, he brought it to his lips and kissed it. Once, twice. He'd never seen a woman go from laughter to shyness so quickly. He heard a twig snap and gave her hand a brief squeeze before letting go. No need in giving Josiah Birch something else to worry about.

Later that afternoon, Daniel led the way through the second pass with Elizabeth and Josiah following. It wasn't nearly as narrow or steep as the first one, but there was a drop-off on one side to a canyon below, so he kept toward the mountainside to be safe. They were nearly through the pass when he noticed his horse's ears prick. The mare whinnied and one of the packhorses reared up. Beau barked from his pouch on the side.

"Quiet, Beau . . ." Daniel searched the ridge and boulders above but saw nothing. Trusting the horse's instincts, he reined in, gripped the tethers to the packhorses with one hand, and reached for his rifle with the other. He released the safety lever with his thumb—and saw it.

From Elizabeth's soft gasp, so did she.

A black bear sauntered out onto the trail, no more than twenty feet away, and stopped. From the looks of him he was still a cub, but he was a large one. Large enough, Daniel hoped, to have left his mama behind. The cub tested his lungs and pawed the snow.

To the left, about ten feet beyond him, a stand of evergreens swayed.

Daniel gauged the shelves of snow overhanging the cliff above and knew that shooting would be a last resort.

"Should we turn around?" Elizabeth whispered.

He shook his head. The trail was too narrow. There wasn't enough time, and he couldn't risk their getting too close to the edge with the snow drifts. The mother bear emerged onto the trail, saw them, and let out a roar. Daniel prayed she and her baby had eaten recently, but from the way she turned to face him and ducked her head low, he doubted it.

She charged.

He dropped the reins to the packhorses and stood in the saddle, taking aim. He would only get one shot.

32

The mother bear dropped. The cub shrieked and ran. And the mountain rumbled.

Daniel looked behind him and saw Elizabeth prodding her mount forward. With surprising agility, she grabbed hold of the reins to the first packhorse while the other took off in the opposite direction. Josiah strained for the bridle as the second animal passed him but missed.

Daniel eyed the snow shelf above them. It started to shift. "Move out!"

With the bear sprawled dead in the trail, there wasn't enough room for him to let Elizabeth or Josiah pass him first. He kicked his horse hard and prayed they followed close behind. He cleared the pass and turned back sharp to check.

Elizabeth was nearly clear when the packhorse spooked and strained against her. Thankfully she didn't fall off. Daniel yelled for her to leave the animal just as Josiah kicked it hard from behind and the horse took off. Daniel tried to grab the reins as the horse passed, but couldn't. He could track him later. Elizabeth cleared the pass with Josiah just as a deafening crack sounded.

The first snow shelf gave way.

Daniel led them farther down the trail and reined in a safe distance away. Breathless, they all stared at each other for a moment before looking back. Snow crystals shimmered in the afternoon sun and an eerie calm gradually settled back over the mountain.

"Are either of you hurt?"

Josiah and Elizabeth shook their heads.

"You done got that bear, sir, right between the eyes. She dropped before she knowed she was dead."

Elizabeth's laughter came out high-pitched and stilted. "I was just praying you wouldn't miss."

Daniel shuddered inside thinking of how differently things could have turned out. "You both did well. Real well." He glanced behind him. "I need to find that packhorse and see what supplies we have left."

Josiah motioned. "That other one make it out, sir?"

Daniel nodded. "But I'm afraid he took most of our provisions with him."

An hour later, Daniel returned to camp with the horse. As he'd suspected, the majority of their food stores were gone, but at least they had their second bearskin, some coffee, and enough hardtack and jerky to get them by for a couple of days, giving him time to hunt. He'd learned young not to pack all the food on one animal.

Josiah had built a fire, and it burned strong and hot, giving off little smoke. Josiah sat huddled beside it with his fur wrapped close about his broad shoulders, shivering. His brow glistened with sweat. Elizabeth pressed a cloth against his forehead and gave Daniel a look.

Daniel put a hand on his shoulder. "How long have you had fever?"

"Since sometime this mornin', sir. But I be fine. I can ride. I won't slow you down none."

"I'm not worried about you slowing us down, Josiah. Where do you hurt?"

"All over, sir."

Elizabeth knelt beside him. "Why didn't you say something earlier?"

Josiah closed his eyes. "No need to, ma'am. Nothin' to be done. Just need to let this work its way outta me."

Daniel calculated where they were. No cave that he knew of for another seven miles or so, and it would be dark soon. The sky was clear blue, which meant the temperatures would be bitter, but at least there was no snow or wind, for now. "We'll camp here for the night. Josiah, you get some rest."

Saying nothing, Josiah lay down, cocooned in the bearskin.

It wasn't until Elizabeth started searching the packs, that Daniel realized what else was missing. She looked at him, then quickly looked away again.

He nodded to her saddlebags. "Do you have any more with you?"

"I meant to get another bottle out at lunch, but I forgot." She mustered a brave look. "I think you said we wouldn't pass another settlement for . . . two weeks. Is that right?" The way she asked it, she already knew his answer.

"And it'll just be a mining camp. They don't carry much in the way of medicine."

She said nothing, and he watched her bravery slip a notch.

She boiled a piece of jerky in melted snow and spoon-fed the weak broth to Josiah, who ate little before falling back into a restless sleep.

Daniel watched her throughout the evening, waiting for the signs, praying he was wrong. But by the time she lay down for the night, he knew he wasn't.

The hot and cold flashes started, mild at first, followed by stomach cramps during the night and the muscle spasms he remembered so well. What little she'd eaten for dinner, her body rejected, and he held her as she alternately shook and perspired. He also checked on Josiah, who was burning up. Cold compresses helped, but the man needed a doctor.

Dawn came, and a wheezing started deep in Elizabeth's lungs and slowly grew more pronounced. Finally, midmorning, exhaustion claimed her.

Just before noon, she stirred. "Am I . . . going to die?" she whispered.

He stroked her hair and kissed her forehead. "No, you're not going to die." But before her ordeal was through, she would wish she could. "It's going to be hard, but you can do it. I'll be here to help you."

Her legs jerked beneath the bearskin, and she pulled them up against her chest. "Did you . . . know?" Her teeth chattered but not from the cold.

Her question was like a hot poker to his gut. He clenched his jaw. "I suspected it. But I wasn't sure." She wrapped her arms around her abdomen and closed her eyes.

By late afternoon, Daniel knew he had no choice. He awakened them both. "We've got to find help. I can't leave you here, so you're both going to have to ride." He decided not to tell them how far they might need to travel. In their state, it would feel like a death sentence.

They broke camp and he helped Josiah onto his horse.

Josiah bent forward, barely holding on to the reins. "My bell . . . I gots to get to . . . my bell . . ."

Daniel had no idea what he was talking about. "Don't you worry about the bell. I'll get it for you."

Josiah nodded, seeming comforted.

Daniel brought his own horse around and lifted Elizabeth into the saddle, unable to tell whether she understood what was happening or not. He climbed up behind her and pulled her against him. She didn't fight anything he did.

Travel was slow, and he kept peering through the trees on the right side of the trail, hoping and praying he was remembering it correctly. And that it was still there. He kept offering the canteen to Elizabeth and stopped to make sure Josiah was drinking as well. It was near dusk when he heard it.

A hawk's screech.

He reined in and looked up. No hawk in sight. The weight inside his chest eased a fraction.

He returned the call, and Makya stepped into a clearing a ways down the path. The Ute stretched out his arm in greeting and started toward him.

"Wait!" Daniel raised his hand, and Makya paused. "Sickness is with me, friend. I come for medicine, and food if you can spare it. I don't mean to bring harm to your camp."

Makya stared. "Do you have the sickness?"

"No, but the dark man does. The woman is unwell, but it's because of white man's medicine, not a sickness."

"I will see them." Makya started toward them.

Daniel lowered Elizabeth into Makya's arms and he laid her on the ground. She groaned and held her stomach as Makya felt her head and throat, then studied her eyes and listened to her chest.

"She has a poison inside." It was more of a statement than a question.

Daniel nodded, helping Josiah off his horse. "Yes, she does. The same poison I told you about that I had years ago."

Josiah's legs buckled, and it was all Daniel could do to support the man's weight. He was heavier than he looked, and his clothes were soaked with sweat. Daniel laid him down and covered him with the fur.

Makya knelt beside him. "He smells bitter. Like death waits to visit."

"Do your people have medicine to help him?"

Makya's answer came slow. "The woman, we can help. The man, I do not know. I will go before you. Wait until I return."

Daniel wanted to tell him to hurry, but there was no need. Makya ran.

33

Sometime during the night, the eldest of Makya's four wives delivered a clay pot with something tangy and sweet smoldering inside it, similar to burning pine needles. The warm air in the tepee grew moist and smoky, and Daniel felt the effects deep inside his lungs. Elizabeth would have too, if she were awake.

He lay beside her in the firelight, listening to her restless sleep and knowing what she was going through. Earlier, the shaman had insisted she drink a dark-colored concoction. Makya explained that the mixture would bring healing to her body. From her reaction, the potion had been none too pleasant tasting, and apparently had a sedating effect, because she'd been asleep ever since.

Makya's eldest wife returned at first light, and Daniel went to check on Josiah. He was located in a tepee pitched farther from camp, one Daniel figured was used in cases of quarantine. The shaman was there when Daniel arrived and Josiah was awake, his eyes wide and watchful of the Ute doctor, his body still racked with fever.

Daniel stood where Josiah could see him, not wanting to interrupt whatever was underway. Beadwork and bunches of dried herbs hung from the sloped ceiling, and the shaman, chanting something, crushed a green leafy plant on a flat stone, then sprinkled the pieces into a cup of liquid and swirled it over the flame. When offered, Josiah drank it without question, just as Daniel would have done.

Once the doctor left, Daniel moved closer.

"Mr. Ranslett . . . glad to see you again, sir. H-how's Miz Westbrook?"

Daniel sat beside him, touched by what his question revealed. "She's resting. She had a rough night and has some rough days still ahead, but she'll be all right."

"What's in that bottle that . . . done her such harm, sir?"

"Morphine, in a syrup, that's supposed to calm the nerves. Her doctor prescribed it, and she's been using it for months. Once you start taking it, your body grows accustomed to it and wants more. When you refuse to oblige, your body rebels. I know because I relied on it for nearly two years, after I was wounded in the war. A friend saw what I was doing to myself and helped me stop. I'm sure I would've died if he hadn't."

"That friend be the sheriff, sir?"

Daniel smiled, nodding. "McPherson and I grew up together."

"I thought I seen a kinship between you two, sir."

Daniel removed the cloth from Josiah's forehead and soaked it afresh in a basin of water. "How are you feeling?"

"Like I'm 'bout to die, but heaven ain't sure they's ready for me yet." Josiah sighed when Daniel reapplied the damp cloth. "That feels good, sir. Thank you. I just so tired . . . my body feels heavy, sir. Like I'm 'bout to sink through the earth."

Daniel watched him, wishing he could do more. "You kept saying something about a bell earlier. Do you remember?"

Acknowledgment showed in Josiah's face. "I don't remember sayin' it, but I ain't surprised I did."

Daniel waited, figuring he would say more if he wanted to.

"You see my clothes anywhere, sir?"

Accepting the turn in conversation, Daniel looked around. He spotted some things set to one side of the tepee and recognized the leather pouch he'd picked up the night he found Josiah by the stream. "I see what was in your pockets, but I'm guessing your clothes are gone."

"You see a pouch, sir?"

"Yes . . ." He rose to get it and pressed it into Josiah's hand.

"Thank you, sir." Josiah's chin trembled, and several moments passed before he spoke again. "You read any of what's in here, Mr. Ranslett?"

Having been tempted to the night he'd first found it, Daniel was glad now that he could answer truthfully. "No, I haven't."

Josiah held it out. "Take it."

Daniel hesitated.

"Take it, sir, please. And you reads it." Josiah nudged it forward. "When a man gets close to dyin' . . . it be a comfort to have a body near who understands what his life was like. Leastwise a little. Makes him feel less like he's by hisself."

Humbled, Daniel took the pouch.

"You keep it and show it to Miz Westbrook, when she's able. And whatever comes, if you need to . . . leave me behind, sir, I understand. Miz Westbrook, she an important woman. She gots her schedule to keep."

"Miss Westbrook's schedule is no longer her own, Josiah. And we're not leaving without you—she wouldn't have it."

A brief smile touched Josiah's mouth. "I sure would like to see them caves she talked about, sir." He shivered. "Seein' things from long ago still standin' . . . gives me hope somehow."

"I feel the very same way, Josiah. You just concentrate on getting well, and I give you my word, I'll get you there to see them."

Over the next three days, as Daniel alternated between caring for Elizabeth and Josiah, he read the frayed pages tucked inside the leather pouch, and quickly began to feel like an intruder. He'd even begun to hear the faintest inaudible echo of a woman's voice as he read. The voice of the woman who had penned the words—only one woman, in his estimation, whose voice was penetrating, fragile with pain, and whose story he wasn't at all sure he wanted to know.

Judging from the journal's personal nature, whoever had written it had probably assumed the thoughts therein would remain private, and with good reason. The handwriting was slow to read and difficult to decipher, and the words were written more from how they sounded rather than with the proper spelling. No dates were given, no names, and the pages weren't in any identifiable order.

But telling by the tattered edges, Josiah had read them often.

Elizabeth stirred on the pallet beside him. Her eyes fluttered open. Daniel laid aside the page he'd been reading and held a cup of water to her lips. She drank the cup dry.

"You want some more?"

She shook her head, wincing. "I want my head . . . to stop pounding." Her voice was hoarse from disuse.

He caressed her forehead. "It will . . . soon. And if it helps any, you're through the worst of it now."

Skepticism knit her brow. "It doesn't feel like it."

"I promise, you are. In fact, I'm so sure of it"—he watched her—"that I'm willing to strike hands on it."

She looked at him. Her eyes narrowed. "I thought you said you'd never strike hands with a woman."

He shrugged. "I did. But . . . people change." He offered his hand.

She stared for a second, then reached out. Her grip was weak, and he kept the exchange gentle, yet firm enough to make it real. She held on for longer than necessary, and a protectiveness rose inside him.

He spoon-fed her some lukewarm broth, and she gradually slipped back into sleep.

He picked up the journal page he'd laid aside, finished reading it, then pulled the next sheet from the pouch. His gaze fell upon the sentence at the top, and a tide of trespassing—and injustice—washed through him.

> i iz maed to stande neked in frunt of him. he did not tuch me at furst. he jus luk at me wit thos eyez thae bern my sken. i tri not to shak but canot hol bak frum it. i pritende u iz tuching me but u wud not be ruf. i clen misef when he dun. i wan to tel u but he sade he kil u if i do.

Daniel winced at the scene forming in his mind. Disgust curdled the pit of his stomach. He smoothed a finger over the page where deep scratches from the quill had indented the paper, and only then did he notice that this particular page appeared different from the others he'd read so far.

It was nicer paper, heavier by the feel of it, a stationery of some sort. But absent of any embossment. He thumbed through the remaining pages and saw a few more sheets like it. He read on. . . .

> peple in tha haus tel me he sint u a wey. it heps sum to no thaet but it stil herts. u r mi hom. i wil nevr b hom agin az longe az u r gon. i mis u. i luk fer u evre dae. wer did u go. if i canot git a wey from heer i think i will di. i prae i will di.

He turned the page sideways and read what was written in the margin.

> this wuz a gud dae. he did not sho hemsef. thae tel mee he is gon for sum tiem an i iz hapie for it. the ladi of tha hous cal me to hr and ast if i wont to lern to rite. she seam hapie to lern i no sum aredi. the ladi iz nis. i liek hr.

Daniel stared at the words and felt his spirits lift. He didn't even know this woman, and yet was glad she'd had a good day, after so many bad ones. She was a slave—that much was clear. And what she revealed on these pages shed a painful light on another side of a world he'd once thought he'd known.

> i woek screemin. u iz stil gon. i luk fer u evre dae but du not se u. he wuz heer agin. he see me to an i node wat wuz in his minde. he tok me to tha wuds. latr i ast god wy he evr maed me. but he do not anser. i thenk he terns his hed bcuz it herts him to se. but he shud not tern his hed. he maed us an he shud fx us.

The words blurred. Daniel blinked, and the tear narrowly missed the page. It took him a moment before he could continue.

The next page was more crinkled, and some of the words were smudged.

> i iz wit chile. i iz sik at first dae but beter az it gos. i hv not tole u yet. bcuz i am not shur it iz yur sed. i prae it iz or prae the chile diez insied me. The ladi of the hous cam an braut presnz todae. she got pritty eyez. i do not thenk she nos wat hr huzbend do to me.

Anger built inside Daniel swift and hot. He realized he was gripping the page and laid it against his thigh to rub out the crinkles, but the paper tore at the corner.

By the time he finished reading the last letter in the pouch, he thought he knew who the woman was in relation to Josiah, and wondered—if she was still alive—if she had ever given birth to the child.

———

Elizabeth awakened, feeling depleted in every way she could imagine. She wasn't hungry, but her body craved something down deep, and she knew what it wanted. She tried to rise up, but pain shot across her forehead, forcing her back down.

"Hey there, take it easy." Daniel appeared over her and she instinctively reached for him. His hands were warm, his grip solid. "They brought you some breakfast, if you're hungry."

Wanting to fill the voracious void inside her with something, she nodded and ate without asking what it was. "How's Josiah doing?"

Daniel smiled. "He's better. He got up and walked around yesterday. The Ute are amazed by him. Most of them have never seen a Negro before, and especially not a man like him."

The Ute men and women she'd seen in recent days were friendly people, always smiling, and they were beautiful with their dark skin, hair, and eyes. She wished again for her camera in order to capture this world that was relatively unknown by *Chronicle* readers.

The consistency of the porridge-like substance was peculiar. It tasted unlike anything she'd had before, but she ate it with gratitude. She teared up thinking of that day at the Tuckers' and how she'd responded to their generosity. She finished chewing and swallowed. "It's not squirrel, but I guess it'll do."

"Who knows . . . It may be squirrel all ground up. I didn't ask." He winked. "But I ate some first, so I know it's all right."

"How long have we been here?"

Daniel dipped the wooden spoon in the bowl. "A week so far. As soon as you get your strength back, maybe in a couple more days, we'll head out."

A week . . . So much time lost. And yet she was so grateful. Every time she'd opened her eyes, he'd been there.

"Thank you, Daniel, again . . . for taking care of me. And for not leaving me behind, or threatening to."

He leaned down and kissed her forehead. "Let's just say I've got a vested interest in you now, Miss Westbrook."

She stopped midchew, his statement resurrecting old suspicions. She swallowed, thinking of men in the past who'd used her to get to her father. "A vested interest?"

"Well, sure . . ." He tugged a curl. "Who else is going to cook for me all the way out here?"

Sighing, she smiled, realizing her suspicions were unfounded.

If there was one man who wasn't after a connection with her father, who didn't care in the least, it was Daniel Ranslett.

—

The view from the ridge was breathtaking. The midday sun angled across the southernmost range of the snowcapped Rocky Mountains and filtered through the pungent forest of evergreen surrounding them. For the hundredth time, Elizabeth wished she had her camera along, wanting to capture a portion of this beauty and share it with others.

She blinked.

For the first time she could remember, her initial thought in relation to photographs hadn't been of Wendell Goldberg or the *Chronicle.* Or even the *Timber Ridge Reporter.* Drayton Turner came to mind and she pushed him out again, wanting as much distance between her and that man as possible. Thinking of him made her wish for her derringer, which she'd lost in the avalanche.

"You about ready?" Daniel walked up beside her. "We need to move on. Rain's coming in, and I'd prefer not to sleep out in it tonight if it can be helped."

"I never thought I'd say it, but I'd be thrilled to sleep in a cave tonight."

"Josiah and I will even let you make the smoosh."

She laughed. "Oh, please, not that again." The corn-bread batter drizzled into hot bacon grease and fried up crisp had been good the first twenty-something times, but she was getting tired of it. And when *she'd* made it twice before, hers turned out so crunchy it nearly broke Josiah's teeth.

Daniel shrugged. "We eat what we've got. If we make good time, I might have a chance to go hunting before dark."

She practically ran for her horse, urging Josiah to do the same.

Josiah beat her into the saddle. "You move pretty quick-like when you're wantin' to, Miz Westbrook."

"When properly motivated by real food, I can do a lot of things."

Two weeks had passed since they'd left the Ute camp. She had asked Makya if they could stop again on their way back through, if there was time. He'd shown interest in learning more about her camera, which she had described to him, and she didn't want to leave the territory without capturing images of his people, of their ancient lifestyle. Makya had spoken with such reverence about the dwellings in the cliffs at Mesa Verde. It was sacred ground to them and many of their children had yet to see the caves. She promised to bring pictures on the return trip.

Josiah's strength had returned more quickly than had hers, and she could still taste the syrup burning a path down her throat. Sucking on Daniel's peppermint helped, as did realizing what her reliance on morphine had been doing to her. She didn't have Dr. Brookston to back her up, but she would swear that her lungs were stronger and that she could breathe more deeply without it.

A couple of hours down the path, they came to a fork in the trail and Daniel glanced back at her. "Which way is south, Elizabeth? If you're right, I'll make dinner. If not, you do."

"Heaven help us all," Josiah whispered behind her.

She laughed. Daniel was testing her, and she took time to study the sun's position along with the direction from which they'd been traveling—and had absolutely no idea. But she wasn't about to admit that. She had a fifty-fifty chance of being right. "The path to the right is south."

Daniel smiled and started toward the right. She felt a moment of triumph until he yanked his reins to the left at the very last minute. "Sorry, Miss Westbrook, but that'll lead us back across the pass we traveled a week ago."

She groaned. "Does this mean you're not going hunting?"

"This means that if I *do* go hunting, you have to cook whatever I bring back."

"Don't you worry none, ma'am, whatever he brings back, I help you with it."

She glanced behind her. "I can always count on you, Josiah."

"Yes, ma'am, you can. Long as you clean up your mess of dishes." His deep laughter encouraged theirs.

———

Elizabeth looked up to see Beau tromping toward her in the cave, with a very dead animal clutched between his teeth. Hearing Daniel's footsteps, she spoke so he could hear. "This is nice, but I think I liked the flowers better."

Grinning, he gave a short whistle, and Beau dropped the animal at her feet.

She picked the rabbit up by the ears. "What do I do with it now?"

"First you skin it—then you roast it."

She eyed it. "Can I do one or the other, but not both?"

Josiah reached around her. "I do the skinnin' for you, ma'am. You search for some sticks and strip the bark clean."

Without complaint, she walked outside to gather branches. It was the middle of May, and spring was finally coming to the high country, as Daniel called it. The temperatures were still on the cool side, especially at night, but nothing like when they'd first set out. Daniel told her it would be another three weeks before they reached Mesa Verde, maybe less with no mishaps.

She found sticks she thought would be appropriate and showed them to Daniel.

"I'm impressed." Using his knife, he showed her how to strip the bark from the branch. "Then you just take it like this and . . ."

He worked the rabbit, now skinned and cleaned, onto the skewer, and Elizabeth didn't even wince. Amazing how hunger could make a person less squeamish and picky.

After dinner, Daniel passed the peppermint tin, which was getting low on contents. She took a stick, broke a third off, and put the rest back. "How did you come to have such an affinity for this?"

Reminiscence shaded his smile. "My mother used to keep a tin of sugar sticks—that's what she called them—on top of the dining room hutch. Every so often she'd hide them from me and my brothers, but we'd find them." A mischievous grin tipped his mouth. "We always found them. She never said anything about the game we were playing. . . ." He reached up and fingered his stubbled jaw. "Not until the very end."

Elizabeth hadn't known they had this in common. "She's gone? Your mother?"

He nodded.

She wanted to ask more about his childhood, about his home, but the wistfulness in his expression kept her from it. As did the knowledge that any memories he might share of Tennessee, of the South, would no doubt conjure harsh ones for Josiah.

A hot spring was located not far from the cave, and they took turns bathing that evening. The warm water felt luxurious, and she washed her hair, twice, not even finding the smell bothersome.

As she lay down on her pallet that night, she noticed Josiah was still awake, which was unusual. Most often he was the first one asleep. He was reading something, and her mind went to the journal pages Daniel had given her to read at Josiah's bidding. Both she and Daniel had agreed not to push him to talk about it. Perhaps he regretted having given them to Daniel—having shared them under extreme circumstances.

But Josiah wasn't reading pages from the leather pouch. He was reading his Bible, and whatever passage he read was encouraging a wistful smile. She watched him, enjoying the expressions moving over his face, while thinking of her own Bible she'd left back in her room at the boardinghouse. She wished now that she'd brought it along. Moments passed, and Josiah finally laid the book aside and closed his eyes. Soon she heard his deep, rhythmic breathing, followed by Daniel's not long after.

But for her, sleep wouldn't come.

She added another log to the fire and brushed off her hands, seeing the small scar from the cut on her palm. She shook her head, recalling when Daniel had removed the sutures. It hadn't been pleasant, but at least she hadn't fainted.

She stretched out on her pallet again. Being here, on this journey, was the fulfillment of her dream. Or she hoped it would be. *"The biggest regrets we have in life, child, aren't the things we do. But the things we don't do."* Those words, spoken by Tillie on her deathbed, were what had finally spurred her to pursue her dream of being a journalist and a photographer. They'd also given her the courage to come west, and she hoped to make Tillie proud.

Thinking of Tillie brought thoughts of Josiah's life close again. She couldn't imagine what all he'd been through. Passages from the journal pages the woman had written played back to her at the most unexpected times. Like now. And having trespassed on such intimate thoughts, such intimate experiences—both those wretched and those precious—bound her to the woman in a way Elizabeth couldn't explain.

Cradling her head on her arms, she prayed God had heard the woman's desperate pleas all those years ago and had answered. Or still would, someday.

34

The mining town was just as Daniel described, filthy and not fitting for any decent woman. After passing some of its inhabitants on the outskirts and watching their reaction at seeing her, Elizabeth decided to stay with Josiah and let Daniel go on in alone. He seemed relieved at her decision.

From where she sat waiting, the mountain looked as though its belly had been gouged out and its insides strewn about with the least of care. Countless stumps remained where towering spruce and pine once ruled, and a sign posted by the stream warned not to drink the water. It was a sobering picture, and she couldn't help but imagine the mountain fifty years ago, or perhaps even a decade ago.

She wasn't sure how long the mining company had been in the area. But she knew with certainty that its presence had brought destruction. Riches too, perhaps, but at what price? She couldn't shake the unexplained sense of grieving inside her, or the image of the hotel Chilton Enterprises wanted to build. But that would be different. She'd seen their resorts, and they were magnificent. It would be a welcome addition to Timber Ridge.

By the time Daniel returned, she was ready to leave. He brought stores of cornmeal and flour to replenish the supplies the Ute people had given them, as well as coffee, a small bag of sugar, dried beans, and other sundry items. What once wouldn't have impressed her now seemed like a feast. Without the extra packhorse, they split the items among their individual saddlebags.

Next morning after breakfast, Daniel approached her, his hand outstretched. In his palm lay a box.

She looked up at him, suspicious, then glanced past him to Josiah, who was saddling the horses a ways down the creek. Apparently this was Daniel's doing alone. He took her hand in his, and for a second she thought he was going to kiss it as he had before.

Instead, he tucked the box into her palm. "I saw this yesterday and thought of you."

A gift? Her interest sparked. "What is it?"

"You have to open it to find out."

"But what's it for?"

He gave her a look and stepped closer. "Does a man have to have a reason to give a woman a gift?"

She giggled. "No, but usually there is one."

A grin tipped his mouth and warmth spread through her. "Just open the box, Elizabeth."

She did and felt a blush of humor. A compass. She ran a finger over the gold etched sides. "Daniel, it's beautiful. Thank you."

"It's so you'll know your way, no matter where you are."

She studied the compass, which happened to be pointing true north, and straight toward Daniel Ranslett. She smiled at the coincidence. "But will it help my cooking?"

"Doubtful. That needs more help than I can fit into a box."

She swatted his arm, then stood on tiptoe to kiss his cheek. He hadn't shaved in days, and the rough stubble of his jaw scratched her cheek in a pleasant way. She dared linger seconds longer than needed and started to draw back when his arms came around her. Their faces were close, their lips almost touching, and she felt the rise and fall of her chest against his. Would he? Oh, she wanted him to. . . . Maybe she should—

"I'm proud of you, Elizabeth."

The statement caught her off guard. She frowned, smiling. "Why?"

He cradled her face. "For a lot of reasons." His hand moved from her cheek down to her throat, and he traced a soft path with his thumb on the underside of her chin. "For coming out west on your lonesome—that took courage. For how you've done out here, with me. I thought you'd be complaining the whole way." His arm around her waist pulled her tighter against him. "But you haven't. You've held your own." His gaze slipped to her mouth. "And breakfast was delicious this morning."

If this man didn't kiss her soon . . . "My biscuits were too brown . . . on the bottoms."

"Your biscuits were perfect." His lips brushed hers, not a kiss, really, but the promise of one. "Bottoms and all."

"Mr. Ranslett?"

Elizabeth stepped back, as did Daniel, though he was slow to release her.

"Yes, Josiah?" Daniel's look said they would continue this later, and she hoped hers communicated the same.

"Horses are saddled, sir." Josiah's attention moved between them, a smile showing through his not-so-guarded expression.

"Thank you." Daniel picked up his rifle and slid it into the sheath on his back. "I guess we'd best be on our way, then."

"Yes, sir. I guess so. 'Less I be needin' to go saddle them horses again or maybe . . . gather more firewood."

With a scoundrel's grin, Daniel slipped his hat on. "I think we're warm enough, Josiah. No need to build another fire."

———

Daniel threw Beau a bone with a chunk of meat still on it. The dog grabbed it before it hit the dirt. "Three days, maybe less, and we'll be there."

Sitting across the fire from him, Elizabeth and Josiah exchanged grins, eating the roasted elk with fervor. Elizabeth licked her fingers, looking more like a girl in that moment than a woman. Though he knew she was all that and more.

"What?" She wiped her hands on a rag. "Do I have something on my mouth?" She dabbed at her lips.

The innocent gesture sent his thoughts down a path he sorely wished he could travel. His thoughts reeled quite often these days when it came to her, especially when she wore her hair down, like tonight. He took a long drink from his canteen. It was June, but the mountain water was still icy cold as he liked it. "It's just good to see you eat like that."

"Like what? A pig?"

"No, ma'am, like you enjoys it." Josiah spoke between bites. "A man likes to provide for a woman in his care." He winked at Daniel.

If Elizabeth caught Josiah's meaning, she didn't show it. But Daniel did, and he leveled a stare in Josiah's direction, which only encouraged Josiah's grin.

Elizabeth took another bite, more delicately this time, with her pinky extended. Daniel grabbed a clean bone and threw it at her. She easily ducked and it missed her. She launched it right back. He caught the bone midair, then tossed it to Beau, who added it to his collection.

"I can't eat another bite." Elizabeth laid her tin pan aside and drank from her canteen. "How far would you say that elk was from us today, when you shot it?"

Daniel lay down and cradled his hands beneath his head, considering the distance. A scant sprinkling of stars dotted the dusky sky above, brave souls daring the sun's fading glow in the west. "Probably seventeen hundred yards, give or take."

"That's a mile away!"

"Not quite, but almost."

Josiah rose and tore off another piece of meat. "How far was you from that bull elk that first day we seen you? That animal was already down by the time we heard your rifle, sir."

"I wasn't nearly that far. Maybe half a mile. And you didn't hear the shot first because the bullet of a Whitworth"—Daniel nodded toward the rifle—"travels faster than the sound of the report. It reaches the target before the sound does."

Elizabeth made a face. "That's a morbid thought. How did you learn to shoot from so far away?"

"Lots of practice. My father started taking me hunting with him when I was six. I brought home my first elk at seven."

"Have you ever come back without anything when you've gone hunting?"

Daniel smiled at her question. Benjamin had asked him something similar when the boy was just a tot. He still remembered the look of wonder in his youngest brother's eyes. "Sure. But it's been a while."

"Is that because game is so plentiful out here?" She cocked a brow in a flirty way that he liked. "Or are you just that good?"

"I know how to shoot, but it's more than that. You can't shoot what you can't track. And you can't track what isn't there. So the fact that this territory has lots of game helps. But that's changing real quick with all the people coming west, and all the mining companies and businesses tearing up the land."

He wondered whether the timing was right to bring up the letters he'd been writing to Congress. With what was transpiring between them, he didn't want to push, but she could help him present his case to Congress in a way no one else could—with photographs. And the connection with her father.

She didn't say anything, and he looked over to find her lying down. Josiah was too. Her legs were crossed beneath her skirt, and he figured she must be considering what he'd said because one booted foot was keeping a steady rhythm. She'd regained her full health and had thanked him more times than he could count for staying beside her during those grueling days when the morphine was leaving her system.

"With progress come challenges, Daniel, I'll grant you that. We just need to find that right balance and work to preserve what's here."

We, she'd said. That was a start. "I agree. But most companies out here don't care much about finding the right balance. When I first came west, herds of buffalo were plentiful. Not anymore. They've been hunted for their skins and sold to folks back east. I've seen the slaughter and the waste. Carcasses littering the plains, with meat that could have fed families through the winter just left behind to rot."

"When did you come out here, Daniel?"

It wasn't the turn in conversation he'd hoped for. "Back in the spring of sixty-six, after the war was over."

The chirrup of crickets blended with the wind in the aspens to create a harmony unique to these mountains. One he'd grown to appreciate.

"Your people hail from Franklin—that right, sir?" Josiah's deep voice cut the night.

"Yes, that's right. I was born and raised there." A nudging thought made Daniel wish he could see Josiah's face better in order to read him. "You ever lived in Franklin, Josiah?" He waited, praying the man would say no. It hadn't occurred to him until that moment that Josiah could have been owned by a neighboring plantation, or maybe even his own family's plantation.

"No, sir, I ain't never lived there."

Daniel let out his breath, then felt guilty over his relief. It mattered little where Josiah had been during those years, because wherever he'd been, he'd been a slave. Just like the woman in the journals.

"Was you in that battle, sir? The one in Franklin?"

"Is that where you got the scar on your back?" Elizabeth's voice came soft on the heels of Josiah's.

Daniel was glad for the darkness. Somehow it made answering their questions easier. "I was in the battle at Franklin, but I got the scar from Chickamauga."

"A man I knowed, he told me about that night in Franklin, sir.

He was there, saw it with his own eyes. Said it looked like the death angel come to reap his last harvest. He told me about that yell you Rebs made too. Said it liked to scare the daylights outta him."

The fire's crackle devoured the silence, and Daniel waited for the tightness in his throat to lessen. As it did, the sounds and images from years past piled on top of one another, just like the dead bodies had.

"What does it sound like, Daniel? The rebel yell . . ."

Daniel found it difficult to speak, and impossible to answer her question. He never wanted to hear that sound again, yet knew he'd carry it inside himself forever.

"I ain't never heard it, ma'am, but what was told to me was that if you heard it and said you wasn't scared, then you's lying. Cuz hearin' it would strip the courage clean outta your backbone."

"What happened that night . . . during the battle?"

Again, Elizabeth's question surprised him. He didn't know where to begin, and didn't want to. He heard her rise up, and he looked over.

She sat with her legs pulled up against her chest and her arms wrapped tight around her knees. Bathed in firelight, her expression held a curiosity that rankled him. Why was it that folks who hadn't been to battle always wanted to hear what it was like, while those who had been would do anything to forget.

"A lot of men died, Elizabeth. That's what happened! They were slaughtered one after the other." Callousness hardened his voice, a tone she didn't deserve.

She drew in a breath. "I only asked because . . ." She looked away.

"Cuz you done lost someone there. Someone you loved, ma'am?"

Elizabeth nodded, her eyes glistening.

"I'm sorry, Elizabeth." Daniel sat up and waited for her to look at him. "I spoke out of turn. But it's a night I don't welcome recollecting. I'd wipe it clean from my memory if I could." He bowed his head. "Men of eighty years lay dead beside boys of thirteen—and younger—the end of life and the beginning, brought to such an unnatural close. Bodies were piled up so high that when the sun rose that next morning we found men who had died where they stood because there was no place for them to fall. And the earth . . ." He closed his eyes and saw it again, heard the sounds. "The ground was drenched with blood. Our boots, of those who had them, were soaked with it."

He lifted his head, wondering if somehow Benjamin could hear him. "My unit arrived south of Franklin the afternoon before and camped on the outskirts. Some of the younger boys who were from around there, whose homes weren't far away, they snuck away for a few hours to see their families. It was against orders, but those of us who knew about it didn't say anything. A lot of them hadn't seen their folks since they'd signed up to fight. All the boys were back before dawn that morning . . . and most were dead by the next.

"The battle started in the afternoon, around four. Night fell fast and it was filled with the sound of bullets. Your heart couldn't take a beat one second but what you wondered whether it would still be working the next." His eyes burned. "It was cold, and dark. Men who'd been cut down right off were lying on the field, hundreds of them. Those still alive were moaning, calling out for someone to help them. Our lines kept pushing forward up the hill, one after another. One line would fall and the next would come right up behind them . . . taking up the charge. And the North just kept gunning us down.

"We were waiting our turn to go, and I kept hearing a sound . . . one I couldn't reckon with. I asked the fella next to me, and he said it was just them—" He caught himself. "Them Yankee guns. But it didn't sound right somehow." A weight settled in the center of Daniel's chest, threatening his composure. "When it came my unit's turn, we formed our line, and I looked uphill. . . ." He shuddered, remembering. "I'd hunted there since I was a boy, so I knew the area well. The Federals had formed caisson tracks, and their cannons lit up the night. Everything would go bright as day one moment, then pitch dark the next. Watching the men push uphill before us—that's when I realized what the sound was. But I . . . I still couldn't make sense of it in my head." He gritted his teeth to stem the tears. "What I heard wasn't gunfire like the fella had told me. It was the sound of bones snapping. As the men climbed the hill . . . they were treading over the bodies of their brothers and fathers and friends."

Daniel wiped his face, fixing his attention on the flames. "Our unit was ordered forward, and that's when I saw him." He took a shredded breath. "My little brother was on the tail end of the formation. Benjamin," he whispered.

Oh, God, would you take away this hurt. I don't want to live "dying" on that battlefield for the rest of my life.

"Word from one of the boys who'd gone home the night before had reached my family, so they knew I was there. Benjamin was carrying one of my old rifles. It was almost bigger than he was. I called out to him, but he didn't hear me. I broke formation and I ran. Ran as fast as I could down that line. I couldn't hear anything—not the bullets, not the bones crunching, not anything—only the sound of my brother's name." He swallowed. "A bullet hit him right before I reached him. In the neck. Last thing he said to me was"—his voice broke—"that he wanted to be like me . . . when he grew up." He ground his teeth. "Sometimes . . . I wake up at night, and I can still feel his blood on my hands. And I can see the light going out of his eyes as I held him there on the field . . . where I taught him to hunt."

The silence lengthened, and Daniel finally looked up. Tears streamed down Elizabeth's cheeks. Josiah's too.

"I'm so sorry, Daniel." She wiped her face. "I . . . I didn't know what I was asking."

"I sorry too, sir, for the burden you been carryin' inside you for so long."

Daniel felt sick. He didn't deserve their compassion. Josiah Birch had every reason to loathe a man like him, to hold so much against him, including life before the war, yet he didn't. And Elizabeth . . .

If she knew how he'd served during the war, what he'd been . . . Her reaction at the possibility of Josiah having murdered a defenseless man hung close, and his gut twisted, knowing he needed to tell her the truth. But he didn't want to. It would change the way she looked at him.

She took a deep breath. "There was . . . or is, a reason behind my asking about that night, Daniel. And believe me when I say that I had no idea how . . . dearly that battle cost you. My intention in telling you this now isn't to cause you more pain. But to . . . to not tell you would feel false inside." She touched the place over her heart. "And I've had enough of that for a lifetime."

He studied her face, not following.

She seemed to have trouble forming her next words. "My father . . . was a colonel in the Federal army. He was the commanding officer in Nashville and"—her voice grew thin—"the tactical commander for the battle of Franklin."

Daniel stared at her as another piece of who Elizabeth Westbrook was fell into place for him. And as another reminder of what he'd done during the war sliced through him. "Your father was a colonel in the Federal army?"

She nodded. "Colonel Garrett Eisenhower Westbrook."

Disbelief stole through him, followed by confusion. "But he's still alive."

She gave a tiny smile. "Yes, he is."

"So . . . he wasn't on the battlefield that day."

Confusion slipped into her eyes. "He orchestrated the battle plans but was called to Washington the morning of the battle. Another colonel, a close friend of my father's, Colonel Henry Jackson, took his pla—" Her frown smoothed. She blinked, then shook her head. "What was your assignment during the war? Were you an officer?"

She said it with such hope. But Daniel saw it in her face. She knew. The threads were pulling taut inside her just as they had for him seconds ago.

"I held the rank of captain . . . but served in a special unit. Our primary mission was to eliminate commanding Federal officers from the field before the start of battle. I was—"

"A sharpshooter," she whispered, looking as though she'd seen a ghost.

"When they realized how well I could shoot, they sent me to Atlanta for more training. And they issued us each a Whitworth."

Her attention moved to the gun propped beside him. "So that means that . . . if my father had been there that day, you would have . . ." Her focus slid back to him.

His jaw went rigid. "Yes," he whispered. "I would have killed him."

"Did you ever miss, Daniel? Even once?"

He was touched by her attempt to absolve him. "No, Elizabeth. I never missed."

She stared at him for the longest time, then lay down on her pallet. He wanted to talk to her, and for her to talk to him. When Josiah excused himself, whether by necessity or to give them time alone, Daniel moved over by her.

He gently touched her shoulder, knowing she was still awake. "Elizabeth, look at me."

She shook her head. "I can't. Not right now."

He smoothed the curls falling down her back and felt her body shake. "I'm sorry, Elizabeth. I'm so sorry. . . ."

She slowly turned over. Tears stained her cheeks. "So am I. . . ."

When he reached for her hand, she pulled away and curled onto her side again, away from him.

"Please leave me alone, Daniel."

He reached for her again, then stopped himself, knowing it was useless. So much for the truth setting a person free.

35

Elizabeth saw him coming and rose from packing her satchel. The sternness in his expression didn't bode well for another attempt at this conversation, but she had to try. He was hurting, and she knew full well that she was the cause. "Daniel, I'd appreciate the chance to speak if—"

"We're late getting on the trail." He strode past her. "If you want to get to Mesa Verde today, I suggest we move out."

She stared at his back, having grown accustomed to seeing it over the past five weeks. What she wasn't accustomed to was the wall between them—and that she'd been the one to lay the first brick only added to her frustration.

He finished loading the packhorse, his movements sharp and defined, more like a soldier's than the man she'd come to know.

When he'd shared with them two nights ago about the war in Franklin and about being a sharpshooter, she'd been too shocked to respond, unnerved when considering what could have happened— what *would* have happened—had her father been on the battlefield that day. Unable to discuss it that night, she'd thought they would talk about it the next morning. But by then, the damage had been done.

His silence was piercing and reeked of resentment. She felt as though she'd taken his trust and, in an effort to handle it more gently, had crushed it instead. But he couldn't avoid her forever, and he was also right. They'd lost a week as she and Josiah had recuperated with the Ute, and her deadline to get the photographs of Mesa Verde to Wendell Goldberg was fast approaching.

She also remembered what the butcher back in Timber Ridge had said about not pushing someone. It had worked for James McPherson with this same man; maybe it would work for her.

She climbed into the saddle, and Josiah fell in line behind her. He also had been subdued since that night. Not sullen, like Daniel, nor evasive, just distant in his own way.

The scenery was still breathtaking but had undergone a transformation. The mountains had grown flatter on their tops, trading their rugged peaks for mesas—tabletops. She could hardly wait to see Mesa Verde and hoped her equipment would be there waiting. But she preferred not to arrive with this tension between them.

They stopped briefly for lunch and to water the horses. She sensed the men's anticipation and guessed they were as excited about seeing the cliff dwellings as she was.

By late afternoon, she was beginning to wonder if Daniel had miscalculated the distance. She checked her compass, then her map. It seemed as though they should be going more toward the south to get to the cliff dwellings, but she wasn't about to question him.

When the sun started its descent, disappointment set in. She'd so hoped to get there today. Daniel paused in front of her on a ridge. He didn't say anything, just stared off to his right. She followed his line of vision, not seeing what he was—

Her breath caught, but only for a second. She jumped from her horse and ran to the edge of the ridge, peering across the canyon. Her body tingled. Palaces, shadowed rooms carved directly into the mountainside, hundreds of feet from the canyon floor, glowed orange red in the setting sun. Remarkable . . .

She framed the scene with her hands, as though she were looking through her lens, and could see it perfectly. She'd have to come back to this very spot to take a picture. This angle was perfect—and Daniel had known it would be.

She turned to look at him. His gaze was fixed on her. She smiled, not expecting him to return it. He did, barely, but his eyes communicated a satisfaction all the same. It would take her time to win back his trust. But she would do it.

Josiah took off his slouch hat and leaned forward in the saddle. "How'd them people do that, ma'am?"

Laughing, she shared his wonder. "I have no idea, Josiah. I'm just so glad they did."

It was well after dark when they arrived in the nearby town, and the mercantile was already closed. When Daniel suggested they stay the night in the hotel, Elizabeth could've kissed him. She took a long, hot bath that evening, wrote a letter to her father to mail the following day, and awakened refreshed the next morning, ready to see if her equipment had arrived.

Downstairs in the hotel lobby, Josiah was waiting, solemn-faced. "We gots some good news, ma'am, and some bad news."

Her excitement went flat. To have come all this way for nothing . . . "What is it?"

"Good news is your equipment is in, Miz Westbrook. Bad news"—his grin broke through—"is I thinkin' you ain't gonna be totin' your camera by yourself no more."

She followed him outside to find Daniel standing by a cart loaded with crates. Next to him, atop a tripod, was a camera whose lens was almost twice as big as her old one! She took the stairs in twos and ran a hand over the polished mahogany. "Did you do this, Daniel Ranslett?"

He glanced at the cart. "I wish I could take credit for it, but I can't. I think somebody's just looking out for you . . . and that you were meant to be here taking pictures of this place, for whatever reason. Just like all the places on our way back to Timber Ridge."

She smiled, and then remembering her calculations from last evening, her enthusiasm tempered. "I thought about that last night. It's already June. I'll need at least a week to take pictures here. And I'm afraid that leaves little time for taking photographs on the way back, and there's still no guarantee the pictures will make it to Washington by the end of August."

"That might be true. . . ." Daniel took off his hat and ran a hand through his hair. "If you didn't take into account that I spoke with the mercantile owner this morning and the same freight company who delivered this shipment will be back through here in four days." A subtle gleam lit his eyes. "They'll pick up whatever you have ready and will take it on to the next town, where it'll meet up with another freighter who'll carry it on to a town with train service back east. So you're guaranteed not to miss your deadline—*if* you can have your photographs ready in four days."

She closed the distance between them. "I can, and I'm giving you full credit for that." She kissed him squarely on his freshly shaven cheek and saw his response, despite his attempt to hide it. "My reaction the other night hurt you, Daniel, and I'm sorry for that. Especially after everything you shared. It just . . . caught me so unaware. Imagining what would have happened to my father had he been there, and knowing what *did* happen to your brother because of my father's leadership in planning that battle . . . I just needed time to sort through it all."

He nodded and took a step back. "That makes two of us."

The scene was perfect, the morning light pristine. Daniel had chosen this morning's ridge with as much care as he'd chosen yesterday's. Elizabeth started to remove the lens from the camera, then hesitated. President Lincoln's familiar address came back to her without falter, no matter that she hadn't uttered it in weeks. She thought about Josiah and Daniel standing behind her.

Josiah stepped forward. "Somethin' wrong with it, Miz Westbrook? You need me to get somethin' for you, ma'am?"

"No, nothing's wrong. I'm just wondering . . . Have either of you heard the remarks President Lincoln gave at the battlefield at Gettysburg?"

"No, ma'am. Can't say that I have. But I sure 'preciate what that man done—God rest his soul. Not right what got done to him in return."

She looked at Daniel, who just shook his head.

She returned her attention to the photograph and to the ancient palaces set within the frame of her lens, and carefully removed the lens cap. " 'Four score and seven years ago our fathers brought forth upon this continent a new nation . . .' "

The words took on deeper meaning knowing they were listening. She could still hear Lincoln's high, clarion tones in her memory.

" 'We are met on a great battlefield of that war. We are met to dedicate a portion of it as the final resting place of those who here gave their lives that that nation might live. . . .

" 'The brave men, living and dead, who struggled here, have consecrated it far above our poor power to add or detract. The world will little note nor long remember what we say here, but it can never forget what they did here.' "

As she spoke, she pictured President Lincoln standing tall on that platform, two or three pages of manuscript in his left hand, and him glancing at them only once as he spoke. The image of a boy of nine rose inside her, one who shared Daniel's green eyes and dark hair, and who wanted to be a man of honor like his older brother.

" ' . . . that we here highly resolve that these dead shall not have died in vain; that the nation, under God, shall have a new birth of freedom, and that the government of the people, by the people, and for the people, shall not perish from the earth.' "

Careful not to bump the camera, she reinserted the lens cap.

Being in such a place, seeing such grandeur, was like a dream all over again—capturing images and sending them home to be published, images that could well garner her the position as the *Chronicle*'s next journalist and photographer. But the opportunity Wendell Goldberg had given her suddenly seemed wistful, somewhat emptied of its importance in light of her experiences in the past weeks. Especially since her interaction with Drayton Turner. She didn't want to have anything to do with Turner's kind of newspaper reporting, and the similarities between him and Goldberg were disturbing. Surely there was something more.

They spent the day taking pictures—ten in all, and six turned out exceptionally well. Late afternoon found them back on the ridge Daniel had chosen the previous evening. All day long, Elizabeth had looked forward to capturing this particular perspective, at sunset, just as Daniel had shown it to her for the very first time.

They camped in the canyon just below the dwellings. The summer day seemed to stretch forever, and after dinner, she leaned back, imagining what life had been like for the people who lived in the cliff dwellings. The wind whispered through the shadowed houses, encircling the ruins and carrying remnants of ancient voices from times long past.

She stole looks at Daniel, wondering how she was going to get him alone to speak with him. But she would before they left Mesa Verde.

Josiah poured himself another cup of coffee and refilled each of their cups. She had learned some about cooking in the past weeks, but after she'd made several attempts at coffee—and failed—Daniel volunteered to keep that responsibility. Josiah had seconded his offer far too quickly.

"Was you there, Miz Westbrook? When Mr. Lincoln gave them words?"

She nodded, blowing across her cup. "It was many years ago, but I remember it like it was yesterday."

"I got times like that in my life too. Where I can still see the faces and hear what's bein' said. Good as if I's standing right there in it again. It was a fine talk by Mr. Lincoln, ma'am, and you give it well."

"Yes, ma'am, you did." From across the fire, Daniel lifted his cup to her.

She returned the gesture, hopeful.

"You two been real kind to me." Josiah's hand dwarfed the tin cup. "Miz Westbrook, you give me a job when most wouldn't. And Mr. Ranslett, sir, you got me to help when I's beaten and then stayed by me when I's sick." He reached for something beside him. "There been days in my life when I thought God himself had turned His face cuz there was too much pain to abide, even for Him. And then others when I know that as sure as the sun'll rise He's with me." He fingered the leather pouch. "Mr. Ranslett, you told us the other night that you held your little brother and saw the light dim in his eyes. . . ."

Daniel's expression was hard to read.

"I know your meanin', sir, but with all respects, I put to you that the light only dimmed from our side. You couldn't see it, but it was there, in the distance, shinin' for Benjamin. It rose inside him that day, full and rich, and he's livin' in it now, just like—" He stopped, his forehead bunched. "Just like my sweet wife, Belle."

36

Belle and I married on a Tuesday in March. Last time I seen her was on a Saturday mornin' in December."

Daniel watched Josiah through the fire. He'd suspected something like this, and had discussed the possibility with Elizabeth, but had prayed he was wrong. Intuition told him something else was coming and that it wasn't good. From the concern in Elizabeth's demeanor, she sensed it too.

"I told you the other night, Mr. Ranslett, that I ain't never lived in Franklin. I answered that way to spare your feelin's at the time, sir."

"So you did live there."

"Not in Franklin, sir, but close. In Nashville. Mr. Stattam, man who owned me and Belle, he showed up one evenin' in December as I's walkin' back to the shanties. He loaded me and five others in a wagon and took us off. Didn't say nothin' 'bout where we's goin', and we had kerchiefs tied round our eyes so we couldn't see. Turns out, we's taken to another plantation he owned, couple hours away. I tried gettin' back to Belle once, and almost made it to Nashville when Mr. Stattam's dogs catched up with me." Hand on his thigh, he rubbed the side of his leg. "After the war, I went to look for Belle. That's when I learnt that Mr. Stattam, he sold her to a man in Franklin not long after he moved me . . . cuz she was carryin' a child."

His suspicions confirmed, shame poured through Daniel. He knew of owners who had forced themselves on female slaves, and in light of knowing Josiah, the knowledge repulsed him now even more than it had back then. Stattam had been a partner to his stepfather, Nathaniel Thursmann, both men devoid of any shred of honor. "I knew Stattam."

Josiah nodded slowly. "I figured you might, sir."

"Do you remember the name of the man he sold Belle to?"

"No, sir. I's never told that. I's only told she ended up in Franklin. I looked for her, but it didn't do no good. Fella by the name of Carter had some lists he got from a white man who was tryin' to help put families together. I went to him, but he didn't have no Isabelle on his papers. No Belle either. Only the age of women when they was sold, and if they's healthy or not. I looked all over Tennessee, down in Georgia, South Carolina, Mississippi. Everywhere I could think that she mighta gone. But no matter where I looked, she wasn't there."

"Belle wrote the journal pages. . . ." Elizabeth's voice was soft.

Josiah nodded. "Yes, ma'am. I gots 'em after the war, from a woman who was friend to her after I's taken away. She's the one who told me 'bout Mr. Stattam sellin' her."

With his boot, Daniel nudged a fallen log back into the flames. "So many of those deeds and records were destroyed in fires or lost when the Federals occupied the homes." Not wanting to get Josiah's hopes up, he was also curious. "Do you know if this man, Carter, used the plantation owners' personal deed books to make his lists? Sometimes the names of slaves were listed in there instead of in the county ledger."

"I can't know for sure, sir. He never did say."

Daniel started to press the matter but stopped. Chances of individual deed records still existing were slim.

"Josiah . . ." Elizabeth's eyes held a sheen. "A minute ago, you said, 'Just like my sweet wife.' What makes you think Belle passed on?"

A sad smile touched his face. "I ain't all the way sure that she has, ma'am. I just think she and I woulda found each other by now, if we's both still here. She used to tell me that I's her home, no matter where she went. She was my home too." The flames from the fire reflected burnished gold on his skin. "She always will be."

As they prepared for bed, Daniel kept turning over what Josiah had said, weighing the possibilities, and watching Elizabeth as she tugged a hairpin still caught in a tangle. Countless times she had pinned those curls up in the morning, taking no telling how long to get them fixed, when they looked so pretty trailing down her back.

They needed to talk, and would. Her reaction to him a few nights ago had jarred him. It hadn't frightened him or scared him off, just made him realize how far-reaching decisions were, and how lasting. Looking back to the first day they'd met, he would never have been able to imagine how intertwined their lives would turn out to be.

"Do you need some help with that?"

She looked over at him. "Yes, if you don't mind."

He circled the fire to her pallet and knelt down, seeing Josiah was already asleep. "Hand me your brush."

"Do you know what you're doing?"

He gave her a look. She gave him the brush. He had the pin out in less than a minute, which was really a shame. He should've taken longer.

"Thank you," she whispered, then looked at the darkened cliff dwellings carved into the mountainside above. "Have you figured out a way for us to get up there?"

"Not yet . . ." Daniel stretched his shoulder, working the sore muscles. He didn't know why, but some days the wound hurt more than others. "But I will."

She twirled her finger. "Turn around."

"Why?"

"Just turn around."

Getting her meaning, he did as she asked, not sure if this was wise.

Her hands were surprisingly strong and went to the exact spot on his back that ached. Then he remembered, she'd seen the wound before.

"Is that too hard?"

He shook his head. "Not at all. Feels good."

"Let your head roll forward."

Her fingers worked across his shoulders and down his upper arms, then to the back of his neck, and to his right shoulder again.

"If I'd known you could do this, I would've asked for my pay in back rubs."

She chuckled and her fingers dug harder. There was no way she could rub too hard for him, but when she moved to his upper neck, then into his hair, he stood.

She looked up at him. "I guess you've had enough."

Was she really that innocent? He looked more closely. Yes, she was. And he planned on keeping it that way. "Yes, ma'am. That was real good, thank you."

"I hope it'll help you sleep."

Not likely. "I'm sure it will."

It took Daniel a while to finally get to sleep, and sometime later, he awakened to a nudge. He opened his eyes and liked what greeted him in the fire's waning glow. His thoughts turned to those of a more intimate nature, and glad she couldn't read them, he rose on one elbow. "What's wrong?"

"Good morning." Elizabeth brushed back her curls, but they paid no heed.

He looked around. "It's not morning. It's not even sunup yet, woman." He lay back down.

"I think I figured out a way for us to get up to the cliffs."

"Does that way involve daylight?"

She giggled, bending over him, which only fed his former musings.

"Yes, of course it does. But I think we can climb to the first ridge—did I tell you that I can climb, I think I did—and then we can . . ."

He stood and stretched, listening but needing to move. Mainly away from her.

By the time the sun shone pink in the eastern horizon, they had walked the perimeter of Mancos Canyon with the aid of a torch, and with Beau trotting along beside them. Daniel had been to the ruins before, but he'd never taken the time to explore like this, and he had to admit, he was enjoying it. Over breakfast, they finalized their plan for scaling the cliffs.

———

Elizabeth made quick work of the breakfast dishes while Daniel and Josiah went into town for more rope. She studied the cliff dwellings above, eager to see inside, to feel the centuries-old rock walls beneath her hands, and to experience the same view as had the people who built the castle-like chambers. If allowed more time, Daniel said he could have built a pulley system to hoist the camera up, along with the rest of her equipment. But the freighter would be back through in two days, and she still needed to take pictures of the sights on their trip back to Timber Ridge. Maybe someday . . .

Daniel and Josiah returned with rope, and by noon they were ready to start climbing. Remnants of rope lay at the base of the cliff, most of it rotted, evidence of climbers who'd come before them.

Daniel removed his boots and looped the rope over his arm and neck, winking at her. "If I start to fall, get ready to catch me."

She didn't find it funny. "If you start to fall, hang on."

"You best be careful, Mr. Ranslett, sir. I don't wanna be havin' to find my way back to Timber Ridge on my lonesome."

Elizabeth swatted Josiah on the arm. "I'd be with you to help."

Josiah raised his brow. "Like I said, sir, if somethin' happen to you, I be on my lonesome."

They all laughed, and she gave Daniel's hand a squeeze. "Please be careful."

He was a good climber, gripping the crevices with his hands and finding footholds. He scaled the first twenty feet of the wall as if he were climbing a ladder, but she didn't realize how good he was until he got to the narrow overhang, roughly sixty feet above the floor of the canyon. She held her breath as he let go of the wall with his right hand and gripped the rock ledge. In one fluid motion, he pushed away from the wall, got a grip with his left hand, and hoisted his body up.

He slipped, and her heart leapt to her throat.

He hung from the ledge, his hands gripping the rock. The muscles in his fingers had to be aching. *Hold on, hold on . . .* Inch by inch, he pulled himself up until his chest was even with the ledge, and then he swung his right leg up, somehow found a grip, and pulled himself onto the ledge. He went down on his back, and she could only imagine the rush of accomplishment he must be feeling.

Still on his back, Daniel stuck a hand over the ledge and gave them a pathetic wave. Josiah let out a whoop, and she clapped along, so proud of him.

She cupped her hands around her mouth. "What took you so long?"

When he finally stood, they clapped again. Daniel took an awkward bow and acted as if he were falling off the cliff. She shook her head at him.

He secured the rope and tossed it down.

Wishing she had her split skirt, Elizabeth bent at the waist, grabbed the back hem of her dress, and tucked it into the front of her waistband. "Not as good as your pants, but it'll have to do."

Josiah snugged the rope around her waist. "You'll do fine, Miz Westbrook. You's made for this kinda thing. I just wish that teacher of yours could be here to see you now."

She smiled and hugged his neck. To her surprise, his expression took on a shy look.

"In the end, ma'am, people is what matters." He glanced at the cliff far above them where Daniel stood. "That's a good man up there. You's a good woman too. Some people's hearts . . . they point true north. You can trust 'em, no matter what comes. Sure is good when you find somebody like that, Miz Westbrook." He shook his head. "And it don't happen often in this life."

Understanding what he was saying, she nodded.

"Now you hurry yourself on up there before he comes down here and gets on to me for huggin' his woman."

"I'm not *his* woman, Josiah."

He just smiled. "Yes, ma'am. Whatever you say, ma'am."

Hiding her smile, she found a grip and started up. It was much harder than Daniel made it look, and she slipped numerous times. Only because he was holding the other end of the rope did she not fall and break her neck. As she continued climbing, she realized how true that was in her career too—God had held her, guided each move. In recent days she'd found herself wanting her writing and her photography to have more meaning, more lasting purpose for Him. Something that would make a difference for the better in people's lives. Something more than simply increasing the circulation of a newspaper . . . But what?

When she reached the height on the wall where she had to let go and grab the ledge, everything within her resisted. Every muscle in her body trembled. Her breath came heavy. Her energy was spent. The thought of letting go of this rock wall—her only certain means of support—scared her to death. She couldn't do it.

"Just let go, Elizabeth, and grab on to me."

It was Daniel speaking above her, but it was God's inaudible voice she heard. God would show her what He wanted her to do with the talents He'd given her—in His time, on His terms. Taking a deep breath, she let go and reached out.

Her right hand connected with the cliff.

"Now quickly—with your left!"

She did as Daniel said and grabbed the ledge, then felt him take hold of her arms. He pulled her up and she clung to him, excited and relieved all at the same time.

He kissed the top of her head and held her for a moment, then slowly encouraged her to turn. "Take a look."

What struck her first was that as high as it had seemed from the ground looking up, it seemed even higher now that she was looking down on the valley below. The ceiling of the dwelling loomed overhead. "Can you imagine living up here?"

"Not if I had to make that climb every day, I couldn't." Smiling, Daniel reached around her waist and pulled the knotted part of the rope toward her front. He tugged the rope playfully, pulling her toward him again, and she took full advantage.

She slipped her arms around his neck, knowing it would get his attention. "We need to have a conversation, Daniel."

Looking only mildly surprised, and mostly pleased, he pulled her close. "I know we do, Elizabeth. But one thing you need to know, darlin' "—his drawl went thick—"is that when we're close like this, talking's not the first thing on my mind."

"I'll try to remember that, when the time comes." She stood on tiptoe. Surely this was enough of a hint, even for the daftest man.

His smile said he understood her desire. The teasing in his eyes said he wasn't going to comply that easily. "So am I to understand, Miss Westbrook, that we're *not* going to have that conversation right now?"

"Daniel Ranslett . . . I've never asked a man to kiss me before, but I promise you, if you don't—"

He complied fully, softly at first, and with a sweetness she hadn't imagined possible, not when he was holding her so tightly. He deepened the kiss, and gradually, she recognized a familiar taste.

She smiled, their lips still touching. "You've been eating peppermint."

Eyes still closed, he kissed her again, more slowly this time, and she got an even better taste.

He drew back slightly. "I got a new tin at the store this morning. Want some?" Flirtation filled his question.

"Yes, but I want my own piece."

"Why does that not surprise me?" He pulled a wrapped bundle from his shirt pocket. Nested inside were three sticks of peppermint. "It just seemed appropriate for the occasion."

"I ain't realized I done tied that rope so good up there, Mr. Ranslett! I sure sorry about that, sir. You havin' trouble gettin' it undone?"

They both laughed, able to tell from Josiah's tone that he wasn't serious.

Daniel untied the rope and let it down again, looking over the ledge. "Try not to tie this thing so tight next time, will you? Took me ten minutes to get it undone."

Josiah's laughter drifted up to them as he started the climb. He lacked Daniel's finesse but matched, or maybe even exceeded, him in strength. Daniel gripped hold of him as Josiah transitioned to the ledge.

Once he gained his bearings, Josiah sighed and looked out over the canyon. "Ain't this somethin' up here." He accepted the candy Elizabeth offered and swirled it in his mouth. He gave her a wink, casting a glance at Daniel. "I'm thinkin' this was worth the wait, ma'am."

She smiled, knowing what he meant and knowing Daniel was listening. "Yes, it was definitely worth the wait."

They spent the afternoon exploring the dwelling. Inside several of the rooms, they found pieces of pottery. Some pieces had been smashed, and remnants of recent fires darkened the rock floor of the dwelling. Some of the pottery was in good condition, as if whoever had used them last had intended to return.

After a brief discussion, they decided to take some of the artifacts back to Makya and his people. They would be safer there, since word of the dwellings' existence was spreading—and would spread even more once her pictures appeared in the *Chronicle*. The thought gave Elizabeth pause.

Using the rope, Josiah fashioned a sort of net, and they lowered several pots to the canyon below.

"I'll ask Makya on our way back if he'd be willing to donate a few pieces of the pottery to the museum in Washington. It would be preserved there for years to come."

"If he says yes, will you mail the pots . . . or take them back with you when you go?"

Daniel's question caught her off guard, and raised other ones she wasn't prepared to answer. "I'll most likely pack them and take them with me on the train. To ensure their safety." She could tell that wasn't the answer he'd wanted. But that was all right. It wasn't the answer she'd wanted to give.

37

Occasional rains followed them for the better part of three weeks on their way back to Timber Ridge. Despite its being July, the mountain air was chilly and damp, and the moisture only served to push the chill deeper into Elizabeth's bones.

She started each day looking forward to stopping again that night. Once dinner was finished and cleaned up, her favorite part of the day began—huddled close to the fire, wrapped warm in Daniel's bearskin, and cradling a cup of his coffee while the three of them talked. She felt more at home in those moments than she'd ever felt in her life.

She'd sent a total of twenty-seven photographs to Wendell Goldberg, via the freighter Daniel had arranged. The trip to Mesa Verde had been more of a success than she could ever have imagined. Makya's prediction had been right—visiting that place, so sacred to his people, had changed her.

Hanging from the cliff that day, as she'd heard the eternal whisper inside her, she'd known then that she still wasn't the woman she wanted to be—but she'd also become aware of God changing her. Little by little. She didn't understand how. She didn't know exactly what He was doing, but she trusted Him to make her into the woman *He* wanted her to be. And she could hardly wait to share her experiences—and the photographs—with Makya and the Ute people on their way back.

Daniel leaned down. "More coffee?"

"No thank you. I'm fine." She drank the last of hers and set her cup aside. She purposefully waited until Daniel settled back down on his pallet before asking her question. "Do we have any peppermint left?"

He looked over at her. "You couldn't have asked that while I was up?" He started to rise.

Smiling, she motioned for him to stay seated. "I'll get it. Where is it?"

"In one of my saddlebags over there." He lay down and sighed, making a show of rubbing one of his shoulders. "My neck sure is tight tonight. . . ."

She shook her head, knowing what he was hinting at, and secretly enjoying that he liked her back rubs. She liked giving them. "Subtlety is not your strong suit, Daniel."

Yawning, he cradled one arm beneath his head and closed his eyes. "Never said it was, ma'am."

Josiah's soft laughter earned her attention, and he smiled up at her from his bedroll as she passed. Pages of Belle's journal were spread out before him. "I ain't sayin' nothin', ma'am."

"Well, that'll be a first." She enjoyed the way his eyes went wide.

"You's one sassy woman, ma'am. And gettin' more so, if you ask me."

"I'm not sassy. I'm just . . . straightforward."

"Mm-hmm . . ." Josiah smiled up at her. "Whatever you says, ma'am."

Giggling to herself, Elizabeth rummaged through three saddlebags before finding the peppermint tin. She pulled it out and a folded piece of paper came with it. She picked it up and was starting to put it back when the salutation caught her attention.

Dear Senator Westbrook, United States Congress . . .

It was a letter, and before it fully registered with her what she was doing, she'd read the first paragraph. A cool wind of reality swept through her.

> I'm writing to you and your colleagues in the United States Congress in an effort to gain attention for the preservation of the Colorado Territory and, more recently, of the ancient ruins at the Mesa Verde Cliff Dwellings. . . .

She scanned the rest of the letter, her sense of trespass eased by an overriding sense of betrayal. Especially upon seeing Daniel's name signed at the bottom.

> If you will permit me, sir, I would appreciate the opportunity to provide photographs of the land that I believe would demonstrate not only the importance of this issue, but the reason why my proposal deserves your serious consideration.

It was clearly a rough draft. He'd marked out sentences and had started them over again, having obviously put a lot of thought—and himself—into it.

She folded the letter and slipped it back into the saddlebag, along with the tin of peppermint. Josiah didn't look up as she walked by. Daniel's eyes were closed, and he didn't move when she lay down. His soft snoring soon confirmed why.

Elizabeth curled onto her side—mostly numb. All this time, she'd thought Daniel's interest in her had been personal. And it had been, in two ways. He wanted to use her photographs—which she would have gladly shared. And he wanted to use her to get to her father—just like many men before him, which is what hurt the most.

She reached for the bearskin, then grabbed a blanket instead and pulled it up close around her chin. She tried to swallow past the ache in her throat and couldn't. Slowly, tears breached her defenses.

Daniel's attempt to preserve this land was noble, honorable. And his passion for the pursuit came across on the page, perhaps better than anything she'd ever written. It was an endeavor she would gladly have assisted him in. She only wished he'd been honest with her from the very begin—

Truth sliced through her and laid her heart bare.

Tears came freely. Upon arriving in Timber Ridge, had her own motivations been any less skewed? Something within told her that her situation had been different, that her circumstances had been unique. But she knew better.

And knowing that only twisted the knife of truth deeper.

———

The rains finally stopped and the sun returned, bringing warmer temperatures and a beauty to the Rockies that Daniel always appreciated this time of year. But he couldn't fully enjoy it, not with this tension that existed between him and Elizabeth. He couldn't place it, but in the past week she'd been different, and it had been an exercise in patience, waiting for the right time to approach her.

They had yet to talk about the battle of Franklin and his connection—or *almost* connection, *thank God*—to her father, and he still needed to tell her about his petition to Congress. Which he dreaded doing.

When Daniel returned from bathing in the stream that evening, Josiah took his turn, with Beau following close behind.

Sensing the timing wouldn't get much better, Daniel joined Elizabeth on her pallet instead of going to his. "We still need to have that conversation."

She took a sip of coffee, not looking at him. "Yes, we do."

Her hair was still wet from her bath, and reddish gold curls hung damp at her temples. She couldn't have been more beautiful, which didn't help the tangle of emotions inside him.

"But before we have the talk about that . . ." He pulled a piece of paper from his shirt pocket, figuring he'd start with the hardest thing first. "I've wanted to tell you something for a while now. Something I'm trying to do. But I didn't want you to get the wrong impression about why I agreed to take you on this trip."

She looked at him, her blue eyes watchful.

"Do you remember what I said to you the first night on the trail? When we shared the bearskin blanket?" He ran a forefinger over a crease in the letter. "You asked me why I agreed to bring you on this trip."

"You said it was because you wanted me to see the land. That you wanted me to feel it inside, so that it would become something I cared about."

She parroted back his response as though she'd written it down that night and had memorized it. He didn't even try to hide his shock.

The tiniest smile tipped her mouth. "I *do* listen to you, Daniel. On occasion."

"Well, that's good to know." Searching for the right words, he prayed for God's guidance as he unfolded the letter. "For seven years, I've been trying to get the attention of Congress." He shared his dream of preserving this territory's land, and about his hopes for what he wanted to accomplish, then handed her the letter.

Her eyes moved across the page, and he waited for the hurt, the sense of betrayal to appear. But it didn't.

"Daniel . . ." She bowed her head. "I found this letter a week ago, when I was searching for peppermint in your saddlebags. And . . . I read it."

He considered her for a minute. At least that explained the tension he'd felt between them. "Why didn't you say anything, if you knew?"

She shrugged. "In case you've forgotten, I, of all people, know what it's like to have ulterior motives. I was hurt when I first found the letter, but after I thought about it, I realized that what you did was no different than what I did when I first came to Timber Ridge."

"But that's just it." He gestured to the letter. "I didn't agree to take you for this reason."

"Are you about to tell me that you did it because you couldn't stand the thought of being without my company?"

He laughed softly, appreciating her wit. "Actually . . . that motivation came sometime later. But it *did* come. My real reason . . . was James."

"James?" She eyed him.

"He helped me through a difficult time after the war, most of which you know about . . . Benjamin's death, my addiction. I owed him a debt—a big one—and when he asked me to take you to Mesa Verde as fulfillment of that debt, I agreed."

She scanned the letter again. "So it wasn't because of this?"

"I give you my word. I started, several times, to tell you about my writing these letters, but I was—"

"Afraid I would think that the only reason you agreed to this was so that I would help you petition Congress and use my father's influence to do it."

"That pretty much sums it up."

"But as it turns out, had you not owed James that debt . . . you wouldn't have taken me."

"No," he whispered. "I wouldn't have. But if it makes any difference, I'm glad now that I did."

"Hellooo . . . the camp!" Josiah returned, Beau trotting alongside him, and Daniel didn't have to wonder why he'd called out. He'd felt Josiah looking between him and Elizabeth this past week, just as he was doing now. "Pretty evenin', you two. You best take a walk b'fore dark and enjoy it."

Appreciating the suggestion, Daniel rose. He faced Elizabeth and bowed at the waist as though at a grand cotillion. "May I have the honor of escorting you this evening, Miss Westbrook?"

She smiled and took his hand. "I would be most delighted, Mr. Ranslett."

They walked down the path, aspen trees clustered on either side, and Daniel covered her hand tucked in his arm. "I'd be lying if I said I didn't hope you'd join me in presenting this petition to Congress. I'd appreciate using your photographs, and benefiting from your obvious influence, but only if you decide this is something you want to be a part of." He paused on the trail, the camp no longer in view. "I won't bring it up to you again, Elizabeth. When we get back to Timber Ridge, you can give me your answer. My goal won't change. I'll still pursue this on my own. Agreed?"

"Agreed," she answered softly, and squeezed his arm.

"Now, about that *other* conversation. I know you think that what I did in the war—shooting defenseless men—was cowardly and without honor, but if I could—"

"What you did, Daniel, killing from a distance, was no different than what my father did. He used tactical measures and wartime strategies instead of a Whitworth rifle. Is there any difference? The result was the same. Except my father's actions killed or wounded over nine thousand men and boys . . ." She moved closer to him. "Among them, your precious brother. . . . And that was just in Franklin, in a five-hour battle. No wonder my father chooses not to speak of the war anymore and of the battle that night. He wants to forget it as much as you do, but he can't. Neither of you can."

Daniel touched her face. Her skin was so soft.

"I have no idea why my father was called from Tennessee to Washington that morning, but I have a feeling, and I know I could be wrong about this . . . but maybe God knew you and I would meet, and that if we'd had that between us . . ." She shrugged and looked away, her vulnerability showing. "If we had such a thing between us, then maybe we wouldn't have—"

He pulled her to him, and Daniel wasn't certain who held the other tighter. He kissed the crown of her head, aching inside for her, and for what it would have cost them if he *had* killed her father that day, and if they'd met now, later in life. How different things would have been.

He drew back and saw her tears. He wiped them away. The way she looked up at him, the gentle yet assertive way she touched him . . . He caressed her face, then dug his hands into her thick curls and tilted her face to meet his. He kissed her full on the mouth, feeling her response. Her eagerness stirred him, and he did his best to banish whatever doubt might linger in the corners of her mind about his reasons for wanting to be with her.

38

Daniel guided the Boyds' wagon across the ridge overlooking town, and Elizabeth was amazed at how civilized Timber Ridge appeared. Not surprising when she'd spent the last three months sleeping in caves, huddling in a tent, or sleeping beneath the stars.

They had returned from Mesa Verde last evening and spent the night with James and Rachel. Rachel had been subdued in Daniel's company, but at least she'd managed to stay in the same room with him, though they didn't speak. As they'd all sat together at breakfast, Elizabeth remembered what Josiah had told her at Mesa Verde—that people were what made the difference. He was right.

It wasn't achievements, however rewarding those could be. It wasn't a career, however necessary earning a livelihood was. And it certainly wasn't fame. What did it matter if people knew your name and yet never really knew who you were? When she whittled her life down to the essentials, to the most important moments, when she imagined what it would be like to stand in the last few seconds of her life and look back in retrospect, it was *people* that mattered most.

And the man sitting beside her now meant more than all the others.

Their last night on the trail, Daniel and Josiah had talked about Tennessee and Franklin, and she'd made a vow to herself that, regardless of what happened between her and Daniel, she would make a journey to that town and that battlefield. To the place of her father's *supposed* greatest victory. To the place where Daniel's and Josiah's lives had been changed forever and where so many men—both Federal and Confederate soldiers—had sacrificed themselves. The thousands of lives had not been "lost" as was so often said. They had been laid down in honor, for family and country.

Daniel reached over and covered her hand on the bench between them. "After we're done in town, I've got something I'd like to show you. If you have time this afternoon."

"It depends on what that something is."

"I'd rather not say for now. Let's let it be a surprise."

Though not certain, she had a good idea of what it was and decided to test the waters. "I've been looking forward to seeing where you live. . . ." She glanced behind her in the wagon bed. "May I bring my camera?"

"Sorry, ma'am. But I don't allow photography."

His smirk gave him away, telling her she'd guessed correctly. He laced his fingers through hers and pulled her closer to him on the buckboard, and her thoughts went to where those of a single woman best not linger overlong. He'd shaved that morning after many days of not shaving, but had kept the mustache and a close-cut beard. She liked it on him. Watching him, she wanted nothing more than to share herself and her life with this man.

He brought the wagon to a halt in front of the Mullinses' store and jumped down. "James said he told you the photograph you wired the *Chronicle* about never arrived."

"I'll send another telegram to Goldberg after I check for my mail. Then I'll take the wagon"—she raised a brow—"and meet you at the boardinghouse."

"Can I trust you to find your way there without me?"

"Have I proven nothing to you in recent weeks, Mr. Ranslett?"

She withdrew the compass from her reticule and held it up. "I'll never lose my way again."

"Not that I'll give you the chance." He winked and untethered his mare from the back. "And for the record, you don't have to prove anything to me, Miss Westbrook. I'm already sold." He made a clicking sound with his tongue and urged the mare on down the street.

Once inside the store, Elizabeth approached the mail counter. Ben Mullins was sorting mail, and she cleared her throat to get his attention. "Any mail this morning for a Miss Elizabeth Westbrook of Washington, D.C.?"

Mullins turned, and a grin lit his face. "Miss Westbrook! Nice to see you again, ma'am. Hope your trip to Mesa Verde was a safe one, and successful."

They spoke briefly, and then he disappeared into the back and returned with a stack of envelopes. "I've got several pieces for you. Some of them came a while back."

Seeing two from Goldberg and two more from her father, she excused herself and went outside to read them on the boardwalk, starting with her father's. He'd received the photograph of her "students" and was quite complimentary but questioned why "their teacher" hadn't been photographed along with them. She didn't look forward to telling her father the truth, and yet she looked forward to the truth being told. His next letter inquired whether she'd received the shipment of school furniture, which she had. Last night James had mentioned it had arrived soon after they'd left for Mesa Verde. She would write her father today and let him know.

Checking the dates on Goldberg's envelopes, she started with the oldest one first. His handwriting had gotten worse. Either that or she was out of practice deciphering his scrawl. She scanned the letter dated April thirtieth, only days after she'd left on her trip.

"Photographs you have sent are spectacular . . . look forward to making the journey myself someday . . ." And the remainder was an update on marketing ideas they had discussed before she'd left Washington.

Since implementing them, it seems the *Chronicle*'s circulation had grown by twenty percent. Impressive, and the shareholders' board was ecstatic.

She opened the second letter, dated the third of June.

> I am growing alarmed at your silence . . . remains to be seen on the position . . . eagerly awaiting your photographs of the cliff dwellings . . . trust you were able to arrange the expedition . . . since you have not responded to my telegrams—

Elizabeth looked up. *Since you have not responded to my telegrams . . .* She frowned. He hadn't sent her any telegrams or she *would* have responded. She finished reading.

> Received your last photograph . . . cannot imagine your shock at coming upon the body . . . outstanding article . . . people will be moved . . . which translates to more sales, our primary concern . . .

Frustrated by more than one thing in his letter, she folded the deckled stationery and headed to the telegraph and newspaper office, leaving the wagon in front of the store.

She needed to send the telegram and deliver the photographs of Mesa Verde to Drayton Turner—whom she wasn't looking forward to seeing again. James said he'd been asking if she'd returned yet and was eager to publish more pictures. She'd not spoken with Turner since the night Josiah was beaten, but both Daniel and James had concluded that Turner's newspaper article had nothing to do with the attack.

Though she didn't approve of Turner's tactics, the people of Timber Ridge deserved to see the beauty of the Colorado Territory, and as Josiah said, perhaps seeing the majesty of Mesa Verde and learning that Ute ancestors had built it would help townspeople to see the current-day Indians in a more favorable light.

From the boardwalk, she spotted Turner's assistant seated behind the counter in the newspaper office. Elizabeth smiled as she opened the door.

"Good morning, Miss Westbrook." The young woman laid aside an envelope.

She'd only met the girl once, and it was so long ago Elizabeth couldn't remember her name. Thankfully a nameplate on her desk provided assistance. "Hello, Miss Cantrell. How are you today?" She saw no sign of Turner, which suited her just fine.

"I'm well, thank you. Is there something I can help you with?" Miss Cantrell rose from her desk, where mail lay scattered.

"I'm here to drop off some photographs for Mr. Turner." Elizabeth handed her the envelope. "I take it he's not in right now." His desk in the back sat vacant.

"No, he's not, but I'll be sure and give this to him." She set the envelope aside. "Miss Westbrook . . ." Shyness crept over the young woman's face. "Ever since I learned about you being a reporter for the *Chronicle,* I've—"

"I'm actually an assistant." Elizabeth softened the correction with a smile. "The *Chronicle* doesn't employ female reporters . . . yet. But I hope that changes in the very near future."

Her expression brightened. "So do I."

"Well, thank you for giving this to Mr. Turner. If you'll excuse me, I need to have a telegram sent." She turned.

"I really admire you for what you're doing out here. Taking photographs, traveling to those cliff dwellings. It sounds so exciting."

Elizabeth glanced back. She detected admiration in the woman's eyes and—not really wanting to spare the time—retraced her steps. "Thank you, Miss Cantrell. I feel very fortunate to be doing what I'm doing. It's taken me a long time to get here, but the journey has been worth it."

"I hope to become a journalist one day."

Elizabeth had gathered as much.

"I know I'll need to start out like you, as an assistant. But then

I want to write my own articles. For a big newspaper in New York, or maybe Boston."

Nodding, Elizabeth had the uncanny feeling she'd been insulted somewhere in the midst of that compliment.

"When you have time, Miss Westbrook, would you consider looking at some articles I've written? I've shown them to Mr. Turner, but he doesn't seem to think too much of them. I'd really appreciate your input, as another woman, on what I could do better."

Aware of Miss Cantrell's true intent, Elizabeth also remembered the many people who had helped her along the way. And the numerous run-ins she'd had with male hypocrisy. "I'd be happy to read your work sometime, and I'll look forward to—"

"I've got them in my desk at home." Miss Cantrell skirted around the counter. "I only live one street over. Wait right here and I'll run get them for you. I appreciate you doing this for me!"

Elizabeth stared as the door closed behind the *New York Times*'s next star reporter, wondering what had just happened. Then she laughed. One thing was certain, Miss Cantrell already had the quality of persistence down to a fine art. Wendell Goldberg had better watch out.

She really didn't want to wait but decided it would be rude to leave, especially with no one else in the office. She stood for a moment, then pulled out her pocket watch to check the time. Something on Miss Cantrell's desk caught her eye. An envelope.

She looked more closely, reading upside down. *Brooklyn Land Development.* The envelope was addressed to Drayton Turner. What was he doing getting mail from a land developer in New York City? A thought came. She immediately dismissed it. It wasn't right.

She stared at the letter, able to think of a hundred different reasons why this was not a good idea. But Miss Cantrell *had* been in the middle of opening the mail anyway. It was next in the stack. Her pulse raced just considering the idea.

She checked the boardwalk to make sure no one was coming.

Both directions were clear. She waited for a wagon to pass on the street. Then she looked back at the envelope, leaned over the counter, and picked it up.

Using Miss Cantrell's letter opener, she slit the envelope across the top, blew into it to separate the papers, and pulled out the stationery. A check fell to the counter. Payee, Drayton Turner. One hundred dollars. No small amount, but not outlandish either. She quickly read the letter.

> Please find the enclosed check which provides payment for services rendered. We appreciate your providing the specifications for the land and for keeping us apprised of the standing with the scheduled auction in Denver.

Footsteps sounded on the boardwalk. Elizabeth threw the letter on the desk and turned, schooling an innocent smile. An elderly woman walking with the aid of a cane smiled and waved to her through the front window. Elizabeth waved in return, holding the fake-feeling smile until the woman passed; then she let out her breath.

She checked the boardwalk again, then snatched up the letter and scanned down. . . .

> The endeavor appears promising. Please inform as to the status of our acquisition at your earliest convenience. We wish to proceed at the soonest possible date. Per our agreement, the remaining compensation for your services is contingent upon full acquisition of the property by year's end.
>
> On a personal note, I have procured the interest of a gun collector and should be forwarding those proceeds in the near future.
>
> Most sincerely,
> H.C. Brickman
> Acquisitions and Mergers
> Brooklyn Land Development

Conclusions quickly forming, Elizabeth turned to see Miss

Cantrell coming back down the street. She tried to stay calm as she folded the letter and slid it back into the envelope, along with the check. She placed the envelope on Miss Cantrell's desk exactly where it had been, then thought better of it and moved it to the opposite stack with the mail that was already opened. Her heart raced as if she'd run a mile.

No one had seen her. Everything was fine. And the letter in and of itself didn't prove anything. All it did was draw a line from Turner to Brooklyn Land Development, a company interested in buying a piece of property in Timber Ridge. A similar line could be drawn between her and Chilton Enterprises for the very same reason.

But where things grew sketchy was in knowing that Travis Coulter—now deceased—had owned a prime piece of property, and that Turner was getting checks from a land development company hoping to acquire land set to go to auction. And that, apparently . . . Turner was selling a gun.

Sheriff McPherson would definitely want to know this information. She just didn't look forward to explaining how she had "accidentally" opened Turner's mail. . . .

Hands trembling, she met Miss Cantrell at the door.

"Thank you so much for waiting, Miss Westbrook. This means so much to me. Here's my portfolio. It contains several articles I've written, and—"

"I can't wait to read them!" Elizabeth took the leather satchel, noticing the woman's name engraved at the top. "I look forward to having lunch with you soon to discuss everything, when both our schedules allow." Eager to leave before Turner arrived, Elizabeth put her hand on the knob.

And felt it turn in her grip.

39

Drayton Turner pushed the door open. "You're back, Miss Westbrook. How nice to see you again."

Sensing his genuine surprise, Elizabeth summoned what little decorum she could. "Thank you, Mr. Turner. We returned yesterday."

"I hope the endeavor achieved the desired outcome."

"It did. It was a very successful trip."

He stepped inside and let the door close behind him. "If you're willing to share your photographs of the cliff dwellings, I'm sure the people of Timber Ridge would appreciate seeing them."

She blinked, staring. The audacity! She wasn't naïve enough to have expected Turner to apologize for what he'd written in the paper about her and Josiah, but she had expected at least *some* form of admittance. A hint of discomfort, maybe. Instead, he offered cordial banter and a request for more photographs. She evened her tone. "I've just left an envelope with Miss Cantrell. There are several photographs inside. You can choose whichever ones you like. There's also a brief article summarizing our trip and highlighting the Ute people's contribution to this area. Now"—she didn't wait for his response—"if you'll excuse me, I need to be going. Miss Cantrell, it was a pleasure speaking with you."

"You as well, Miss Westbrook. And"—the woman glanced at

the portfolio—"I look forward to hearing what you think." Behind Turner's back, she mouthed, *"Thank you for watching the office."*

Elizabeth managed a smile and closed the door.

A few steps down the boardwalk she spotted a sign posted in the window of the telegraph office—TELEGRAPH DOWN. *Infuriating!* Recent rains must have caused more problems. She sighed. So much for thinking of Timber Ridge as civilized. Apparently *civilized* was a relative term.

She was returning to the store for the wagon when she saw Dr. Brookston waving her down.

"You're back from your trip, Miss Westbrook! I trust things went well?"

Realizing that would be a common question, she encapsulated their experiences in a brief answer, seeing the interest spark in Rand Brookston's eyes. "I believe Mr. Turner will be publishing some pictures in the *Reporter*. If not, I'll get some to you. The cliff dwellings are magnificent."

"Very good. How's your health? And your hand?"

Carefully, Elizabeth broached the subject of her addiction, feeling safe with him. Sure enough, he'd seen it happen many times in cases such as hers. They spoke for a while longer and he examined her hand, complimentary of Daniel's removal of the sutures. Then Elizabeth excused herself, eager to see Daniel and tell him what she'd learned in the letter to Turner.

She drove to the boardinghouse, but Daniel wasn't there yet. Josiah had offered to come and carry her equipment back to her room, but James had discouraged it, feeling his presence in town wouldn't be welcome quite yet. The fervor over Travis Coulter's death had settled down after they'd departed for the cliff dwellings, and no new evidence had surfaced. A similar murder had occurred in Denver, where a man's body had been found behind a saloon, and once people read about that in the *Timber Ridge Reporter,* their attention shifted. Still, James was home for the morning repairing the barn, and he didn't want Josiah returning when he wasn't in town, which she appreciated.

She grabbed a lighter box of journals and records from the back of the wagon and made the two-flight trek to the third story. The *Chronicle* was paying for her lodgings while she was in Timber Ridge, so she'd kept her personal items in her room while she was on the expedition. By the time she reached her door, she had a renewed appreciation for all that Josiah had done for her.

She set down the crate and fished for the room key in her reticule. Her hand brushed against the compass, and she pulled it out along with the room key.

Fighting a reluctance to be inside this room again, she drew strength from her recent experiences. If she could survive what they'd been through on the way to Mesa Verde and back, she could do this.

She pushed open the door and stepped inside.

The curtains were closed. The room was dark. It had a musty scent and smelled of disuse, but wasn't as bad as she had imagined. She thought she could still detect a faint chemical odor. She walked to the window to see if she could see Daniel coming down the—

Someone grabbed her from behind and lifted her off the floor. Hands fisted below her rib cage delivered four hard thrusts, one after the other, and expelled the air from her lungs. She clawed and scratched, struggling to breathe.

A moist cloth came over her mouth and nose. The smell was bitter and overpowering. Her eyes teared, and she shut them tight. She tried to cough but couldn't. The fumes burned her nostrils and singed the back of her throat. She was spinning, spinning—yet how could she be when her feet were still on the floor?

She cried out, or thought she did, to the One who could save her.

A fleeting thought surfaced before darkness pulled her under—if God saw to it that she got out of this room alive, she was never coming back in here again.

40

D aniel saw the box sitting in the hallway. "All right, now . . ." He picked it up and knocked on the door. A portfolio was balanced on the top, one he didn't remember packing. A name was printed on the upper edge—Miss Laura Cantrell, *Timber Ridge Reporter*.

No answer on the door.

The knob turned easily in his grip. "If you can carry this box all the way up here, then you can—" The room was dark. "Elizabeth?" He stepped inside.

A chemical smell still lingered. He would've thought Miss Ruby would have had things aired out better, but in the woman's defense, she hadn't known when they were returning. Crossing the room to open the window, he kicked something with the tip of his boot. It hit the wall opposite him with a crack.

Thinking that a rug had been in this room before, he rested the box on the bed and walked over to see what he'd kicked. He bent down to pick it up, and alarm shot through him.

He ran back to the hallway. "Elizabeth!" He strode to the window and flung back the curtain to allow in some light. Nothing else seemed out of the ordinary, except that she wouldn't have left her compass behind. And certainly not on the floor.

He grabbed the portfolio and took the stairs down by threes, shoving the compass in his pocket. He found the proprietor's quarters on the first floor and pounded the door. "Miss Ruby!" He jiggled the knob. Locked.

He ran out front. The wagon wasn't there. Another wagon, almost identical to it, with supplies in the back, was parked nearby. But it wasn't the one they'd borrowed from Rachel. How had he not noticed that on his way in?

He covered the short distance to the general store.

When questioned, Mullins shook his head. "No, she left here a good forty-five minutes ago. Maybe longer."

"Did you see her head to the boardinghouse?"

"I didn't follow which way she went, but I did give her some letters. From Washington, if that helps."

It didn't. He left instructions for Mullins to keep Elizabeth there if she showed up. He checked the telegraph office, but it was closed.

He spotted a young woman seated at the front desk in the newspaper's office. "Sorry to bother you, Miss"—he recognized the name on her nameplate and found his first question needless—"Cantrell. Can you tell me how long ago Miss Elizabeth Westbrook left here?"

"A half hour perhaps." Her attention went to the portfolio in his grip. "How did you get that? I gave that to Miss Westbrook."

"I found it outside of her room at the boardinghouse. I was supposed to meet her there. Did she say where she was going after she left here?" He scanned the office for any sign of Turner.

"No, but she seemed in a hurry when she left."

"May I ask what's in here?" He held up the portfolio.

"Miss Westbrook agreed to read some of the articles I've written. She's going to tell me whether they're any good or not." Something in the woman's eyes said she already thought they were.

Daniel set the leather case on her desk. "Is Turner here?"

She shook her head. "You just missed him. A member of the town council called a special meeting this morning. Mr. Turner had to leave and said he wouldn't be back for quite a while."

Daniel glanced out the front window. That didn't make sense. Ben Mullins was on the town council, and he was at the store. James was part of the council too, and he wasn't coming into town until around noon. If a special meeting had been called, they would be there. He thanked the woman and returned to the boardinghouse.

He and James had discussed Elizabeth coming back into town and decided it would be fine. James assured him things had blown over, that people had moved on in their concerns. But now he wondered.

He knocked on Miss Ruby's door again.

Muffled footsteps sounded before the door opened. "Good morning, Mr. Ranslett—"

"Morning, Miss Ruby. Have you seen Miss Westbrook?"

The proprietor shook her head. "No, I haven't. I'm sorry."

"Would you know if anyone's been in her room?"

A frown shadowed the older woman's face. "I was out for a while this morning, but I haven't given anyone a key, if that's what you mean. I would never do that with her renting the room."

"No, ma'am, of course not. I didn't mean to insinuate—" He nodded. "Thank you." He walked down the hallway, trying to think of where to look next.

"If you'd like for me to tell her you came by, Mr. Ranslett, I'll be happy to. I'm thinking she'll be here sometime soon."

Daniel stopped and retraced his steps. "What makes you think that?"

She smiled. "Well, I saw a wagon with her camera and all her things parked out front of the general store. It sure is nice to have her back in town. Mr. Turner said the very same thing when I met him out front. I—"

"Drayton Turner was here?" Unexplained warning scuttled through him.

"Why yes, he brought me a newspaper. Hand-delivered at no charge. He said he was giving out papers this morning, seeing if people would like to advertise. But why would I want to advertise, I told him, when my rooms are always occu—"

"Much obliged, ma'am." Daniel took a backward step. "I really need to be going."

"I'll be sure and tell her you came by."

He ran across the street to the butcher shop. He'd just been by the general store and the wagon wasn't there. Elizabeth wouldn't have just up and decided to take the wagon and go somewhere. Not when they had planned to meet. And how could Turner be at a council meeting *and* be hand-delivering his newspapers? "Lolly!"

"Ranslett! Welcome ba—"

"Have you seen Elizabeth?"

"Who?"

"The woman photographer."

He shook his head. "Sorry." His eyes narrowed. "Is something wrong?"

Daniel relayed his concern. "Would you get word to the sheriff's office and tell Willis or Stanton what I've told you? I'll ride up the ridge and see if I can spot anything from there."

Already out the door, Daniel heard Lolly's affirmation behind him.

He swung into the saddle and kicked the mare's haunches. If Elizabeth *was* with Turner, his gut told him it wasn't good. But what reason would Turner possibly have to harm her?

As he rode toward the ridge, he checked the streets. He pushed the mare hard, and she flew up the mountain trail toward Rachel's home. Reaching the ridge in record time, he jumped down and pulled his scope from his saddlebag. He searched the roads closer up, then focused across town on the only route leading to Denver.

Starting at the base of the mountain, he followed the switchback trail as it wove back and forth through the evergreens. It was a steep climb for a loaded wagon, and he didn't think one loaded as heavily as theirs had been with Elizabeth's equipment could have made it to the top of the pass and over in the time elapsed.

He moved the scope to the right and spotted a wagon—headed up Old Barnes Hill Road. His pulse kicked up a notch. The wagon disappeared behind a stand of aspen, and he waited for what felt like forever before it reappeared on the other side. One person on the buckboard. The image was blurry and he gave the cylinder a slight turn to adjust the focus. It looked like a man, but he couldn't be sure.

Whoever it was, they rode at a leisurely pace, and the wagon bed was stacked with crates and boxes. He had packed Elizabeth's equipment himself, and that wasn't it. His unease expanded.

He searched the area again with his naked eye, just in case, then ran a short way down the ridge to get a different perspective. With the aid of the scope, he roved the mountainside. There—

He moved the scope back a fraction. A wagon. A single rider on the buckboard.

The wagon moved along at a good clip and went behind a curve before he could get a good look at what was in the back. It was on the road leading around to the backside of Maroon Lake. He followed the road in his mind, reading the twists and turns from memory. It ended abruptly in a bluff overlooking the lake. Remote, not easily accessible, and it didn't get much wagon traffic because the path got real narrow at the top, and it was quite a hike to get to the picturesque view. Just the kind of place Elizabeth would've braved for a photograph.

For some reason, that thought sat ill within him.

He watched through the scope, waiting for the wagon to reappear. And when it did, he stepped forward and nearly slipped off the ridge. It *was* Turner, he was certain. And no doubt that was Elizabeth's equipment in the back. But where was she?

A closer look at the wagon bed and he realized his earlier instincts had been right. Dread coursed through him. He ran back to his horse.

Getting to that bluff meant riding back through town and following the same path up. At least a half hour to get there on horseback. Too long. As he rode on up the mountain, he cursed Drayton Turner, fearing what the man might do. Or what he might already have done.

41

She could breathe.

That was the first thing Elizabeth noticed when she began to awaken. She tried to open her eyes but quickly closed them. The sunlight was excruciating. Her eyelids felt swollen, and they burned on the inside. Her throat ached as if she hadn't had anything to drink for days. She tried to swallow and would've cried out, but the lining of her throat refused further abuse.

She was seated on the ground with what felt like a rock at her back. Her arms were tied behind her. She tried to move her feet, but her ankles were bound as well.

"You're awake, Miss Westbrook. I thought possibly I'd lost you there for a while."

She went still, recognizing the voice.

Sensing shade on her face, she chanced a look and blinked. Not so much to see him better but to make sure she was seeing correctly. She closed her eyes again; the light and air on her eyes was too painful.

"I apologize for the way I had to escort you here, ma'am. Considering our past, I doubted whether you would've come if I'd asked you straight out. Especially not once I told you the purpose of our visit." Turner laughed softly. "You know, Miss Westbrook . . . it's not nice to open someone else's mail."

His voice, his manner, sounded so normal. It sent chills skittering up her spine.

"Didn't make sense to me at first when I realized the letter had already been opened. Miss Cantrell didn't say a thing about it . . . because she didn't open it. I remembered you having her portfolio in your hands when you left, and that's when it all came together. She had to go home to get that for you, and you went snooping."

Elizabeth cringed, listening. If only she could talk to him. Then again, she wondered if it would make any difference.

"Miss Cantrell never opens my personal mail, but then . . . you had no way of knowing that. Did you, ma'am? I'm actually quite impressed, in a way. I didn't realize you had the gumption to do something so . . . beneath you."

Without her sight, sounds became more distinct, and Elizabeth tried to identify what she heard. The wind in the trees, a rustling somewhere behind her, and in the distance, a hawk's cry. She tested the ropes binding her wrists.

"The ropes aren't overly tight, Miss Westbrook, because—" He paused. "May I call you Elizabeth? I feel like I've learned so much about you in your absence."

She didn't respond.

"I know it probably hurts you to speak, but perhaps you could nod. That would only be proper, I think."

Wishing she had her derringer, Elizabeth nodded as she rubbed her wrists together behind her back. Daniel had to be wondering where she was by now. She didn't know how much time had passed, but surely he would come looking for her. But how would he know where to look? Even the best tracker in the territory couldn't track what he hadn't seen.

"Thank you . . . Elizabeth." The crunch of gravel. Turner was moving around. "The ropes aren't overly tight because I don't want any marks on your wrists. Not that it matters much in the end, but I'm trying my best to—What are you doing?"

She continued to work against her bindings.

He set something down. A crate? "Stop that, Elizabeth."

Unexpected fury filled her. At his tone and demeanor, at who he was, at what he'd done to her. To Josiah. She kept rubbing.

Pain exploded across the left side of her face and she fell hard to the ground, feeling her right shoulder pop. She gasped, groaning aloud, wishing now that she'd done as he'd asked. Dust coated her tongue.

"That's part of your problem. You simply don't listen." He sighed. She heard something behind her. A twig breaking. Or maybe a squirrel in the brush. "And you have this . . . air about you. I noticed it the first time we met. You look down on us, Elizabeth. The people of Timber Ridge. We are somehow . . . less in your mind, but that's of little importance now."

She felt certain that if she could see him he would look maniacal. But all she could picture was him in that feathered bowler, and the image in her mind didn't fit with the term. But what he'd done to her back in her room—and what he was doing now—did.

She started to shake, not on the surface, but inside, deep down, in the center of her belly. It was a nauseating fear, one born of fatigue and regret. *God, I don't want to die.* Not here, not yet, not like this. She tried to sit up and couldn't. She heard clicks and scrapes. It took her a moment to realize what he was doing. He was setting up her camera on the tripod. . . .

"You're the daring woman photographer come to tame this vast western frontier, Elizabeth." He said it with the same dramatic flair he'd used the night he interviewed her. "Everyone in town knows how you travel these mountains, braving the wild to get your self-serving photographs. And they know of your breathing problems, so I don't think this will be too much of a shock for them. Or much of a disappointment."

Eyelids closed, she moved her eyes from side to side, trying to ease their sensitivity. Whatever he'd laced the cloth with was not quick to forgive, and she didn't think she would stand another bout with it. She imagined what a cool cloth would feel like laid over her eyes, and unexpected tears rose in response.

She blinked and finally managed to keep her eyes open for a few seconds at a time.

Turner's back was to her. From this odd sideways angle, she watched him. She saw her equipment set up at the edge of the cliff and slowly realized what he was going to do—he was going to push her off the cliff. And make it look like an accident.

Fear coiled inside her. She shivered and remembered something Josiah had said. Something about fearing what was ahead. *"Knowin' Jesus has already sifted through what's comin' before it gets to me . . . Well, I reckon that ought to be enough."* Thinking of all the hardships Josiah had faced in his life, tears slipped down her cheeks. She prayed for the same faith he had to be in her. Jesus knew where she was. He'd sifted through this moment before it had gotten to her. She clung to that thought, repeating it over and over. *Jesus knows where I am. He knows where I am. . . .*

Tillie had been right about regrets. It wasn't so much the things she'd done that Elizabeth regretted in that moment—other than opening that letter—it was the things she hadn't done. And if given only a handful of moments to live, she would have spent every one of them with the people she loved, letting them know—some for the very first time—just how much she cared.

Turner angled toward her, and she quickly closed her eyes.

He raised her to a sitting position and reached around behind her. "Try my patience again, Elizabeth . . ." His tone was cordial. "And next time I'll use my fist."

He untied her wrists, and she didn't dare open her eyes. He untied her ankles, and she took inventory of her body. Her right shoulder throbbed. She moved it slightly and fire shot down through her back and arm. It would take a few seconds to regain her balance once she stood, so running was out of the question. Unless she could hit him with something first, and she needed to open her eyes to do that. But if she opened her eyes at the wrong time, her element of surprise would be lost. And if she *did* try to hit him, she needed to hit him hard enough to knock him out. Because he'd already proven that, if it came to a fight, he would win.

With confusing gentleness, he helped her stand. Her legs were unsteady from lack of use and tingled as the blood rushed down into them. She tried to swallow, wanting to scream in case someone was within earshot, but the dust in her mouth made it impossible.

He took hold of her arm and pulled her forward. Chancing it, she opened her eyes again. He was looking ahead, pulling a cloth from his pocket. The cliff where her camera was set up was no more than fifteen feet away. She tried to dig in her boot heels, but he just pulled harder.

"One advantage of housing the only telegraph office in town, Elizabeth, is that it gives one insight into the goings-on within a community. Return . . . first . . . photograph . . . of . . . body. Stop. Attention . . . Sheriff . . . McPherson."

He was quoting one of the telegrams she'd sent to Wendell Goldberg.

Turner paused and turned. She squinted her eyes tight. His grip threatened to cut off the circulation in her arm.

"You simply can't be assured of privacy in such a rustic little town, can you, ma'am?" He was facing her. She felt his breath on her cheek. He made a *tsk*ing noise. "Pity . . ."

She caught a whiff of the same acrid scent she'd smelled back in her room. If she would have any opportunity, this was it. She opened her eyes, saw his widen, and went for his face, clawing, scratching.

Anything cordial about Drayton Turner vanished.

His fist came at her and she pulled back, but he caught her on the chin and everything went fuzzy for a few seconds. She tried to push him away and he gave her right arm a vicious tug. Her knees buckled from the pain and she went down.

"Your problem, Elizabeth"—he dragged her closer to the cliff, his grip viselike—"like so many others, is that you underestimated my—"

An eerie screech, unearthly and primal, rose from the mountains. The air trembled with the sound, and so did she. The squall washed over the canyon, crashing against the walls and echoing back. Her flesh crawled, and she imagined not just one voice, but thousands of rebel voices joined in the primitive chorus. Brothers readying for battle, readying to die, and she knew that what Josiah had said about the cry was true.

Turner went stock-still. Seizing the moment, she twisted away from him and turned to run. But he recovered and grabbed her by the hair, pulling her back. He pressed the cloth over her mouth and nose. She held her breath, but fumes still worked their way inside. Rawness burned in her throat.

She grabbed at his hands and arms, digging in her nails, fighting for air, aware of consciousness slipping. She opened her eyes and saw the canyon far below—

Then time stilled. The world took on a slower pace.

Turner jerked and his grip on her went slack. She looked over at him. His eyes were wide, his mouth frozen in surprise. Blood issued from a hole in his chest. Choking, she pried his hand from her hair and quickly moved away. Disbelief whitened his face as he staggered back. And plunged into the ravine.

Only then did she hear the report of the Whitworth rifle.

42

"They's ready for the photograph, Miz Westbrook. And gettin' a mite impatient too, if you askin' me."

"Thank you, Josiah. I've almost got things ready." Focusing the image, Elizabeth wished there were a way to capture the golden brilliance of aspen and the burnished red of maples skirting the Maroon Bells in the distance. Not certain yet which season would prove to be her favorite in the Rockies, she had a feeling it would end up being autumn.

She knew the science behind the leaves changing colors as the trees went dormant, "dying" for a season, but the transformation represented a time of reflection for her. A time when that which was once hidden was laid bare, and she couldn't help but wonder if that had been part of God's design in this particular season—giving people a chance to see the intricacy of His design. That's what He'd done with her in recent months. He'd stripped away, layer by layer, until He'd shown her what was most important.

She bent to peer through the glass viewer again. Residents of Timber Ridge had turned out en masse for the dedication of the new school. Now all they needed was a teacher. James had placed newspaper advertisements for interested parties in all the major cities back east, and the town council was currently accepting applications.

It had taken some time, but she'd finally penned the details of that day on the cliff with Turner. Though she had dreaded doing it, the process turned out to be cleansing, and she thought she'd laid that memory, and that man, to rest. Yet she wasn't naïve enough to think she would never be bothered by it again—she knew about Daniel's dreams.

"That's a mighty nice bustle on that dress, ma'am."

She felt a bold hand on the small of her back and slowly straightened. She'd worn this dress—her favorite, the red with the black cummerbund—for him, remembering how he'd commented on it in the store when she'd first arrived in Timber Ridge. "Mr. Ranslett, as a Southern gentleman, you really ought not to be looking at my bustle, sir."

A scoundrel-worthy smile tipped his mouth. "I reckon you're right, but tell me now . . . just why are you wearing such a thing if not to attract a little more attention to it?"

She bit her lip to keep from smiling. "Don't you have someplace you're supposed to be?"

He tipped his hat and turned to go, but not before she felt a swift tug on her backside. That man . . . She bent again to peer through the camera's lens only to see him walk straight into her line of vision, along with Beau.

Daniel took a place beside Rachel and her boys. Not too close. Mitchell and Kurt smiled up at him, but Rachel did not. Her face showed her struggle, though Elizabeth guessed she tried hard to hide it. Rachel was, after all, a proper Southern belle. Her hands on her sons' shoulders, she moved away from Daniel, ever so slightly. No one else seemed to notice, but Elizabeth did. And so did he.

Seeing Josiah waiting, Elizabeth motioned for those occupying the left side of the lens to scrunch closer. The Tuckers and their children scooted in, and she noted Rand Brookston standing by them. That handsome young doctor had worked a miracle for her, and it seemed he was working one for little Davy too.

The afternoon she'd walked into her room at the boardinghouse and discovered her equipment destroyed, she thought her dreams had been destroyed as well. What she hadn't known then was that God loved her enough to intervene in her dream—to shatter it, to shatter *her*—only so He could put her back together and give her an even bigger, better dream. *His* dream for her life.

She'd thought her coming to the Colorado Territory had been for her career. And who knew, maybe it would still turn out that way, in part. But her real passion lay with Daniel Ranslett in a shared dream—one they hoped would gain the attention of Congress.

The photograph she'd taken, the one James had hoped would reveal a clue about Travis Coulter's murder, had revealed nothing. But in the end it didn't matter. Going on a tip from the letter she'd read, the one Turner had destroyed, James traveled to New York and tracked the sale of Coulter's pistol to a gun buyer there, who had acquired it from an unsuspecting employee at Brooklyn Land Development. Coulter had made a deal with Turner to sell his land to the New York–based company, but apparently changed his mind at the last minute. And the decision cost him his life. Turner had also had a contact inside the Denver Commissioner's Office who was going to swing the bid in the auction to his favor. He would've gotten away with murder, if not for her curiosity.

Daniel smiled at her through the camera lens, and she knew it was time. Certain the image was focused, she carefully slid the protective plate holder into place and removed the slide. She reached for the lens cap.

"I know what's to do now, ma'am, so you just run on."

She pulled her hand back. "I'm sure you do, Josiah. You're a quick learner, and the best assistant I've ever had. But are you sure you'll know how long to—"

"Trust me, ma'am." He gestured. "Now you just get on over there on that side for once."

She hesitated, then did as he bade.

Daniel held out his hand. "You're the loveliest thing I've ever seen, Elizabeth Westbrook, and I have a spot for you right here beside me." He pulled her close. Kurt and Mitchell smiled from where they stood, and she reached over and tousled their little red heads. Wordlessly, she reached behind her for Rachel's hand. Rachel gripped hers tight and held on.

"All right, everybody, stop all that talkin' and hold them smiles."

Everyone grew quiet except for a stifled giggle here and there throughout the crowd.

Josiah removed the brass cap from the lens, and Elizabeth was certain she saw his lower lip tremble before he began. " 'Four score and seven years ago our fathers brought forth upon this continent a new nation, conceived in liberty and dedicated to the proposition that all men are created equal . . .' "

EPILOGUE

Elizabeth reached for Daniel, seated beside her. His hand was warm and large and rough, and enveloped hers completely. "Are you ready?" she whispered.

He stroked the underside of her wrist with his thumb. "Thanks to you . . . I am."

She looked around the chamber. Nearly a year had passed since she'd been in this room, and it was every bit as resplendent now as then but felt far more intimidating to her today.

People filled the hall and conversation rose to a hum. Every gallery ticket was spoken for, the clerk had told her. Men occupied every elected seat. But someday—she held hope—women would fill these seats as well. Perhaps in her lifetime. She thought of the days ahead, then just as quickly thought of those most recently past.

She and Daniel had married at his family plantation in Franklin in early December, then had spent the following weeks there in the family home where he'd grown up. They'd walked the now peaceful fields where Benjamin and so many others had died years ago. It was hallowed ground beneath their feet, and as they'd traced those paths—all the way from his home to nearby Carnton Plantation, where so many were buried—they'd spoken in hushed tones, when they'd spoken at all.

The pound of a gavel from the front of the chamber drew everyone's attention, and everyone took their places. Gradually, the din of conversation fell away.

"The Senate will now come to order." The president of the Senate presided from the central dais, with the assistant secretary, the journal clerk, parliamentarian, and legislative clerk on the tier below him. "On this twenty-first day of January, in the year of our Lord eighteen hundred and seventy-six, we yield the floor to Senator Garrett Eisenhower Westbrook, of the grand state of Maryland."

Elizabeth looked on as the president of the Senate nodded in distinguished fashion to her father, who made his way to the podium, and she could not have been prouder. Not only of him but of what he was about to do.

Her father looked out over the crowd. "President of the Senate, distinguished colleagues, and honored guests . . ." He found her in the audience and a look of pleasure moved across his face. "I am present before you today to propose a bill designed to protect one of our nation's grandest vistas. Being distributed to each of you now"— he nodded to clerks at the side, and Elizabeth smiled as Daniel squeezed her hand—"is a gold-embossed volume that contains nine of the finest photographs on record of the untamed splendor of the Colorado Territory and the sacred Ute tribal lands of Mesa Verde. These photographs were captured by one of the—" He stopped and cleared his throat. "By one of the most gifted and . . . extraordinary photographers of our day, Mrs. Elizabeth Westbrook Ranslett."

Elizabeth's throat swelled with tears, and she was grateful she didn't have to make a presentation today.

"These bound volumes are presented to each of you as a gift in the hope that you will see for yourselves the magnificence and unequaled grandeur of this nation's Rocky Mountains."

The creak of fresh bindings filled the chamber, and Elizabeth leaned forward in her chair to catch the senators' expressions. Collective awe and amazement accompanied their hushed whispers, and an unequaled depth of pride swept through her for Daniel and his accomplishment—for *their* accomplishment.

"I am proud to introduce to you a gentleman," her father continued, "whose acquaintance I am most pleased to have made at this particular point in my life."

She heard Daniel's deep breath beside her and felt her own chest rise and fall. *Thank you, Father, that these two men, so dear to me, didn't cross paths at an earlier and more fateful time in history.*

"A gentleman who has dedicated himself to the preservation of these lands, and who has written to many of us in this very room over the past seven years. It is with deep regret that I tell you he never received a single reply. And as much as many of us would like to cast that blame on our illustrious Postmaster General . . ." Laughter filled the chamber. "The blame is laid at my feet . . . and yours." The laughter slowly faded. "Only now are we recognizing the significance of his selfless endeavor." Her father nodded in their direction, their signal. "Mr. Daniel Wayne Ranslett is here today to tell us about this land and the magnificent cliff dwellings you see in the pages before you. . . ."

Daniel leaned close. "We made that journey together, Elizabeth." Amid applause from the chamber, he rose, inviting her to stand with him. "We're going to make this one together too."

Elizabeth paused outside of Rachel's barn, and Daniel took her hand. "You ready?"

Gripping her reticule, she nodded and blew out a breath. "I think so."

Josiah looked up when they walked in. He laid aside the cloth in his hand and stepped back from the saddle on the workbench. Elizabeth first read surprise in his expression, then endearment, and was certain she'd never forget how he grabbed them both in a huge bear hug, his arms nearly wrapping around them both.

"Welcome home, Mr. and Missus Ranslett. I got your letters while you's gone." His grin stretched wide and was true to the man he was. "Them letters was just like sittin' round the fire, talkin' to you both. 'Cept your letters didn't go on as long as you do in person, Missus Ranslett."

She nudged him in the arm. "Plainspoken truth . . . I've missed that from you."

"There ain't no other kind, and I reckon I's too old now to change." He dipped his head. "Sure is good to have you back, the both of you. This place ain't been the same with you gone."

Daniel motioned to a bench and stool. "Can we sit for a minute, Josiah, and talk?"

"Yes, sir, Mr. Ranslett, sure we can. I likes to hear all about your trip. Missus Ranslett told me in her letters that you donc real good in Washington 'fore all them important white men."

Daniel smiled, settling on the bench beside her. "They were more impressed with Elizabeth's photographs than they were with me. Which is as it should be."

She scoffed. "That's not true. Daniel did a marvelous job. I was so proud of him." She briefly described that day, giving Josiah the high points.

"That sounds real fine, ma'am. Maybe someday, sir"—he turned to Daniel—"you might give me that speech you gave that mornin'. I sure like to hear it."

"Uncle Daniel—" Mitchell appeared in the doorway. "Uncle James wants to know if you can help him with something for a minute."

"I'll be right there." Daniel turned back. "I kept a copy of the speech for you. We'll read it together after dinner tonight." Slowly, he stood and extended his hand. "I'd consider it an honor . . . *Josiah*."

Josiah stared, and Elizabeth could see the power of Daniel's simple invitation reflected in Josiah's response. Josiah's composure wavered; then he stood and gripped Daniel's hand. "Thank you, Mr. Ranslett. I be lookin' forward to it, sir." Daniel left and Josiah eased his weight back down. "You gots yourself a good man there, ma'am."

"Yes . . . I do. And I'm looking at an equally good man right here." Enjoying his grin, she took another breath and let it out slowly, half wishing Daniel were still there for this part. "Speaking of my husband, there's something I'd like to tell you." She watched Josiah's face. He was a perceptive man with a discerning spirit, and it wouldn't take him long to understand.

"After we returned from Mesa Verde, Daniel wrote letters to plantation owners who lived in Franklin during the war, and to those still in the area today. Neither of us said anything to you at the time because . . . we didn't want to raise your hopes needlessly. Daniel checked everywhere, Josiah. He went from home to home and searched every plantation's private deed book he could find. He talked with all the owners or their heirs, and—" Her voice broke, thinking of all Daniel had undertaken, and to what end. She watched Josiah's expression cloud and reached out to him.

Josiah's work-worn hands covered hers. "That's all right, ma'am. I understand what you's sayin'. And I appreciate what you done for me—same for your husband."

A creaking drew their attention, and without conscious thought, Elizabeth rose. She looked toward the door. Josiah followed her gaze, and slowly, unsteadily, he came to his feet. Tender yearning softened his rugged features.

Daniel stood in the doorway, with Belle. He covered her hand on his arm and drew her forward with him. "Belle, may I present Mr. Josiah Birch of Timber Ridge, Colorado Territory. And Josiah . . ." Daniel's eyes grew moist, his voice more gentle. "It is with deepest honor that I present . . . your wife, Mrs. Isabelle Birch of Franklin, Tennessee."

For a moment Josiah's lips moved, but nothing came out. He blinked, tears coursing down his cheeks. His broad chest rose and fell in quick succession. "Belle . . ."

His wife took the first step, her eyes radiant with love for her husband. He took her in his arms and held her for the longest time. When they finally parted, Belle gently touched his face. "After all these years," she whispered, "I'm finally home."

Elizabeth looked across the room at Daniel and found him watching her. What she felt in her heart, she read in his eyes. After all these years, she, too, was finally home.

A Note from Tamera

Dear Friends,

Thank you for journeying back in time with me to experience the adventures of those whose spirit and determination helped forge this great country. Their sacrifices, accomplishments, and collective memory echo around us even now. Yet we don't often reflect on just how much their contributions impact us.

Having grown up in the South, I've long held a love for its history, much as living in Colorado led me to appreciate its rich heritage. Weaving those two passions into one story was pure privilege. In writing *From a Distance*, I learned much about the early days of photography, and how arduous and painstaking it was to take even a single photograph! With our modern world of disposable and digital cameras, not to mention cell phone photography, we snap pictures left and right, rarely giving thought to the pioneers in this field and how their life's work now enriches our lives.

That appreciation goes to a far deeper level when we reflect on the sacrifices men and women made in the Civil War. The Battle of Franklin referenced in this story took place on November 30, 1864. Often referenced as "The Gettysburg of the West," it was one of the few battles fought at night. The battlefield was only two miles long and one and a half miles wide, and though the battle lasted only five hours, some 9,500 soldiers were killed, wounded, captured, or missing. Nearly 7,000 of that number were Confederate. The battle centered largely around the Carter House, which still stands today. If ever you're in Nashville, I'd encourage you to take the time to walk those grounds and tour the home. The Carnton Plantation mentioned in this story is also a historic landmark. The Confederate Cemetery at Carnton (where Daniel's brother, Benjamin, is fictitiously buried) is the largest privately owned military cemetery in the nation, and walking those grounds is a moving experience.

Lastly, I pray that as you've read this book, you gained a glimpse of what power lies in giving God your dreams. Elizabeth's journey and the lessons she learned along the way are familiar to me, and I'm so thankful God loves us enough to intervene in our dreams—only to give us even bigger, better dreams. *His* dream for our lives.

As always, I'd love to hear from you. Please stop by my Web site at *www.tameraalexander.com* and leave me a comment on my guestbook. You'll also find discussion questions for all my novels there.

Until next time,

Tamera Alexander

ACKNOWLEDGMENTS

My thanks . . .

First and always, to Jesus—who gives me undeserved life, both here and in the hereafter.

To Joe, Kelsey, and Kurt—without you guys, none of this would be doable. Much less, worth doing.

To Natasha Kern, my agent—my gratitude and highest respect. God's ways surely are higher than our own.

To Karen Schurrer, Charlene Patterson, Helen Motter, Sharon Asmus, and Ann Parrish, my editors at Bethany House—your insights are treasured and I look forward to writing many more books together. Special thanks to Karen, for donning your photographer's hat and for capturing Kelsey's curls for this cover. That was such a fun afternoon spent "dodging the sun."

To Deborah Raney, my writing critique partner—I cannot imagine this journey without you, friend.

To Doug and June Gattis, my parents, and Fred Alexander, my father-in-law—I appreciate your reading through the manuscript before publication. Your comments, catches, and suggestions were so helpful, and your encouragement . . . so timely.

To my Uncle Ben and Aunt Lyda (Mullins)—thank you for the summers spent with you on your farm in Dellrose, Tennessee. Those were exciting times for a city girl from Atlanta, and are treasured memories to me now. Aunt Lyda, I know you're looking forward to joining Uncle Ben "at Home," but I'm so grateful you're still with us here. I love and appreciate you.

To the CdA women—I look forward to our plotting, playing, and praying together every summer.

And to my readers—how could I have known that the sweetest thing about writing would be connecting and interacting with you? You've given me so much through your notes and e-mails. Connecting with you "through these characters" is a joy I'd not expected and that is so fulfilling!

Join me again in spring 2009 for *Beyond This Moment,* the next book in the TIMBER RIDGE REFLECTIONS series.

———

Tamera Alexander is a bestselling novelist whose deeply drawn characters, thought-provoking plots, and poignant prose resonate with readers. Having lived in Colorado for seventeen years, she and her husband now make their home in Tennessee, where they enjoy life with their two college-age children and a silky terrier named Jack.

Tamera invites you to visit her Web site at *www.tameraalexander .com* or write her at the following addresses:

Tamera Alexander

P.O. Box 362

Thompson's Station, TN 37179

tameraalexander@ymail.com

Looking for More Good Books to Read?